# A FAIR EXCHANGE

## ANN PORT

Books by Ann Port

*It's All in the Title*

*The Bernini Quest*

ISBN: 1470153807
ISBN 13: 9781470153809

# A
# FAIR
# EXCHANGE

## ANN PORT

*Dedication*

*A Fair Exchange is dedicated to seven special individuals:
To Royal Oakes, who believed in me when I first
wrote the book years ago
To Susie Gilfix, who provided invaluable insight
from a unique point of view
To Taylor West for her encouragement, wisdom, and vision
To Cynthia Siegle, who accompanied me to
Munich to do my research
To Ken Moe for his scholarly advice
To Warren Isabelle, who urged me to publish
To Louise Turner for her continuing enthusiasm and
belief in my literary endeavors*

# PREFACE

Although *A Fair Exchange* is primarily a work of fiction, I have attempted to remain as historically accurate as possible within a broad framework. With few exceptions, the major characters of the novel are fictitious. I attempted to portray them as realistically as possible within the limits of the information available and the scope of fiction.

Of course the leaders of the Third Reich are infamous, as is Doctor Sigmund Rascher, who played a major role in the Luftwaffe high-flight tests and a series of freezing experiments conducted at Dachau between May and October 1942. Though I took some liberty with the time line for the purpose of literary unity, these tests occurred within several months of the dates specified in the novel.

The Dachau camp experiences described in the book are representative of concentration camp practices in that location and all over Hitler's Germany. The atrocities committed against the Jews and the Reich's political enemies have been well documented.

Special mention should be given to the excellent works that provided the background necessary in order to write about this period. Some of these include: *Hitler: A Study in Tyranny* by Alan Bullock, *The Rise and Fall of the Third Reich* by William Shirer, *What Was It Like in the Concentration Camp at Dachau?* by Doctor Johannes Neuhausler, *Hitler and Munich* by Brian Deming and Ted Iliff, *Hitler's Munich* by Joachim von Halasz, and *Berlin, 1933-1945* by Mark Kopleck.

I contend that in the Third Reich there were, even among Hitler's fanatical supporters, a few individuals who searched their consciences and called upon their fundamental beliefs and values to guide them in their decision-making process. Though history has shown there were not enough of these people to prevent the atrocities that occurred at the Nazi death camps, perhaps they made small contributions and, unknown to history, helped a few who were suffering.

# CHAPTER 1

E rich Riedl pushed open the massive front door of the Braunes
Haus, paused, and inhaled a deep breath of the frigid air.
"Another exciting day," he grumbled, grateful that the mind-
numbing afternoon had finally come to an end. As he crossed the
short distance from Hitler's Munich headquarters to Konigsplatz,
a blustery blast of cold air all but stopped him in his tracks. He
removed his cap to keep it from blowing away and tucked his
chin tightly to his chest. "Of all days to forget my raincoat," he
growled. "It has to be twenty degrees colder than when I left
home this morning. Now if the rain would hold off—"
    Erich's hopes of staying dry were quickly dashed as a jagged
flash of lightening lit up the ever-darkening sky. Seconds later he
flinched, when a booming clap of thunder exploded, an ominous
portent that pouring rain was imminent. The first drops of rain
spattered the ground as he turned left toward the Verwaltungsbau,
the Nazi administration building. He hurried by the first of the
Ehrentempel, the twin limestone honor temples that housed the
sarcophagi of Nazi martyrs who were killed in the failed Beer
Hall Putsch in November 1935. A group of women, who were
about to climb the stairs to the monument, slowed down and
waited for him to pass. Their considerate act was not uncom-
mon, though Erich was hardly naïve enough to believe they were
displaying deference to an officer of the Reich. Rather they were
wary of the twin lightning bolts on his Waffen SS uniform, symbols of his membership in Germany's chosen elite.

Uniform aside, Erich was the epitome of the Fuhrer's ideal. At six-feet three, his broad shoulders tapered to a thin waist and slender hips. Always athletic, he took special pride in his physical conditioning and worked out regularly to keep his body toned and sleek. His thick, slightly-wavy hair was the color of ripened wheat, a trait valued in the new Germany. Other attributes aside, his eyes were his most striking feature. Pools of blue, bold, and piercing, they mirrored his many moods. Quick to flash anger, they were equally apt to twinkle with pleasure, or to express his quick wit and sense of humor, which, friends and colleagues complained, had been nearly non-existent in the preceding months.

Erich blamed his moodiness on the pressures of work, though in his heart he knew he was making an absurd excuse for what was really going on as he struggled with impossible supply problems, and, at the same time, grappled with weighty personal struggles which often kept him awake at night and pressed on his mind during the day. It had been another fitful night, followed by a late start that caused him to leave his apartment that morning without his topcoat. "I'm paying now," he complained, as he picked up his pace. Eager to be indoors, he raced up the stairs and blew into the building to greet the officer of the day, who frowned as he had to endure yet another blast of cold from the constantly opening door. "Good afternoon, Scharfuhrer," Erich mumbled, his lips numb from the cold air.

"Hauptsturmfuhrer," said the young man. "Commandant Mueller is waiting for you. You're to report to his office *immediately*."

"Thank you," Erich replied, thinking the last thing he needed was another pointless meeting, especially at 4:30 in the afternoon, a half-hour before he'd officially be off duty. *I should have followed my first instinct and gone home,* he thought, as walked up the first flight of stairs, but the prospect of returning to his lonely room after a frustrating day wasn't appealing, so to prolong the inevitable, he'd decided to return to headquarters to ask his best friend, Joachim Forester, to join him for a beer at the Hofbrauhaus.

At the second floor landing Erich hesitated, thinking it wouldn't hurt to take a quick side-trip down the hall to Joachim's office before reporting to the commandant. He quickly reconsidered. *Not a good idea,* he thought as he climbed to the third floor. *Muller already knows I'm in the building. There are no secrets in the Verwaltungsbau.*

The staccato sounds of typing emanating from the offices of the SS secretaries drowned out the sound of his footsteps as Erich approached the commandant's office in the center of the hall. He had barely knocked when he heard a raspy, "Enter, Hauptsturmfuhrer," resonate from behind the door. He entered an office bare of furniture except for a gun-metal gray desk with two straight-backed chairs, an austere table near the window, and a row of metal file cabinets set against the wall near a closed closet door. The only ornamentation in the otherwise antiseptic room was a clock, the regulation picture of the Fuhrer that hung in every office and in most buildings throughout the Reich, and a blood-red banner bearing the bold, black swastika of the Nazi Party.

Erich quickly focused on the officer sitting behind the desk. Commandant Mueller was the image of the perfect Prussian officer: his spine straight, his hair smoothed tightly against his skull, and his demeanor rigid and stiff like his appearance. He remained seated as Erich clicked his heels, raised his arm in the modified salute adopted by the SS—elbow bent, hand raised toward the ceiling—and snapped; "Heil Hitler."

"Heil Hitler," Mueller responded. He gestured to a coffee pot and cups on the table near the window. "Coffee, Hauptsturmfuhrer?" he said.

"Yes, thank you," said Erich. As he crossed the room, he was inexplicably nervous. The sturmbannfuhrer was a stickler for channels. Junior officers were rarely summoned to his office; yet here he was. He poured the bitter brew that was passing as coffee during the war and turned back toward the commandant. "Would you like a cup, Sturmbannfuhrer?" he asked.

"Not now," Mueller said sharply; his tone exacerbating Erich's unease. "Now, shall we could get down to business?" He pointed to the chair opposite the desk. Taking his coffee with him, Erich briskly crossed the room and sat down. Wasting no time with pleasantries, the commandant pushed his papers aside and said: "You're familiar with the SS detention camp at Dachau, Hauptsturmfuhrer?"

"I am," Erich said tentatively. While Mueller spoke, Erich recalled his only visit to the ancient country town. Several months before, he'd been ordered to deliver a document pouch to the Schulzstaffel, the SS training camp adjacent to the detention camp. He remembered his surprise as he approached the designated drop-off point. The base exuded energy and vitality. Asphalt streets were lined with sturdy modern barracks, lovely red-roof homes for the senior officers, crowded garages, and bustling workshops. There was a swimming pool and a large sports field for the officers. The only drawback to the otherwise unsullied scene was a layer of grime that clung to the windows and buildings. The soot-like substance was unlike anything Erich had seen in other meticulously clean SS camps, and he wondered how the men who trained there, despite their modern, well-equipped quarters, could adjust to the soot and the pervasive stench that appeared to be emanating from the nearby detention camp.

Mueller's sharp tone and cold glare jolted Erich back to the moment at hand. "Hauptsturmfuhrer," he said impatiently. "I asked if you're familiar with the camp at Dachau."

"I haven't actually been inside the compound," Erich said, feeling increasingly apprehensive. "But I have visited the Schulzstaffel."

"The compound, as you call it, Hauptsturmfuhrer, was built to detain communists, socialists, Catholic priests, and intellectuals, who refuse to accept the philosophy of the Fuhrer and the party, and who, because of their teachings, are deemed dangerous to the unity and order of the Reich. Two-hundred of these Dachau detainees have been selected to participate in a series of Luftwaffe experiments."

Mueller paused as if expecting a response. When Erich only nodded, he continued. "You have been reassigned to the Totenopfuerhande, the Death's Head Unit, at Dachau, where you will serve as the special administrative assistant to Untersturmfuhrer Doctor Sigmund Rascher, the officer overseeing the tests."

Erich tried to mask his astonishment. He'd never expected this sort of assignment. Known for their intolerance and brutality, the Totenopfuerhande were ardent fanatics who managed the concentration camps. Suddenly his tedious administrative job seemed infinitely preferable to a place he knew little about, but intuitively dreaded.

Mueller's frown and his harsh tone once again brought Erich back to the moment at hand. He didn't know what the commandant had said or how many minutes had passed since he'd been advised of his transfer, but Erich guessed it was his turn to respond. His eyes met Mueller's. What he saw suggested that his less-than-eager response to the news was unacceptable. Figuring a show of enthusiasm was essential, he thundered: "Heil Hitler. I'm proud to be a part of the Luftwaffe experiments, Commandant."

Mueller glared and shifted papers on his desk. "Of course you are," he said sarcastically. "Your orders will be ready later today."

He looked at his watch. "Or considering the hour, more likely tomorrow morning. I know very little about the tests, though I've been told the doctor is engaged in high-flight research designed to assist our pilots who are being shot down over the North Sea. What I also know is the experiments at Dachau are of personal and continuing interest to Reichsfuhrer Himmler, and I can't see how being involved could hurt your career." Mueller's contemptuous grin oozed as much sarcasm as his words.

"Erich realized he was once again required to show some gratitude for the assignment. "Please thank the appropriate people for their confidence in me, Sturmbannfuhrer," he said, wondering if Mueller realized how difficult it was for him to feign excitement about his new duty. He was thankful when the commandant ignored his contrived gratitude and returned to the papers on the desk.

It was obvious the meeting was over, so Erich stood, barked, "Heil Hitler," and receiving only a nod in return, turned and left the room. He shut the door behind him, and with renewed clarity, recalled Dachau—the grime, the smells, the secrecy. He had no idea what was going on behind those barbed-wire fences near the Schulzstaffel, and, truth be told, he had no desire to find out. In an instant the reams of paperwork he'd been generating and the insoluble issues he'd been struggling to resolve seemed idyllic.

Thinking Joachim had likely left for the day, Erich went to his own office at the end of the third floor hallway. He hung his hat on the rack by the door and plopped down at his desk. For the next fifteen minutes he sorted through the messages he'd received while at the meeting. Finally, unable to concentrate, he gave up, stared out the window at the pouring rain, and speculated about what could have recommended him for his new assignment.

His first position as a full-fledged member of the SS had been under SS Obergruppenfuhrer Reinhard Heydrich, the chief of the Reichssicherheitshauptamt, the main security department of the government. Erich thought back about the direction his career had taken under Heydrich's direction. At first he'd handled routine administrative duties, but toward the end of his tenure, he had begun to work on preliminary research for several of Reichsfuhrer Himmler's personal projects. His immediate boss was Wolfram Sievers, the one-time bookseller who had risen to the rank of SS colonel and executive secretary of the Institute for Research and Study of Heredity. Erich's job had little to do with the actual experiments being conducted. Instead, he processed the mountains of paperwork justifying anthropological skull measurements. He wasn't privy to specifics about the testing procedures, but he'd discovered a great deal on his own, and what he learned had been disturbing.

Erich quickly pieced together the link between Dachau and his two bosses. Heydrich was responsible for converting the abandoned munitions factory at Dachau into a concentration camp for political prisoners, and, for a while, Sievers conducted his gruesome experiments at the camp. As he thought back, Erich was filled with increasing trepidation. It was one thing to be involved with the experiments in an administrative capacity and quite another to be participating in their implementation.

After completing Siever's project, he had been promoted to the rank of Hauptsturmfuhrer and was transferred to Munich as a systems analyst. Busy with problem-solving in his new job, he never dreamed he might again work on human experimentation, at least until now. Suddenly a carefree evening with Joachim sounded even more appealing, but for a different reason. He was no longer seeking a friendly ear to listen to his complaints about his supply issues. Joachim was able to find a bright side to every predicament, no matter how troublesome. Erich hoped his friend could find something positive to say about Dachau.

# CHAPTER 2

Feeling an ever-increasing need to forget about his new assignment, Erich left his office and descended the stairs to the second floor to see if perhaps Joachim was working late. This time the utter stillness and cessation of sound in the halls was disturbing. Any kind of commotion would keep him from thinking about the conversation in Mueller's office.

Joachim's door was closed. Erich knocked, and, without waiting for a response, walked in. The room was empty, but Joachim's topcoat was still hanging on the rack by the door. *At least one person had enough sense to dress warmly today,* he thought as he sat down at Joachim's desk.

As he stared at the door, willing it to open, he thought about his friend. Over the years he had come to rely on Joachim. Their friendship had been shaped during the early days of their membership in the Hitler Youth, and it matured as they grew. Though their personalities were polar opposites, for some inexplicable reason, they worked. Joachim, with his quick wit and *laissez faire* approach to life, was a foil for Erich, who was more serious-minded and practical. Because of Joachim's *joie de vivre*, Erich learned to relax and be more flexible, and, in turn, he helped keep his always-mischievous friend out of trouble.

Each day after school or Hitler Youth activities, they would ride their bikes several miles to a rugged lean-to, a clubhouse of sorts, they had built in a secluded corner of three barren acres several miles outside Berlin. Erich's grandfather had named the property Unser Traum, "Our Dream." In the dilapidated shed, the one remaining legacy from his own father, Erich and Joachim dreamed and planned their glorious futures in the party. It was here they began to feel they belonged to each other and also to a greater cause.

After graduating from the university, like countless other young men ready to take their places in the world, Erich and Joachim realized there were few prospects and little hope. Once again they found the answer to their unrest in the Nazi Party, and their youthful zeal exploded into a fanatical devotion. In Adolf Hitler they found their answer. They eagerly became full members of the party, proudly taking their binding oath of allegiance to the Fuhrer, promising "at all times to show respect and obedience to him, and to any leaders he may appoint." Now, for the first time in his career, Erich wondered if that oath was coming back to haunt him.

When they enthusiastically joined the SS, Erich had worried that Joachim wasn't cut out for his chosen career. His easy-going nature hardly fit the perception of the SS "man of iron." He questioned some of the more drastic Nazi principles, and, despite Erich's warnings, he verbalized his opinions too frequently. However, despite Erich's reservations, Joachim had remained faithful to the SS motto, "Loyalty Is My Honor." That was except for one occasion.

Erich leaned back in the chair, folded his hands behind his head, and thought about the horrible day; the only time both he and Joachim violated their sacred oath. They had been full-fledged members of the SS for a little over a week and were awaiting orders to their first posts. The arduous training and repetitive, mind-numbing indoctrination had been both physically and mentally challenging. But no matter the problems they encountered, they were sustained by their unwavering dedication to the Fuhrer and the party. Their beliefs were uncompromising; their enthusiasm for Germany's future under the Fuhrer's leadership was unwavering; their ideology was unflagging. But for the first time on that decisive day in April, all of their beliefs and principles were challenged.

Erich recalled that the weather was frigid for the time of year, but despite the chill in the air, he and Joachim were excited about enjoying some much-needed leave-time. A fellow officer, a loner who rarely interacted with others, asked to tag along as they headed for the local beer halls. Neither Erich nor Joachim knew Ernst Halder well, but they welcomed him anyway.

After several stops and numerous rounds of beer, it was clear that Joachim and Ernst had downed a few too many. Since they all had to report to work early, Erich decided to take them back to the barracks. After unsuccessfully arguing that they were only getting started, the two inebriates agreed to go home. As they staggered down the nearly empty sidewalk, a young girl unexpectedly appeared from out of nowhere. Erich noticed she walked quickly with her head lowered, so she didn't see the approaching men until it was too late for her to step aside.

At the last minute the girl made a futile attempt to get out of the way, but Ernst staggered, and she ran full force into him. When he recovered from the unexpected contact, the young officer, partly in anger and certainly from embarrassment, grasped the obviously terrified offender by the shoulders and shook her vigorously. Being more lucid than his companions, Erich realized the reason for the girl's panic. Pinned to her breast was the yellow Star of David, the symbol of her shame in the new Reich.

When he saw the patch, Ernst became even more abrasive. He grinned salaciously and shoved the shocked girl toward the street. "This Jew-bitch needs a lesson in manners," he snarled. "I'll teach her to respect an officer of the Reich." He glanced around, and, spotting an alley separating two nearby buildings, he grabbed his prey, who began to moan as she struggled to escape the SS man's vice-like grasp.

Erich recoiled in disbelief as Ernst tugged the trembling woman toward the secluded spot. "Come watch the fun," he said, glancing back at his stunned companions. "To save her life, this slut will service all of us." He pulled the woman's face close to his. "How about it, Jewish whore?" he roared, grinning arrogantly as he threw her to the ground.

Without warning, Joachim grabbed the out-of-control officer's lapel. "She's learned her lesson, Ernst," he shrieked. "She'll watch where she's going from now on."

Ignoring Joachim's words, Ernst tore at the girl's skirt with one hand, while with the other he fumbled to loosen his own belt buckle. He dropped his pants and ripped the blouse from the sobbing Jew's shoulders, revealing her bare breasts. She struggled in vain to hide her nakedness as she thrashed about, trying to fight off the ever-increasing threat looming above her.

Erich stood dumbfounded and conflicted by the scene playing out in front of him. He instinctively knew he should right the wrong he was watching, but then the girl was a Jew, a subhuman, who could be punished however Ernst wished. Unsure how to respond, he froze, wanting to act, and, paradoxically, not daring to violate the teachings he accepted without question.

Joachim quickly solved the problem. He lunged, grabbed Ernst by the shoulders, and spun him around. Pulling his hand back, he struck him hard to the jaw and again to the mouth, spun him around again, and kneed him in the groin. Ernst gasped and fell back against the wall, unconscious and bleeding profusely from the place where Joachim's second blow had landed.

When Joachim resumed the attack, Erich grabbed him in a bear hug, pinning his flaying arms to his chest. "Stop it, Joachim," he yelled. "Think about what you're doing."

As the two men grappled, Joachim seemed to recognize it was Erich who was holding him back, and he began to calm down. Erich held on for several more minutes before slackening his hold. When Joachim made no move to break free, he let go. Both men stared down at the practically-nude, hysterical girl and the bloodstained officer lying nearby. As Joachim staggered toward her, the Jew cowered, obviously fearing an attack from him too. He grabbed her arm and pulled her to her feet. "Get out of here," he bellowed. "And for God's sake, from now on watch where you're going."

The girl didn't move. "Go!" Joachim yelled. She turned and stumbled from the alley. Just as she rounded the corner and disappeared from sight, Ernst began to stir. He rose to his knees, clinched his jaw, and sneered as he wiped the blood from his split lips. "Consider this the end of your career," he snarled at Joachim; "maybe your life. Attacking a fellow officer won't be sanctioned. I was lawfully punishing an enemy of the Reich."

Joachim lunged again, but before his blow struck, Erich seized his arm and held him back. "Get out of here, Joachim!" he shouted. "Now! I'll handle this."

Joachim fought to break free from Erich's grasp. As he held Joachim's arm, Erich spoke again, calmly and firmly. "I said go home! I'll see you later."

Joachim reluctantly straightened his uniform coat, picked up his cap from the ground, and hobbled from the alley. When he was out of sight, Erich bent to help the bloody and embarrassed officer, who was rising on wobbly legs. "Your friend will pay for this attack," Ernst roared as he pushed Erich's arm away. "If it's the last thing I do, I'll see to it."

If he hadn't known before, Erich quickly realized that Joachim was in serious trouble. He had to do something. But what? He could barely get his mind around what was happening, and he had a cold sense of foreboding in the pit of his stomach. His heart pounded in his chest as he tried to gather his thoughts. It was all he could do to speak calmly as he tried to reason with the humiliated man, who was obviously bent on revenge. "You know Joachim, Ernst," he said calmly. "He loves women and Jew or not, your reaction to an accidental encounter was excessive."

"I'm sure you'll find yourself in the minority in that regard," Ernst said, staring angrily as he wiped the flowing blood from his lips.

Thoughts raced through Erich's mind. If Ernst reported the incident, at the very least Joachim's career would be over, and his life could be forfeited as an example to other officers. He couldn't let Joachim suffer for an act of conscience and the belief that no woman, regardless of her religious beliefs, deserved to be raped. He felt responsible for what happened. He should have acted sooner. He thought for a few minutes and then, choosing his words carefully, said: "Maybe we can find a way to make sure this incident isn't reported."

"I can't imagine what could keep me from informing the sturmbannfuhrer about the occurrence," Ernst said huffily. He paused. "Any ideas?"

Erich heard an inviting rather than angry tone in Ernst's response. The smirking man was clearly open to a bribe. To Erich that was an offense far worse than Joachim's foolish effort to help the unfortunate Jew.

As a result of the ensuing conversation, the incident was never reported. After completing their training, Ernst was stationed in Dresden, Erich remained in Berlin, and Joachim was assigned to SS Headquarters in Munich. Numerous times in the succeeding months, Joachim asked Erich how he'd been able to persuade Ernst to keep the incident with the Jew to himself. Erich never revealed what it took to make the mess go away. His only comment when Joachim asked was: "Trust me, my friend. It was a fair exchange."

Every once in a while Joachim tried to catch Erich off guard, but no amount of trickery could get him to reveal the cost of silencing the SS officer. But from that moment on, the already strong bond between the childhood friends was permanently sealed, and even though the episode hadn't been mentioned in recent months, Erich knew Joachim often thought about what had occurred in the alley and was grateful for his help; for Erich, that was enough.

Both Erich and Joachim were disappointed when they were separated after training. Ten months later, Erich was transferred to Munich, and the two men quickly picked up where they'd left off. Only Joachim knew of the struggles and conflicts plaguing the seemingly confident and poised officer. Only Erich knew that Joachim wasn't always the cheerful man he was perceived to be. Both men were totally at ease when they were together. There was no need to prove anything.

The sound of the door opening startled Erich and jarred him from his thoughts of times that seemed so long ago. He grinned as Joachim sauntered into the room. Definitely the most popular officer on the Munich staff, Joachim was not really what one would call handsome. Slightly shorter than Erich, he was leaner, though just as muscular. His dark golden hair was beginning to thin, and youthful fights had left his nose broken more than once, making him look ruggedly masculine. Like Erich's, his eyes were his most striking feature. Blue-green, sparkling, and usually smiling, they reflected captivating charm.

Joachim's rise in the SS hadn't been as rapid as Erich's, but he didn't seem to mind. They never competed for glory or position. Joachim enjoyed life too much to worry about someone else's career. He really gave little care and concern to his own.

Joachim tossed a file on his desk. "I heard Mueller summoned you to his office," he said. "I decided to stick around to see why."

"It seems our beloved commandant thought he should be the one to break the good news about my new orders. As of tomorrow or the next day, I'll be joining the Death's Head Unit at Dachau."

"Dachau!" Joachim shook his head. "Now that's a surprise. I figured the Nazis would eventually transfer their fair-haired boy, but being one of Himmler's favorites, I figured you'd be headed back to Berlin. Any idea what you'll be doing?

Erich nodded no. "Mueller was vague which leads me to believe he may not know."

"Really?" Joachim said, feigning shock. "The Imperial Prussian actually admitted he's out of the loop? What exactly did he say?"

"Only that I'll be involved in high-flight experiments scheduled to begin at the camp in a few days. Obersturmfuhrer Doctor Sigmund Rascher is the officer in charge. Have you heard of him?"

"No, but it doesn't appear you're excited about your new assignment.

"I'm not unhappy. Perhaps 'unsettled' is a better way to put it."

"Maybe it won't be as bad as you think."

"Sure," Erich said sarcastically. "Joining the Death's Head Unit is something anyone would be thrilled to do."

"Point made. You said you may have to report as early as tomorrow?"

"They're processing my orders as we speak. I originally came back to headquarters to drag you to the Hofbrauhaus for a beer. It seems I could *really* use the diversion."

"Say no more," Joachim removed his coat and hat from the rack. "Shall we go?"

"I'm right behind you," Erich said as Joachim opened the door.

# CHAPTER 3

As Erich and Joachim exited the building and descended the stairs to Arcisstrasse, the pouring rain had dwindled to a light drizzle. "It's freezing out here," Erich grumbled.

Joachim glanced up at the sky. "From the looks of those clouds, we're about to be hit with another downpour. I suggest we get moving."

Erich had to sprint to keep pace with his friend as they raced along Brennerstrasse through Karolinenplatz. When they turned off Odeonsplatz on to Theatinerstrasse, the drizzle turned into a light rain, and when they passed the now-silent glockenspiel in Marienplatz, the rain began to fall in torrents. "Damn it's cold," Joachim said as he pulled the collar of his topcoat tightly around his neck. "Where the hell's your trench-coat?"

"Don't ask."

By the time they reached the Hofbrauhaus three minutes later, Erich was drenched. As Joachim pushed open the door to the Schwemme, the crowded beer hall, an inviting blast of warm air and the smell of stale beer welcomed them. "Heaven on earth," he said as they entered the loud, smoke-filled room.

"Where to?" Erich asked as he acknowledged a few officers who stood and conversed in small groups.

Joachim pointed to long wooden picnic tables and benches near the far end of the hall. "Follow my lead," he said.

"Is there anyone you don't know?" Erich shouted as they pushed their way through the densely packed crowd.

"I certainly hope not." Joachim held up a key to the beer-mug safe. "I'm a regular now. I recently qualified for my own stein." He pulled a coin-like object from his pocket. "And I pay for my beer with tokens."

"I take it I should be impressed."

"Under the circumstances, I'd say that might be an appropriate response."

They approached a sign announcing they were in an area reserved for the "Stammtisch." "And now you have your own special table?" Erich said.

"I do, and I'm proud of it."

They barely had time to take off their caps when a cheerful buxom barmaid wearing a traditional Bavarian costume and carrying ten one-liter steins of Hofbrau Dunkel approached the table. Joachim playfully pinched her cheek. "Two of those dark beers, Gretchen," he said, "and two orders of weisswurste with sweet mustard," He looked at Erich for approval.

Erich nodded yes. "Sounds good to me," he said. "I didn't have much lunch." He watched the barmaid deliberately swing her ample hips as she went to deliver beers to the officers at the next table. "All body and no brains." He shook his head. "She's not my type."

"I'd be fascinated to meet a woman who *is* your type, my friend," Joachim said. "To date I haven't met anyone who could come near to your idea of an ideal woman."

As Joachim conversed with the two of the other regulars at the table, Erich waved away the betzel lady carrying her basket of pretzels and concentrated on the oompah band. The men, dressed in lederhosen and feathered caps, were playing the traditional drinking song, *In Munchen Stent ein Hofbrauhaus.* Erich tapped his foot and gently swayed with the others as they sang:

*In Munich stands a Hofbräuhaus: one, two—cheers!*
*There run out so many steins: one, two—cheers!*
*There are so many brave men: one, two—cheers!*
*Show what he can endure*
*Already early in the morning he begins*
*And late at night he comes out*
*So beautiful it is in the Hofbräuhaus!*

When the band struck one, hundreds of gathered guests raised their thick, one-liter steins and, simultaneously repeating the words, clinked the mugs with everyone in the vicinity. The same process was repeated for two. When the band struck cheers, Erich joined in as everyone took a gulp of the bronze liquid. The chorus was repeated four times in less than four minutes, and when the song was over and the applause had stopped, it was clear that many of their fellow officers were already drunk.

While Erich and Joachim enjoyed their beers and white sausage, more people, military and civilians alike, who seemed to be seeking an escape from the pressures of the day, packed the Schwemme. Here in this haven there was no talk of rationing, no watered-down beer, and no depressing conversation.

As the evening progressed, Erich was both amused and amazed as he watched Joachim flirt with several young women at the same time. He marveled at his friend's ability to keep each and every lady oblivious of his attention to the others. When one curvaceous brunette, obviously one of Joachim's previous conquests, left her seat at a nearby table, he called out: "I'll be over in a while, Gerta. Keep the fire blazing."

Erich watched several more of Joachim's assignations before giving up. "There's no way I can compete with your countless female fans," he said. "So I'm heading home." Joachim opened his mouth to protest, but Erich nodded no. "Enjoy yourself," he said. "It seems I'm not in a party mood after all."

He was about to open the Schwemme door when a woman pushed it toward him. She was tall; Erich guessed about five-feet eight. As she removed her coat, he admired her slim figure. Her skin, though obviously fair, was deeply tanned. Her light ash-blonde hair, streaked blonder by the sun, was long and tied loosely at her neck with a blue ribbon. As she walked, she exuded an air of aloofness and yet, paradoxically, smoldering sensuality. But despite her extraordinary beauty, there was no apparent arrogance in her demeanor.

Passing Erich without even a glance in his direction, the lady crossed the room and joined an elderly man sitting several tables away from Joachim. Preoccupied, Erich nearly knocked over a barmaid carrying a tray of foaming beer as he abruptly turned and retraced his steps. He grabbed Joachim's arm. "Have you seen that woman before?" he asked.

Joachim looked around. "I'm not sure what woman you're talking about, my friend, but I'm sure I've seen all the ladies here tonight, if you know what I mean. I doubt even one of them could have escaped my eye."

"How about the woman who came into the Schwemme a minute ago?" Erich pointed to the table where the lady was intently conversing with her companion. "Do you know her?"

Joachim glanced in the direction Erich was pointing. "You mean the blond knock-out?" he said. "We were introduced, but I don't know her well. She's a staff writer for the *Völkischer Beobachter,* but if you hope to make time with her, forget it. She's ice, my friend. There's no warmth in that gorgeous body, and what a waste. She reminds me a little of you; all work with no time off for play."

"Tell me more about her," Erich said as he stared at the woman.

"There's not much more to tell. When she first came to head-quarters, I tried to impress her with my great looks and indefatigable charm, and I know a few others who were initially interested in getting to know her. So far no one's had any luck. She's definitely not the party type."

"You mean she didn't have time for the idol of the Hofbrauhaus?" Erich joked. "Maybe I'll be luckier than you were. Do you think you could finagle an introduction?"

"After all those insults you actually expect me to help you?"

"Come on," Erich pleaded.

"Stop pouting. Yes, I can introduce you, but, I repeat, it's a lost cause. She turned me down, and we both know how irresistible I am. The man she's with is the liaison between the Propaganda Ministry and the *Völkischer Beobachter*. I know him well enough to approach them."

As Joachim spoke, Erich's regard for the stunning blond escalated. *The People's Observer* was the most influential newspaper in the Third Reich. Known for its exaggeration and hyperbole, it had become Goebbels's instrument for imparting the party line to the masses. If the woman wrote for that paper, she was not only beautiful and talented; she was surely a dedicated party member.

While Erich reflected, Joachim slid off the bench. "Come on," he said, motioning for Erich to follow him to the table where Beck was sitting. As they approached, the woman looked up. Erich noticed a smattering of freckles across the bridge of her nose, her lively dark-blue eyes, and her sharply etched cheekbones. He stared at her almost rudely as Joachim said: "Good evening, Herr Beck."

"Good evening, Obersturmfuhrer," Beck said. There was a pregnant pause until he realized both men were looking at the woman sitting with him. "May I present Fraulein Inge Friedrich, who was recently reassigned from Berlin to the *Völkischer Beobachter* office here in Munich."

Inge looked at Joachim. "We've met before, Obersturmfuhrer," she said coolly.

"We have, Fraulein," Joachim said. "May I present Hauptsturmfuhrer Erich Riedl? Erich, meet Herr Karl Beck and Fraulein Inge Friedrich."

"Would you like to join us, gentlemen?" Beck asked, realizing the men weren't going anywhere.

"We'd be glad to," Erich said a little too quickly. He grinned when Joachim squeezed in beside Beck, leaving him the empty space beside Inge.

Beck, his eyes glinting behind steel-rimmed glasses, directed his attention to Erich. "We haven't been introduced before, Hauptsturmfuhrer," he said, as he fished in his pocket for a cigarette and then paused to light up.

"I've had no occasion to work with the Propaganda Ministry, Herr Beck. Until now, my job has been with Systems and Procedures of SS Operations in Munich."

"Until now?" Inge said, making conversation, but clearly not interested.

"Yes, Fraulein. An hour ago I was given a new assignment. Poor timing, since I met you tonight."

From the frown on Inge's face, Erich could tell his flirtatious comment wasn't positively received. Unsure of what to do next, he looked at Joachim. As expected, his friend raised an eyebrow as if to say, "I told you so."

"Then you're leaving Munich?" Inge said.

"I report to the SS facility at Dachau within the week."

At the mention of Dachau, Inge flinched. Erich looked at Joachim and Beck. Clearly the two men hadn't seen her reaction. Joachim was watching him, and Beck was grounding out his half-smoked cigarette in the ashtray. As he again turned to Inge, Erich recalled his own reaction when Mueller first mentioned Dachau. He wondered what had made Inge react so intensely.

There was a lapse in the conversation as Gretchen approached. "Two more beers, my love," Joachim said. He looked at the others at the table. "Fraulein? Herr Beck?"

"Nothing for me, Obersturmfuhrer," Inge said. "I really must be going." She reached for her purse, stood up, and turned to her boss. "I'll see you in the morning, Herr Beck. Perhaps we'll be able to finish our discussion without interruption." She looked from Eric to Joachim. "Gentlemen," she said coolly.

Erich stood to let Inge slide off the bench. Instead of sitting back down, he followed close behind as she made her way through the crowd. "Herr Beck said you recently arrived in Munich," he said as they approached the Schwemme door. "Do you often come to the Hofbrauhaus?"

"My job leaves me little time for a social life, Hauptsturmfuhrer," Inge said curtly.

"Erich, please, Fraulein."

Ignoring Erich's request, Inge continued: "Hauptsturmfuhrer, you heard me arrange an early-morning meeting with Herr Beck, so I must say goodnight."

"Would you join me for dinner tomorrow evening, Fraulein?" Erich persisted. "I'd like to see you again."

Inge nodded no. "I'm sorry, Hauptsturmfuhrer. That won't be possible." She looked at her watch. "My aunt is expecting me for dinner, and I'm already late. She abruptly turned and walked away, leaving Erich self-conscious as he saw Joachim watching the encounter. He turned and walked slowly back to Joachim's table. Beck had left, so he sat down in his place.

"That obviously went well." Joachim said, his voice oozing sarcasm. "An icy one, huh, my friend?"

"I suppose I'm going to hear an 'I told you so.'"

"From me? Never!" Joachim laughed. "But I hate to be the one to mention—"

"Then don't."

As Joachim droned on, Erich's enthusiasm for the evening once again dwindled. He tried to convince himself that his failure to solve the supply issue combined with news of his new assignment had made him tired and irritable. His original purpose in coming to the Hofbrauhaus had been to unwind, and now he was anything but relaxed.

He looked up to see Gretchen carrying another stein-filled tray. "No more for me," he said. As he got ready to leave, he couldn't resist one last sarcastic comment to Joachim. "Have a great time with your little barmaid. At least one of us will have a stimulating evening."

Joachim patted Erich on the back. "Tough luck, my friend," he said. "But look around you. You can't let one cool female get you down. I see numerous ladies who would love to spend time in your company. Any one of them would do her part to help you forget the frosty reception you got from the ice queen."

Joachim's sly grin irritated Erich even more than his sarcastic tone. "Not tonight," he grumbled. "See you tomorrow." He made his way through the crowd. As he pushed open the Schwemme door, a blast of wintry air slapped him in the face. He momentarily considered turning back to the warmth of the Hofbrauhaus, but instead, he pulled his collar around his neck and faced the frosty cold. At the moment, confronting the weather seemed preferable to facing Joachim and his I-told-you-so mentality.

As he walked along the narrow, dark, deserted streets leading to his apartment on St. Annastrasse, Erich felt an overwhelming sense of loneliness. It was too wet and cold for pedestrians to be strolling on an October evening, and with the strict gas rationing in place and the blackout requirements, few cars were on the road. Munich looked and felt like a ghost town. The people were hiding from life behind their blackout curtains. *War has sapped the life out of a usually vibrant city*, he reflected grimly. *Maybe that's what's wrong. It's sapped the life out of me too.*

With two short blocks to go, he passed Anna Kloster. Suddenly the skies opened and the rain fell in torrents. He began to run as quickly as the battering wind would allow, but the gusts only drove the rain harder, impeding his progress. By the time he splashed the final yards to his apartment, his clothes were saturated and he felt like a walking icicle.

Hoping to generate some body heat, he hustled up the stairs to his third-floor room. The door creaked as he pushed it open to face the Spartan surroundings he called home. Without turning on the lights, he walked to the window and peered out at the torrents of hammering rain assaulting the glass. Nothing was visible in the dark night; the rain hid all.

With the blackout curtains firmly in place, he turned on the lights, removed his soggy clothes, and hung them on the hook that served as his closet. He vigorously toweled himself dry and put on a thick robe. Still chilled, he moved around the room to generate some warmth in his body. As he walked back toward the bed, hoping that crawling under the inviting down comforter would warm his chilled body, the single picture on his otherwise empty dresser caught his eye. As he gazed at the distinguished-looking man with the thick mustache who stared back at him from the frame, the loneliness he had felt as he walked along the nearly deserted streets returned. In the man's face he could see his own features. He looked into twinkling eyes, and, as he often did in moments of reflection, he wondered what his life would have been like had his father not committed suicide. He took the picture with him to the bed and placed it beside him on the nightstand. Because he was so chilled, he left his robe on as he nestled under the thick comforter.

Settled in the ever-increasing warmth, Erich picked up the picture again and thought about his father. The family was wealthy, the third generation to produce steel in the Ruhr valley. In his mind's-eye, he could still see his great house bustling with servants and friends. Then, without warning, his life changed. He was too young to realize his country's humiliating defeat at the end of World War I had brought about the radical changes in his life. He didn't understand why the friendly servants were leaving him, but he knew there was something really bad happening. His loving and perpetually cheerful father no longer smiled, and his usually happy mother cried all the time.

It was only after he joined the Nazi Party, that Erich began to comprehend the enormous strain the war and the ensuing, peace had put on his father. Hitler Youth leaders finally put it plainly in words he could understand. In 1923, Germany failed to pay the reparation payments required by the Versailles Treaty, so French and Belgian troops marched into the Ruhr.

In retrospect it wasn't hard for Erich to figure out how the invasion personally affected his family. Because his father made steel for the German war machine, the victors accused him of criminal activity and seized everything he owned. That was all except for the property outside Berlin, the place where he and Joachim once played and dreamed. Years later his mother explained how his father hid the deed to Unser Traum, the land that had been his father's and his grandfather's before him. The defeated man staunchly refused to allow anyone to take his son's only remaining legacy.

As an adult, Erich began to understand his father's all-pervading feelings of guilt and despair when his family was abruptly reduced to a state of near poverty. His inability to provide for those he loved caused him to put a gun to his head and pull the trigger. Even now, when he thought of his family, Erich's recollections were not of the happiness he enjoyed during his youth in the big house, but rather of the sorrow and hopelessness pervading his home after his father's death. He clearly recalled the changes the suicide made in his mother's face; the dark circles under her beautiful blue eyes that were usually red from crying. He remembered the efforts she made to be courageous as she carefully packed their few remaining personal possessions. He remembered her attempts to be cheerful and confident when they were forced to move to Berlin after the big house was stolen out from under them. He remembered her tears as he huddled against her and stared at the bare walls in the small apartment which a family friend had kindly rented to them. He remembered, but it wasn't until he was much older that he understood his mother's pain and fear and the desperation that drove his father to an early death.

As he curled up in his now warm bed, Erich pictured his mother. After the anguishing move, she found a job as an assistant to a newspaper printer. The publisher, another family friend, took pity on the penniless woman with the small child to support. Her meager salary allowed her to maintain the small apartment and to meet Erich's basic needs. Their home was clean but certainly not fancy. From time to time Erich wondered if growing up in the sterile atmosphere had shaped his own Spartan tastes.

But it wasn't the sparseness of their apartment that haunted him. It was the change he saw in his mother. Night after night she'd return home from an arduous day, exhausted and dejected. Yet despite her perpetual fatigue, she always managed to make a decent meal for the two of them. For Erich's sake, she struggled to remain optimistic, though when she smiled her eyes were dull and lifeless. Over the years she grew increasingly wan and gaunt. Except for her beloved son, there was no joy in her life.

As he matured, Erich began to understand that financial worries were the primary cause of his mother's distress. He pleaded with her to sell Unser Traum and quit her job, but she adamantly refused. It was, she argued, all that remained to secure his future. He'd been robbed of everything else. She would not let him lose Unser Traum.

When she died of pneumonia in 1936, Erich finally realized his mother never overcame the trauma of his father's death and the ensuing changes it made in her life. He felt overwhelming love and gratitude for a woman who had done everything in her power to make his life as pleasant and comfortable as possible. During these lonely intervals, he missed her the most.

Erich put the picture back on the table. He closed his eyes and listened to the pounding of the rain, hoping the monotonous sound would lull him to sleep. After twenty minutes of tossing and turning, he decided it was ridiculous to lie there doing nothing. He got up, turned on the light, and crossed the room to pick up a magazine. As he moved past the door, he bent and retrieved his cap, which had fallen from the hook holding his dripping clothes. Before hanging it back up, he paused and fingered the skull and crossbones so prominently displayed on the black fabric. "Obedience and loyalty to the Fuhrer and to one another unto the grave and beyond." For years this ancient credo of the Teuton Knights had been a driving force in his life. It was the reason he would go to Dachau and carry out his duties, whatever they proved to be. Erich's thoughts turned again to his father. Would he approve of his son's political leanings and his membership in the SS? Somehow, Erich doubted he would.

He took the magazine back to bed, but reading provided no relief from the strange combination of restlessness and boredom he was feeling. His mind drifted from the words on the pages to the evening he'd spent at the Hofbrauhaus. For a fleeting moment he considered dressing and going back to find Joachim, but the ceaseless sound of the rain battering the window and the thought of putting on his frosty clothing and trudging into the frigid night were definite deterrents. So, instead of getting up, he put down the magazine and reflected on the event-filled day. His anxiety about going to Dachau mingled with thoughts of Inge, and he became increasingly uneasy. What would the future bring? Afraid to speculate, he closed his eyes and, once again, tried to sleep.

# CHAPTER 4

The dark clouds and pelting rain were of little concern to Inge as she left the warmth of the Hofbrauhaus. Her heavy wool-lined raincoat and the umbrella she carried kept out the dampness. Eager to be home, she walked briskly up Theatinerstrasse toward Odeonsplatz and her aunt's house on Jagerstrasse.

As she neared the familiar front door, she thought about how glad she was to be back in Munich; the town where she spent most of her life. Her father, a foot soldier in the Kaiser's army, had been killed during the Second Battle of the Marne in August 1918, and her mother died of tuberculosis a year later. Because there were no other relatives to care for her, she came to Munich to live with her father's only sister, her maiden Aunt Sigrid. Two years after her arrival, Sigrid adopted Rosel, the child of friends who were tragically killed in a train wreck. Over the years, Sigrid, Inge, and Rosel had become a family in the real sense of the word.

"Is that you, darling?" Sigrid called from the kitchen when she heard the door close.

"It is, Aunt Sigrid."

The pungent aroma of schweinebraten, Inge's favorite pot-roasted pork, and kraut filled the house. With the rationing going on, Inge wondered how her aunt continued to serve meat. *I guess it's her old-time contacts at the local markets,* she mused as she headed toward the kitchen.

Inge loved the home, probably because it was much like her aunt, warm and practical with few frills. In the parlor, comfortable chairs and an overstuffed eiderdown couch sat cozily beside a large fireplace where logs blazed. Behind the plain curtains at the windows, drawn tightly to help keep out the dampness, were the unpleasant black shades, grim reminders of the war raging all around them. When the order to block out the light had been issued, Sigrid refused to comply with the directive. After several arguments, she acquiesced, but as she said with a sneer on her face, "only to keep Rosel safe."

When Inge reached the cozy kitchen, her fifty-three-year-old aunt was standing at the stove, her back to the door. Her gray hair, which had become considerably grayer over the past few months, was tightly coiled in a bun at the back of her head. Sigrid turned, and her eyes, so lately troubled, strained, and tired, smiled in greeting. Like Inge, Sigrid initially seemed aloof, even standoffish, but as acquaintances became friends, they quickly discovered the woman was warm, generous, and caring. Though middle-aged, her figure was still firm and slim, and Inge often teased her about the men who looked at her admiringly.

"Why don't you sit and relax for a few minutes, darling?" Sigrid said. "Dinner's almost ready."

"It smells delicious," said Inge. "If you're sure you don't mind, I'll kick off my shoes and read the paper, unless I can do something for you."

"The work's finished, so enjoy the fire and unwind."

Inge returned to the parlor. She tried to focus on the paper's cover story, but instead, she thought about the reasons she'd returned to Munich. She wished the circumstances surrounding her homecoming could have been happier, but then life at the Friedrich household hadn't been cheerful since Hitler first seized power. Inge realized she bore much of the responsibility for the incessant quarreling. Despite her aunt's vehement protests, she'd remained resolute. She would play a role in the new Germany.

Finally, tired of battling, Sigrid allowed her to join the Bund Deutscher Madel, the state-sponsored group for girls fourteen to eighteen. In her mind's eye Inge could still see Sigrid's tears when, under great duress, she signed the permission form. As she handed her the papers, she reiterated her fervent wish that the values she'd instilled over the years would take precedent over the teachings of Adolf Hitler, or as she irreverently spit out, the "Pied Piper of Hamlin."

Inge placed the newspaper on the table, lay her head on the back of the chair and continued to think about the past. For as long as she could remember, she'd wanted to be a journalist. She planned and dreamed about a career covering all the important events of the day. To the impressionable teen, one of the principal appeals of the BDM was the chance to pursue her goal, and now, after years of hard work, she was a successful and respected writer for one of Germany's most important papers.

*Journalist?* She smirked as she thought about what being a newspaperwoman in the Third Reich really meant. *I can't remember when I've written a truly important story,* she mused. *When did the enthusiasm instilled in me as a girl begin to fade?* With increasing disdain, she'd come to realize her dreamed-about career was not what she envisioned it would be. All she *really* did was regurgitate the propaganda Goebbels and the party provided.

Inge vividly recalled early days of training and indoctrination in the BDM. Though she wasn't fond of the arts, crafts, childcare, cooking, and sewing, she loved learning the folklore and traditions of the party. Kinder, Kuche, Kirche; children kitchen, church, was the group's slogan. Though she rejected the concept that the primary role of young females in Nazi Germany was to give birth to healthy, racially-pure boys, she enjoyed the camaraderie among the girls, particularly the sports competition. She excelled at the long jump, and she loved to swim in the summer and ski in the winter. Over the three years she was a member of the BDM, she wholeheartedly accepted the importance of self-sacrifice for Germany. She was taught to avoid racial defilement and, sadly for Sigrid, learned to rebel if her aunt didn't fall in line with the party philosophy.

When Inge was eighteen, Sigrid won the next battle in their continuing war. Inge wanted to join the Belief and Beauty Movement, an organization for girls eighteen to twenty-one. Thinking her niece had been exposed to enough propaganda, Sigrid forbade her from participating, and instead, insisted she enter the university.

After graduation, excited to begin work and eager for the chance to do something important for Germany and the Fuhrer, Inge took a job as a cub reporter for the *Völkischer Beobachter* in the Munich office. It didn't take long for her to embrace the party philosophy: the public needed to be tested; the truth manipulated selectively and twisted to give it new life. The use of constant repetition, posters, and blaring loudspeakers—and a total monopoly of all printed words—became a customary and acceptable way of life.

When she successfully completed a six-month training period, she was permanently assigned to the paper's Berlin staff. At first, her job was almost as exciting and challenging as her training had been, but soon the deadly conformity that began to unfold in the nation's press as it was harnessed to serve the propaganda needs of the state began to temper her enthusiasm. There was no longer room for creativity or individual analysis of events, and reporting the truth became a forgotten concept.

Every day Inge received directives from her editor, Alfred Rosenberg, who was given his orders by Goebbels or one of the reichsfuhrer's aides. She was forever being told what to write and what to suppress, how to slant the headlines, which editorial lines to emphasize, and what to delete from the paper altogether. She began to think if she heard about Section Fourteen of the Press Law once more, she would scream in frustration. She could quote the words verbatim: "Nothing can be included in the newspaper that could weaken the will of the German people or the defense of Germany. Nothing can be included which will offend the honor and dignity of the country." Now with the course of the war changing for the worse, what a problem the law had become for every legitimate journalist; if any remained.

Sigrid's voice interrupted Inge's musings. "Dinner is served," she called from the kitchen. "Come and eat while it's hot."

Inge got up from the comfortable chair and went to join her aunt. She paused in the kitchen door, recalling with a great deal of shame and regret the numerous tension-filled meals she, Sigrid, and Rosel had shared at the table that had once been an escape, even a refuge from the outside world.

Throughout the months before Inge moved from home to a dorm on the Munich campus to pursue her political and career goals, the family dinners had, more often than not, turned into angry confrontations. What had once been the highlight of each day became so distressing that, though she lived only a few kilometers away from home, Inge made countless excuses for staying away, and eventually she stopped having dinner with her aunt and her adopted sister altogether. She dreaded, even feared, recurrences of the loud arguments that typically had her storming away from the table leaving Sigrid and Rosel in tears.

*How ironic,* Inge thought as she watched her aunt dish up the steaming food. *Sigrid tried to use Rosel's love of the classics, history, art, and music, as well as her political neutrality to shame me into giving up my dream. Yet her efforts made me even more determined to live my life my way.*

Though the two women had put the confrontations in the past, Sigrid's angry denunciations were etched in Inge's memory. "Why can't you be more like your sister?" she would shout at the height of a dinner-time argument. "You no longer have a mind of your own." Inge remembered how furious those words and Sigrid's tone had made her feel, but instead of achieving their intended purpose, they only served to make her more determined to persuade her family that Hitler's way was the right path for all of them.

Finally, after months of being apart and missing their time together, the members of the Friedrich household had agreed that Hitler and the merits or shortcomings of the Nazi Party would no longer be debated, particularly during meals. But despite the truce, when Inge once again came back to the family table, the underlying tension lingered, and an awkward silence often replaced the once-lively conversation.

After Inge was assigned to the Berlin office, the three rarely saw each other, so when she could get home, her visits with Sigrid and Rosel were tranquil and satisfying. That was until the day when Inge's world was shattered and the joyful serenity that had once again become a way of life abruptly disappeared.

Three months before, Sigrid had called; her voice panicky and tremulous as she begged her niece to come home. Inge pleaded for an explanation. What was so important that she should take time off from work and return to Munich? Though she urged and cajoled, Sigrid, too unnerved to provide any information over the telephone, became even more agitated. So, with a sinking feeling in her stomach, Inge took the train to Munich, where upon her arrival, she quickly learned their lives had drastically changed; Rosel was missing.

For two days, stopping only to sleep for a few hours at night, Inge and Sigrid searched for a clue to Rosel's whereabouts. They went from door to door, asking friends and strangers alike for information. One neighbor thought she'd seen Rosel leave the house with a shopping bag, but no storekeeper where she regularly shopped remembered if she'd been in that day. Apprehension and frustration mounted as their search went nowhere. They were part of a frightening mystery, and every clue led to a dead end. Both were sure that Rosel wouldn't leave for any length of time without telling them, and she had nowhere to go. Her life was in Munich. Reluctantly, they could only conclude she'd been taken by someone—but by whom, and why?

When Sigrid first called, Inge applied for and was granted a four-day leave of absence from the paper. With the time almost up, there was still no trace of Rosel nor a hint of what happened to her. Sigrid was inconsolable, and Inge, realizing she had no choice but to remain in Munich, asked for and was given more time at home.

Day after day they searched, but they encountered only dead ends. As Inge's fears for Rosel grew, so did the enigma. There was no rational explanation for the woman's disappearance. As each day passed, Inge became increasingly sure that Sigrid was holding back essential information. Over and over she appealed to her aunt to tell her if there was a reason Rosel might leave, or if she knew of anything that might help them in their investigation. Each time Sigrid changed the subject, but Inge could see the distress in her eyes as she denied knowing anything more than what she'd already shared.

Despite the fact that Sigrid reacted negatively to Inge's probing, she persisted with her queries. Finally, with only hours of her leave remaining and sure Sigrid was privy to a secret, Inge threatened to abandon the investigation and return to Berlin if her aunt refused to tell her whatever it was she was hiding. With no other option, Sigrid reluctantly acquiesced.

Inge would never forget the discussion that made such a profound impact on her life. The dinner dishes had been put away and the two women were having coffee in the parlor. A deafening silence persisted as they sat and stared into the dying fire. Sigrid finally broke the impasse. "I've given this matter a great deal of thought over the past few days, Inge," she said tentatively. "You deserve to know what I've been hiding from you. I should have told you earlier, but I was frightened. I only hope I'm not too late for us and for Rosel." Perhaps to avoid the subject for as long as possible, Sigrid rose and added two more logs to the fire. She stared pensively as the flames leapt up, casting eerie shadows on the walls.

Feeling an unexpected twinge of trepidation, Inge shifted nervously on the couch. Sigrid, sensing her niece's growing uneasiness, her impatience to know what was being hidden from her, and her unwillingness to prod, sat down. At last freeing herself from the burden she'd been carrying, she began to speak: "I've never spoken about Rosel's past," she began. "But now it's time for you to know everything. When Rosel first came to live with us, you were both very young and there was no need for me to say anything. When you were old enough to understand, because of your deep commitment to those horrible Nazis, I couldn't talk with you, Inge, and I certainly couldn't tell Rosel and ask her to keep my secret."

"What could my political association have to do with Rosel, Aunt Sigrid?" Inge said, feeling both confused and irritated. "Are you blaming me for making you keep your deep, dark secret?"

Sigrid's eyes spit fire and her anger was evident when she spoke. "I suppose in a way I am, Inge," she said. "Because of your 'Pied Piper,' I had to keep my secret, and worse, deny Rosel her ancestry and her heritage."

When she saw the anguish in Sigrid's eyes, Inge's anger abated, and, instead, she became increasingly confused by the direction their conversation was taking. "I have no idea what you're talking about, Aunt Sigrid," she said, her frustration growing.

"I'm trying to explain," Sigrid said, her voice wavering as she clasped her hands in her lap. "Until this moment, your party affiliation forced me to keep important information from both you and Rosel. Lord knows, I wanted to discuss this matter years ago, but I was afraid if I shared my secret, I'd be putting you in a difficult position. You would be forced to decide whether your loyalties lay with Rosel and me or with your chosen party. I loved you too much to ask you to make a decision, and, I confess, I was too frightened by your fanatical belief in the Fuhrer to test your loyalties." Sigrid paused, inhaled, and exhaled deeply. "Speaking truthfully, I'm still frightened." Sigrid watched Inge's reaction, and seeing her niece's distress, quickly added: "Though now I don't doubt what your choice would have been and will be now. I'm confident you would have picked your family over your Fuhrer."

"I don't understand, Aunt Sigrid," Inge said hesitantly.

"You will, Inge. Let me finish. You know my dear friends Johann and Eva were killed in a dreadful train wreck outside of Lucerne. You also know they left their only daughter, Rosel, at home while they vacationed. Eva asked to take the baby with them, but Johann wanted her to have a break from the duties of motherhood. He said the trip was to be their second honeymoon, so they left Rosel with her nanny, and I checked in on her every day."

"That's old news, Aunt Sigrid," Inge said curtly, her renewed sympathy for her aunt once again giving way to irritation. "You're not telling me anything I haven't heard dozens of times before."

Sigrid continued calmly. "I also told you when Eva and Johann died there were no grandparents, aunts or uncles to take the child."

"I'm waiting to hear something new; information that will help us locate Rosel."

Sigrid clinched her jaw, and the color drained from her face. "That's what I'm trying to tell you, Inge. You need to know that I lied to you."

Not sure she heard correctly, Inge waited for her aunt to elaborate. When she didn't, Inge reached over and took her hand. "What are you saying, Aunt Sigrid?" she said. "I've never known you to lie about anything."

"I'm trying to explain, Inge, but it's so difficult. Eva's and Johann's families didn't approve of the marriage and disowned them."

"Why did they object?"

"I'll get to that in due time. As I was about to say, when they left Rosel in my care, Eva and Johann also left me a considerable sum to care for her and a large trust she can claim when she turns thirty-five."

"So that's how we've lived so comfortably all these years," Inge reflected aloud. "All along I assumed the money was yours, but it wasn't my place to ask. You know if Germany loses the war, German currency won't have any value, so—"

"That won't be a problem, Sigrid said. "I keep only enough cash in my Munich account to provide us with day-to-day necessities. In 1931, when Hitler began to consolidate his power, Johann's accountant, who has invested and more than doubled the money over the years, transferred the bulk of the funds into Swiss accounts, so it will be there for us and Rosel if and when we need it, but that's beside the point. The money played no part in my decision to adopt Rosel. She had nowhere to go and no one to love her. I couldn't let the authorities put her in an orphanage, and I thought she would make a wonderful companion for you. From the first moment she came into the house, I knew I'd made the right decision. The two of you became fast friends."

"This is all well and good," Inge said, still impatient. "But I can't figure out where all this is leading. I need to know what you've been hiding from me for all these years."

"I'm getting there, Inge. Please bear with me. You must see how hard this if for me to talk about."

"Please trust me, Aunt Sigrid," Inge implored.

"I do trust you, darling." Sigrid looked down, avoiding eye contact as she continued. "From the day Rosel arrived I raised you both as my own children. In their will, Eva and Johann also stipulated that, if anything happened to them, Rosel would legally keep the name Dollman, so I was never able to adopt her. For convenience's sake I called her Rosel Friedrich. No one besides you knows I'm not her real aunt, which makes her disappearance all the more puzzling. I intended to tell you both the story about Rosel's parents when I felt you were old enough to understand."

"Understand what? And what stopped you?"

Sigrid hesitated again before slowly resuming her explanation. "For one thing, while you were growing up the timing never seemed to be right. You and Rosel were happy, and I wanted her to concentrate on the love I was giving her and the future I would provide, not on a tragedy that occurred when she was a baby. Then you became enthralled with the teachings of the Nazi Party."

Inge glared at her aunt. "I can't understand why you keep referring to my political affiliation," she said irritably. "What could politics have to do with whatever it is you're trying to say? You've never hidden your distaste for the Fuhrer, but I can't see how he or the party has anything to do with why you couldn't share your deep, dark secret until now."

"If you'll stop interrupting, I'll try to make you understand."

Duly admonished and regretting her sharp outburst, Inge sat back down on the couch. "I apologize, Aunt Sigrid," she said. "Please go on, but I wish you'd get to the point."

Sigrid dropped her chin to her chest. "I *will*, darling, though I continue to wish this conversation didn't have to take place."

Inge took her aunt's hand. "What is it?" she pleaded. "What's the secret you've kept for so long? You realize nothing you say could make me love you less."

"I hope that's true, Inge." Sigrid sighed. "I told you that I always planned to share my secret, but not like this. Now Rosel's disappearance forces me to bring everything out into the open sooner than I'd have liked. I don't mean to hurt you, Inge, but after you became an ardent Nazi, it was too late to confide in you. During the early days of your membership in the Bund Deutscher Madel, I considered broaching the subject, but every night you'd come home more excited about the Fuhrer and the party. Each time you did, I put the discussion off for another day, but another day never came. I suppose I was a coward, but Rosel was happy and my secret was safe, so why take a chance?"

"A chance on what?"

"A chance that my revelation would ruin all of our lives. Only days after you joined your girls' club I realized that, however much you loved her, ideologically speaking, Rosel had become your enemy."

Inge let go of Sigrid's hand. "How could you say such a thing?" she said, her eyes flashing. "I may have been obstinate from time to time, but if Rosel were my real sister, I couldn't love her more."

Tears fell down Sigrid's face. "Rosel was the reason I tried to keep you from becoming a part of the Nazi movement," she cried. "I tried every argument I knew, except the right one. I didn't tell you the truth before it was too late. I should have said something the minute I realized Herr Hitler's plan for the Jews."

"I don't understand," Inge said, feeling increasingly concerned as she waited to hear what Sigrid had kept from her for so long.

"Listen and you will." Sigrid took a breath and finally said the words: "How could I reveal that our Rosel was a Mischling?"

Inge recoiled. Crossbreed? Of mixed blood? Blood Shame? These were words Hitler used to describe German intermarriage with other races, especially the Jews. But these were other people who had nothing to do with her. They were strangers.

As soon as she shared her secret, Sigrid seemed to regain her composure, and there was newfound resolve in her voice. "Rosel's mother was Jewish," she explained. "Johann, who was one of my closest childhood friends, loved Eva and married her in spite of their differing beliefs. Her religion wasn't a problem for him, but both families refused to have anything to do with them or Rosel when she was born."

"That's why they were disowned?"

"Yes, and why I was chosen as Rosel's guardian."

Sigrid stared at Inge, waiting for her to respond. For a while Inge seemed lost in her thoughts. "And all this time," she finally said.

Sigrid completed the sentence: "We've both loved Rosel because she's a valued member of our family. I had no problem with Eva's faith. She was a wonderful woman and a loving mother. I wish Rosel had known her, but that's not important now. I couldn't tell either of you because I waited too long. When your Fuhrer began to preach his hatred of the Jews and enacted those horrible Nuremberg Laws in 1935, Rosel's secret had to remain mine alone. I couldn't even share it with her for fear she would tell you. That's another reason I'm telling you this now. If the Nazis discovered my secret, you and I could be in jeopardy for harboring a woman whose mother was a Jew."

Her mind filled with conflicting thoughts, Inge trembled at the full realization of the conflict and misery her aunt must have endured when those laws were passed. For the first time she truly understood Sigrid's vehement objections to her alliance with the Nazi Party. She thought of the times when, as a journalist of the Reich, she'd supported the Nuremberg Laws in her articles and reports. Now she tried to apply their significance to Rosel. Because of Eva's religion, her marriage to Johann was strictly forbidden, and Rosel, the offspring of their illegal union, was less than a citizen; she was subhuman, a vermin to be despised.

Inge didn't immediately respond, but racing through her mind were the specifics of the laws. "Give me a minute to take all this in," she said. She rose, put another log on the fire, and watched the leaping flames. So many times she'd written about the directives that were created to "safeguard the nation and the people." She knew the propaganda angle by heart. Marriage between Jews and German citizens was forbidden. According to the law, Rosel would have been banned from public parks, libraries, and beaches. She would have been forced to wear the yellow badge of shame in Hitler's Germany and because her name, Friedrich, didn't sound Jewish, she would have had to add the name Sarah to her given name. Rosel Sarah Friedrich. It seemed inconceivable.

Inge assessed Rosel's situation. Having two Jewish grandparents coupled with maternal legitimacy, meant she would have been a Mischling of the first degree. What did this mean? Though she was still worried, she felt slightly better. She was relatively sure that Berlin hadn't made a decision about the disposition of the Mischlinge. *Maybe that's why Sigrid and I are safe for the moment,* she thought. *They wouldn't want to arrest a Völkischer Beobachter journalist unless there was a valid reason. And maybe,* she reasoned, *they're not sure of Rosel's status. That bodes well for us, at least for the moment.*

In an instant Inge finally understood the full significance of what Sigrid had shared and her reluctance to tell Rosel's story. Fighting the tears welling-up in her eyes, she spoke quietly; her voice pleading and sorrowful. "Did you actually believe I would report your secret to the Gestapo, Aunt Sigrid?" she asked. "For even a moment, did you think the party or the Fuhrer were more important to me than you and Rosel?"

Wringing her hands, Sigrid looked down. Her resolve again disappeared as she choked out the words: "I don't know, Inge, I wasn't sure how you'd react. All I knew for certain was your enthusiasm for your newfound cause was unwavering. I suppose, in my heart, I doubted you'd do anything to jeopardize our safety, but I couldn't test your resolve, nor, as I said, could I ask you to choose. So many times you asked—no, you insisted—that I keep my objections about the Nazis to myself. You even told me it was your obligation to report any irregularities in my behavior to your superiors at the BDM. After all the years of indoctrination you'd received, how could I be sure?"

As she listened, Inge realized Sigrid's fears had been justified. Because of her newfound insight, the initial indignation she'd felt when she heard her aunt's allegations evaporated. She had been an ardent Nazi, but would she have chosen the party line over her family? Would she have reported Rosel? *Definitely not,* she thought. Despite her passionate political convictions, she would have kept her aunt's secret. She would have picked Rosel over the party.

Sigrid interrupted Inge's musings, bringing her back to the moment at hand. She'd covered years in a matter of minutes.

"Come sit," Sigrid was saying. "I'm sure you're hungry after such a long day."

"That I am, Aunt Sigrid. The pork roast smells delicious."

Inge sat down while Sigrid served the meal. "I'm glad you're home, darling," she said. "You're rarely out this late, and I was beginning to worry. Did you get your new assignment? I know you were hopeful."

"Not yet. That was why I stopped by the Hofbrauhaus for an after-hours meeting with Herr Beck. I'm late because I ended up staying longer than I originally planned. While we were talking, he introduced me to a young man, an SS officer named Erich Riedl."

"And you liked him?" Sigrid said anxiously.

Inge smiled. "Not in the way you're thinking."

"I can't believe I'm hearing this, Inge. I've encouraged you to meet a nice young man and settle down, but not with an SS fanatic. I hardly think the word 'nice' would apply to anyone in that horrible group."

"Aunt Sigrid, you're not listening to me. I'm not interested in Erich, at least not for personal reasons."

"I'm afraid you're not making much sense."

"I'm trying to explain, so listen before you jump to conclusions."

"I'll try, darling, but you know me."

"I certainly do." Inge smiled. "As I was saying, in the course of our conversation, I learned that Hauptsturmfuhrer Riedl has just been reassigned to Dachau."

"Inge—"

Inge held up her hand. "I said no comments until you've heard everything I have to say. I know you hate it when I mention Dachau, but as I said when you trusted me with the particulars of Rosel's background, I'm convinced that if either the SS or the

Gestapo is responsible for her disappearance, she would have been taken to the nearest detention facility, and that's Dachau. Since I've yet to find out anything about the fate of the Mischlinge, my assumption is she's still there. That's one of the reasons I stayed here in Munich instead of going back to Berlin."

Quickly realizing Inge's intent, Sigrid scowled. "For God's sake, don't tell me you'd even consider using this SS officer to help in your search," she said. "I absolutely forbid it, Inge. This man could cause terrible problems for us and for Rosel. SS men are zealots, and they detest Jews. If Erich Riedl knew we'd been harboring—"

Inge put her hand on her aunt's arm. "You're getting way ahead of yourself, Aunt Sigrid," she said calmly. "I have no idea if I'll ask Hauptsturmfuhrer Riedl's to help us search for Rosel, but honestly, I'm at a dead end, and I don't know what else to do. Despite my best efforts I can't get anyone to tell me about Dachau and who's being held there. Over and over, using a different angle each time, I asked Beck to let me write a story about the camp, but each time he turned me down with no explanation for his decision. Until I have a new angle, I can't ask again. When I met Erich, a possible solution to my problem stood right in front of me."

"But Inge—"

"Please stop worrying. Would it help if I promise not to jump into anything without thorough planning, especially if it means putting Rosel or you and me in any danger? Had I known how upset you'd be, I wouldn't have mentioned Erich Riedl, and you're right, he's probably an extremist. Whatever my decision, I promise to proceed cautiously."

Sigrid opened her mouth to protest, but Inge nodded no. "There's been enough talk of Dachau and the SS for one evening," she said. "Tell me about your day."

Seemingly glad to change the subject and talk about trivialities, Sigrid mentioned Frau Oberhausen's concern about the shortage of food at the local market, and she talked about Herr Koch's fear that the early October frost would kill the last of the summer vegetables in his garden. To Inge, her aunt's day epitomized pleasure. It had been a long time since she had shopped or stopped to talk with friends or neighbors.

"Are you listening to me, Inge?" Sigrid said. "You seem to be somewhere else. I hope you're not thinking about Dachau or that SS man again."

"Not at all, Aunt Sigrid. I'm thinking how I'd like to spend my leisure hours."

"Then why don't you take some time off? I'm sure Herr Beck can function without you for a little while."

Inge sighed. "I'd love to," she said. "But we both know it's impossible, at least not now. I have to locate Rosel and find a way to her home." Inge stroked her aunt's hand, not daring to let Sigrid know what she was really thinking: *Hauptsturmfuhrer Riedl. You may be the only hope I have for bringing my family back together.* She smiled at Sigrid, once again noticing the exhaustion and anguish on the face she loved so much. "We'll take everything a day at a time. We can't get too far ahead of ourselves." She got up from the table. "Come on," she said. "I'll help you with the dishes."

# CHAPTER 5

Erich spent a restless night. The rain was still pounding against the windowpane when he dragged himself out of bed. He walked to the window and raised the blackout curtain. There was no sign of blue on the horizon, and the menacing gray-black clouds offered no promise of a respite from the storm. He shivered, crossed the room, and felt his clothes. *Still wet with little chance of drying today,* he silently complained. After washing up in the basin in the bathroom down the hall, he returned to his room and grudgingly pulled on his damp trousers. As he buckled his belt, he paused to read the engraving on the metal buckle: "Unsere Ehre Heisst Treue," My Honor Is Loyalty." *There's nowhere an SS man can go in Germany nowadays without being reminded,* he reflected, *not even his own bedroom. As if I need to be reminded.*

When he finished dressing, the only dry clothes he had on were his shirt and tie, and the moist uniform jacket was quickly saturating them with an uncomfortable dampness. He took his trench coat from the hook. "If I'd worn this yesterday, I wouldn't be so miserable now," he muttered as he locked his apartment door behind him.

An icy blast of moist air slapped him in the face as he pushed open the outer doors of the apartment building. Reluctant to face the elements, he paused in the doorway. With the soggy uniform underneath his coat it wouldn't be an enjoyable walk to work, but he had no choice. He turned onto St. Annastrasse and headed to the office.

By the time he got to Arcisstrasse, Erich was waterlogged. He tugged open the heavy door and dripped his way along the first-floor corridor to the radio room. An enlisted man sitting hunched over the short-wave radio barely looked up. "You're early today, Hauptsturmfuhrer," he said.

"I'm expecting new orders, Wagner. Any chance they're ready?"

"Let me check." Wagner sifted through the information on the paper-strewn desk. "They're not here yet," he said. "Try again in a few hours."

"I'll have breakfast and check when I get back." As he started down the steps, Erich thought about skipping breakfast altogether, but on cue, his stomach growled. Braving the elements, he jogged to the Café Luitpold on Brennerstrasse. "I should have realized my orders wouldn't be ready and stopped here on the way to work," he grumbled as he silently cursed the wretched weather.

The smell of ersatz coffee greeted him as he entered the cheerful room. *I wish the horrible stuff tasted as good as it smells,* he thought as he made his way to a table in the corner by the fireplace. A frumpy middle-aged waitress waddled toward him. "Coffee, Hauptsturmfuhrer?" she quacked sourly. "And perhaps you'd like to look at the morning paper? It just arrived."

"Yes to both questions," Erich said. The woman poured the hot brew and handed Erich the morning edition of the *Völkischer Beobachter*. The news on the front page was a near duplication of what he'd read the day before, the only difference being the dateline. He perused an article enumerating the glorious conquests of the German Navy. The Mediterranean was now an "Axis Lake." Germany and Italy held most of the sea's northern shore from Spain to Turkey, and the southern shore from Tunisia to within ninety-five kilometers of the Nile River. German troops occupied the territory from the North Cape of Norway on the Arctic Ocean to Egypt, and from the Atlantic at Brest to the southern end of the Volga River on the Asian border.

A headline about Field Marshall Rommel taking sick leave at his mountain retreat caught his eye. According to the journalist, the Reich hero was suffering from a nose infection and a liver problem. Erich theorized about the actual reason for the leave and shook his head. *When did I become such a cynic,* he wondered as he turned to the local section.

The second page featured a report about a Munich businessman who'd been arrested for smuggling foreign currency into Switzerland to aid a group of Jewish refugees. The offense was particularly shocking because the smuggler was an Abwher agent. According to the reporter, additional counterintelligence agents would soon be implicated in the scheme, which he said, "could have far-reaching repercussions."

Erich laid the paper aside as the waitress refilled his coffee cup and took his order, dark rye bread and his favorite leberwurst, a sausage spread. He sipped the bitter brew, thankful for the warmth. Once again he began to peruse the paper. On the bottom of the third page of the local section, he spotted an article about the Munich Hitler Youth. The by-line on the column was Inge Friedrich. Ordinarily Erich would have ignored the propaganda piece, but his interest in the indifferent woman, who had crossed his mind so frequently since their meeting at the Hofbrauhaus prompted him to read. The article was well written and ended with the statement of loyalty he'd so often professed during his own days in the Berlin Hitler Youth Organization. "You, Fuhrer, are our commander! We stand in your name. The Reich is the object of our struggle. It is the beginning and the amen."

Erich paused and contemplated the words that had once given him chills. *What happened,* he wondered, as he had the day before and the day before that. *Where's the zeal?* He thought about the journalist who had repeated the lines. *Better she was indifferent to me,* he rationalized. *I'll be leaving Munich and her behind in a day or so anyway.*

Still reading the so-called news of the day, he enjoyed the tasty food. When his plate was clean, he tossed several coins on the table, tucked the paper in his uniform pocket, and reluctantly faced the cold dampness as he returned to headquarters. There hadn't been sufficient time for his orders to arrive, so he passed the radio room and went to his own third-floor office. As he hung his cap and coat on the rack by the door, he looked around for what he presumed would be one of the last times. Except for the increasing monotony he'd been feeling about his job of late, he'd enjoyed his time in Munich.

Ironically, he had felt differently when he first received his orders to report to the Bavarian capital. Except for the chance to be with his friend, he hated to leave Berlin where all the action was taking place. His face must have mirrored his disdain, because, soon after Joachim arrived at the central train station to pick him up, he couldn't resist a comment. "Does Himmler's fair-hair boy have a problem being stationed in Munich?" he had asked sarcastically.

As he sat looking out the window at the dismal sky, Erich recalled the ensuing hours, which taught him a great deal about Munich and even more about his friend. His first response to Joachim's question was a slap on the shoulder and a condescending response. "I'm glad to be here with you, but you've got to admit; being assigned to this irrelevant place isn't exactly a career booster."

"You're kidding," Joachim said sarcastically. Waiting for Erich to refute his assertion, he paused. When Erich didn't respond, he continued. "Apparently, you're not."

Chapter 5 | 51

"Obviously I've offended you," said Erich. "You know I wasn't disparaging your assignment."

Joachim's response struck Erich. It was definitely out of character: "Sure you weren't," he muttered, a frown on his face.

"I'm sure Munich is a great place to serve—"

"My God, you're unbelievable!" Joachim said indignantly. "All I've heard for months is how *vital* it is for an SS man to be stationed in Berlin. You know I could care less about my rank or how quickly I advance, but frankly, I'm sick of your derogatory comments about Munich, and, by extension, me."

Erich remembered he opened his mouth to protest, but Joachim shook his head. "No comment, please," he said angrily. "I intend to show you how wrong you are. Berlin may be the center of government, but Munich is the heart of the party. For once in your life, let me be the expert."

In all the years he'd known Joachim, Erich had never seen this side of the man. Except for the episode with Ernst and the Jewish woman, Joachim had never appeared irritated, much less angry. Sure they'd both complained during their rigorous training and the non-stop indoctrination, but, for the most part, Joachim took even the tough times in stride. Erich quickly realized it wasn't a time to joke. "I had no idea you felt that way," he said. "I'm sorry if I offended you. Maybe if you show me *your* Munich, I'll better understand how you feel."

Erich pushed his chair away from the desk, leaned back and kept thinking about that day.

"Our first stop is Schleissheimerstrasse 34," Joachim said; still clearly irritated. "That's where Hitler lived from 1913 to 1914. "He was twenty-four when he came here to evade military service in the Austrian army. Prior to that, he'd been living in Vienna where he hoped to become an artist and architect. In Austria his philosophy of anti-Semitism, nationalism and racism began to evolve. While he lived in this building, he paid the rent by painting watercolors of the tourist sites, like this one." He pulled up in front of the Feldherrenhalle at Odeonsplatz. "After the Beer Hall Putsch, this monument eventually became important to the Nazi Movement."

"I know the story," Erich said, perhaps with a little too much exasperation.

Joachim reacted with equal annoyance. "Good, then I'll remember to keep my version short when we come back to the place later on."

Erich looked at Joachim quizzically. "Why the hell are you so damn irritated?" he said. "I've never seen you like this."

"I'm not irritated, but I'm not going to spend the weeks and months ahead listening to you sing the glories of Berlin and denigrate Munich. Let's say I'm putting a halt to your braggadocio before you get started."

Erich quickly realized that, though unintentionally, he'd been belittling Joachim's assignment as he bragged about how lucky he was to be stationed in the capital. "I look forward to the rest of the tour," he said, trying to make peace. "But how do you know all this stuff?"

"I made it a point to learn. I love this city. After the war I may live here permanently, though I haven't forgotten about Unser Traum and our dream to build houses on the property. Maybe I'll live there and spend holidays in Munich." Erich laughed. "What's so funny?" Joachim said impatiently.

"Are we actually arguing?" Erich said. "If so, it's a first."

Oddly Joachim didn't smile. "I don't know, but if we are, the argument is long overdue," he said crossly as he stopped the car on Elisabeth Platz. "This is the school where Hitler lived from August 16 to October 1914."

"Are you going to show me every place where the Fuhrer spent time?" Erich said, trying to break the tension. Joachim grinned, and Erich silently sighed. *That's more like Joachim,* he thought as his friend continued.

"Not everyplace, just spots on the way to the office," Joachim said. "Though I'm tempted to extend the tour until you say uncle."

"Uncle," Erich said, smiling.

"Too little too late," said Joachim. "We're turning onto Thierschstrasse to go by the offices of the *Völkischer Beobachter,* the right-wing newspaper the party bought in 1920."

Coming back to the moment at hand, Erich thought about Inge. *When I first saw those offices, I had no idea I'd be interested in a woman who works there,* he thought. *Though I probably won't see her again.*

As he returned to memories of the now infamous tour, Erich recalled he quickly began to understand Joachim's pride in Munich and how his friend felt about his unintentional disparagement of his city. He berated himself for his holier-than-thou attitude.

The next stop on the tour was Pappenheimerstrasse 14, where Hitler went on trial for high treason after the Putsch, and then Schellingstrasse, the 1925 home of the party headquarters and the place where Hitler met his future mistress, Eva Braun. Telling Erich he'd show him Eva Braun's home and the villa the Fuhrer bought her—the love-nest they still shared on Delpstrasse—at a later date, they turned up Brennerstrasse. "This will be your world while you're stationed here," Joachim said as he pointed out the Brauneshaus, the party headquarters; the Fuhrerbau where Hitler maintained his offices; and the famous Ehrentempel, the shrine for the fallen of the Beer Hall Putsch. "So this is Munich," he said when he parked the car in front of the Verwaltungsbau. "And your office is here in the administration building."

Erich put his hand on Joachim's shoulder. "Thanks for the tour," he said. "But more importantly, thanks for putting me in my place. I deserved your disdain, and I sincerely apologize for my attitude. You'll hear no more from me about the merits of Berlin and the insignificance of Munich. I'm sold on your city." Joachim grinned, but he didn't respond. However, in an instant, he was again seemingly carefree and happy-go-lucky.

Erich returned to the moment at hand. Thankfully, he hadn't seen the ill-tempered, snappish Joachim again, but then he hadn't given his friend reason to show his serious side. He was packing personal objects when he heard a sharp rap on the door. "Come in," he called, expecting to see a sturman bringing him the dreaded orders. The door opened only partially, and a head appeared. Joachim's toothy grin was incompatible with his tired-looking eyes. "You must have had quite a night," Erich said.

Joachim pushed open the door and moved sluggishly to the nearest chair where he dramatically dropped down. "You can say that again," he moaned. "I might not recover for weeks, and I doubt Gretchen will be able to walk for days." As he laughed, Erich was again astonished by his friend's ability to find life so carefree and amusing despite the gravity of the war going on around him.

Joachim propped his rain-spattered boots on the corner of Erich's desk. "Any news about your orders?" he asked.

"Not yet, but I expect they'll be here any minute. When you knocked, I thought it might be the sturman."

"Any idea when you'll be leaving this gorgeous office for who knows what?"

"Not precisely, but I imagine I'll have a day or so to pack and move out of my apartment."

"Which is why I came in at this ungodly hour."

"Judging by the smirk on your face, I'm sure nothing I say will keep you from telling me your reason, so don't keep me in suspense any longer."

"A party," Joachim bellowed. "We're going to have a real send-off."

Erich rolled his eyes. "Now why would we do that?" he said. "I'll be less than thirty-kilometers away. I'll be in Munich so often you'll think I still live here. Admit it. You're using me as an excuse to have a good time."

Joachim grinned. "Why would you ever think that?"

"Gee, I don't know, but who am I to deprive you of your fun?"

"I never dreamed you'd be this easy," Joachim said. "Though I figured you'd eventually see it my way." He stood up, leaving drops of dirty water from his boots on Erich's desk. "Now if you'll excuse me, I need to finish my menial work so I can get on with the critical business ahead, the plans for our party. Tonight, seven o'clock at the Hofbrauhaus. I'll stop by and pick you up."

"I'll be waiting," Erich said. "I wouldn't miss *our* party for anything."

Joachim left, and, feeling slightly more light-hearted at the prospect of the night ahead, Erich returned to the tedious job of sorting through his desk drawers. He'd worked for an hour when there was another knock on the door. "Enter," he called out.

A scrawny sturman barged in, snapped to attention, and blared enthusiastically, "Heil Hitler."

*He must be new around here,* Erich thought. "Heil Hitler," he said. "What can I do for you, Sturman?"

The young man handed Erich a manila envelope. "Your orders, Hauptsturmfuhrer."

"Thank you, Sturman." Erich opened the envelope and quickly examined the papers. As anticipated, he would have two days before he had to report to Obersturmbannfuhrer Weiss at Dachau. *October 20th,* he thought, *the beginning of a new phase of my life.* For no specific reason he felt a sinking feeling in his stomach.

He dismissed the Sturman. Still holding the envelope and needing some solace, he went downstairs to find Joachim. He didn't have far to go. Joachim was standing close to the stairwell with an alluring secretary from the mailroom. "Here comes the guest of honor now," Joachim said. He kissed the blushing woman on the cheek.

"Good morning, Hauptsturmfuhrer," said the girl. "Joachim tells me he's throwing a change-of-orders party for you tonight at the Hofbrauhaus."

Erich chuckled. "The gathering's not for me, Anna. My transfer is just an excuse for Joachim to have a party."

"Well, no matter the reason, we could use a little fun around here," Anna said petulantly. "The reports have been so discouraging lately. Frankly I'm tired of seeing gloomy faces. Everyone's sick of the war. Most of my friends thought Germany would have been victorious long before now."

After an admonishing glance from Erich suggesting Anna's remarks were dangerous, Joachim addressed the girl. "Well, my love," he said. "We'll all forget the war tonight. I'm looking forward to having a party after the party with you."

"Count on it," Anna murmured seductively as she wiggled free of Joachim's grasp. As she sauntered down the hall, she occasionally glanced back seductively at Joachim.

"Don't forget to bring all of the other beautiful women you know," he called out, and then added: "For the other men, of course." She waved as she turned the corner toward the mailroom. Joachim sighed. "The hours around here move much too slowly. I'm already ready for the party to start."

"It does my heart good to see you enjoying this transfer so much," Erich said.

"Do I detect annoyance in your tone?"

"I suppose you do. I got the official word a few minutes ago. I'll be reporting to Obersturmbannfuhrer Martin Weiss day after tomorrow."

Joachim's eyes widened. "Weiss is the Dachau commandant?"

"He is. Do you know him?"

"Not personally, but he's in and out of the Fuhrerbau all the time. A friend of mine said he's an arrogant, heartless bastard who enjoys watching people suffer. I hate to say it, old buddy, but after learning who's running the camp, my guess is that horrible things are happening at Dachau."

Erich's misgivings rapidly turned to dread. "What exactly did your friend say?" he asked, wanting yet not wanting to know.

"Not too much, and that's the problem. He mentioned some rule that prevented him from talking about what's going on at Dachau. Let's just say I don't envy you."

"Did I give you the idea I'm thrilled to be working in a detention camp? And this conversation isn't making me feel any better."

"Then I'll gladly change the subject. I probably should have kept my mouth shut in the first place, but you know it's not my style to keep quiet."

"I'm sorry," Erich said. "It's not your fault that I'm so grouchy. Let's talk about this party. I assume everything's set for tonight."

"Need you ask?"

"I guess it was stupid to question your organizational skills, so I'm going back to work, or your excuse for a party won't be there."

Erich started back toward the stairs when he abruptly turned back. "Hey, pal," he called out. "Any chance you can get Inge Frederick to come to this party of ours?"

"Can't get the ice queen off your mind, huh?" Joachim said, chuckling. "Funny what rejection does to you."

"Don't remind me. So, can you accomplish the impossible?"

"Let's just say if anyone can get Inge to the party, I can." Joachim turned toward his office, leaving Erich staring after him and shaking his head at his friend's audacity.

# CHAPTER 6

Inge gazed out her bedroom window at her aunt's neatly planted garden. She'd been awake for an hour, but the chill of the morning air kept her under the eiderdown comforter until she had no choice but to get up or be late for work.

She watched the raindrops bounce in the puddles dotting the ground. Looking up at the sky, she sighed. The dark, menacing thunderclouds showed no sign of clearing. *What a wonderful day to stay in bed and read*, she thought. She looked around the cheerful room, admiring the worn, green-and-pink chintz curtains, the matching comforter, and the huge over-stuffed chair where she'd spent pleasant hours reading.

"Are you up, Inge?" Sigrid called from the hall. "Will you join me?"

"I'll be right there, Aunt Sigrid."

The irresistible aroma of freshly baked bread wafted through the air as Inge washed up, dressed, and joined her aunt in the kitchen. "Tea?" Sigrid asked.

"Yes please."

Inge watched her aunt pour the delicious-smelling, pale-brown liquid into the cups. "What's the occasion, Aunt Sigrid?" she asked. "I thought you were hoarding your precious tea for a special celebration."

"I was, but somehow this morning seems like a good time for a treat. It's cold and dismal outside, and I thought we could use some additional warmth in here."

Inge placed her hand over her aunt's and squeezed. "Who am I to argue?" she said, smiling at the dear woman who had tried so hard to create some semblance of normalcy despite her fears for Rosel.

Sigrid cut a generous slice of the crusty bread and a piece of salami, handed the plate of food to her niece, and joined her at the table. "Do you have time to talk for a few minutes before you have to get ready for work?" she asked.

"Not as much time as I'd like." Inge took a bite of the bread. "Delicious as usual and exactly what I needed to get my morning off to a good start."

"You seem preoccupied," Sigrid said. "Are you expecting a difficult day?"

"Not really, at least not in terms of the work I have to do. I finally put my article on Munich's Hitler Youth to bed. If it ran in the morning paper, I'll bring a copy home."

"So you'll be working on a new project."

"I hope so, and that's why I can't sit and chat. I'd like to catch Herr Beck before his day gets crazy and he doesn't have the time to hear my proposal. I'd hoped to talk with him in an informal atmosphere at the Hofbrauhaus last night, but we didn't have time to finish our conversation. What I'm asking is critical if we're going to find Rosel, and getting Beck's approval for what I want to do won't be easy."

"Tell me you're not going to ask for an assignment at Dachau again, Inge. You know how I feel."

"I know you're worried, Aunt Sigrid. I wasn't going to tell you about my plan, but we agreed there'd be no more secrets between us. You need to understand what we're facing and why I have no choice but to persist."

"But there must be another way—"

"Then what is it? For the life of me, I can't come up with anything." Seeing Sigrid's distress, Inge backed off. "Anyway there's probably no need for concern," she said. "I doubt Beck will give me permission to write about Dachau."

Despite Inge's attempt to sound reassuring, Sigrid wasn't through. "Please try to appreciate my feelings, Inge," she said. "I'm frightened."

"I know you are, Aunt Sigrid, but why don't we stop worrying until we have something to worry about." Inge stood and picked up her plate. "Let me help you clean up."

"There's no need, darling," Sigrid said glumly. "Sit back down and drink the rest of the tea. We can't let one drop go to waste."

As Inge sipped her tea, she thought about all she'd done to find Rosel since moving back to Munich. Soon after Sigrid shared Rosel's story, she had used her press credentials to try and find out all she could about the camp. She quickly learned that Dachau was off limits to anyone not directly involved with camp business. Most of the files she attempted to access were classified, but she *was* able to discover that the facility was initially used to house political prisoners, though more recently it had been converted into a Jewish detention center. She wondered if what Sigrid said was true. Had the SS learned about Rosel's Jewish heritage and arrested her? If so, she would have been taken to Dachau for processing. But how had the agents learned about her in the first place?

It was no secret the SS kept meticulous records, so Inge knew Dachau would have files chronicling Rosel's seizure, as well as information about her current whereabouts, but how could she gain access? Each time she asked Beck for authorization to write about Dachau, he steadfastly refused. In her most recent memo she had offered several justifications for writing a feature article that would run in the Munich edition of the paper and be available for wider distribution. The first and least controversial option was an article about the SS Death's Head Squadron serving at

Dachau. The second possibility was an in-depth story focusing on the incarceration of the enemies of the Reich and the ongoing and stepped-up efforts of the SS to purify the German race by separating the Jews from the population at large. If Beck vetoed both suggestions, which, considering the direction the war was taking, Inge imagined he might, her final suggestion was for a shorter, special-interest piece detailing Himmler's recent visit to Munich and the Reichsfuhrer's keen interest in the SS camp at Dachau.

Disappointing yet not surprising, Beck rejected all of her ideas without even suggesting she expand one of her proposals. How could she broach the subject again? She figured excess curiosity about Dachau and too much urging on her part would only make Beck wonder if she had an ulterior motive for requesting the assignment. If he was suspicious, would he inform the Gestapo about her unusual interest in the camp?

Now with no more ideas, it seemed that fate had intervened in her favor. Erich's Dachau assignment could give him access to the files she so urgently needed to see. Inge remained conflicted. One minute she decided to use the man, and minutes later she realized how dangerous it would be to try to enlist an SS officer's help. He was a member of Hitler's privileged few, a brazen fanatic. She remembered the stories of SS extremism that recently crossed her desk at the office. Many had been so troubling that Beck censored them rather than unduly alarm the public. She shook her head. *And now I'm thinking about asking the extreme of the extremists for help. That's definitely not smart.*

She finished the last of her tea and looked at her watch. "It's getting late, Aunt Sigrid," she said. "You know Herr Beck doesn't tolerate tardiness." She walked through the parlor with Sigrid close at her heels, removed her coat from the rack, and slipped it on. Sigrid handed her the brightly-colored scarf that she tied around her head to keep out the morning chill.

"Will you be home for dinner?" Sigrid asked.

"I hope so. Wish me luck. Today's important for all of us."

"I always wish you luck and a good day, darling." Sigrid opened the door. "Stay warm. I don't want you to get sick."

Inge slipped on the gloves that had been in her coat pocket and opened her umbrella. "I'll see you tonight," she said.

As she passed Gestapo headquarters and approached the *Völkischer Beobachter* editorial offices, the steady rain had turned to a drizzle. No longer having to deal with the deluge, her thoughts returned to Erich Riedl. "I'm playing a deadly game," she whispered. *How could I even consider asking an SS man to help me find Rosel? There's no way this strategy will work, and I could put Sigrid and me in jeopardy. What good would we be to Rosel if we were arrested and transported to Dachau?* In seconds she changed her mind yet again. *But at this point I have no other alternative.*

She reached 39 Schellingstrass, so there was no more time to rehash her dilemma. Relieved to be in out of the cold, she made her way through the bustling halls to the news department. Josef Halder and Werner Kramer, two of her colleagues, looked up from what they were doing to greet her. Both were ambitious young newsmen who, on her first day in Munich, made it clear they didn't believe a woman had a legitimate place in the working world, let alone as a journalist reporting the stories that would influence public opinion. This antiquated attitude was irritating, but what annoyed Inge even more were their flirtatious attempts to charm her. Fortunately, after several rebuffs on her part, they began to see she was in the office to work, and when she submitted several first-rate stories, their animosity turned to respect.

"You look like a walking icicle," Josef said. "Coffee?"

"Please," Inge said as she removed her coat. "It's nasty out there. Is it my imagination, or is it colder than usual for this time of year?"

"I've lived in Munich for most of my life, and I can't remember a nippier fall," said Werner.

From the looks of their desks, Inge knew the men had been at the office for some time. "Any electrifying news today?" she asked, though she already knew the answer.

Josef shook his head. "Beck isn't back from his meeting with Goebbels's representative, but I'm sure we'll get our daily dose of scintillating information when he returns." He looked at Inge's puckered brow. "Are you alright?" he asked. "You seem preoccupied."

"I suppose I am," Inge said. "I'm ready for a new assignment, and I'd like to get started instead of sitting around here trying to figure out how to present the news that crosses our desks with a positive spin."

"Any idea what you'd like to tackle?" Werner asked.

"I have a few thoughts, but I'd rather tell you about them after I get Beck's approval."

"Holding out on us?" said Josef.

"Just being smart. You men get all the scoops and this could turn out to be the story of the year."

"You won't even give us a hint?" Werner said.

"Not the slightest clue, but thanks for the coffee."

Inge took a sip and sat down at her desk. She began to study the mounds of repetitive reports in front of her, including the latest news releases. "Pretty dismal stuff," she said.

Josef nodded. "It won't be easy to write anything positive about this crap."

Inge skimmed a release calling for additional volunteers to help the Reich's cause. The plea had an ominous and foreboding tone. "There's no way I can make a call for more volunteers sound optimistic," she pondered aloud. "If additional 'volunteers' are needed, things aren't going well, or they wouldn't be needed."

Josef laughed. "Sadly, I understand your round-about logic, but of course you'll make it look like the Fuhrer is asking for more patriotism; for more dedication to him and the cause. Forget the real reasons. They're not worth mentioning."

"I believe that's called 'stretching the truth,'" said Werner.

"Whatever it is, I don't like it," Inge said. "This isn't the way I envisioned my journalistic career."

"I question your use of the word 'journalism,'" Werner responded. "What we're being asked to do doesn't resemble responsible reporting."

Inge didn't comment. From her earliest days in Berlin, she knew the office wasn't the place to disagree with the propaganda guidelines of the Reich. Instead, she continued to peruse the piles of reports on her desk. From time to time she glanced at her watch, paradoxically eager for, and yet dreading, Beck's return from the morning briefing. The more she pored over the news summaries, the more preposterous seemed the task of writing an optimistic article. All of the news coming out of Berlin was discouraging. As she tried to come up with a positive spin on an article about the need for additional food rationing, the phone rang. She rarely received personal calls, and was surprised when Josef held the receiver in her direction. "It's for you, Inge," he said. "Your caller says his name is Joachim Forester."

Inge took the receiver. "Heil Hitler!" she said.

"And a Heil Hitler to you, Fraulein" came the casual and almost mocking response from the other end of the line. Inge was amazed that anyone could make the stiff greeting sound humorous. "Fraulein Friedrich," he said. "This is Joachim Forester."

"So I've been told," Inge responded coolly, as Josef smirked.

"I'd like to invite you to a party at the Hofbrauhaus tonight, Fraulein."

"I'm sorry, Obersturmfuhrer," Inge said without hesitation. "Attending a party is out of the question."

"I'm sorry too, Fraulein," Joachim said. "You remember Erich Riedl, the man you met last night? He was hoping you'd be able to join us. He told you he's leaving Munich for a new assignment in a matter of days, and a few of us—"

"Of course, I'll be there, Obersturmfuhrer," Inge interrupted.

"Really?" Joachim said, sure he sounded as astonished as he felt. "You'll come?"

"Of course," Inge said.

When Joachim didn't respond, Inge realized she'd been too eager to accept the invitation after her initial refusal. "What I meant to say, Obersturmfuhrer, is I appreciate the invitation. What time will festivities begin?"

"At seven o'clock."

"Until tonight then." Inge smiled as she hung up the phone, wondering if fate had again interceded on her behalf. She tried to work, but found it hard to concentrate. Plans and counter plans raced through her mind. She finally decided she couldn't make any decisions without getting to know Erich better, so she forced herself to edit one of Josef's articles for the next addition.

# CHAPTER 7

As he sifted through papers on his desk, Erich's frustration grew. The lengthy meeting with the Economic and Armament Committee the day before had come closer than ever to producing the results he'd been struggling to achieve. He had nearly completed his part in the creation of a new system for channeling goods and supplies to the Waffen SS Panzer Divisions operating in Europe. Though there were still a few issues to work through, he had formulated the basic strategy and solved some of the pressing problems. Now he was preparing the final report for Berlin so others could implement the suggested procedures.

In addition to the supply project, he'd begun preliminary work on a plan for reorganizing the staff of SS Munich Headquarters. Streamlining procedures could make each individual more valuable to the unit and, in turn, generate more all-around effectiveness. Now his replacement would complete both projects. It wasn't concern that someone else would get credit for his work that bothered him; rather, he didn't like to walk out on an assignment before he brought it to a successful conclusion.

After completing his report on the economic and armaments meeting, he persisted in the almost insurmountable task of sorting through the endless stack of papers on his desk, filing some and trashing others. He recalled that just before the news of his transfer he'd felt the same annoyance while doing exactly this sort of work. How paradoxical that the task he disliked seemed infinitely preferable to the challenging new assignment he'd soon begin. His desire to escape was the reason he'd come back to headquarters to find Joachim. He had found his friend, but he'd also been given new orders which he knew would change his life.

He was about to take a break when the door opened and Joachim walked in. "Good timing," Erich said. "I was just thinking about you." Without responding, Joachim leaned against the door with his arms folded and a smirk on his face.

"You look like a proud peacock," Erich said impatiently. "I know you're dying to tell me why. So explain why you're looking so smug."

Still silent, Joachim remained in place. Not being in the best of moods to begin with, Erich's disposition went from bad to worse. "Either tell me why you're being an ass, or get the hell out so I can work," he said irritably.

Still grinning, Joachim finally crossed the room and plopped down in the chair opposite Erich's desk. "I, my friend, have achieved the impossible, the greatest feat of our time, the *coup-de-gras*."

"Of course you have," Erich said sarcastically. "So stop with the bravado and tell me what you're talking about. What have you done, though maybe I should be afraid to ask?"

"What have I done? You mean what task have I expertly and brilliantly fulfilled? What problem have I shrewdly solved?"

"Cut it out, Joachim," Erich growled. "It must be obvious that I'm not in the mood for game-playing, and anyway, you know you're dying to tell me about your extraordinary accomplishment, or you wouldn't be smirking like an idiot and acting like an ass. From the hints you're dropping, I'd say you've single-handedly figured out a way to win the war."

Joachim grinned. "Not quite the entire war, but I may have won a battle in your own private conflict."

Erich picked up a folder and slammed it back down on his desk. "Damn it," he said. "Tell me what you're raving about or get the hell out."

"Do I detect an element of aggravation in your voice?" Joachim smirked. "How could you possibly be annoyed with the man who has managed to coerce the ice-queen of Munich to come to your farewell party?"

"You're kidding," Erich said, his anger giving way to disbelief. "Inge Friedrich's coming to the Hofbrauhaus tonight?"

"She is, and you owe your old buddy an apology for being so testy."

Erich shook his head. "You're impossible," he said. "But this time I'll gladly give you the credit you deserve. I doubted even *you* could get Inge to come to the party."

"Underestimated again. So, old buddy, I've done my part, and quite well I might add. Now it's up to you to charm the lady, though I'll lay odds you won't succeed. Better practice your approach. I noticed the lines you used last night didn't work so well."

"If you'll get out of here, I'll do just that," Erich said, but this time he was smiling.

"I'm going! I'm going!" Joachim chuckled as he walked over and opened the door. "But you have to admit I'm great?"

"Yes, you're the greatest and I'm sure I'll never hear the end of it."

Joachim was laughing as he left the office, leaving Erich staring at the door. Knowing how much he had to accomplish in order to finish by five o'clock, he threw himself into his work.

———————————

Inge waited nervously and impatiently for Beck to arrive. She'd been at the office for over an hour, and he still hadn't returned from his morning briefing. One part of her plan had been put into motion with Joachim's invitation to Erich's party. Now she had to face the next obstacle. She needed her boss's permission to write an article about Dachau, and she knew there was little likelihood she'd get the go-ahead.

Paradoxically excited and bored, she kept skimming the repetitious news briefs. Most of the write-ups weren't worth examining, and she didn't read beyond the headline. Suddenly one piece caught her eye, and she caught her breath. There, facing her in print, was her invitation to write the article. The headline read; "Daring Experiments to Begin at Dachau."

Dachau! The name jumped off the page. In a vague synopsis, the news-brief described soon-to-begin research experiments based on a need to save Luftwaffe pilots who were regularly being shot down over the North Sea. The men were dying from exposure to the cold, and the Dachau study was designed to help them survive for longer periods, thus increasing their chance of being rescued.

Inge was instantly energized. Before her was a unique approach to solve her predicament. If she could find a way to emphasize the positives of the tests, maybe Beck would relent. She felt her hands and feet grow cold, as thoughts raced through her mind: *What if this current request is one too many, and Beck suspects my motives? Worse, what if he turns me down again? There won't be another opportunity.* She stared at the clock on the wall, her apprehension increasing with each passing minute.

By 11:30, she'd all but given up and was about to go home, when, looking beleaguered and annoyed, Beck dashed into the newsroom. "Good morning, or since it's almost noon, perhaps I should say good afternoon, Fraulein," he said, his expression exuding annoyance.

"You're later than usual," Inge said, trying to hide her nervousness with small talk.

Beck scowled. "Inane interruptions slowed us down. Inge, would you take the news releases to the printer? There's no need to edit or rewrite. We're to print them exactly as they're written."

Inge rose and took the papers Beck held out. "I'd be glad to." She paused at the door and looked back. "Herr Beck," she said. "When I return, I'd like to speak with you about a new assignment."

"Certainly," Beck said without looking up. "I'm sorry we didn't get a chance to finish our discussion last evening. I take it you have some thoughts about what you'd like to do."

Suddenly Inge was glad they hadn't had time to talk at the Hofbrauhaus and that Beck was late coming to the office. Had he been on time, she wouldn't have seen the article about the Luftwaffe experiments. "I have an idea I'd like to discuss," she said.

"Deliver the papers for me, and then we'll talk."

As she walked down the hall, Inge considered how best to approach the topic of the experiments. *I can't be too enthusiastic or Beck will suspect I have ulterior motives, especially in light of my past requests,* she reflected. *On the other hand, I have to be resolute enough to make him believe this assignment is valuable and useful, both as a special-interest piece and a propaganda tool. Somehow I have to find the precise words to make my point.*

At the news desk she handed the papers to Alfred Dressen, the head printer. "Today's meaningful articles," she said with a hint of disgust.

"I'm sure this news will be as exciting as what we printed yesterday," Dressen replied with equal disdain. "One thing for sure; it won't cause an increase in circulation."

Her mission successfully completed, Inge said goodbye to Dresser and headed back to the office. At the door she paused and took a deep breath. "It's now or never," she said under her breath as she walked in.

When she saw Beck, her heart sank. He was talking with Josef. With someone else in the office she wouldn't have a chance to present her case for writing an article about the upcoming tests at Dachau. Hearing the door close, Beck looked up. "I'll only be a minute, Inge," he said. "Josef and I are almost finished with our business." Inge sighed with relief. She wouldn't have to delay the discussion after all. She tried to hide her angst as she perused the news from Berlin.

Fifteen minutes later Josef finished talking with Beck. "Bye, Josef," Inge said.

"Good luck," Josef whispered as he passed her desk.

"Thanks." Inge turned to her boss. "Well, Herr Beck," she said. "Are you ready to hear my idea for a sensational story?"

"I am, and I apologize for the delays." Beck pointed to the chair opposite the desk. "Please sit down and tell me what you're thinking."

"I'd like to report on something meaningful for a change," Inge began, weighing every word as she spoke. "Something that will extol the efforts our leaders are making to protect the brave men fighting for the Reich."

"Another propaganda piece?"

"Yes and no. What I have in mind would be a factual report that could also be used as propaganda. While reading through the news-briefs, I came across information about Luftwaffe experiments about to get underway at the Dachau detention facility. The research has real possibilities for a story, and since the Munich office is closest to the camp, we're the staff that should cover the tests."

Beck frowned and shook his head. "You know Dachau's off limits to all civilian personnel," he said. "I've told you several times before; you'll never be given permission to write this sort of article, even if I personally appealed to Berlin on your behalf."

Inge persisted. "I'm aware of the rules regarding Dachau, Herr Beck. I believe the restrictions apply to individuals who are seeking information about the operations of the camp. This assignment would have nothing to do with the camp itself. I'd only be covering the Luftwaffe experiments." She was sure she could hear her heart beat as she spoke, and she wondered if Beck heard it too. She continued, outwardly calm and inwardly shaking. "I believe the German people want to know what's being done to rescue the pilots when they're shot down."

Beck kept resisting. "But Inge," he said. "Apart from the modicum of news we've already been given, we know nothing about what these experiments entail; the nature of which is probably unsuitable for public consumption."

"It's precisely because they are so mysterious that I'm asking for permission to investigate, Herr Beck." Inge leaned in toward her boss. "The secrecy surrounding Dachau has intrigued me since I came back to Munich. I guess it's my nose for news telling me there's a story here."

Inge waited while Beck thought about what she'd said. After what seemed like an eternity, he began: "I'll admit, I've been puzzled by your preoccupation with Dachau," he said. "But honestly, if I had time to give the camp a second thought, my journalistic instincts might drive me as yours have driven you."

Though not ready to declare victory, Inge felt somewhat encouraged. "The secrecy intriguers me, but I have to say, the work I've done lately makes a story about Dachau more appealing," she said. "The news, if you can call it news, we've been asked to print lately, is mundane and repetitive. Don't you think the public would like to read something encouraging?"

Beck thumped his pen on his desk. *At least he's considering my proposal,* Inge reflected. She held her breath as he began to speak. "Inge, perhaps your idea has possibilities, but I can't give you permission to enter Dachau."

"I figured that might be the case but—"

"Let me finish. I'm not sure this is in your best interest, but your idea has merit. There's not much reason for celebration and enthusiasm at the moment and, though we try to spin the news, our articles aren't doing much to make the people believe Germany will win the war. So I'll contact the Berlin propaganda office as well as the newspaper chief, Herr Rosenberg, and see if they will grant permission for you to cover the experiments. I should have an answer for you in a day or so."

Inge tried to hide her excitement. "Thank you, Herr Beck," she said as professionally as possible. She was pleased, but she was also frustrated. If Berlin was making the final decision, her chances were slim, and this created another dilemma. Should she approach Erich Riedl? He said he'd be leaving for Dachau in a few days, so she had very little time to decide.

"Until we get word, I'd like for you to assist Josef with his assignment," Beck was saying. "He's working on a story about the new art exhibition at the Alte Pinakotek, the show Reichsmarshall Goring is sponsoring."

*Another critical task,* Inge reflected with contempt. She suspected Herr Beck felt the same way, but she wasn't going to verbalize their feelings. "Of course, Herr Beck," she said. "You'll let me know as soon as word comes down from Berlin."

"As soon as I hear something, Inge, you'll know. Now I have some outside work, including a meeting with Herr Juenger from the Reich Foreign Office, so if you'll excuse me?" He got up from his desk and reached for his coat that was draped over the chair behind him.

"Have a nice afternoon," Inge said. "If you need me, I'll be at the museum with Josef."

Beck left the office, leaving Inge excited, troubled, nervous, and annoyed. She rested her head in her hands. Could she stand to wait? So much was riding on her getting this assignment. "I can't sit here feeling sorry for myself," she whispered as she looked at the clock. "Before I join Josef at the Alte Pinakotek, I'll go home for lunch and tell Aunt Sigrid as much as I can about my discussion with Beck and my plans for the evening." She put on her coat and scarf, took her umbrella from the stand, and left the office.

It was still cold and misty outside, but no rain was falling as she dodged the puddles on the slippery sidewalk. Eager to be in the warmth of her home, she was lost in thought as she walked the last few blocks to the house. *Will Berlin let me write about tests taking place in a detention camp,* she wondered. *Will my motive be suspect?* "I'll drive myself crazy if I keep thinking like this," she said. "I have to forget about Dachau until I get the final word." She knew that would be an almost impossible task.

Before she had time to take out her key, Sigrid opened the front door. "I saw you coming up the walkway, darling," she said. "This is an unexpected but welcome pleasure. What brings you home at this time of day?"

"I'm on my way to an art exhibit at the Alte Pinakotek and I thought I'd stop by and join you for lunch. We need to talk."

"Take off your coat and come warm yourself by the fire. We'll talk before lunch. You know I'm a curious woman who doesn't want to wait to hear your news. Would you like tea?"

Inge hung her coat on the rack and removed her boots. "Twice in one day?" she said. "Are you expecting the end of the war and a fresh supply?"

"I can only hope for a speedy end to the war," Sigrid said over her shoulder as she disappeared into the kitchen.

While she waited for the water to boil, Inge stared into the hypnotic flames. *Fires are so calming,* she thought, *at least the ones in fireplaces.* That morning she'd read about the conflagration caused by increased bombing of Cologne by British and American planes. In June, 1940, British bombers had attacked Munich for the first time, but since the city was on the outer periphery of the planes' range, most of the bombs landed on the outskirts of the city, causing only minor damage. She wondered if Munich would soon experience the full-blown violence and destruction of war. She put aside those distasteful thoughts as her aunt returned with a pot and two cups. Sigrid poured the steaming tea, handed a cup to Inge, and took a cup for herself. "Now, dear," she said. "Tell me your news.'

"It's not news, at least not yet, but I thought you should know that I asked Herr Beck to let me write the article about Dachau. If my request is approved, I'll have access to the camp and hopefully discover if Rosel was taken there."

Sigrid inhaled sharply. "Do you think Herr Beck will approve the assignment?" she asked tentatively. "And if he does, won't writing such an article be dangerous? From what I'm told, the goings-on at Dachau aren't fit for publication."

"I hope I'll be given permission. If I am, I'll likely be confined to one particular area, but I may have an ally at the camp."

Sigrid looked perplexed. "An ally?"

"I hope so. Remember I told you about Erich Riedl, the man I met at the Hofbrauhaus? Tonight I'm attending a going-away party his friend, Joachim, is throwing for him. I hope speaking with Erich in a relaxed atmosphere will help me figure out what kind of man he really is."

Sigrid walked to the fireplace and took a picture of Rosel off the mantle. "I hate this, Inge," she said anxiously. "If you go ahead with your crazy idea to use an SS officer to help you search for Rosel, I may lose you too."

Inge walked over, took the picture, and stared at the face smiling back at her. "Trust me, Aunt Sigrid," she said. "I won't do anything stupid. But you know we can't give up. We have to find Rosel, and until now, I had no idea how to proceed. You also know I won't say or do anything that could put us in danger."

"Not intentionally, but what if you slip?"

"I won't. I know you're unhappy, but would you have me give up?"

"I don't know," Sigrid said softly. "I'm so torn."

"I know you are. At the moment my plans are tentative. It's possible that after tonight I'll decide I can't risk asking Erich to help us obtain the information we need. We'll just have to wait and see."

Sigrid sighed and, once again, her customary resilience triumphed over her apprehension, at least outwardly. "Don't worry about me, Inge," she said. "If you're going to make your plan work, you'll need your strength, so come have lunch. If you help me with the final preparations, I'll give you another cup of tea."

"How can I resist?" Inge said, glad her aunt was no longer objecting, at least for the moment.

# CHAPTER 8

Rather than going directly to the museum after lunch, Inge returned to the office. She read through Josef's background file on art in the Reich, and specifically the exhibit at the Alte Pinakotek. It didn't take long for her to realize the rules and philosophy governing printed news also applied to the arts.

With little expectation of seeing a worthwhile exhibit, she walked through Karolinenplatz toward the Alte Pinakotek. As she battled the blustery wind, her thoughts turned from art to the party for Erich. *I'll have to be more congenial than I was when we first met,* she thought, *but I can't be too friendly. Any radical change in my behavior might make him question my motives.*

She turned onto Theresienstrasse and approached the museum from the rear. Despite her coat and scarf, she was chilled when she finally reached the front of the building. A gigantic banner hanging from the second floor advertised: "Hundreds of Works by Famous Nazi Artists." *Not much of a story here*, she speculated, *merely another propaganda piece.* As she entered the first-floor gallery and began to look around, Josef's familiar voice echoed her own thoughts: "Fascinating isn't it?"

Inge rolled her eyes. "I don't imagine any of these so-called works of art will stir anyone to action, unless it's action to leave the exhibit."

"But nevertheless, I'll write a stimulating article about the glorious and talented painters of the equally glorious Reich."

"And I'm here to help you figure out how to do just that, but before I do, I need to wander around and look at these alleged masterpieces. If you need me, yell. I'll be between this gallery and the one next door, which used to house the Italian collection."

"I'd tell you to enjoy the exhibit, but I'm not sure it's possible."

"Don't waste your breath," Inge said as she moved toward the far-side of the gallery.

Large nude sculptures spaced evenly around the room seemed to jump out at her as she walked past them. She paused and read the card describing one of the strong, virile men who was supposed to represent the new generation of Germans. She moved back to study the display as a whole. To her the figures appeared rigid, unyielding, and lacking in grace. "How appropriate," she commented under her breath as she left the hall and moved into the next room.

The new toys created for the children of the Reich weren't exciting either. There were several versions of a stuffed doll with arms raised in the Nazi salute. *Again, propaganda, not art,* she pondered, *but is any of this stuff really art? There's nothing I can do to help Josef write a positive review about this nonsense.*

She joined Josef, who was standing beside a huge sculpture of a nude athlete hurling a spear. "Magnificent, isn't it?" he said sarcastically.

Inge shook her head. "I doubt you could print anything I'd have to say about this figure or any of the other so-called art. That said, do you mind if I go home early? I'm going out tonight, and I'd like to change first."

"Sure. I'm about finished anyway." Josef grinned. "Do you have a date?"

"No, I don't have a date. I'm merely attending a going-away party, and I need a few minutes to pull myself together before the festivities begin."

"By all means, go. There's nothing you can do to make this pointless nonsense seem any better than it is. I'll see you in the morning."

"Have a good evening." Inge turned to leave and then looked back. "And thanks, Josef."

She was about to open the door when Josef came up behind her. "I've been looking at this dismal display for too long," he said. "Why don't I drive you home?"

Inge nodded. "I accept your kind offer," she said. "I wasn't looking forward to walking in this dreary weather."

It was cold, but the rain had stopped when they exited the building. Josef opened the passenger door for Inge, walked around, and slid behind the wheel. After several tries, the cold engine turned over and he edged away from the curb into the sparse traffic moving along Arcisstrasse. During the first few minutes of the drive, he concentrated on avoiding the huge puddles in the road. As they neared Karolinenplatz, Inge broke the silence. "Do you know anything about the SS facility at Dachau?" she asked.

Josef was obviously caught off guard, and Inge wondered if it was her imagination, her own apprehension, or a genuine wariness in his voice when he responded. "I was on assignment in the Dachau area several weeks ago," he said. "Driving to meet the couple I was scheduled to interview, I passed the camp. When we were through discussing their son's valiant service to the Fatherland, I asked them about the SS facility. They either didn't know or were afraid to say much."

"My guess, the latter," Inge said.

"Exactly what I thought. On a whim, I decided to use my press credentials to see if I could get into the camp and take a look around. As soon as I pulled up to the Jourhaus gate, I was turned away by an extremely antagonistic guard."

"So you didn't learn anything?"

"Only what I already know; that the facility is off limits to civilians. My journalistic curiosity was piqued, so I went back to the town and stopped at a local café. I thought maybe some of the diners would have something to say. Every person I spoke with was friendly and cheerful until I mentioned the camp. As soon as I did, the tenor of the discussion changed. Frankly, most of them seemed troubled by my questions. If they knew, they definitely didn't want to discuss what was happening nearby. As we talked, it became clear that they were terrified of the Gestapo and thought they'd be arrested, imprisoned, or worse if they answered questions."

"So you think they were in denial."

"I felt they were thinking 'if I don't acknowledge what's happening, it won't be true,' but I'm rambling on about my experiences, and though I have an educated idea about what's going on at Dachau, I can't say for sure. Why the interest?"

"This morning I asked Herr Beck for permission to write about some Luftwaffe experiments about to begin in the camp. He submitted my request to Berlin for approval."

"You're not serious," Josef said incredulously. He paused, waiting for Inge to respond. When she didn't, he said: "Apparently, you are. I can't say I wish you luck. Journalistic curiosity aside, I'd leave well enough alone. Instead, help me write something positive about this horrible art exhibit here in Munich."

"You don't get it, do you?" Inge said crossly. "It's this art, though I hesitate to call it art, along with the insipid article I wrote about the Hitler Youth, that makes working on a story about Dachau so appealing. Maybe there's bona fide news to report for a change, and if not, at least the work will be more interesting than what I'm doing now."

"But hardly safer. The party has gone to great lengths to conceal the truth about what's occurring in camps like Dachau. As

# #

# # # # # # # # # # # # # #

you know, very little news crosses our desks. Be careful you don't get in over your head, Inge. From what little I've seen and what I immediately sensed, Dachau is a dangerous place. I urge you to stay as far away from there as possible."

"I'll keep your warning in mind, my friend," Inge said. "I appreciate your concern and advice. I promise not to do anything stupid."

When Josef pulled up in front of Sigrid's house, Inge was glad to bring the conversation about Dachau to an end. She got out of the car, leaned down, and looked through the open window. "Thanks for the ride," she said. "See you in the morning."

"I can't wait to see what exciting assignment awaits me," Josef said with disdain. "Enjoy your party."

"I will thanks." Inge waved as Josef drove away. His revelations about Dachau exacerbated her concern for Rosel, but it didn't make her question her tentative plan to enlist Erich's help. *Bottom line,* she mused, *despite Josef's warnings, I have to get into the camp.*

Erich finally finished putting the last of his personal papers in his briefcase. He glanced at his watch. Surprised it was already six o'clock, he snapped the briefcase shut, retrieved his cap from the top of the file, and went to find Joachim.

As he reached out to open the door, it crashed into him, and he jumped back to avoid a collision. "I was expecting you," he said to Joachim. "Though I thought you'd show up hours ago."

"Despite what you may think, I do work," Joachim said. "And hard as I try, I can't always find an excuse for quitting early. Seriously, and you know how I hate the word, I had a few problems to work through. I wish you were staying in Munich long enough to finish developing your new plans for supply movements from Berlin. I could use the help."

"You're my replacement?"

"I am, and, sadly, I may be forced to work harder than I'd prefer."

Erich rolled his eyes. "What a pity," he said sarcastically, "but not to worry. The notes I'm leaving should guide you through the process until the new system is implemented. Before you start, look through the thick file marked, 'preliminary findings' in the third drawer of the file cabinet."

Joachim sneered. "I repeat," he said. "It sounds like too much work for me. With this drudgery I'm facing, when will I ever find time for life's true pleasures and challenges?"

"You mean like the barmaid at the Hofbrauhaus?" Erich joked.

"Ah yes, Gretchen. She'll have her work cut out for her tonight if she expects to enjoy my attentions. Anna promised to bring a bevy of beauties to your party. Selecting the right woman will require considerable skill and intense concentration."

"Have you considered that one or two of the women might not be interested?"

"You mean like Inge Friedrich wasn't interested in you? Not on your life, my boy, and speaking of Inge, she won't be the only potential prize at the party tonight. Keep that in mind in case the ice queen shows up in a frigid mood and rejects you yet again."

"Like she rejected you?

"Did I say that? I must have spoken under duress or lied to make you feel better." Joachim opened the door. "Shall we go? I don't want to leave the ladies waiting for too long."

When they reached the Hofbrauhaus, the Schwemme was teeming with people, most of them SS officers. Cigarette smoke swirled in the air, giving the room a murky appearance. The oompah band was apparently taking a break, but a tinny-sounding piano could be heard over the raised voices of the men gathered around it, who were loudly singing, *"Deutschland Erwache"*—Germany Awake. Erich paused and listened to the rousing words, which had prompted his initial enthusiasm for the party.

> *Peal out—that thundering earth may know*
> *Salvation's rage for honor's sake*
> *To people dreaming still comes woe,*
> *Germany Awake! Awake!*

The smell of stale beer, the jovial crowd, and the spirited camaraderie in the room took Erich's mind off his new assignment. "Looks as if you've done a great job organizing this event," he said loudly enough for Joachim to hear over the din. "However, I don't see your so-called *'coup-de-gras.'*"

"Patience, my friend." Joachim grinned. "How could you doubt me? Inge Friedrich will be here. Keep your eyes on the door while I rest my eyes on the beauty around us." Joachim glanced around the room. "Now if you'll excuse me, I've spotted the love of my life." He sauntered over to a blond who was standing by the windows. Erich watched his friend engage the girl in conversation and wondered how many times Joachim had met the "love of his life."

For the next fifteen minutes, Erich wandered from table to table, chatting briefly with other officers who had come to say good-bye and wish him well. As time passed, he became increasingly discouraged. He began to wonder if Inge had changed her mind and decided to skip the celebration. He'd lost much of his initial enthusiasm when he caught sight of Joachim, who was grinning and pointing. Erich turned toward the door just in time to see Inge enter the room. The woman was stunning; her blue dress emphasizing her perfect figure. He caught his breath and tried to compose himself as he walked over to greet her. "Good evening, Fraulein."

"Good evening, Hauptsturmfuhrer," Inge said, hoping her nervousness wasn't evident.

"Erich, please, Fraulein."

Not wanting to appear aloof, Inge corrected herself. "Erich," she said.

"I was pleasantly surprised when Joachim told me you were coming," Erich said. "Last night I got the distinct impression you don't like parties."

"And exactly what impression did I make on you, Hauptsturmfuhrer?" Inge questioned.

*Off to another terrible start*, Erich thought. "I'm sorry, Fraulein. That didn't come out as I intended. I was trying to say you seemed more interested in work than in socializing."

"Perhaps because I was here to conduct business, Haupts, um, Erich." Inge smiled, but her response was chilly. "I was trying to discuss an upcoming assignment with Herr Beck, so naturally I was disappointed when we weren't able to finish our meeting."

"Then again, I apologize. We've gotten off to a poor start, not once but twice. Why don't we try again?"

Inge smiled, and this time her eyes smiled too. "An excellent idea," she said.

"Shall we sit down, Inge?" Erich watched for a response to his use of her first name. When she didn't react, he began to relax.

"Please," she said. Erich escorted her through the ever-growing crowd. As they passed Joachim, he looked up, grinned, and immediately turned back to the blond he was charming.

Erich took Inge's elbow and led her to a nearly-empty table near the far wall of the room. As soon as they sat down, a barmaid placed two beers on the table. Deciding it would be better to try to put Inge at ease by talking trivialities rather than asking personal questions, Erich began the conversation. "I enjoyed your article about the Hitler Youth," he said. "The story reminded me of my own experience in the organization."

Inge began cautiously, choosing her words with one purpose in mind, to learn everything she could about the man she might eventually ask to help her find Rosel. "There's perhaps a little more fanaticism among the members today," she said. "When you were a member, the Fuhrer was beginning his rise to power. Since the conquests of Poland, Austria, and Czechoslovakia, and with the help of the state propaganda machine, the adoration of his young followers is even more intense."

Erich too tested the waters, wanting to find out all he could about the woman who'd impressed him so greatly in such a short time. "Your article said the leaders of the group still stress physical training," he said. "My favorite activity was the speed-hiking competition. One day after our group won the race, we were taken for an audience with the Fuhrer. I still remember his eyes. When we were introduced they seemed to grab and hold me; not allowing me to glance away. I was amazed when I met the man several years later. Though I had changed considerably, he remembered my name and spoke of the circumstances surrounding our first meeting. He has quite a gift for recollecting names and facts. I was so excited when I took my oath in front of Reichsjugendfuhrer von Schirach, who gave a speech proclaiming: "Whoever marches in the Hitler Youth is not a number among millions, but the soldier of an idea."

"When did you join the organization?" Inge asked.

"In 1934, before membership became mandatory. I was one of the older members. Though I was already at the university in September 1938, I, along with 80,000 other enthusiastic boys and young men, marched into the city stadium. We listened in awe as the Fuhrer spoke, his arm extended in response to our reverent salute. He said: "You, my youth, are our nations' most precious guarantee for a great future, and you are destined to be the leaders of a glorious new order.'" Shouting into the microphone, he finished with 'Never forget that one day you will rule the world.' Back then I thought he could do no wrong."

"And now?" Inge probed.

Before Erich could respond, Gretchen interrupted, placing two more steins of beer on the table. "Joachim said to keep the beer coming, Hauptsturmfuhrer," she said. "Here's your next round."

"Thank you, Gretchen." Erich nodded as Joachim waved.

"Would you like anything else?" Gretchen asked.

Erich looked at Inge. "Are you hungry?"

"Actually, I'm starving. I stopped by my aunt's for lunch before covering the art exhibit at the Alte Pinakotek, but that was hours ago."

"What would you like?"

"Whatever you recommend."

Erich turned to Gretchen. "We'll have an order of wiener schnitzel and some of your famous weisswurste." He looked back at Inge. "Is that alright with you?"

"It's perfect. You were talking about your time in the Hitler Youth," she said as Gretchen left to place the order.

"That's in the past. Let's talk about today. Have you been given a new assignment?"

Inge took a deep breath. This was the moment she'd been waiting for; her chance to begin the discussion about Dachau. She began tentatively. "If I'm given the project I've requested, I'll be working with you. I'm hoping to write about the Luftwaffe tests that are about to begin at the camp. Herr Beck signed off. Now we're waiting for the final word from Berlin."

"Do you expect to be given permission?" Erich asked. "I don't know much about Dachau or what the experiments will entail, but from what I've been told, it's highly irregular for a civilian to be privy to anything taking place at the camps."

Once again Gretchen interrupted as she served the food and two more beers. Conversation during the meal turned away from Dachau, but when they finished eating and the plates had been cleared, Erich continued where he'd left off. "I was surprised when you said Herr Beck's forwarding your request to Berlin," he said. "I've never read an article about the detention camps."

"That's the point. I'm not asking to report on the camp itself, only on the Luftwaffe tests. Realizing you've only recently received your orders, any idea what you'll be doing at Dachau?"

Erich nodded yes. "Ironically, I'll be a part of the team conducting the experiments you're hoping to cover, so if you do get the go-ahead from Berlin, we'll be working together. And it would be nice to see a familiar face."

*Oh my God! How much better could this be?* Inge mused. All of a sudden her relief was two-fold. Even if she wasn't given the assignment, she'd have a contact at the camp, and though it was a long-shot, perhaps someone who'd be willing to help with her search for Rosel.

As the evening progressed, by tacit agreement, they dropped the subject of Dachau. Later, when Erich thought about the time they spent together, he remembered little besides the refills of beer Joachim sent to the table and the friendly, at times even warm, conversation with the woman opposite him. She told him about her childhood and about her aunt who had raised her. Erich found himself responding to her disclosures with revelations about his life. There were times when she seemed to pull back, and he wondered why, but each hesitation seemed only momentary, and, overall, she seemed to enjoy the opportunity to get to know him better.

It was as if there were no one else in the room as the two talked, ignoring all of the party guests around them. After what seemed like only moments, Inge looked at her watch. "I really must go," she said. "It's late, and my aunt worries."

"May I walk you home?" Erich asked.

"No, but thanks for offering. We live about a block off Odeonsplatz, so I don't have far to go. Besides, I've kept you from your other guests for too long, though I've enjoyed our time together." She smiled, realizing, almost reluctantly, that she meant what she said.

"I hate for the evening to end," Erich persisted. "Let me see you home. I couldn't enjoy myself if I thought you were out on the streets alone after dark."

*Maybe a short walk will give me more time to get to know the man,* Inge rationalized. "I suppose I would feel better with an escort," she said. "If you're sure you don't mind—"

"Not at all," Erich quickly responded. "I'll tell Joachim where I'm going so he won't think I've disappeared for good. I'll be right back."

He wound his way through the crowd until he found Joachim snuggling up to Gretchen. "I'm impressed." Joachim grinned slyly. "I didn't think you could, but it seems you've melted the ice queen. Maybe you could give me a few pointers."

"She's hardly icy," Erich protested. "I'll walk her home and be back shortly."

"Take your time. I'm not going anywhere."

Erich put on his coat and made his way back to Inge, who was waiting by the door. As they left the Schwemme, he took her arm to keep her from slipping on the wet pavement. The biting wind and frosty air made conversation difficult, so there wasn't much talk along the way. When they arrived at Sigrid's door, Inge extended her hand. "Thank you for walking me home," she said. "And thank you for a pleasant evening."

Erich placed his other hand over hers. "It's been a pleasure," he said.

"If all goes well, perhaps we'll meet again at Dachau." She withdrew her hand, and without saying anything more, opened the door and went inside.

Erich stood on the porch for several more minutes. Finally, he turned, placed his hands in his pockets, and sauntered back to the Hofbrauhaus, not caring that the rain had once again begun to fall.

# CHAPTER 9

When Erich returned to the Schwemme, the room there were fewer people milling around. He located Joachim, who was standing with Anna on the far side of the room. "I'm sorry I took so long," he said as he approached his friend. "But I'm back now and ready to be the life of the party."

"Unfortunately, it may be too late for you to charm the ladies tonight." Joachim said. "Sturmbannfuhrer Mueller stopped by while you were otherwise engaged."

"Nice try," said Erich. "The Prussian Peacock would never come to the Hofbrauhaus to find me."

"Ah, but he did, old buddy. He said to tell you a staff car will pick you up at your apartment tomorrow morning at nine o'clock. Apparently you have a meeting with your new boss at ten."

"You're serious," Erich said incredulously.

"I am. Do you need help packing? For you, old buddy, I'd leave this delicious morsel behind."

Erich nodded no. "I appreciate your willingness to make the ultimate sacrifice, but there's not much to pack," he said. "And I'd feel guilty if I deprived Anna and the other women of your company. No doubt it would be too much for them to endure." He patted Joachim on the back. "Take care of yourself, and make my apologies to our guests. I'll be in touch."

Once again it was pouring when Erich left the warm beer hall. He tucked his head into his coat collar and, pushing against the wind, plodded through the deserted, dark side-streets toward St. Annastrasse.

---

Inge stretched out on the couch in Sigrid's parlor and gazed into the warmth of the glowing embers. A sense of calm enveloped her as she pushed her head deeply into the soft cushions. She shut her eyes and thought of Erich Riedl. She was surprised how comfortable she felt with the man. Unlike most of the SS officers she'd met, he wasn't arrogant or self-centered. He was pleasant and warm.

When the red embers began to fade, she rose, added another log, and watched the blaze flare again. Several times during the evening she'd felt her heart leap like these flames were leaping now. *I could be attracted to this man if he weren't merely a means to an end*, she thought as she tried to focus on her original purpose for going to the party. *As it is, I have to be interested in him only because of what he might be able to do for me at Dachau.*

---

After a restless sleep, Erich woke before the alarm blared. Reluctant to get up, he wondered if the morning cold was keeping him in bed, or the thought that he'd soon be reporting to his new assignment with no idea what he'd find at the end of his twenty-minute ride to Dachau. As he lay under the warm covers, he recalled several conversations he'd had as he left the Hofbrauhaus. Some of his friends seemed troubled when they wished him good fortune. Was it his imagination, or had he really detected concern on their faces when he talked about his transfer?

He'd finished most of his packing before going to bed, so after washing up and dressing in his still-damp uniform, he stuffed the rest of his clothes into his duffel bag. The last item he packed was the picture of his parents. He wedged it between clothes to prevent the glass from breaking and looked around the room one last time for anything he might have forgotten. Finding nothing, he picked up his bag and left for what, despite the ever-present feeling of uneasiness, he hoped would be a positive chapter in his life.

The sun was shining as he emerged from the apartment building, but though it was bright, the rays did little to lessen the chill in the air. He only had to endure the cold for five minutes, as a black Mercedes displaying a SS skull-and-bones flag on each fender approached and stopped in front of him. An SS scharfuhrer wearing the same insignia on his black tunic opened his door, leaped from the car, clicked his heels, and roared; "Heil Hitler."

"Heil Hitler," Erich said as the young man opened the car's rear door and stepped aside so Erich could slide in.

Any hope of conversation during the ride quickly dissipated. Finally, when they crossed the Amper River, the scharfuhrer, who had been so reluctant to converse during the earlier part of the trip, seemed eager to talk. "Have you been to Dachau before, Hauptsturmfuhrer?" he asked.

"I've been to the Schulzstaffel, but not to the camp," Erich responded as he continued to look out the window.

As they crossed the Wurm River, Erich had his first glimpse of the Jourhaus. He studied the words carved in large black letters on the gate separating the lower floor of the building: "Arbeit Macht Frei;" Work Makes You Free. *Free from what?* Erich wondered. As he observed the guard towers scattered around the perimeters of the camp and the jagged barbed wire marking the outer boundaries, he wondered at the irony of the message.

Freedom was clearly not an option for those being detained at Dachau.

Looking to his right toward what he surmised was the administration building, another sign caught his eye. "There is one road to freedom," he read. "Its milestones are: obedience—diligence—honesty—order—cleanliness—temperance—truthfulness—sacrifice and love of one's country." Erich didn't have time to dwell on the meaning of message, because the driver stopped a few meters inside the gate. "The Jourhaus will be your residence while you're at Dachau, Hauptsturmfuhrer," the scharfuhrer announced. "Your room is on the second floor."

"I look forward to bunking here," Erich said, trying to appear enthusiastic.

"Below your room are the guardroom and the office of the report leader. Look ahead and to your right. The large building is the administrative office. That's where we store prisoners' personal belongings. The building also contains the showers, the kitchen, the laundry, the enlisted men's mess, and a clothing store."

"What's the huge, open space in front of us?" Erich asked.

"That's Roll Call Square. It's the area where the general population of the camp is counted twice daily, morning and evening."

Erich looked out at row upon row of men standing at attention. "Is there a roll call taking place now?" he asked.

"Not a scheduled one. The prisoners who remain in the square are awaiting punishment for acts against the Reich. I'd like to tell you more, but we're out of time. Obersturmfuhrer Weiss doesn't tolerate tardiness."

As they passed more closely to the prisoners in the square, Erich was stunned by what he observed. Standing in the damp cold in striped prison garb with no jackets or coats, were obviously brutalized human beings of all ages. Erich couldn't help himself. He gasped as he stared at shaved heads, gaunt faces, and sunken eyes reflecting their terror. The SS officers bundled in warm topcoats and wearing heavy gloves and boots, looked obese in contrast to the freezing, disheveled creatures they guarded. Willing himself to look away, yet unable to do so, Erich was relieved when the driver turned to the right, and the gruesome scene was behind him.

When the car came to a halt in front of the administrative building, the enthusiastic scharfuhrer jumped out and opened Erich's door. Two guards stood at attention, but said nothing as he led Erich past them into the building to a closed door to the right of the main entrance. "This is the commandant's office," he said as he knocked.

Erich heard a gruff "Enter." He opened the door and went in. "Hauptsturmfuhrer Riedl, I presume," said the man behind the gray metal desk.

"Heil Hitler," Erich barked.

"Heil Hitler. Sit down, Hauptsturmfuhrer." The commandant motioned to the metal folding chair opposite the paper-strewn desk. "I'm Martin Weiss." Weiss placed his right elbow on the desk and rested his chin on one finger as he studied Erich, who immediately noticed the Death's Head ring on the commandant's finger. When he worked in Berlin he had watched a ceremony when Reichsfuhrer Himmler presented one of the coveted symbols to a senior officer. The ring was not a national decoration that could be earned, but rather a symbol of extraordinary loyalty to the Fuhrer and the party.

"I'm the commandant of camp operations," Weiss was saying. "Welcome to Dachau, Hauptsturmfuhrer. Though you'll be working for Obersturmfuhrer Doctor Rascher, who will be conducting the Luftwaffe experiments, you will report to me should you have a military question."

Erich nodded as Weiss forged ahead. "It's our policy to inform any incoming enlisted man or officer of Article Eleven of the Dachau Regulations, issued by Oberfuhrer Eicke, the first commandant of the camp. By doing so before your camp orientation, we can be certain you're aware of the consequences should you discuss any aspect of our work here at Dachau."

*The man gets right to the point*, Erich thought as he tried to recall what he knew about the first Dachau commandant. *Ah yes*, he thought to himself. *Above all else, Eicke was famous for his brutality.*

The rustling of paper as Weiss picked up a sheet from his desk interrupted Erich's thoughts. He listened as the commandant read: "The following offenders, considered agitators, will be hanged: anyone who politics, holds inciting speeches and meetings, forms cliques, loiters around with others, who for the purpose of supplying the opposition with atrocity stories, collects true or false information about the concentration camp; receives such information, bares it, talks about it to others, smuggles it out of the camp into the hands of foreign visitors, etcetera."

As Weiss droned on, Erich's hands grew cold, though he was perspiring. He wasn't surprised that SS officers or citizens of the town of Dachau wouldn't discuss the camp. How many men who came to the party to say goodbye knew about Article Eleven? He wondered about the atrocities the commandant spoke about, and he remembered what he'd witnessed as he crossed Roll Call Square.

He tried to concentrate, but his mind wandered. "Do you have questions, Hauptsturmfuhrer?" Weiss asked.

"Excuse me, Obersturmbannfuhrer. I didn't hear you," Erich responded.

"That's obvious," Weiss said huffily. "I asked you if you understood the punishment should you reveal anything about what you see here at Dachau."

"The consequences are perfectly clear," Erich said.

"In that case, I'm sure you're eager to unpack, see the camp, and meet Doctor Rascher." He picked up the phone. "Send Obersturmfuhrer Wolfers to me immediately," he ordered.

Moments later the door opened, and a young lieutenant entered. "Heil Hitler," he screeched.

"Obersturmfuhrer Heinrich Wolfers, this is Hauptsturmfuhrer Erich Riedl," Weiss said. "Wolfers, take the hauptsturmfuhrer to his room in the Jourhaus. When he's had time to unpack, commence a modified tour of the camp."

"Yes, Sir," Heinrich responded. He turned to Erich. "Hauptsturmfuhrer, follow me."

"Thank you, Obersturmbannfuhrer. Heil Hitler," Erich said to the commandant, who nodded dismissively and opened the folder on his desk.

The word "modified" stuck in Erich's mind as he appraised his escort. About five-feet-ten, Heinrich was muscular and stocky. Erich figured he was probably twenty-two or twenty-three. His hair was light blond, and his eyes pale-blue, but what struck Erich was the man's baby-like face, which was nothing like most of the manly SS officers he knew.

As they walked behind the administration building toward the Jourhaus, Erich was acutely aware of the stench permeating the air. He wondered if he was already violating Article Eleven, but he decided to broach the subject anyway. "What's that rancid smell?" he asked. "I first noticed it a few months ago when I delivered papers to the Schulzstaffel."

"It's a combination of things, Hauptsturmfuhrer. It may take a while, but you'll get used to it. Eventually you won't even notice."

Heinrich hadn't answered the question, but Erich didn't ask for further clarification. They arrived at the Jourhaus and went inside. "This is where you'll be quartered," he said when they reached a room on the second floor.

Erich figured he'd be bunking with several other men, but the room contained two metal cots, each with a dresser beside it. One of the bunks was obviously occupied, so Erich moved to the empty one and placed his gear on the bed. "Will fifteen minutes give you enough time to unpack?" Heinrich asked.

"I don't have much," Erich said. "So that should be sufficient."

When Heinrich left, Erich began to put his clothes in the chest of drawers. As he did, his eyes traveled around the room. There wasn't a touch of warmth in the stark surroundings. He was amazed the room was so impersonal. It was as if its occupants were expected to remain separate entities without distinctive personalities, values, and beliefs. Besides the cots and chests, only a large swastika and a clock decorated one side of the room. On the opposite wall was a four-foot replica of the skull and bones of the Death's Head Unit. The ever-present picture of the Fuhrer adorned the connecting wall.

His barrack-mate had no personal objects on display, so Erich left the picture of his parents in his bag he stowed under the bed. He barely finished unpacking when Heinrich returned. "I'm ready for the *modified* tour," Erich said.

As they crossed Roll Call Square, Erich looked toward the men he'd observed when he first arrived. *Their tattered uniforms would make scarecrows look elegant by comparison,* he thought, as they neared the first row. Several prisoners looked up, though not directly at him. *Is it apathy, melancholy, or fear etched on their faces,* he pondered, and he felt oddly conflicted. As before, he wanted to look away, but he couldn't tear his eyes from the pitiful mass of humanity. The macabre scene both mesmerized and disgusted him. *They're like the stickmen I used to draw as a child,* he thought as he studied the walking cadavers, their emaciated bodies devoid of fat and muscles. *These men are no longer individuals. They've become depersonalized and virtually dehumanized.*

Repulsed by what he saw, Erich struggled to hide his distain. He turned toward Heinrich, wanting desperately to understand what was happening. "Why are these people out here in this cold?" he asked, realizing there was an edge in his voice.

"It's punishment, Hauptsturmfuhrer," Heinrich said matter-of-factly. "The prisoners are counted twice a day, morning and evening. Last night one of the men went missing. The rest were ordered to remain here until the offender was located."

"And he still hasn't been apprehended?" Erich asked; thinking the SS guards had to be more efficient than Heinrich implied.

"Of course he was," Heinrich said smugly. "He was discovered early last night. Turns out he was ill and couldn't make it to roll call."

"Then why are these prisoners still out here this morning?" Erich asked in disbelief.

"They're being used as examples for the other prisoners. This time they got off easily. They only had to remain outside for one night and will be returning to work at noon."

Erich was stunned by Heinrich's use of the word "only." *The prisoners "only" had to stand still in the freezing cold without food or water from five or six o'clock in the evening until noon the following day. They "only" had to suffer this punishment because a man was sick and couldn't report. They "only" had a short time remaining before they were allowed to return to work.* He wondered if the chill rushing through his body was from the frigid air or the horror he was watching. Heinrich made going back to work sound like an escape, a privilege, and a reward for surviving the eighteen-hour ordeal. With some trepidation, Erich wondered what returning to work would entail. He wasn't sure if protocol permitted him to ask, but he decided being new to the camp would be a good excuse if he were breaking the rules. "I noticed the sign on the camp gate," he said. "It says, 'Work makes you free.' What kind of work do the prisoners do?"

Heinrich didn't refuse to answer, so Erich figured his question wasn't out of line. "There are several groups of workers, Hauptsturmfuhrer. You'll learn more later—"

"Because this is the *modified* tour," Erich said, trying to hide his contempt.

Heinrich nodded. "I'm not authorized to—"

"Just tell me what you can," Erich said.

"Very well," said Heinrich. "Ordinarily, we have work crews who roll the camp streets and others who work in the gravel pits. As you know, Dachau is close to the Alps and almost six- thousand meters above sea level, so the winter weather can be quite severe. Snow is not tolerated within the limits of the camp, so if flakes fall during the day, they must be removed from all of the open places and streets. The snow is piled on the carts by the insurgent clergy incarcerated in the camp. We call the group the Snow Commandos." Heinrich looked up toward the cloudy sky. "With this frigid weather the unit may be activated sooner than expected."

Erich nodded, but he didn't respond. He was literally speechless. "Some of the prisoners carry food containers from the kitchen to the barracks," Heinrich was saying. "It was recently suggested that we use wagons instead, and the commandant is considering the proposal. There are many other meaningful tasks the prisoners who remain in camp are asked to perform."

*Meaningful?* Erich again marveled at the irony in Heinrich's choice of words. *Does the man really believe the jobs he described are meaningful?* He thought about the Snow Commandos and stifled a laugh. *How could there be a rule prohibiting snowflakes in the compound?* He remembered Heinrich had said snowflakes, not piles of snow. *Removing piles of snow would make too much sense.* In his mind's eye he imagined members of the Snow Commandos flailing their arms to prevent flakes of snow from landing. *It can't be that bad,* he thought, *or could it?*

"Have I satisfactorily answered your question?" Heinrich asked.

"You have, but I do have one more query if you don't mind. You mentioned the prisoners who remain in the camp. Do some of the men work outside the gates?"

"Those who are in better condition work in the munitions factories in the Dachau area. These are usually the new detainees. Eventually, they're unable to do the factory work and are then assigned duties here in the camp."

"I see," Erich said, and he did see. Repulsed, yet strangely fascinated, he stared at the defenseless multitude thinking, *what futile lives they lead and what pointless tasks they're being asked to perform.* Suddenly he felt an overwhelming sense of compassion and empathy for the miserable men; emotions he knew a dedicated SS officer should never experience.

Knowing they were being watched, none of the prisoners moved as much as a hair. They were clearly freezing, but they didn't shiver. To a man, they remained statue-like, their eyes lowered as if staring at their shoes. Consciously or unconsciously, these pathetic human beings, who epitomized weariness, misery, despair, and defeat, were struggling to remain a part of the mass in order to avoid the attention of the brutal guards, who seemed eager to punish or murder for any offense, however minor.

Erich noticed an empty space in the third row of the otherwise uniform formation. He looked more closely. A corpse sprawled out grotesquely on the ground in front of the other prisoners, had caused the gap. Though the shriveled and emaciated body was a distance away, Erich could make out the spreading pool of blood coming from the gaping wound on his forehead. Aware of Erich's interest in the prostrate body, Heinrich offered an answer to Erich's unasked question. "The prisoner didn't number off quickly enough," he said. "Of course with groups of this size, discipline is crucial. Guards must set examples, and often the weak don't survive."

Though he tried not to react, once again, Erich was stunned by the evident lack of concern in Heinrich's voice. He already knew he'd never get used to the suffering around him. He wasn't just feeling uneasy; he was feeling contempt. He was thankful when, instead of turning back to the prisoners, Heinrich led him away from the square toward the poplar-lined main camp road. As they walked, they encountered heavily armed guards, many leading snarling German shepherd dogs. Heinrich paused in front of Block Two. "The living quarters are divided into blocks, and each block is divided into two parts," he said. "Each side has a living room and a dormitory. Shall we go take a look?"

Erich nodded, and Heinrich led him into the Block Two living room. Erich quickly counted forty-five chairs around four tables. He didn't have time to see much else because Heinrich motioned toward the dormitory, a room tightly packed with military, three-tiered wooden bunks resembling white oblong boxes. Each had a blue-checkered cover with a uniform hand-width of white sheet exposed on each side. "The beds are precisely the same height," Heinrich boasted. "I pity the prisoner who makes his bed a fraction lower. It's a punishable crime."

Erich wondered if he'd heard right. Were men really punished if their beds weren't precisely made? "Considering the number of prisoners confined here, the room is very clean," he said. "The floors are shining, and I don't see a mark on the walls."

"Our prisoners are highly motivated to keep the place spotless," said Heinrich. "You mentioned the clean walls. One mark means at least an hour of pole hanging."

"Pole hanging?" Erich said, though he wasn't sure he wanted to hear Heinrich describe the punishment.

Again Heinrich seemed eager to explain. "It's a method the guards use to keep the prisoners in line," he said. "The guilty party is suspended on a pole with his hands tied behind his back until he learns his lesson."

Erich swallowed hard. How could Heinrich be so blasé about human suffering? *I might as well hear it all now,* he thought, feeling more disgusted by the minute. "What determines the type of punishment the SS officers dispense?" he asked.

"There are no predetermined guidelines, Hauptsturmfuhrer. Punishment is left to the guard's discretion, and it's impossible to predict what might provoke any one guard at a given time. It might be a button missing from a prisoner's jacket, or perhaps a lengthy pause before a question is answered. In the camp, tolerance shows weakness. Death's Head guards learn this concept during the first day of training. Even the threat of punishment establishes control. We've found the most dreaded punishments are flogging, the standing punishment, withholding of rations, and, for the worst offenders, relegation to the Strafblocke, where they're chained and deprived of food. Of course death is the ultimate threat."

Erich thought about the prisoners who were still suffering the standing in Roll Call Square. Obviously, the threat of punishment was working at Dachau. Not eager to hear more, he walked toward the door leading to a washroom containing two huge white sinks. He crossed the room and peered into an annex. Brown toilets lined the wall. *No privacy or room for dignity here*, he reflected. "How many prisoners live in here?" he asked, hoping his disgust wasn't obvious.

"The dormitories were originally built to accommodate ninety prisoners, but lately we're packing in one to two-hundred in each one. Over the past months the camp population has swelled because we're taking in more Jews from Poland." Heinrich motioned toward the door. "Now that you've seen where the prisoners live, shall we go outside so I can show you the physical layout of the camp?"

"Of course," Erich said, grateful to be leaving the abysmal block. Heinrich paused outside the door. "I don't imagine too many prisoners try to escape from the camp," Erich said as he surveyed the scene in front of him.

"Escape from Dachau is impossible," Heinrich said proudly. "The first deterrent is the nine-meter neutral zone surrounding the camp buildings. It's hard to see from here, but at the far edge of the open space is a wide ditch. That's prevention number two."

From where they were standing, Erich couldn't determine the depth of the trench, but it appeared to be at least three-meters wide, too large for anyone to leap across. A barbed-wire fence lined the far side. If the jagged metal wasn't enough to dissuade anyone who might get that far, warning signs posted every few meters affirmed that the menacing barrier was electrified. Behind the fence, the final deterrent was a thick wall separating the camp from the road, and around the entire perimeter, watchtowers rose ominously along the sides of the blocks and at all the corners. On each was a mounted machine gun, its barrel pointed toward the neutral zone surrounding the camp.

Heinrich noticed Erich watching a tower guard aim his machine gun toward one side of the neutral zone and slowly move it toward the other. As if anticipating a question, he explained: "Anyone who is not authorized to be in the neutral zone is shot at once, Hauptsturmfuhrer. The guards must be constantly alert and ready to act if a prisoner tries to escape."

Erich realized Heinrich was waiting for him to respond. There was no way he was going to voice his opinion, so he changed the subject. "I'd like to see the rest of the camp," he said.

"Of course. If you'll follow me."

The gusting wind was doing its part to announce the early onset of winter. As the two men walked along the main camp road, it seemed to be raining leaves. *I wonder if there are Leaf Commandos,* Erich thought. *If there aren't at this point, I'm sure it's only because the guards haven't thought of it yet.*

"The prisoners did all the landscaping, Hauptsturmfuhrer. We're very proud of our beautiful camp."

Erich was shocked by Heinrich's choice of words. *Beautiful,* he thought. The tree-lined road was attractive, but to enjoy its beauty, he had to look straight ahead. If he turned only slightly, the surroundings were stark and ugly.

At the end of the road, Heinrich turned left and pointed. "The forest up ahead forms the northwest corner of the camp," he said.

Erich couldn't see much through the dense foliage, but he could tell there was some sort of activity occurring behind the trees. He was about to ask what was going on, when a strong gust of wind blew in from the west. He inhaled the putrid air. "The disgusting odor I mentioned earlier seems stronger in this area of the camp," he said.

"It's coming from Barracks X," said Heinrich. "A visit to that part of the camp isn't on the modified tour, Hauptsturmfuhrer, though I imagine I'll be given permission to take you there once you're acclimated to the camp practices. We've all very proud of the new building being constructed in the area."

"I imagine you are," Erich responded curtly, sure that whatever was hidden in those trees wouldn't be any more to his liking than what he'd already seen.

As they turned back toward the front of the camp, Heinrich saw Erich's scowl. "It's always difficult at first, Hauptsturmfuhrer," he said. "But it does get easier. Someday what you're seeing now won't affect you, especially if you remember these people are the enemies of the Reich, subhuman vermin who aren't fit to live among decent people."

*My God,* Erich thought, *the man sounds like a walking propaganda manual.* He was astonished to hear the euphemisms Heinrich was using to disguise the reality around him. *Do these propaganda phrases separate the SS men's personal lives and feelings from the jobs they're doing,* he wondered, *or have they become used to dealing in stereotypes?* Now, as he listened to Heinrich, he doubted he could ever be apathetic when it came to the plight of other human beings, Jews or not.

As they walked, he thought back. From his first days in the Hitler Youth he'd been trained to fear the Jews; to avoid anyone who wore the yellow Star of David. He was taught to hate what the leaders called "corrupt and inferior" individuals who, at the end of World War I, had caused Germany's humiliating defeat, and, in Erich's young mind, brought about his father's suicide. Now he was wondering why he never questioned the party's Jewish policies. *Did I bury my head and refuse to see what was going on? I suppose even if it were true in the past, there's no way I can escape now.* He sighed as, all of a sudden, an unfamiliar feeling took him by surprise. He was afraid. He wondered if he'd lose his soul at Dachau.

Erich didn't have time to reflect on his startling insight, because they arrived at the next stop on the modified tour, the medical center. "Normally an infirmary houses prisoners who are ill," Heinrich explained. "But at our facility, volunteers submit to medical experiments for the good of humanity. Normally I would be allowed to take you inside, but important experiments with typhus and jaundice injections are currently underway in the building. You'll be able to see the place another time."

Erich was certain the prisoners taking part in the infirmary experiments hadn't volunteered. He remembered his meeting with

Weiss and the infamous Article Eleven. Within a short time, he'd realized why the need for such a rule. With increasing apprehension, he wondered what kind of experiments he'd be conducting.

Heinrich accompanied Erich to Block Five near the front of the camp road. "This is where you'll be working, Hauptsturmfuhrer," he said, as he opened the door and stepped aside, allowing Erich to enter. There were three desks in the office. A woman, who looked to be in her mid-thirties, worked at the center desk. *Wow,* Erich thought, when she looked up at him. There was little softness in her face, and the steel-rimmed glasses perched on her nose made her appear more masculine than feminine. Her dull brown hair was pulled back in a tight bun at the back of her neck. As she stood to greet the men, Erich saw she was lean, with few curves showing through her crisply-ironed, tailored, white shirt and gray wool skirt. Erich immediately noticed her shoes. *They look more like combat boots than women's apparel,* he reflected, and though he had no idea why, his thoughts drifted from the secretary to Inge Friedrich. The contrast was astonishing.

While Erich was mentally comparing the two women, the secretary spoke. Her voice was deep and melodious, and he mentally gave her a positive mark. "Obersturmfuhrer?" she said.

"Fraulein Hambro, may I present Hauptsturmfuhrer Erich Riedl? He will be working with you and Doctor Rascher." Heinrich turned to Erich. "Hauptsturmfuhrer, this is Fraulein Erna Hambro, Doctor Rascher's secretary."

"Good afternoon, Hauptsturmfuhrer," Erna said.

Erich looked at the clock on the wall. It was already 12:30 p.m. He thought about the horrific scenes he'd witnessed over the past few hours as he greeted his secretary. "Good afternoon, Fraulein."

Erna smiled, and her plain face lit up. Her green eyes, which only moments ago seemed dull and lifeless, twinkled. *Not all that bad*, Erich thought, and he gave his secretary another positive point. *She's not as homely as I first thought. Her smile is definitely her best quality.*

"I'm afraid Doctor Rascher isn't here at the moment," Erma was saying. "He's in Berlin meeting with Gruppenfuhrer Doctor Hippke, the medical inspector for the Luftwaffe. They're making last-minute schedule adjustments before we begin our project. The doctor told me to say he regrets not being here to greet you personally, and asked me to provide preliminary information. You'll find it over there." She pointed to the desk on her left. "The doctor will give you an in-depth briefing when he returns to camp tomorrow." As Erna talked, Erich walked over to what he assumed was his desk. "Before you begin, Hauptsturmfuhrer, may I have some food delivered?" she said.

After his modified tour, Erich didn't feel like eating, but he knew nothing about the camp schedule or when he'd have the opportunity to eat again. "Thank you, Fraulein," he said. "I missed breakfast."

Erna turned to Heinrich. "Obersturmfuhrer, on the way to your office, please stop by the kitchens and have a tray delivered to Block Five."

"Right away," Heinrich said.

"Thank you for the camp tour, Obersturmfuhrer," Erich said, once again wondering what a full inspection of Dachau would reveal.

Heinrich nodded and left without responding. When the door closed, Erna turned to Erich. "Now, Hauptsturmfuhrer," she said. "You can familiarize yourself with our project while you wait for your food."

Erich nodded and began to read.

# CHAPTER 10

Hoping to tie up loose ends in case Berlin approved the Dachau assignment, Inge reported to work early. She spent the morning jotting down her thoughts on the art exhibit for Josef, completing routine rewritings of the news-briefs, and reviewing the current bulletins from the front. Now all she could do was wait for the decision to come down from Berlin.

Beck sat at his desk working on a story about Rommel's extraordinary successes, prompted no doubt, by the previous day's article revealing the field marshal's illness. *Nothing negative in the press,* Inge thought. *Why scare people with the truth? Rommel's sick.* She thought for a moment. *Or is he? Maybe he's out of favor. I'll bet even Beck doesn't know what's real and what's misinformation.*

Beck's phone rang, shattering the silence in the room. "Heil Hitler," he said nonchalantly. Normally, Inge wouldn't have paid attention to what her boss was saying, but this time she listened intently to his side of the conversation, hoping this was the news she'd been waiting to hear.

Beck responded to the caller with terse answers. After several minutes he hung up and sat silently, clearly contemplating the information he'd received. After what seemed like an eternity, he turned toward Inge, who held her breath. "That was Goring's private secretary," he said. "He met with Goebbels and Herr Rosenberg. It seems you've been given permission to cover the Luftwaffe experiments."

It took everything Inge had to stifle a sigh. She tried to remain outwardly composed and unemotional as she listened to Beck, who seemed to be talking to himself as much as to her. "I didn't think you'd be given the okay to write this article," he said pensively. "The Luftwaffe experiments involve Jews, and even though they're reportedly being conducted to benefit our fighting men, I'm amazed that, beyond a casual mention like the one that caught your attention the other day, the leaders would want to reveal the test methods and results in a comprehensive article." Continuing to reason aloud, Beck continued. "But can whatever you learn be printable?" Realizing he was arguing with himself, he shook his head. "I'm sorry, Inge. I didn't mean to go on like this. I was told if the information in your proposed article is acceptable, it will be printed."

Inge's heart was pounding. "Thank you, Herr Beck," she said breathlessly.

"You know you're to report only the optimistic and encouraging results of the experiments."

*How ironic,* Inge thought. *My boss is telling me to report the positives before the experiments begin.* "I can do that," she said. *I'll do anything to get into the camp.*

Because she was thinking about Rosel, Inge didn't hear much as Beck explained the ground rules for her article; that is until he neared the end of his spiel. "And, Fraulein," he said. "It's crucial that you abide by the Dachau directives, including Article Eleven that, in essence, makes it an offense punishable by death should you report any unfavorable occurrences taking place at the camp."

Inge struggled to remain expressionless. "Of course, Herr Beck," she said. "I understand." She did, but she didn't. *What's going on at Dachau,* she wondered. *What actions could possibly be so terrible that they would necessitate such an extreme regulation?*

Inge had no idea what Beck had said during her musings, but he'd apparently moved on to another topic. "And since you won't be allowed to live at the camp, the paper will provide you with an official car," he said. "There's an apartment house near the Dachau castle, which should do quite nicely as your head-quarters." He wrote an address on a piece of paper and handed it to Inge. "The rooms are rented on a weekly basis, so you needn't worry about having to sign a long-term lease. The car will allow you to travel back and forth between the camp and the office as the need arises."

"I appreciate your efforts on my behalf, Herr Beck." Inge said. "When may I begin?"

"Special permit papers are being couriered from Berlin. As soon as they arrive, you'll be cleared to proceed with your new assignment. I'll make arrangements for the car to be delivered to your home tomorrow morning. Spend the afternoon completing your work here, and use the evening to pack whatever you need for your stay in Dachau."

"I will thank you."

"You're welcome, but one more thing, Fraulein. Against my better judgment I submitted your request to the Luftwaffe general staff. I expected—no, I hoped—you'd be refused, but since you weren't, I advise you to use extreme caution. I don't pretend to know what's happening in the camp, nor do I wish to be told. In this particular instance, ignorance seems preferable. But whatever you learn, I don't imagine it will be easy to write a positive, printable report. That thought aside, I'm apprehensive."

"I appreciate your concern, Herr Beck. I'll be sure to heed your warning."

"Please do. Now if this article about Rommel is going to run in tomorrow's paper, as it must, I need to go back to work. When you're finished, go home. No need to work until five o'clock."

Despite her excitement, apprehension, and desire to leave right away, Inge tried to focus on the work at hand, but every few moments, thoughts of Erich Riedl intruded and prevented her from concentrating. Though not a fatalist, she decided it had to be destiny of some sort that she was introduced to the SS captain at that point in time. If not, it was at least a fortunate coincidence.

*But how do I proceed*, she wondered. Even a tentative plan of action totally escaped her. "Okay," she whispered. "I could sit here and focus on the problems I might encounter at Dachau, but that's a waste of time and energy. One step at a time is my new philosophy. So step one. Erich told me to let him know if I got the assignment. I'll call him as soon as I get to my new apartment."

Right before leaving the office, she called Sigrid and told her about receiving permission to write about the experiments. Anticipating her aunt's disapproval, she was prepared for an intense debate, if not a fierce argument, and, for the first time since the dinnertime quarrels about her party membership, she wasn't looking forward to going home.

At four o'clock Inge thanked Beck again, said she'd be in touch, and walked home. No familiar greeting came from the kitchen as she hung her coat in the hall. *There's going to be hell to pay*, she mused as she walked into the parlor. It became instantly clear that she was right. Sigrid sat rigidly on the couch, her knitting needles flying. Realizing the only time her aunt took out her knitting was when she was exceedingly agitated, Inge tried to take control of the conversation and begin the evening on a positive note. "How was your day, Aunt Sigrid?" she said cheerfully.

Sigrid didn't respond to her niece's question or her smile. "Come in, Inge," she said; her tone ominous. "I've been waiting for you to get home."

Inge walked over to the couch, sat down, and kissed her aunt on the cheek. "That's not a friendly greeting," she said. "I'm home earlier than usual. I thought you'd be happy to see me."

"Don't try to make me feel guilty, Inge," Sigrid said. "Your tactic won't work. You know I'm upset, and no amount of disingenuous optimism on your part will appease me."

"I'm hardly being insincere," Inge said. "I haven't seen you in a while, and I've missed you. Isn't that reason for an affectionate hello?"

Hardly pacified, Sigrid continued. "Inge, I've made a decision. I won't allow you to go to Dachau. When you shared your proposed plans with me, I didn't argue—"

"Excuse me," Inge said huffily. "I'd say you did an excellent job of making your feelings known."

"Not really. That's because I didn't believe Herr Beck would be foolish enough to grant your request. I kept my counsel and didn't share what I know."

"What you *know*, Aunt Sigrid, is probably nothing more than conjecture."

"What I *know*! So please be quiet and listen to what I'm saying. You remember Frau Magda Ott?"

"The grocer's wife?"

"Yes. Her husband occasionally delivers food to the camp."

"Okay, but I don't see what that has to do with my assignment."

"Pay attention and you'll soon learn."

The edge in Sigrid's voice startled Inge. "I'm listening," she said.

"Herr Ott's store is one of the largest in the Munich area, so he carries more goods than all other Dachau markets combined. When the British or American bombers destroy a supply train, Herr Ott provides whatever supplemental supplies he can spare until the next train arrives. For that, he receives special compensation from Berlin."

Inge often wondered how Ott's store always managed to stock goods termed "scarce" in the news releases. "I didn't know. Go on, Aunt Sigrid," she urged, suddenly interested in what her aunt had to say.

"Good. I finally have your attention. Before he could begin delivering to Dachau, Herr Ott was sworn to secrecy. Magna mentioned something about an Article Eleven; at least I think that was the number. Anyway, the penalty for telling anyone about what he saw or heard was death."

Inge was instantly concerned. If Sigrid knew about Article Eleven, there was something to Frau Ott's story. "Tell me what Herr Ott saw, Aunt Sigrid," she said calmly.

"I'm trying to, Inge. Herr Ott was distraught by what he saw taking place at the camp, and he began to act strangely. He wasn't sleeping and refused to eat. After several heated arguments Magda convinced him to tell her what was so upsetting.

"And how did you learn of this mysterious and disturbing business that's supposedly going on at Dachau, Aunt Sigrid?"

"Don't make light of this, Inge," Sigrid warned. "After listening to what her husband had to say, Magda was terrified. She needed a friend, and I was the person she decided to trust, though God knows, what she said terrified me too, especially since you told me Rosel could possibly be incarcerated in that dreadful place."

Inge put her arm around her aunt's shoulders. "Tell me what Frau Ott told you, Aunt Sigrid."

"For your sake, Inge, for mine, and for Magda and Herr Ott, you must never repeat what I'm about to tell you."

"Of course not," Inge said calmly. "That goes without saying."

Sigrid sighed deeply and continued. "Magda told me her husband saw hundreds of prisoners. Many were being mistreated by

SS guards, and he witnessed two murders. One man was flogged, and the other was strangled."

Though she was stunned, Inge made a concerted effort to remain composed. "If Herr Ott witnessed these incidences, and if there really is an Article Eleven, how did he get out of the camp without being arrested?" she asked. "And how was he in a position to see what he says was happening if the goings-on at Dachau are kept so secret?"

"Magda said when her husband delivers the merchandise, he's usually taken to the kitchens along the back route. This time the guard who regularly escorts him was called away. Herr Ott got out of his truck to smoke a cigarette and wandered up a side road. In front of him was a huge square containing hundreds of prisoners lined up in long rows. That's where the murders took place. Herr Ott was shaken and immediately raced back the way he came. He got into his truck before the guard returned. And that's not all. He saw SS guards with guns, and there were vicious dogs patrolling barbed-wire fences that enclose the entire camp. Dachau isn't a place for you to be, Inge."

"Aunt Sigrid, I told you I won't be involved with anything Herr Ott thought he saw," Inge said.

"Inge, Herr Ott is old, but he isn't blind or senile, so don't be so condescending. He witnessed unspeakable acts of cruelty inflicted on the prisoners."

Though Inge believed what her aunt was saying, she wasn't going to exacerbate Sigrid's fears. "Whatever Herr Ott saw, I won't encounter. I repeat; I won't have anything to do with the actual camp, only with the special experiments being conducted there."

"Are you deceiving yourself or trying to fool me?" Sigrid asked huffily.

"I don't know what you're talking about," Inge said.

"Yes, you do. You're a smart woman. If, as you say, you won't be involved in camp activities, how do you expect to learn about Rosel? Isn't that the reason you pressed Herr Beck for this assignment?"

"I was planning to tell you before you told me Magda's story. I spent last evening with Erich Riedl. By virtue of his membership in the SS, he'll have access to information that, as a civilian, I'd be denied."

Sigrid stood up and walked to the mantle. As before, she picked up a picture of Rosel, studied it for a moment, put it back, and turned to Inge. When she spoke, her tone was more anguished than angry. "I don't know how many ways I can say this, Inge," she said. "You cannot ask an SS man to help. No matter how amiable Erich Riedl may be, if put to the test, he'll side with his own. Any association with him could put you in jeopardy, or worse, it could cost your life."

Inge walked to the fireplace and took her aunt's hand. "Aunt Sigrid, we both know I have no choice. Neither of us could be happy knowing we hadn't done everything possible to bring Rosel home. I understand your concerns. I wasn't going to admit my anxiety, but I'm frightened too. However, I can't let personal fears keep me from what we both know has to be done. Now come and sit down."

"Will you at least tell me what you plan to do?" Sigrid said when they were settled on the couch.

"I wish I could, but I don't know. I'm sorry my uncertainties make it more difficult for you."

"But you're a journalist," Sigrid pleaded. "Can't you make discreet inquiries from the safety of your office?"

"I've already done all I can without raising suspicions, Aunt Sigrid. If I'm going to make any progress in our search, I have to go to Dachau."

"Then nothing I say will make you change your mind."

"Nothing. I'm sorry Frau Ott's news kept me from assuaging your fears, but in spite of our misgivings, and note, I said 'our,' not yours, I have to proceed."

When Sigrid didn't respond, Inge sat quietly, letting her aunt ponder the situation. Several minutes later she spoke: "Regardless of what I feel about what you're planning, I *do* understand, darling," she said as she wiped the tears pooling in her eyes. "You know I don't want to add to your anxiety, but as I've said so many times over the past months, I'm terrified I'll lose you too, and I couldn't bear it." She paused again, and, again, Inge waited for her to collect her thoughts. "You will promise to keep in close touch?" she finally said.

Inge put her arm around Sigrid's shoulder. "I'll do better than that. The paper is providing a car. I'll come home every chance I get."

Sigrid smiled, but Inge saw no real relief in her expression. "That would be nice," she said, her thoughts clearly elsewhere.

"Why don't we agree to stop talking about fears and dangers for now? Unless you need help fixing dinner, I'll start packing. While we eat I'll tell you about my living arrangements. It sounds like Herr Beck found a lovely place for me to stay."

Sigrid nodded, but Inge knew she hadn't eased her aunt's fears. She had only postponed another inevitable confrontation.

# CHAPTER 11

While Erich ate his lunch, Erna Hambro sat quietly at her desk. Mindful of her new associate's wan appearance, she presumed what he'd witnessed during his camp-orientation tour was bothering him. Having dealt with other officers newly assigned to Dachau, she decided to give him time to read and digest the information about the upcoming experiments without interference from her.

At two o'clock, explaining that she had an appointment in town, she cleared her desk and removed her coat and scarf from the hat rack near the door. Her hand on the doorknob, she turned back. "One more thing, Hauptsturmfuhrer," she said. "It's best if you remain in the office until Obersturmfuhrer Wolfers comes to take you to dinner. Wandering around the grounds could be dangerous."

"Thank you, Fraulein," Erich said. "I appreciate the advice."

Glad to be alone, Erich continued to look through the information in the file. The papers describing the upcoming research contained a brief summary and justification for each of the tests they'd be conducting, though there were very few specifics about the means or methods to be utilized. The first were tests designed to measure the effects of high altitudes on flyers. The alleged objective of the decompression experiments was to examine the effect of the sudden loss of pressure or lack of oxygen that pilots experienced when they had to parachute from great heights.

The high-flight tests were to be followed by freezing experiments, prompted by difficulties facing two groups of fighting men, Luftwaffe pilots and the Wehrmacht on the ground. Pilots shot down over the North Sea were dying in the freezing water, and thousands of German ground forces, ill prepared for the bitter cold, died or suffered debilitating injuries due to icy conditions. Though there was little definitive information about the third element of the testing, it appeared some sort of warming experiment would be held in conjunction with the freezing test.

Erich read through numerous reports from the pilots. Most of the stories in the file were matter-of-fact and similar in nature, so rather than scrutinizing the material, he began to skim the pages. That was until he came upon a series of letters from Doctor Rascher to Reichsfuhrer Himmler and from SS Sturmbannfuhrer Karl Brandt, Hitler's personal physician, to Obersturmbannfuhrer Sievers.

"So that's it?" he said when he saw Siever's name. "Our association when I worked in Berlin is the reason I was chosen for the tests at Dachau." Rascher's reason for supporting the high-flight tests became immediately evident. Besides being an SS officer, he was also an obersturmfuhrer in the Luftwaffe. That's why Inge was given permission to write the article," he whispered. "Rascher wants to highlight the Reich's efforts to assist their heroes, and he's using a widely-read newspaper to do it."

Several pages into the testing protocol, Erich came to a diagram for a small compound. It showed an office on one side of the building, "which is probably where I'm sitting now," he said. Behind the wall to his right was a room marked, "High-altitude chamber," and beyond that was a yard identified as the "Testing Compound" where, he assumed, the freezing tests would take place.

As he read, Erich was paradoxically interested, and, at the same time, bored by the redundant material. The plan called for the use of two hundred test cases, the justification for the large number being the desire to achieve accurate results. He was hardly naïve enough to believe, as the manual suggested, that the Dachau prisoners were "volunteers."

The more he read, the more apprehensive he began to feel about the weeks and months of testing ahead of him, but, he rationalized, *if the trials could make a difference to my comrades in arms, weren't they worth the sacrifice of a few prisoners?* When he realized the absurdity of that notion, he was dumbfounded. After only a few hours in Dachau, could he really be thinking like Heinrich? "God no!" he said aloud. *The forfeiture of any life can't be justified.*

He was deep in thought when Heinrich sauntered into the office. Again Erich wondered how the man could be so cheery in such a dismal place. He closed the folder. "Isn't it rather early to eat?" he said.

"It's camp policy," said Heinrich. "There's a 6:30 p.m. roll call, which many of the officers are required to attend. We never know how long the process will take, so everyone eats before it begins. As the prisoners have no work to do and no place to be, the evening assembly usually lasts longer than the one that's held every morning. So if you're ready to go."

"I am," Erich said. *How soon we forget the problems of others and think only of our own needs*, he reflected as he followed Heinrich out of the office.

As they strolled through the now-empty square, Erich heard the shouts of the guards from the watchtowers at the corners of the walls and on top of the Jourhaus as they reported in: "Tower A, no incidents, Tower B—"

Once again he looked up at the ominous machine guns mounted on the structures, their threatening barrels directed toward the area he was passing through.

When they neared the administration building, the flood-lights on the outermost walls began flashing to life, bathing the square and the blockhouses with the brightness of daylight. *Yes,* Erich mused as they walked the final few steps toward their destination, *escape from Dachau would be effectively impossible.*

"Here we are," Heinrich said. He stepped aside and gestured for Erich to lead the way into the spacious dining hall. As he looked around, Erich thought how strange that there would be such a pleasant, cheery room in the otherwise grim camp. Brightly colored cloths covered several rows of tables, and curtains with matching fabric hung at the windows. Adding to the overall sense of coziness, a fire blazed in a round pot-bellied stove in the center of the room.

The liveliness in the room was perceptible. The men chatted good-naturedly, and from what Erich could hear of the conversations around him, there was no talk about camp activities. It became immediately clear that mealtime was for enjoyment and relaxation. The foreboding atmosphere in the rest of the camp was nonexistent in this unofficial sanctuary.

Heinrich ushered Erich to a table occupied by three other officers and made introductions. "Obersturmfuhrers Georg Roenne and Wilhelm Riess, Hauptsturmfuhrer Curt Rath, may I present Hauptsturmfuhrer Erich Riedl," he said.

Instead of saying "Heil Hitler," the men greeted Erich with handshakes and friendly hello's, making it more apparent that all formalities were ignored at mealtime. Accepting Curt's invitation, Erich sat down at the table. In minutes, a Jewish girl, recognizable by the yellow star on her left breast, served the food. As she placed the plate in front of him, Erich noticed she was clean and well-groomed. Had he not seen the fear in her protruding green eyes, made even larger by her close-cropped hair, he would have believed she'd been hired to serve, but when she opened her mouth to ask if he wanted more coffee, he saw her jagged, broken teeth. He shivered, wondering what atrocities had caused her to be in this state.

The girl served rapidly and expertly, yet she seemed to be in a trance or state of shock as she moved from table to table. Erich saw two other women dressed in the same prison uniforms and wearing the Star of David waiting on the other tables. As a group the women weren't as thin as the prisoners on the outside, and their uniforms weren't as threadbare. *Probably because they're lucky enough to steal food and don't have to stand outside for lengthy periods of time,* he thought. He shook his head. *Lucky? How could that particular word ever apply to these women?*

As they ate, Erich began to realize that, in the eyes of the other men, Heinrich didn't exist. For all intents and purposes, they ignored him. "New to camp today?" Georg asked.

"I arrived this morning," Erich said. "I'm Doctor Sigmund Rascher's new administrative assistant for the special experiments in Block Five." Though he expected questions about the experiments, none came.

As he listened, Erich was surprised his tablemates rarely mentioned activities outside the camp walls. Though they spoke about families and friends, they said nothing about trips to Dachau or Munich. Puzzled, he decided to find out why. "Have you been to Munich recently?" he asked Curt.

"We're restricted to the camp because of the nature of our work," Curt said.

"Doesn't the threat of Article Eleven allow freedom of movement?" Erich asked. "Certainly knowing the penalties for speaking about Dachau, no man would be foolish enough to discuss what's occurring here." When he saw the frown on Rather's face, Erich knew, by questioning policy, he was breaking the tacit agreement to avoid talk of work at meals.

This time Rather ignored the unspoken rule. "Despite the threat, or should I say the promise of Article Eleven, Commandant Weiss feels the less contact we have with the outside populace, the less chance we'll reveal too much. That's why town visits are rare. We have a sports field and a swimming pool at the Schulzstaffel, and we try to provide entertainment for the officers here in camp." He nodded toward the girls who were busy clearing the dishes.

Understanding the implication, Erich chose not to continue. Instead he shared stories about Munich and answered questions about his activities at headquarters. As the meal progressed, he began to relax in the pleasant atmosphere. For a while he almost forgot where he was and what he was about to do for the "good of the Reich" in this refuge from harsh reality.

When the last empty plate had been cleared away, Rather turned to Erich. "Care to join me for tonight's roll call?" he said. "I'm the duty officer. Every evening when the prisoners finish work, we count heads to make sure they're all present and accounted for."

Erich hesitated, but seeing Rather's expression, he quickly understood if he was going to get along with the other officers, he'd be obliged to participate in camp activities, even those he might find personally unsettling. And more, as a member of the SS, he'd be expected to hide any revulsion he might feel. *In fact,* he thought, *as an SS officer, any mistreatment of a prisoner, especially a Jew, shouldn't affect me at all*. "Thank you, Hauptsturmfuhrer," he said. "I'd be glad to join you."

"There's no need for formality in here. Please call me Curt. May I call you Erich?"

"Of course, Curt," Erich said; glad to be enjoying an element of comradeship in the cold, hostile surroundings of Dachau, even though there was an apparent lack of honesty among the men who gathered at the tables. He wondered if they were hiding their true feelings or if, like him, they were mentally conflicted.

Erich followed Curt toward Roll Call Square. Nearly all of the prisoners were assembled, though a few were still marching in from the blocks in rows of about ten. As the men tramped in, Erich strained to hear what they were singing. He was astonished to hear the words of a popular German love song.

"Have you been told much about our camp routine?" Curt asked as they waited for the last prisoners to enter the compound.

"Not really," Erich said. "Though Heinrich took me on the modified tour."

"Then you realize discipline and order is the primary rule at Dachau. The prisoners are on a rigidly enforced schedule. Rising time, depending on the season, is between three and five o'clock. Within thirty-minutes they must wash, make their beds, tidy their lockers, and eat. After breakfast, some prisoners go to work outside the gates, some are assigned to the chore of straightening the barracks, and the rest report to Block Street to wait for roll call."

"And this same routine is followed in winter and summer?" Erich asked.

"In summer the morning roll call is conducted between six and six-thirty a.m. The workers are then divided into gangs. They work either inside or outside the walls and report back at six p.m. for the evening roll call, which lasts until the numbers are correct."

There was no more time to discuss camp routines, as all of the prisoners had arrived in the square. The officers moved forward to a position in front of the first row, and Erich surveyed the mass of humanity before him. Old and young alike, the universally frightened men, with tired eyes set in shrunken and gaunt faces, stood in countless, silent rows. A guard to Erich's right barked an order: "Stand still! Caps off!"

"That's the senior member of a block," Curt explained. "Next he'll report the number present to the camp leader."

Curt moved closer to a frail man, and Erich approached with him. When they neared the pathetic specimen, the prisoner dropped his eyes to avoid the officers' stares. Erich reached out, took the man's trembling wrist in his hand, and studied the tattooed numbers that corresponded to the large numbers on his striped, raggedy uniform. Curt noticed Erich's interest in the tattoo. "Here at Dachau, a man counts only because of his number," he said. "His name and his life history are irrelevant."

Erich dropped the prisoner's wrist, and, feeling a knot in his stomach, moved on. He thought he perceived a trace of relief on the emaciated face as he departed. *It's as if the man appreciates the smallest of miracles.* Erich thought. *He's still alive.*

The two men walked down a second row until they approached a prisoner who was swaying and having difficulty remaining upright. "He has dysentery," Curt said unemotionally. Erich moved forward to look more closely. The man's eyes were wide with fear as he made what appeared to be a tremendous effort to stand motionless and erect. Perhaps the guards would have noticed had they not been distracted by another skeleton-like figure standing nearby in the same row. The prisoner sneezed. Erich focused on the offender as a scharfuhrer approached, and, with his rubber truncheon, struck several sharp blows to the living cadaver's head.

Erich flinched and turned to gauge Curt's response. The man watched impassively. Even though Heinrich had indicated as much during the modified tour, at that moment Erich understood that the wretched prisoners were nothing more than playthings of fate, who were dependent on the whims and moods of the guards. The art of survival hinged on their being inconspicuous and not drawing attention to themselves.

The roll call finally ended with no additional episodes. Erich declined an invitation to play cards. Instead he crossed the empty square toward the Jourhaus. Searchlights from the guard towers crisscrossed the area, and he wondered how much the prisoners actually rested at night. Surely they were tortured with the suspense of what might happen during the day ahead. Jew or not, he pitied these excuses for human beings. Once more he realized his feelings violated SS doctrine and years of ceaseless indoctrination.

------------

Inge finished a quiet dinner with her aunt. Though both women tried to act as if nothing was wrong, there was an unusual amount of tension at the table. After clearing the dishes, Sigrid took Inge's arm. "Come into the parlor, darling," she said. "I have something I want to say."

"We do need to talk," Inge said. "I can't leave for Dachau with the underlying animosity between us."

While Inge put another log on the fire, Sigrid settled on the couch. For a while, the two women were lost in their own thoughts as they watched the leaping flames. Sigrid finally broke the awkward silence. "I understand why you have to go to Dachau, Inge" she said. "You need to do everything possible to find Rosel. I want you to know that, despite my fears for your safety, I accept your decision."

Inge sighed and put her arm around her aunt's shoulder. "I appreciate your support," she said. "We both know that finding Rosel will be difficult, and perhaps impossible, but with you on my side it will be easier. If it helps you feel better, I'll keep you informed every step of the way." She smiled. "Who knows, I may need your help."

Sigrid brightened. "Do you really think I could assist with the search?" she asked.

"Absolutely, and you can begin right now. Will you help me pack?"

"I'd love to, darling. You start while I make tea."

Inge was thankful the disagreement with her aunt was over, at least for the moment. She was sure Sigrid hadn't finished with her yet, but at least she'd be leaving Munich on a positive note. She went to her room to pack for her trip to Dachau.

# CHAPTER 12

A loud knock on the front door woke Inge. She rolled over, looked at the clock, and realized she'd overslept. *Oh well,* she thought as she pulled the covers up around her chin. *Staying up late with Sigrid was more important than getting my much-needed beauty sleep.*

The previous night while she packed for her trip, she and her aunt had shared anecdotes and special memories of Rosel. Their recollections about their cherished days together gave rise to outbursts of laughter and more than a few tears. They also exacerbated Inge's resolve to locate the woman she'd grown up with, learned to love as a sister, and with whom she shared so many happy times.

The sound of the front door closing disrupted Inge's musings. Seconds later, Sigrid knocked. "Come in, Aunt Sigrid," she called. "I'm awake."

Sigrid opened the door. "This just arrived for you." She handed Inge an envelope. "There's also a car parked out front. It's one of those little Volkswagens."

Inge took the envelope. "Thanks, Aunt Sigrid," she said. "You're already dressed. Have you been up for long?"

"For a little while. I decided to let you sleep. When do you have to leave?"

"Not for another hour. I'll wash up and have breakfast with you before I go."

Sigrid smiled. "Breakfast will be ready when you are."

Seconds later Inge heard pots and pans rattling in the kitchen. Throwing back the comforter, she emerged from her warm cocoon. She crossed the room, raised the blackout curtain, and peered out at the dark clouds hanging heavy over the city. "Is it too much to hope there could be sun two days in a row?" she mumbled.

Feeling the chill of the morning through her skimpy nightgown, she hurried to the bathroom, washed her face in the tepid water, and dressed in a tailored brown suit. She looked around the room one last time, picked up her suitcase, and joined her aunt.

"No more tea?" Inge said.

"Unfortunately, not this morning. We drank the last of my supply last night, but I'll pick up more from Herr Ott later today." When Sigrid mentioned the grocer, Inge thought about Dachau. Her apprehension intensified as the time to begin her project grew near.

After a cup of coffee and a piece of toasted brown bread, Inge got up and put her dishes in the sink "I have to go," she said. "Will you walk me to the door?" The women linked arms and left the kitchen. When Inge turned to hug her aunt, there were tears in Sigrid's eyes. "Everything will be fine," she said. "After I've settled into my apartment, I'll call and let you know how to reach me. This won't be a long separation. I promise."

Sigrid choked back tears as Inge picked up her suitcase. "I love you, Inge," she said. "Please be careful."

"I promise I will. I'll call you later."

*The weather's appropriate,* Inge thought as she left the warmth of her home behind and faced the cold, battering wind. Knowing it wouldn't take much to turn back, she put her bag in the car and slid behind the wheel. After studying the controls for a few minutes, she turned on the engine and jerkily departed for Dachau.

Erich awoke to the sound of reveille blaring over the Jourhaus loudspeakers. He sat up and looked at the clock on the wall. It was only five. He groaned, shut his eyes, and lay back down. "I don't think I slept for even an hour," he mumbled groggily. Throughout the night, images of the macabre events he'd witnessed flashed through his mind, keeping sleep at bay. Despite the chill in the room, each time he woke from a gruesome dream, he was sweating profusely. He couldn't get the visions of haggard and wasted human beings out of his head.

When he could linger no longer, he got up and staggered to the bathroom to wash up and shave. Feeling only slightly refreshed, he returned to his room, put on his uniform, and left the Jourhaus. Hungry and ready for coffee, he walked swiftly past the pathetic throng gathered in the square for roll call. When he entered the dining hall, he spotted Heinrich Wolfers sitting apart from the other officers and walked over to the table. "Good morning, Obersturmfuhrer," he said. "May I join you?"

"Please do." Heinrich motioned to the seat across from him. "But it's Heinrich in here. Remember, we're informal in the dining hall."

This time a male prisoner wearing a yellow Star of David served breakfast. As they talked about subjects unrelated to Dachau, once again Erich marveled at the ability of his fellow officers to shut out the gruesome occurrences just outside the dining hall doors. "Shall I accompany you to Block Five?" Heinrich asked as Erich pushed his empty plate aside.

"No thanks. I can find my own way."

Immediately after Heinrich left, a serving girl came to remove the dirty plates. Erich compared the pathetic creature to Gretchen, who happily and willingly served at the Hofbrauhaus. How strange something as personal as religion could put these two girls in such contrasting situations. Gretchen, a Christian, enjoyed freedom and spent her nights as she chose with whomever she selected. On the other hand, through no fault or choice of her own, this girl, because she was born to Jewish parents, had a closely cropped head of hair, was practically starving to death, and unwillingly served her subjugators. As he stared at the waitress, Erich once again wondered at the tricks of fate. Here was a pitiable child-woman very much like the girl Joachim had saved in a Berlin alley so long ago. She too was terrified and at the mercy of a brutal SS officer.

He finished his coffee and checked his watch to see if there was time for another cup. It was close to nine and he couldn't be late for his first full day of work, so, without a refill, he left the dining hall, and crossed the now-empty Roll Call Square. As he walked quickly up the Lagerstrasse toward Block Five, he marveled at the tranquility of the scene in contrast with what was happening all around him. The almost-leafless trees lining the road swayed gently in the breeze as he passed beneath them. Had he been able to keep his eyes focused on his immediate surroundings, he would have thought he was walking through a lovely Munich park, but as he turned toward Block Five, he became acutely aware of where he was; and it wasn't in a park.

As Erich entered the office, Erna glanced up. "Good morning, Hauptsturmfuhrer," she said. "Did you sleep well?"

Erich doubted Erna wanted to hear about his restless night. "I did, Fraulein," he said. "Thank you for asking. Is the doctor in yet?"

"No, and as it turns out, he won't return today. His meeting with Reichsmarshall Goering was postponed until this afternoon. If all goes well, he'll be back tomorrow morning."

Erich removed his hat, hung it and his coat on the rack by the door, and took a folder out his briefcase. "I've read all the preparatory material," he said. "Did Doctor Rascher leave instructions about what I should be doing until he returns?"

"He didn't," Erna said. "I'm going to town for supplies. Would you like to ride along? There's no reason for you to remain here?"

"I would," Erich responded quickly, not relishing the thought of a free day in camp.

"Before we go I'll let the office know you'll be away. Though you're on special assignment and don't require permission to leave the grounds, the commandant expects to be notified when you do. The same holds true for Doctor Rascher and me."

"Thank you," Erich said; surprised but then not surprised that his comings and goings would be monitored. "If there's nothing more I need to do here, I'll return to the Jourhaus and be back in thirty-minutes."

"No need to come back. I'm parked just inside the Jourhaus gate. I'll meet you there."

"In a half-hour." Looking forward to a pleasant day away from the camp and its gruesome scenes, Erich left the office and walked rapidly to his room.

---

A little after ten o'clock, Inge arrived at the address Beck had provided. To get to her destination, she had wound up a hill and bumped along narrow, cobbled streets lined with small houses. As she drove, she made mental notes of places she might need to know about in the future, including two cafes that looked pleasant and inviting. The Cafe Bieglebrau was near the base of the hill, while the Schloss Cafe was very close to her apartment.

She had no more parked the car in front of the building when an enormous woman with heavy jowls and twinkling eyes waddled out to greet her. "Good morning, Fraulein," she said warmly. "I've been waiting for you."

"Thank you." Inge said. "You must be Frau Heiden."

"I am, my dear. Herr Beck thinks very highly of you, but I'm sure you know that. He asked me to look out for you, and now that I've seen how beautiful you are, I know why. Let me show you to your room. I'll take one of your bags."

Inge picked up the heavier suitcase and followed Frau Heiden inside and up the stairs. She waited while the landlady opened a door in the middle of the second-floor hallway. "I hope this will be acceptable," Frau Heiden said, a broad grin on her face.

The room reminded Inge of a charming country inn where she'd spent an idyllic weekend several years before. The bed was covered with several quilts, "to keep out the autumn chill," Frau Heiden announced. There was a comfortable-looking, overstuffed chair by a lamp-table in one corner, and a small desk with a chair on the wall opposite the bed. "This desk should be perfect for your writing," said the landlady. "And I believe this chest will adequately hold your belongings."

"The room is lovely," Inge said.

"But I haven't shown you the best part." Frau Heiden walked over to a large casement window and beckoned for Inge to join her.

Inge pushed the sheer curtain aside and gazed out over the town of Dachau. The red rooftops of the houses blended with the vibrant reds, oranges, and yellows of the seasonally changing trees. She could see quaint winding streets in the foreground, and in the distance, a vast and beautiful valley leading all the way to the base of the Alps. "What a beautiful view!" she exclaimed.

"I'm glad you approve." Frau Heiden turned and walked to the door. "And now I'll leave you to unpack."

"Excuse me, Frau Heiden," Inge said as the landlady opened the door to leave. "Is there a telephone I can use while I'm here? I promised Herr Beck I'd check in daily, and I'll probably need to make additional calls associated with my work."

"We have one telephone in our building. I planned to have another installed on this floor, but the war prevented me from following through. The phone is downstairs near my apartment, which is right beneath your room. Feel free to use it whenever you have a need. If you receive a call, I'll come up to get you, and if you're out, I'll take a message."

"Thank you so much," Inge said.

"You're quite welcome, my dear. I'm sure I'll see you later."

Inge unpacked before walking the short distance to the Schloss Cafe for lunch. The smell of home cooking greeted her as she entered the small, cozy room containing about twelve tables, each covered with a red-and-white-checkered tablecloth. An older woman, who, like Frau Heiden, wore a traditional costume, seated her by the window. Inge ordered leberknodel soup, which, the waitress explained, "is a bread dumpling seasoned with liver and onions."

"And I'm going to splurge," Inge said. "I'll have mil-lirahmstrudel for dessert." While waiting for her food, she gazed out the window and watched the passersby. There weren't too many smiles on the faces of the pedestrians. *The war's beginning to take its toll on everyone*, she pondered. *Will it ever be over?*

The soup was delicious and the dessert scrumptious. When Inge finished, she knew the Schloss would be one of her favorite Dachau cafes. She paid, and with the increasing cloudiness bringing a wintry chill to the air, she abandoned her plans to take a walk. Instead, she returned to her room to call Erich and make her plans.

---

Erich spent a pleasant morning exploring the town of Dachau. The narrow cobblestone streets and picturesque neighborhoods were an extreme contrast to the nearby camp, and best of all, the people were smiling, unlike the wretched Jews and the brutal guards at the SS facility. He climbed to the hillside Schloss of the Wittelsbachs. For the moment, the skies had cleared, so he wandered to the east terrace and looked out at the Zugspitze, the Wendelstein, and the Alpine chain of mountains. As he gazed out at Munich in the distance, he wondered what Joachim was doing. He wished he could be with him, solving the supply problems he'd found so mind-numbing only days before. *Anything would be better than what I'm about to do at Dachau,* he thought as he roamed through the palace gardens. In spite of the near absence of the summer scents, the tired-looking plants, and the chill in the air, he savored the garden's tranquility.

As the clouds again covered the blue sky, he strolled back down the hill, exploring the quiet corners and sleepy town squares along the way. Hungry, he stopped for a late lunch at a sidewalk cafe, delighting in the peaceful atmosphere and the taste of the rich Bavarian beer.

Four o'clock came all too quickly. Disappointed he'd soon be leaving the peaceful town and not looking forward to returning to the horrors of the camp, he walked slowly to the marketplace. Erna arrived on time, and as they drove back to camp, Erich felt better. The day had been what he needed, a respite from the realities he was facing: the SS camp, death, and talk of war. The small town was an island in a turbulent sea, a haven in a crazed universe full of death and hate. He wondered if the citizens of Dachau knew what was occurring so close to their idyllic world. *If they do, how could they be so seemingly carefree?*

Erna dropped Erich at the Jourhaus gate. Worried that the perfect afternoon might be spoiled if he crossed Roll Call Square, he went to his room. He didn't want to think of experiments, of Jews, or of anything unpleasant. He lay down on his cot in the empty room and shut his eyes. For the first time in days, he refused to give into negative thoughts, and he relaxed.

---

When she returned to her room, Inge's mind was buzzing with ideas about how she'd approach Erich. He had told her to call if she got the Dachau assignment. "That's what I'll do," she said. "But only because it's necessary. *It may be unladylike, but I'll invite him to dinner. I can learn so much more about the man in a relaxed, informal setting.* With her strategy in place, she went to the phone, dialed the camp number Beck had given her, and asked the operator to connect her to Erich's office. "I'm sorry, Fraulein," the operator said. "Hauptsturmfuhrer Riedl and his secretary are in town for the day and can't be reached until tomorrow morning."

Finally ready to put her plan into motion, Inge was disappointed she'd have to wait a little longer, but what surprised her even more was that, for an instant, she wasn't bothered because she couldn't get right to work; she was jealous. *Of course I can't expect him not to see other women merely because we had one enjoyable evening together,* she thought, *and I'm definitely not emotionally involved with the man.* Unexpectedly she felt a twinge of disappointment when the thought crossed her mind.

# CHAPTER 13

After a refreshing night's sleep and a hearty breakfast of wurst, his favorite fried potatoes, brown bread, and coffee, Erich was ready for his first full day of work. When he left the dining hall, there were no prisoners in Roll Call Square. There had been two full days without morning incidents. *Maybe my expectation that every day will bring additional violence is groundless after all,* he hoped rather than believed.

Erna was on the telephone when he entered the office. He hung his coat on the rack, sat at his desk, and opened the files on the impending experiments. Before he had a chance to begin reading, Erna hung up. "Good morning, Hauptsturmfuhrer," she said pleasantly.

"Good morning, Fraulein. Thank you again for the trip to town."

Erna smiled, but her momentary affability quickly gave way to her customary professional demeanor. "I hate to begin your day with more distressing news," she said. "But it appears we're facing yet another delay. I just spoke with Doctor Rascher. He'll be in Berlin for another week, and would like for you to join him."

"Did he say why?" Erich asked.

"Only that you'll be interviewing Luftwaffe pilots about the problems they face at high altitudes. The doctor believes information you gather from personal interaction will help us further refine our plans for the tests."

"I see," Erich said, though he didn't think there was much more he could learn beyond what he'd already read in the preliminary report.

"A military transport will meet you at the Munich-Reim airport at 11:30" Erna was saying. "Plan to be away for a week, perhaps a little longer. I reserved a room for you at the Aldon."

Erich was surprised. The Aldon was the preferred hotel of foreign diplomats and the German aristocracy. "Will I be meeting the doctor at the hotel?" he asked, wondering if that was the reason he was being afforded such luxury.

"No, at the Air Ministry. The doctor is staying at his private residence outside the city. Here's his office number." She handed Erich a slip of paper. "Call him when you're settled."

"Then I should pack." Erich stood and put on his coat and hat. "I'll see you in a few days, Fraulein."

He'd just reached the door when Erna called out; "Hauptsturmfuhrer, I almost forgot. There's a message for you from a Fraulein Friedrich. She called a few minutes ago."

"Is she in Dachau?"

"The number she left is local. She said she represents the Propaganda Ministry and the *Völkischer Beobachter*, though she didn't give me a specific reason for wishing to speak with you." She stood and handed Erich a paper containing the number. "You may use my telephone if you'd like. I'll be in Commandant Weiss's office."

Erich's vague concern for Inge's safety suddenly turned to dread. What he'd seen over the previous two days had validated his initial belief that Dachau was no place for Inge to work. He called the camp operator and had her dial the number. After several rings a woman answered. "Heil Hitler," he said. "I would like to speak with Fraulein Friedrich, please."

"May I tell her who's calling?" the woman said.

"This is Hauptsturmfuhrer Erich Riedl returning her call."

"Just a moment, Hauptsturmfuhrer," said the woman. "I'll get her."

Several minutes later Inge answered. "Erich, thank you for calling me back so promptly," she said breathlessly.

"I'm sorry I missed your call. When did you get to Dachau?"

"Yesterday morning. I spent most of the day settling into my apartment. I called the camp to tell you I was here, but you were out."

"I spent the day in town. Had I known you were here, we could have met for coffee. Apparently you got the assignment?"

"I did. I was hoping you'd help me with my story. Could we meet for dinner tonight?"

"I'd like to have dinner, Inge, but unfortunately it can't be tonight. I'll call you next week, and we'll set up a time to get together."

"Fine," Inge said, trying to hide her disappointment. "In the meantime, I'll begin the background research necessary to write the article. I'll talk with you soon."

Though he wanted to warn Inge to be careful, Erich remained silent; sure the camp phones weren't safe. "Take care of yourself," he said.

"You too," said Inge.

As he hung up, Erich realized he hadn't thought much about the beautiful reporter over the past two days. Suddenly, in his mind's eye, her image became the face of the Jew who served meals in the dining hall. "This place must be getting to me," he whispered; again thinking he had to find a way to keep Inge from writing about the experiments."

Erna returned, interrupting Erich's thoughts. "You'd better pack, Hauptsturmfuhrer," she said. "You don't want to miss your plane. There isn't another one today, and your orders clearly say you're to be in Berlin tonight. Obersturmfuhrer Wolfers will drive you to the airport." She handed Erich a folder. "Hopefully this information will help with your interviews. It arrived by courier a few minutes ago."

Erich took the folder. "Thank you, Fraulein," he said. "I'll see you when I return."

———————————

Inge hung up and, her hand still on the receiver, stood quietly by the phone. She felt frustrated and disappointed, not only because her efforts to find Rosel would have to be postponed, but also because it didn't occur to her that Erich would decline her invitation. *Was it presumptuous on my part to believe he would chivalrously come to my assistance,* she mused. She didn't know him well enough to guess what his reaction would be if she told him about her problem. She wondered if his loyalty to the party would supersede his personal feelings. Would he report her to the Gestapo for harboring a Jew?

Her mind raced. *I'm a pretty good judge of character,* she reflected. *The man I spent time with at the Hofbrauhaus would never turn me in, but helping me in my efforts to find Rosel is another matter.* She paused in her musings. "My God," she said incredulously. "I'm making Erich Riedl the basis for my success or failure. I have to do this on my own, as I intended before I met the man. I was going to succeed without him. I still can! I'm going to Dachau today to begin my research. I can't count on Erich."

She released the receiver and went upstairs to her room, pleased that once again she was depending entirely on herself and formulating an independent plan of action. She decided the first step would be to meet Erich's secretary and see what she could discover about the actual experiments.

Reasoning a trip to the detention camp was hardly a time to look glamorous, she dressed in a dark-blue tailored suit and arranged her blond hair in a bun at the nape of her neck. Pleased with what she saw in the mirror, she left her room and began the long-anticipated trip to the camp.

The driving was easier than it had been the day before, giving Inge the opportunity to think as she drove. She recalled her aunt's story about Herr Ott. Though she wrote about death in her articles, and realized fatalities were the price a nation paid for making war, she wondered how she'd react if she witnessed an incident like the one Herr Ott described.

Arriving at the camp gates, Inge rolled down the window. She took a deep breath to calm herself and inhaled a putrid aroma. Was it rotting garbage? She couldn't figure out what could cause such a stench. The guard waved the car to a stop. "This facility is strictly off limits to civilians, Fraulein," he said gruffly. "Did you see the posted sign?"

Inge reached for her papers. "I believe these will explain," she said confidently, trying to hide her nervousness.

The guard took the envelope. While he studied the papers, Inge gazed at the huge iron gate and considered the words; "Arbeit Macht Frei." She peered beyond the barricade. Though she couldn't see much, the tall watchtowers with pointed roofs, walls that seemed to surround the entire camp, and a barbed-wire fence, hardly suggested freedom. She shook her head, thinking the structures were inconsistent with the word "free."

The guard's voice interrupted her thoughts. "If you'll excuse me, Fraulein, I must verify your orders," he said. "Remain here."

*What, no "please, Fraulein?"* Inge thought, as the man turned his back, leaving her sitting in the car as he went into the Jourhaus. Once again she strained to see beyond the gate. She noticed numerous single-storey buildings surrounding a vast, empty area. There was another guard tower visible on the far side of the square. "If I were writing about the camp I'd lead with six words," she whispered: "Dachau is frightening, stark, and depressing."

Five minutes passed before the guard exited the Jourhaus. He folded Inge's papers and handed them back to her. "I'm sorry, Fraulein," he said. "You will not be permitted to enter. The principal participants in the project are away on business."

Inge was both surprised and disappointed. Erich hadn't said anything about leaving camp. She tried again. "Is Doctor Rascher's secretary in?"

"I assume she is," the guard said. "Her car is parked in its usual spot."

"Then I would like to meet with her. She should be able to provide the background information I need to begin my article."

"Fraulein, I said you may not enter the camp," the guard said sternly.

"But my papers are in order—"

"Papers or no papers, Fraulein, Obersturmbannfuhrer Weiss decides who will or will not be admitted. You have been denied access."

Realizing she was pushing too hard but not yet ready to give up, Inge tried once more. "Would it be possible for me to speak with the obersturmbannfuhrer?" she asked.

"That is not possible, Fraulein. Doctor Rascher is your contact, not Commandant Weiss. The doctor's secretary is not authorized to provide information without his consent."

"Thank you for making the effort, Scharfuhrer." Clearly the sarcasm in Inge's final statement didn't go unnoticed, because the angry guard abruptly turned and entered the Jourhaus. Inge jammed the car into reverse and backed away. She was furious. *What do I do now,* she wondered. *Am I supposed to give up and return to Munich?*

As quickly as it rose, her fury subsided and she began to feel sorry for herself, for her aunt, and especially for Rosel. She would never give up her search, but now she was even more concerned. Could the extra time before she gained access to the camp possibly be the difference between life and death for Rosel? She thought of what little she'd seen at Dachau. Instinctively, she knew that, if Rosel was living in the camp, she was in imminent danger.

By the time she pulled up in front of her apartment house, Inge's resolution had turned to despair. "What can I do when I can't even get through the front gates?" she whispered. As she opened the car door, she had a thought. *If I can't get into camp to see the secretary, perhaps I can get her to come to me. I can try to set up a meeting in town. Why didn't I think of that before wasting my time and energy being angry? I may not find out about Rosel as quickly, but at least I'll be starting the process.*

---

Erich looked down at the panorama below. The cold October wind had already done its job. None of the brilliant reds, greens, and oranges of fall remained. The earth had taken on a gray-brown appearance.

The dreariness of the scene and the dark clouds the plane passed through matched Erich's somber mood. He'd never experienced such ambivalence. He didn't want to go to Berlin, but he didn't want to remain at Dachau. He wanted to support SS policies and fundamental principles, yet his conscience bothered him when he contemplated the atrocities being committed in the camp. He wanted to see Inge Friedrich, but he didn't want her anywhere near Dachau. He wanted to work on a worthwhile project for the Reich, but he knew this "worthwhile project" was going to involve the death of the "volunteers," and it bothered him. He'd never felt so confused and so alone.

He tried not to dwell on his personal struggles and began to peruse the papers Erna had provided. He couldn't concentrate, so to pass the time, he tried to sleep. He couldn't drift off. He considered striking up a conversation with other passengers making the flight, but no one seemed eager to converse.

Time passed slowly; minutes seemed like hours. Finally, the plane made its final approach to Tempelhof, landed, and taxied to the terminal. Erich deplaned and walked through the building to the street, where a large black Mercedes waited by the curb. As he approached the car, a scharfuhrer leaped from the driver's seat. "Heil Hitler," he screeched.

Erich recalled his early days in the Hitler Youth. He too had been enthusiastic. *Does age temper fervor, or is it that reality interferes with idealism?* Erich wondered. "Heil Hitler," he responded with less fervor.

"If you'll wait in the car, I'll pick up your luggage," the young man said. He quickly returned and deposited Erich's bag in the trunk.

As they drove up Nieder Kirchnerstrasse and turned left onto Wilhelmstrasse toward the hotel, Erich looked out at the familiar buildings. When they passed the New Reich Chancellery, he remembered what Hitler had said when he moved into the building after his election to Reich chancellor in 1933. "No power in the world will ever get me out of here alive." *Considering the state of the war, that's a portentous statement,* Erich mused as they passed the Fuhrer Bunker.

Near the Reich President's Palace he noticed there were fewer vehicles on the streets. He knew gasoline was being severely rationed in the capital, so he wasn't surprised to see horse-drawn wagons mingling with the automobiles on the road, and there were more bicycle riders than normal. "Are there numerous shortages in Berlin?" he asked the driver.

"Food rationing has become a way of life, Hauptsturmfuhrer. Only replacements for necessary clothing like shirts and underwear are available for most people. You'll definitely notice the shortage of soap if you take a walk on a warm day."

Erich laughed. "Still, conditions don't look too terrible," he said.

"Overall we've been lucky. We haven't been hit hard since March of last year when the British bombs fell on the Unter der Linden. That was when the State Bibliotek on Friedrichstrasse and the Old Royal Palace were severely damaged."

The conversation ended when the car pulled up in front of the stately hotel. "If you can afford it, this is the place to stay," the young man said as he opened Erich's door. "I heard a luxury bunker was recently built beneath the building."

*I wonder who'll be left in the city to use it if it comes to that,* Erich thought as his driver removed the suitcase from the trunk. He thanked the young man and went inside. His reservations were in order, and, after checking in, he followed a youthful bellboy to his room. "Aren't you awfully young to have a job?" he asked as the elevator ascended to the sixth floor.

"Not too young, Hauptsturmfuhrer. My name is Kurt. I'm filling in for the regular bellman who's fighting on the Eastern Front." He smiled proudly. "Next year I'll be old enough to join the army and fight for the Fuhrer, and our glorious Fatherland."

*As eager as I once was,* Erich reflected. Kurt unlocked the door. As he placed the bag inside, Erich quickly surveyed the room. Except for the blackout curtains, there was no evidence a war was raging throughout Europe. The furnishings were elegant. A couch and coffee table occupied one corner. On the adjoining wall was a large bed covered with a dark blue spread that matched the floor-length blue draperies hanging at the two windows. Blue rugs accented the highly polished hardwood floor. Beside the bed was a table holding a lamp with a blue shade. A chest and armoire stood against the wall to the left of the bed. On the right of the entrance, a door opened into a private bathroom. Erich peeked in. There seemed to be an ample supply of soap and toilet paper, and there was even a shower. *That alone is enough to make this trip worthwhile. Rationing must not apply to the elite.*

He rewarded Kurt for his assistance with a small tip and quickly unpacked what little he'd brought with him. He washed the travel grime from his hands and face, put on his coat, and left for Luftwaffe Headquarters. He was told to call first, but having been cooped up in an airplane all day, he decided a walk would be enjoyable.

He exited the hotel onto Wilhelmstrasse and headed south toward the Air Ministry entrance on the south side of the Leipziger Strasse-Wilhelmstrasse junction. He climbed the steps past the guards standing stiffly at attention, and entered the reception area. Sitting at a desk was a prim secretary. "Heil Hitler," he said. "I'm Hauptsturmfuhrer Erich Riedl. I'm attached to the SS Tokenkopfuerhande Unit at Dachau. I was told Doctor Rascher would be in the building."

"Doctor Rascher has a temporary office here," the woman said. "I'll check with his secretary to see if he's available." She dialed an extension. "Hauptsturmfuhrer Erich Riedl is here to see Doctor Rascher," she said. "Is the doctor in?"

Erich waited while she listened. She hung up and looked at Erich. "The doctor's in a meeting with Gruppenfuhrer Doctor Hippke and can't be disturbed, Hauptsturmfuhrer. I'm told he didn't expect you today."

"I arrived in Berlin about an hour ago and needed some exercise after a long flight," Erich said, "so I thought I'd take a chance. Did the doctor leave instructions for me?"

"He'll meet you in the Aldon dining room for breakfast at eight o'clock tomorrow morning. Gruppenfuhrer Doctor Hippke will also attend. The doctor will then brief you on what he expects you to do while you're in Berlin."

"Please let the doctor's secretary know I'll be there, and thank you, Fraulein."

Erich checked his watch. It was 5:30. He was hungry, but he didn't feel like eating out. He retraced his steps to the Aldon, went to his room, and immediately called room service. With an hour to wait before the food would arrive, he took off his jacket and shoes and lay back on the bed. As his head molded into the soft plush pillows, he began to feel depleted of energy, both from the long trip to Berlin, and from the challenges he'd been forced to confront since arriving at Dachau. He closed his eyes and slept.

In what seemed like only seconds, he heard a knock. Feeling like he'd been drugged, he dragged himself off the bed, trudged to the door, and opened it to greet Kurt, who pushed a cart into the room. The boy placed the food on the table in front of the couch and took off the warming lids. "Will there be anything else, Hauptsturmfuhrer?" he asked.

"No, thank you, Kurt." Erich tipped the boy again, sat on the couch, and began to pick at the food. The short nap between calling room service and the arrival of his meal had left him too tired to eat. Despite the enticing aromas, exhaustion won out. He peeled off the rest of his clothes, set the alarm for 6:30 a.m. and fell into the warm, comfortable bed.

---

Inge was unsuccessful in her efforts to reach Erich's secretary. Each time she called, the office phone rang five or six times before the camp operator came back on the line to report there was no one in Doctor Rascher's office. On her third try, she began to wonder if Erich's secretary was also prevented from working in the camp because her bosses were away.

She took a break from calling and walked to the Schloss Café for a quick bite before returning to the apartment to try the elusive secretary one more time. She dialed the now-familiar number and asked the operator to try Rascher's office yet again. The phone rang four times. On the fifth ring, the camp operator would come back on the line to tell her no one was in the office. Discouraged, she was about to hang up when she heard a winded; "Hello, Heil Hitler," on the other end of the line.

"Heil Hitler," she said cheerfully. "This is Inge Friedrich, Fraulein. It is Fraulein?"

"This is Fraulein Hambro."

"We spoke yesterday when I called for Hauptsturmfuhrer Riedl."

"You're with the *Völkischer Beobachter*," Erna said. "How may I help you, Fraulein?"

"I'm working on an article about Doctor Rascher's Luftwaffe experiments. I came to the camp today in hopes of meeting with you and obtaining some background information, but I was denied access."

"That's not unusual," Erna said. "Even with the proper papers, it's difficult for a civilian to gain admittance to Dachau. Has the doctor approved your article?"

"I assume he has," Inge replied. "Final permission came from Berlin, and I doubt I'd be given the assignment without the doctor's consent."

"I suppose not," Erna said pensively. "But, Fraulein, the doctor won't be in for at least a week."

Inge considered the time-frame. She recalled that Erich said he'd be away for a week or more. *Is he with Rascher,* she wondered as she responded: "I hate to wait, Fraulein Hambro. Would you be able to provide the preliminary data I need to get started?"

"I suppose, with Doctor Rascher's approval, I could give you a general overview of the tests," Erna said. "Of course, it will be up to the doctor to provide specific details."

"I understand, Fraulein. Since I can't get into the camp, would you meet me for lunch in town tomorrow noon?"

"I could do that." Again Erna hesitated. "That is if I get Doctor Rascher's consent by then. I expect to hear from him within the hour, which is the reason I'm still at the office. If the doctor approves the meeting, shall we say noon at Café Bieglebrau?"

"I know the place," Inge said. "I'll meet you there. In the meantime, I'll be in Dachau at Frau Heiden's apartment house." She gave Erna the number. "Until tomorrow."

*I've finally begun,* she thought as she went upstairs to her room to prepare questions for Erna.

# CHAPTER 14

E rich woke up before the alarm could do its job. Feeling like he was nursing a bad hangover, he groaned, reluctantly threw back the covers, and staggered to the bathroom. Without waiting for the water to heat up, he lunged into the shower, his body recoiling as the icy flow struck him in the face. Instantly wide-awake, he shivered while he waited for the warm water to replace the cold. Feeling more alert, he shaved, dressed, and, with time to spare before his driver was due to arrive, sat down on the couch to review the materials Erna had provided.

The folder contained a list of names of Luftwaffe aces he was supposed to contact in Berlin. Beside each name was a short biography of the pilot. Erich selected eight men who, as Erna indicated with a star, were reputed to be in the city. They had all participated in high-altitude flight missions and complained of physical problems as a result. After reading enough to speak knowledgeably with Rascher and Hippke, he left for the long-awaited meeting with his new boss.

As in the bedroom, there was no hint of war in the Aldon's dining room. Crisply dressed waiters moved from table to table, placing dishes of steaming food on white, stiffly-starched linen tablecloths. All of the servers were older, almost at retirement age. *They're sacrificing so that young men can fight for the Reich,* Erich thought as the maître'd led him to Rascher's table.

Neither man rose as Erich approached. Rascher extended his hand, and Hippke nodded. The doctor pointed to the empty chair, and Erich sat. As soon as the coffee arrived and Erich ordered, Rascher got down to business. "Hauptsturmfuhrer, if you've finished reading the preparatory materials Fraulein Hambro provided, you know what we'll be doing at Dachau," he said.

"I've read the reports, Sir."

"Then we'll come right to the point," Hippke said. "The course of the war is changing."

Erich was shocked that a high-ranking officer of the Reich, and one of Hitler's inner-circle, would verbalize his opinion to others; particularly to someone he'd just met. *That kind of negativity is hardly conducive to living a long life,* he mused as the general continued. "This last spring Reichsfuhrer Himmler expressed concern that the research on the effect of high altitudes on our flyers was at a standstill. There were no human volunteers for the dangerous experiments, and the monkeys being used for the initial tests failed to provide acceptable results. In May of this year, Field Marshall Erhard demanded additional high-altitude testing which would take into consideration the extreme cold an aviator faces if shot down in an icy sea, but of course you're aware of his request."

"I am, Sir," Erich said, "but I don't understand what the need for more tests has to do with the turnaround in the momentum of the war?"

"With additional pressure from Allied air forces, our pilots have to climb to higher altitudes to avoid both the planes and the flak from guns on the ground," the general explained. "Since the United States entered the war, more pilots are being shot down. Some are forced to parachute into the icy seas, and we have to find a way to help them survive in the cold water until a rescue team arrives."

"We've agreed to provide information to the Luftwaffe about how they might prepare the pilots to face these problems of high flight and frigid seas," Rascher added. "I take it you've seen our equipment at Dachau?"

"I haven't been in the actual testing area," Erich said. "Though I have seen the Block Five blueprint."

"The section to the right of the office is the decompression chamber," Rascher said. "Prisoners will be placed in the enclosure, and the air will be pumped out until oxygen and air pressure duplicate conditions the pilots face. There's a glass partition that will enable us to observe the prisoners' reactions in the simulated atmosphere. For this phase of the testing, we plan to use two hundred men. The large number should give us a clear picture of what our flyers have to tolerate during their missions."

Erich strained to remain expressionless. Apparently he failed because Hippke was glaring. "You weren't aware of the testing methods, Hauptsturmfuhrer?" he asked.

"I haven't been briefed on exact procedures, only on the justification and criteria to be used in the tests," Erich said.

"We will be utilizing asocial individuals, criminals, and Jews for these experiments," said Hippke.

The conversation was interrupted as the waiter served the meals. When he left the table, Erich asked: "And what about the other tests, Herr Doctor?"

"We will conduct tests to see how much cold a human being can endure before he dies, and then endeavor to determine the best means of re-warming a soldier or airman who has survived the exposure to the extreme cold," Hippke said.

"How will these last experiments be conducted?" Erich asked the question, but dreaded the answer he'd likely receive.

"As you saw on the plan for Block Five, there's a compound behind the office," Rascher explained. "The second and third phases of the tests will be conducted there. They will begin when it's cold enough and continue until we have definitive answers.

We need to provide the Luftwaffe with results at the earliest possible date, so we'll need to move quickly. We will be utilizing two freezing methods. The first group of prisoners, some dressed in Luftwaffe uniforms and some naked, will be placed in groups of two in a tank of ice water. A second group, ten or twelve at a time, will be left unclothed in the snow." Rascher chuckled, his laughter totally incompatible with the events he was describing. "So you can see why cold weather is necessary."

Erich nodded and forced a smile as Rascher continued. "We will record the results of our observations as well as what the doctors discover when they perform autopsies on the dead. The Dachau morgue is being readied to handle our corpses."

Erich felt the food he'd just ingested rise to his throat, and he took a sip of water to force it back down. "And what about the warming experiments?" he asked, reasoning he might as well hear it all right then instead of in bits and pieces. As dramatic as it sounded, he knew his life could depend on his reaction to what Rascher said. He already knew too much. If he refused to participate, he was expendable. Regardless of the threat of Article Eleven, he was sure the two men seated at the table would never allow him to walk around freely knowing as much as he did. He'd have to keep any concerns and fears to himself and act the part of the unfeeling SS officer he was supposed to be.

"The third area of the research is the warming experiment," Rascher was saying. "We need to find the best method of warming a half-frozen man. We'll bring in women from Ravensbruck for this phase of the experiment." Erich quickly realized the method to be used to warm the men.

Grinning salaciously, Rascher explained: "We will use these women in one set of tests and hot baths in the other, after which we will compare the results."

*So this is the "worthwhile work" I'll be involved with*, Erich thought. "And my job, Herr Doctor?" he asked, hoping Rascher would confirm what Erna had said, which was that he wouldn't be involved in the actual testing.

"You will record our findings and prepare the final report for Berlin. We're counting on your organizational and administrative ability." Rascher looked at Hippke and smirked. "After all, we are only scientists." He turned to Erich. "Any more questions, Hauptsturmfuhrer?"

"Only one, Sir. Why was I selected for this important project?"

"It's quite simple," Hippke said. "We need an officer with unique administrative abilities. Reichsfuhrer Himmler personally recommended you for the job. I believe you worked on one of his special projects in the past. Apparently the Reichsfuhrer was pleased with your work ethic as well as your loyalty to the party and the Fuhrer."

"I'm flattered the Reichsfuhrer would remember me," Erich said. "Please assure him that I will try to continue to prove my worth and my loyalty to him, to the Fuhrer, and to the Reich."

"I'm sure you will, Hauptsturmfuhrer," said Rascher. "You have been given an assignment to complete while you're in Berlin waiting for me to conclude my work. I see little reason for us to meet again, but should the situation change and the need arise, I will contact you here at the hotel or you can reach me at the Air Ministry. I'm fairly sure both of us will be able to complete our work within a week's time. If the weather remains cold, we will return to Dachau on October 29th and begin the actual experiments shortly thereafter. In a few days, my secretary will contact you with the flight information. In the meantime, you have a car and driver at your disposal. You need only notify the desk clerk at the hotel when you wish to use them."

"Thank you, Herr Doctor," Erich said. "I'm sure I'll be able to complete my task in the time allotted."

"Then if our business is finished." The doctor dropped some money on the table and stood.

Erich rose but made no move to leave. "If you don't mind, Herr Doctor, I would like to have one more cup of coffee before I get to work," he said.

"Certainly." Rascher turned to leave and then abruptly turned back. "And one more thing, Hauptsturmfuhrer," he said. "You may or may not be aware, but the Propaganda Ministry has taken an interest in our experiments. A reporter from the *Völkischer Beobachter*, a woman named Inge Friedrich, will be covering the experiments. Of course she won't be privy to our methodology. You will keep the woman from finding out or reporting anything that could shock or negatively affect any citizen of the Reich. Her local editor, Herr Beck, knows if she learns too much or stumbles onto information we feel is detrimental to our program, she'll be eliminated before she's able to report her findings. Berlin fully understands and accepts this condition of allowing her into Dachau. So you see, Fraulein Friedrich will be walking a tightrope. Let's say that whether she remains erect or falls off will, to a great extent, depend on your guidance. Do I make myself clear?"

"Perfectly," said Erich. "I'll do my best, Herr Doctor."

"I am certain you will," Rascher said.

The two men said their terse goodbyes and left the table. Erich's mind was on overload. What he'd just heard was far worse than he initially envisioned, and, in addition, he was responsible for Inge's life. "Damn," he whispered. *Why was the woman given permission to report on these experiments in the first place?* Taking care of her would make his already-stressful job even more difficult. He wondered if Inge had already gone to the camp. She was clearly eager to begin her work, and he doubted she'd wait until he returned to Dachau. Hoping he still had the number Erna gave him, he reached into his pocket. Relieved it was still there, he left his half-finished cup of coffee on the table and hurried to his room.

It was 10:30 when he asked the hotel operator to connect him with Inge's apartment building. The same woman who answered the phone a few days earlier picked up again. "Fraulein Friedrich, please," Erich said. "It's important I speak with her."

"I'm not sure she's in her room. I'm her landlady, Frau Heiden. I'll go upstairs and check. May I tell her who's calling?"

"Erich Riedl. Please tell her I'm phoning from Berlin."

Frau Heiden seemed flustered to receive a call from outside the Dachau area. "You're the Hauptsturmfuhrer who called yesterday," she said.

"I am," said Erich, with more calm than he felt.

"Please wait." Erich heard her drop the receiver and bustle off to look for Inge. *She has to be there,* he said to himself as he waited.

In what seemed like hours rather than minutes, he heard Inge's voice. "Erich? Frau Heiden said it was you. You're in Berlin?"

"I am," Erich said, skipping the niceties. "I wondered if you've been to the camp yet."

"I tried, but I didn't get beyond the Jourhaus gates. I didn't know you were leaving Dachau."

Inge's last statement was lost on Erich as he audibly sighed with relief. "Good," he said.

"I would hardly say it's good."

"I meant—"

Inge didn't wait for him to explain. "I'm pleased to say that, despite the SS guard's refusal to allow me access to the camp, I've found a way to begin my research. I'm meeting Fraulein Hambro for lunch later today. I'm hoping she'll provide the background necessary for me to begin work on the article."

Erich tried not to over-react. "I'll provide all the information you need when I return to Dachau next week," he said.

"You expect to be away for a week, and you don't want me to do anything until you return?" Inge said with disbelief.

"That's right. Except for me, please don't speak with anyone at Dachau. How about joining me for dinner at the Hotel Wagner at 6:30 on the 30th? As it stands now, I'm due back on the 29th, though as yet I don't have specific flight information. If there's a change of plans, I'll contact you through Herr Beck."

"You don't even want me to have lunch with Fraulein Hambro."

"I don't. Please Inge."

"Alright," Inge said reluctantly. "After we hang up I'll call Fraulein Hambro and cancel our appointment, but if I have to sit around and wait, I'll do so in Munich. I'll be at my aunt's house, or, as you said, you can reach me through Herr Beck." She gave him Sigrid's number. "I hope you'll eventually provide a valid explanation for what you're asking me to do or rather not do."

Erich breathed a sigh of relief. "I definitely will," he said. "So unless you hear from me regarding a schedule change, I'll see you on the 30th."

"Enjoy the rest of your time in Berlin," Inge said. As she put the receiver on the hook she was still torn; wanting to meet with Erna, but, at the same time, remembering Erich's warning tone and her promise to wait for him to return before she began her research. *Would it really hurt to meet with the secretary outside the camp?* She answered her own question. *It undoubtedly would. It could cost me Erich's help in the future, and if what he implied is true, it could cost me my life.*

Deciding she had no choice but to abide by Erich's wishes, Inge dialed the camp operator, who put her through to the office. When Erna answered, she explained that her editor needed her in Munich, so she'd have to cancel lunch. Still disappointed but reconciled to the delay, she packed, slipped a note explaining her departure under Frau Heiden's door, and drove home.

# CHAPTER 15

The week in Berlin passed swiftly. Erich interviewed all of the flyers on his list, though none of them provided additional information which would influence the upcoming experiments. Though the meetings were held in the Air Ministry building, he didn't see Rascher or Hippke again. With the week nearly over, he decided the trip had been a total waste of time.

When he returned from his final interview on Monday the 28th, there was a message confirming his flight at eight o'clock the next morning. He was thankful the unproductive trip would soon be over. With no interviews scheduled for the evening, he decided to take a walk. He strolled south along Wilhelmstrasse past the Ministry of Justice, the Reich Presidential Palace, and the Old and New Reich Chancellery. No lights escaped from the blackout curtains covering the windows of the building. The darkness of the usually lively city was a confirmation of the direction the war was taking. Like the government offices, the usually well-lit windows of familiar restaurants and shops that still remained open after sunset were covered with heavy curtains lined with leather to prevent light from spilling out when anyone entered or left. It was dark everywhere. The only bright sparks in the black night were the blinding blue flashes from an occasional passing tram car.

There were few cars on the road, and drivers who were brave enough to venture forth moved at a snail's pace. With only the light of a narrow beam showing through a slit in the black felt covering each headlight, they strained to see in front of them. A small number of white double-decker buses, their headlights also hooded and their interiors lit only by a faint blue light, crept through the darkness. *The passengers look like ghosts,* Erich reflected as he made his way along the dark sidewalk. *How appropriate. Ghosts in a nighttime ghost town.*

Only a handful of pedestrians were strolling the nearly deserted street. Many wore luminous buttons on their coats, some in the shape of Nazi swastikas. Others, virtually blind in the darkness, tapped their way with white canes. Erich paused to watch as a policeman pounced on a man who was lighting a match. *Yes,* he thought. *Berlin had changed with the reversals of war and the threat of night bombings.*

Tired of looking at the dismal scenes all around him, Erich returned to the hotel and ordered room service. While he waited for his food to arrive, he tried to finish his reports, but his thoughts turned to Inge. Had she gone to Munich to spend the week with her aunt as she'd promised? He was worried about the headstrong woman. He wanted to dissuade her from writing about the experiments, not make her persist because she was angry with him.

At the Hofbrauhaus she had mentioned the many arguments she had with her aunt about joining BDM. He reasoned her allegiance to the Fuhrer would have to be extraordinary if she was writing for the *Völkischer Beobachter*, the party's mouthpiece. Would her loyalty to the cause compel her to report everything he said to Beck? He was sure she would wish—no, demand—to know far more than he was willing to reveal. As Rascher suggested, she was walking a tightrope, and he had to be sure she kept her balance.

"There's no time like the present," he said as he picked up the phone and asked the hotel operator to connect him to Inge's apartment house. He was relieved when Frau Heiden said her tenant had been in Munich all week. He left a message confirming the dinner meeting on the 30th.

With a temporary respite from worrying about Inge, he had time to wrestle with his own demons. During his stay in the city, he'd done little to resolve his dilemma. He hadn't really allowed himself time to think. Now, as he sat quietly waiting for his dinner, he thought about the gruesome experiments Rascher described. He couldn't imagine participating in such brutality. He wondered if there was any way out. *I'd have to leave the country,* he thought. *A few days ago, that might have been an option, but now Inge's life is in my hands. No. However disgusting, I'll have to see this through.*

---

Erich woke up early, shaved and dressed. Before leaving the room he checked his briefcase to make sure the results of the interviews were easily accessible should he need them on the plane. At 7:00 a.m. he carried his bags to the curb to meet the driver. Seven-fifteen came and went and the car hadn't arrived. Erich was growing more nervous by the moment. A little before 7:30, a different driver pulled up to the hotel entrance. Not waiting for him to get out, Erich opened the door and slid into the back seat. "The regular driver was transferred to the front," the young man said contritely. "I was just given the assignment. I apologize, Hauptsturmfuhrer."

"I'm sure it's not your fault," Erich said. "Just get me to Tempelhof before the damn plane takes off."

They sped along Wilhelmstrasse toward the airport. Fortunately, there were few cars on the road at the early hour, though at one point a horse-drawn wagon turned in front of the car, impeding their progress. The driver bypassed the terminal and pulled onto the tarmac as the propellers on the transport plane were spinning. Erich grabbed his luggage, jumped from the car, and raced to board through the open cargo door. He spied Rascher sitting in the aisle seat and chose a seat directly across the aisle. "You nearly missed the flight, Hauptsturmfuhrer," the doctor growled. "A moment ago I ordered the pilot to take off without you."

"The regular driver was transferred to the front, and his replacement was late," Erich said as he put his bag in the overhead compartment and stuffed his briefcase under the seat in front of him. "The way he drove through Berlin, I wondered if we'd end up in the hospital instead of the airport."

Rascher didn't respond, so Erich buckled his seat belt and sat quietly through the takeoff. "Was your stay in Berlin beneficial?" Rascher asked when they were airborne.

"I interviewed all the pilots on the list," Erich said. "But I didn't learn much beyond what we already know." He briefly summarized the information he'd garnered from the sessions. Rascher seemed to half listen, and Erich began to wonder why he'd really been summoned to Berlin. It seemed the doctor knew the interviews would be meaningless.

The trip was uneventful. Rascher slept most of the time, leaving Erich to his own, less-than-comforting, thoughts. During one of the rare times they did converse, the doctor reported that the next two days would be used to select the two hundred prisoners who would take part in the first phase of the tests and then move them to a common block. Erich wouldn't be involved in the selection process and would be free to spend his time as he wished until the actual testing began.

Erich was pleased he'd have time to meet with Inge. His renewed concerns for her mingled with the excitement he felt at the prospect of seeing her again. She'd been in his thoughts during the trip, and even more so as he flew back to Munich. Her safety had become his primary concern and the reason he'd take part in the tests. He turned to speak to Rascher, but seeing the doctor was again sleeping, he moved to the window seat and looked down at the landscape below.

---

The week dragged for Inge. At first the often-dreamed-about days of leisure were enjoyable, but it wasn't long before everything changed. By the fourth day she wasn't sure she could stand another minute doing nonsensical activities. In an effort to do something meaningful, she went to the office. Josef and Werner were out on assignment and Beck had been summoned to Berlin by Alfred Rosenberg. *Nothing seems to be working out today*, she thought. Irritated she returned home to face more monotony and frustration.

The next few days were identical to the ones before. The only meaningful moments were those she spent with her aunt. During their time together the two women renewed their relationship which had been strained before Inge's departure for Dachau. Inge was careful not to mention Erich's unsettling warning that she stay out of the camp. Her excuse for being home was a delay in the start of the tests.

On the morning of the 29th, Inge got up later than usual. She put on her robe, went to the parlor, added a log to the fire, and headed to the kitchen to make coffee. Before she could turn on the stove to heat the water, there was a knock on the door. She pulled her robe tightly around her and went to see who had come to visit. "Good morning, Josef," she said. She looked beyond the man. "You walked, so you must be freezing. "Come in. What brings you out so early on such a dreary day?"

"It seems I've become the official office delivery boy. I bring a message from Beck. Sorry I missed you at the office yesterday. I was out on a crucial assignment."

"Another art show?"

"Preliminary work for the November 9th holiday." He paused. "Come to think of it, why aren't you at Dachau?"

"Because my assignment was postponed for a week. What's the message?"

"Here." Josef handed Inge a folded note. She opened it and read. For the first time in days, she felt hopeful. "Good news?" he asked when he saw her smile.

"Confirmation that a friend will be returning to Dachau today, which means I'll be able to start working on the article. After a week in Munich with nothing constructive to do, I'm feeling useless."

"Funny." Joseph chuckled. "That's how I feel every day."

"I wish I could help, but—"Inge grimaced. "I hate to be rude, Josef, but I have to pack and leave for Dachau as soon as possible."

"So the message means the messenger gets the boot?"

"It's not that. I have a great deal to do and—"

"I understand. I realize I've said this before, but take care of yourself, and remember, if there's anything you need, don't hesitate to call."

"Thank you," Inge said. "I'll be in and out of the office, so I'll see you soon."

Inge shut the door and went to the kitchen to look for a note to explain her aunt's absence. She found what she was looking for. Sigrid was shopping and would be back around noon. Excited the lengthy delay was coming to an end, she dressed, and packed. She was just about ready to leave when Sigrid bustled in carrying a bag of groceries. "You're dressed up," she said. "I thought you planned to stay in today."

"Plans have changed, Aunt Sigrid. I'm returning to Dachau this afternoon, and I'm meeting Erich Riedl for dinner."

"I see," Sigrid said glumly. "I knew this time would come, but I suppose I hoped our visit wouldn't end."

"If everything works out, we'll be together all the time," Inge said cheerfully. "And Rosel will be with us."

Apparently Inge's reassurances weren't helping, as Sigrid's frown deepened. "There's no need to worry, Aunt Sigrid," Inge said with all the confidence she could muster.

Tears welled up in Sigrid's eyes. "I'm trying to be strong," she said. "But it isn't easy, Inge. Isn't there anything I can say to persuade you to give up your crazy plan?"

Inge nodded no. "I'm afraid not," she said. "Unless you have a better idea, Erich Riedl is our best chance to find Rosel."

"Promise you'll phone if you need me," Sigrid cried, showing none of her usual resolve.

Inge hugged her aunt. "You know I will, but I really have to leave. I'll call you in the morning." She hugged Sigrid again, picked up her bag, and left for Dachau.

---

Erich was glad when the plane finally landed in Munich. Rascher reiterated that they would meet in Block five at 9:00 o'clock on October 31st. He then left in his chauffeur-driven Mercedes. "Are you ready to go?" Heinrich said. "I'll have you back at Dachau in no time."

"I am." Erich slid into the back seat. "Anything new at the camp?" he asked. *What a stupid question,* he thought as soon as he said the words. *Why would anything be different?*

"Only that more and more prisoners are arriving daily," Heinrich said. "And most of the incoming detainees are Jews."

"I see." He wondered if any of the new arrivals had been transported for the Luftwaffe tests.

To avoid unwanted conversation, Erich slept during the short drive. In what seemed like minutes Heinrich announced: "We're at the Jourhaus gate," Hauptsturmfuhrer." Erich presented his papers to the guard, who waved the car into the compound. "Shall I drop you at Block Five?" Heinrich asked.

"Please. I need to check in with Fraulein Hambro before I unpack."

As they entered Roll Call Square, Heinrich stopped and waited for a prisoner work crew to pass. Erich noted that one of the men lagged behind the others. Unfortunately for the straggler, an ever-alert guard also noticed. He leaped toward the laggard and struck him two short yet powerful blows to the head. "You pig," he snarled. "I'll teach you to keep up." He shoved the prisoner to his knees. "Now dig with your hands. It's good practice for the gravel pit tomorrow."

As they neared the camp road, Heinrich had to change course to skirt another group of prisoners. Erich looked out at a ridiculous scenario playing out in front of him. The men had been divided into two teams. Team A carried sand from one point to another, and team B carried the same sand back to the original location. As Heinrich maneuvered the car around the group, Erich could hear the SS men yelling: "Tempo, tempo, faster, faster, faster. Begin, you lazy dogs. You! Come here! You! Go there!" Despite the chilly air Erich could see the perspiration on the anguished laborers' faces.

When they finally reached the office, Erna was straightening her desk and preparing to depart for the day. "Hauptsturmfuhrer," she said, looking surprised. "I didn't expect you back in the office for two days."

"I'm not officially here." Erich removed the files from his briefcase and put them on Erna's desk. "I brought the transcripts of my interviews so you can type the results for the doctor, and truthfully, I was hoping for a ride to town."

"I'd be glad to take you. Does the commandant know you're leaving?"

"I haven't reported in yet, though I imagine Heinrich did it for me."

Erna smiled knowingly. "I imagine he did," she said. "Before we go I'm taking a file to the administrative building. While I'm there, I'll tell the commandant's secretary you're here, but are leaving immediately. We'll meet at the Jourhaus gate in, shall we say, fifteen-minutes?"

"Excellent," Erich said. "And thank you for the ride."

---

Inge parked near the apartment house and went to her room. She unpacked, pleased she'd soon know why Erich frantically urged her to wait before beginning the article. She wanted to rest, but found it impossible to relax. She finally gave up, washed her hair, and toweled it dry. When she returned to her room and checked her watch, it was only 4:30. "I'll go crazy if I stay here any longer," she whispered as she chose her most attractive dress, a green print on a white background with a tight waist, a snugly fitting bodice, and a flared skirt. She tied her hair back with a green ribbon that matched the green in the dress, and selected a pair of dark pumps to complete the outfit. *I'll drive to the Wagner and take a walk to pass the time,* she decided. *That's better than sitting here doing nothing."*

It was 5:15 when she parked near the hotel entrance. Before beginning her walk, she went inside to locate the dining room. She was ten steps into the lobby, when she saw Erich sitting on a couch across the room reading the paper. Embarrassed she'd arrived almost two hours early, she turned to sneak away, but before she got to the door, he looked up. "Inge," he called out.

"She turned back and crossed the room to where he was standing. "Erich," she said. "I came over early to make sure I could find the hotel before I took a walk." She paused. "But why are you here? Your message said 7:00 o'clock."

"I know, but without a car of my own, I had to catch a ride with Fraulein Hambro. She leaves the office around four." He smiled. "Seeing you here makes me glad she didn't opt to work late. May I walk with you? I've been cooped-up in an airplane all day. I'd like a little fresh air."

"Of course I'd enjoy your company, but if you have other business, I can certainly go by myself."

"I can't think of anything I'd rather do. Maybe we could finish our business while we walk and later enjoy a pleasant dinner."

"That sounds like an excellent plan, but I have another idea. It's getting cold, so instead of walking around town, how about a ride through the countryside in a warm car. You drive." She held out the keys. "I hope you do better than I did when I first drove from Munich to Dachau. I got off to a rather shaky start."

Erich laughed. "In that case, I won't be too embarrassed when I stall."

You're right, it is cold," he said as they exited the lobby. He helped Inge into the passenger seat, walked to the driver's side, and slid behind the wheel. For the first time in months he felt happy and content, and though the initial part of the trip wasn't the smoothest, he soon got used to the clutch.

The clouds hung low and a damp autumn fog filled the air as they turned onto the highway toward Stuttgart. They'd been driving for fifteen minutes when Erich pulled the car off the road into a quiet spot overlooking the Amper River. He turned off the engine and turned to face Inge. "It's time to talk about Dachau and your article," he said. "I'm sorry I couldn't tell you about my trip to Berlin. We have to be cautious when I'm on the camp phone; any phone for that matter. Did you have a good week in Munich?"

"It was restful but unproductive. You said you'd explain everything when you get home. I'm ready to listen."

Still unsure how specific he should be, Erich began tentatively. "Inge, as a member of the Reich press corps, you've participated in the propaganda crusade to make the news look positive."

Inge nodded. "True, but—"

"Let me finish. At the beginning of the war there was a campaign in the press aimed to persuade skeptical citizens that 'protective custody' camps are necessary in order to restore public order and provide security to the Reich. But what hasn't been reported, at least to my knowledge, is that the camps are being utilized for purposes totally unrelated to the restoration and maintenance of order."

"I don't understand—"

"The tests you want to write about will be performed on prisoners interred at Dachau, and it's not likely any of guinea pigs will survive."

"But the news releases said volunteers will be used."

"Most of the participants will be Jews, but they won't have a choice in the matter."

Inge's worst fears about Rosel's were coming to fruition. "Are there many Jews being held in the camp?" she asked hesitantly.

"As far as I can tell, Jews make up the majority of the prison population. In any case, most of the prisoners wear a Star of David patch."

"My God!" she whispered, her voice shaking with emotion.

Erich was confused by Inge's response. He reached over and took her hand. "You must realize the methods we'll be using in these tests can't be made public, Inge. Honestly, I don't know why you were given permission to report on any aspect of these damn experiments, but I assure you, whatever article you submit will be carefully redacted, and since I'll be acting as the liaison between you and the office, I'll do the initial editing. I've already said too much, so I'm not doing my job very well."

"No wonder I was turned away at the camp gates," Inge reflected aloud. "But why didn't you want me to meet with Fraulein Hambro in town? Does she know what you just told me?"

"Of course she does. Erna has worked with Doctor Rascher for years. She lives here in town, but she travels wherever he goes as part of his testing team. She's unquestionably loyal to her boss and totally dedicated to his programs."

"Are you telling me she approves of the testing methods?"

"I'm not sure, but my gut says she'll enthusiastically embrace all of the doctor's projects. Had you too met, I don't think she would have given you much information."

"So that's why you didn't want me to have lunch with Erna. You thought a meeting would be futile."

"Partly, Inge, and I'm going to be blunt. The particulars of these tests are so sensitive and classified that if Erna or any civilian not bound by Article Eleven of the camp code should say too much, he or she will be eliminated." Erich watched the color drain from Inge's face. He knew he'd made his point.

Continuing to hold Erich's hand, Inge quickly processed what he'd said. Sigrid had mentioned Article Eleven when she told Herr Ott's story. She couldn't let Erich know she'd already heard of the infamous directive, because it could put her aunt in danger. "You mentioned something about Article Eleven," she said. "What's that?"

"You realize what I'm about to tell you is classified?" Inge nodded. "Article Eleven is the reason why no one outside the camps knows what's going on inside. Everyone involved in camp operations faces death if he or she reveals any particulars about what's happening behind the Jourhaus gate. That includes me, and I've told you far too much already. So you see, my life is literally in your hands."

Inge ignored Erich's effort to inject a little humor into a serious discussion. She squeezed his hand as she thought aloud. "Since these tests are new and Article Eleven seems to have been the procedure for some time, I assume there are other equally gruesome events occurring in the camps."

Erich moved closer and placed his free hand over hers. "I can't answer that question, Inge. I can only say that the article you want to write isn't worth the danger you'll face if you go through with your plans to work in the camp."

"I asked what else is occurring in the camp, and you didn't answer, so I'm asking again," Inge said.

Again Erich tried to hedge. "I'm not privy to all camp practices, and you know why. I can't discuss anything but the Luftwaffe tests. Even then I'm limited in what I can say."

Inge frowned. "Your refusal to respond is my answer, but you need to know that first and foremost, I'm a journalist. I *will* cover these tests no matter what the danger to me personally."

Erich was dismayed. "Why do you insist on writing this article after I've repeatedly told you how dangerous it could be for you?" he asked. "You know whatever you give to Herr Beck has very little chance of being printed. At best you'll be permitted to present a few statistics when the testing is complete and you'll be required to put a positive spin on whatever you learn."

"I can't give up, Erich, no matter the risk," Inge said, a hint of desperation in her voice.

Realizing he couldn't change her mind, Erich tried another approach. "If you must know what's going on in the camp, go back to Munich and I'll call you every day with a report. I'll provide test statistics and give you as much information as I can without putting you at risk."

"I can't," Inge said. "I have to stay here, and I don't mean in town."

"You realize I have the authority to prevent you from entering the camp gates."

Inge let go of Erich's hand and glared. "You wouldn't," she said angrily. "I'm going to Dachau. If you won't help me, I'll find another way."

"Damn it, Inge, you're being ridiculous," Erich said, his tone revealing the frustration he was feeling.

Realizing she'd overreacted, Inge tried to calm down. It was apparent that Erich didn't wholeheartedly support the tests, but there was no way she could trust him with her secret. "You have to understand," she pleaded. "I want to write an important story for a change. I'm tired of reporting on inane topics like the Hitler Youth and a Munich Art Exhibition."

From Erich's expression, she doubted what she said sounded believable. "A week ago I asked you to trust me and go to Munich, and you did," he said. "Can't you trust me now?"

Without thinking, Inge lashed out. "Trust you, a Tokenkopfuerhande SS Officer?" She shook her head. "That's like trusting a Gestapo agent. I know about your code: duty and loyalty and honor above all. I have no reason to believe my problems would take precedence over your fanaticism."

Erich was shocked at the intensity of Inge's outburst. The word "problems" echoed in his ears. "I'm not asking you to trust an SS officer, Inge," he said calmly. "I'm asking you to believe in me, Erich Riedl. I'm able to separate the man from the uniform. Can you find a way to do that?"

Inge didn't answer. Instead she looked at him with desperate and pleading eyes as tears rolled down her cheeks. He moved closer and put his arm around her shoulder. "I realize it's too soon in our relationship to expect you'll trust me, Inge," he said. "I only hope you'll realize a man isn't always what he appears to be on the outside, or what his uniform says he is. But I think we've exhausted this topic for now. I know I have. How about a pleasant meal with no more discussion of Dachau, at least for now?"

Inge knew it wasn't the time to press. "I'd like that," she said quietly. Erich started the car, turned around, and headed back to town.

# CHAPTER 16

Though the atmosphere wasn't exactly cheerful, the dinner was enjoyable, Inge and Erich's inability to trust one another kept them from sharing what they were so eager to reveal, so for the most part, the discussion was little more than a continuation of the conversation they'd begun at the Hofbrauhaus the night before Erich left for Dachau.

For Inge, caution was key as she struggled to determine what would happen if she decided to share her secret with the SS man. Would he help her find Rosel, or were his beliefs so deep-rooted that he'd have no choice but to betray her? For Erich, his inability to penetrate the wall Inge had created was frustrating. What reassurances could he give her? How could he make her see she could trust him?

When they could linger no longer, Erich suggested they take a walk. "It looks like we might have at least one day without rain or snow," he said as they left the warmth of the lobby. "The stars are beautiful, but it's freezing."

"What about tomorrow," he asked. "I have a free day."

"I'm going to see my aunt. Would you like to join me?"

"Absolutely," Erich said without hesitation. "And maybe later in the afternoon we could meet Joachim at the Hofbrauhaus for a beer."

They soon discovered it was too cold for a lengthy stroll, so they turned back toward the hotel. "Would you like to come upstairs?" Erich asked. When he saw Inge frown, he added: "Just to continue our talk, nothing more."

"I should get back to my apartment before Frau Heiden begins to worry," Inge said. Erich put his arm around her and she rested her head on his chest. "I wish I could stay this way forever," she whispered. "It's so nice to forget my problems, if only for a minute."

"I'd like for you to stop worrying altogether," Erich said. She looked up and he lowered his mouth to hers. She responded, hesitantly at first, and then eagerly as she wrapped her arms around his neck.

A passing car interrupted the moment. Erich reluctantly loosened his grip, took Inge's hand, and walked her to her car. She slid behind the wheel and rolled down the window. "What time tomorrow?" she asked.

"Whenever you like."

"I'll pick you up at nine o'clock."

"I'll be ready, and in the meantime, I think I'll miss you."

Inge laughed. "I think I'll miss you too." She lowered her eyes and realized she really would.

As Erich took the elevator to the third floor, he thought about what Inge had said. The word "problems" was telling. *Could her "problems" be why she's so determined to write about the experiments? But what could be so troubling that she'd risk her life for the story?*

The room was a far cry from the luxury of the Aldon, but a great improvement over the barracks at Dachau. He plopped down on the bed and continued to try and make sense of their conversation. He was positive Inge was hiding something. He remembered her reaction at the Hofbrauhaus when he'd first told her about his upcoming transfer. Tonight confirmed his initial suspicions. Something about the camp was both tormenting and motivating her. Her response when he asked her not to write about the experiments had been too adamant for a person who was just interested in writing a good story. *But why*, he asked himself again.

---

When the sun's rays burst through Inge's window, she was already dressed. She went downstairs, called her aunt to let her know that Erich would be coming to visit, wrote a note to Frau Heiden, and left the apartment with plenty of time to get to the Wagner by nine. When he pulled up to the hotel door, Erich was waiting out front. He slid into the passenger seat, leaned over, and kissed her on the cheek. "I called Aunt Sigrid this morning," she said. "She's looking forward to our visit."

"That's encouraging. The lady must like me if she's taking me home to meet the family."

"You never know my ulterior motive," Inge teased. *No, you really don't,* she thought, *and I'm sure you'd be shocked if you did.* "Did you speak with Joachim?"

"I called this morning. He'll be at the Hofbrauhaus at five o'clock. I can't wait to see his face when I walk in with you."

"You think he'll be surprised?"

"Stunned, mystified, and, I hope, tortured. He said I wouldn't have a chance with you because you rejected him. For once he was wrong, and I can't wait to rub it in."

"You're awful. You actually enjoy torturing your friend."

Erich laughed. "When you get to know Joachim, you'll understand."

The drive to Munich passed quickly. Erich picked up where he'd left off at dinner, entertaining Inge with more anecdotes of his college days and experiences with Joachim during the early days in the SS. As they talked, Inge wondered how the friendship between the two men had become so strong and meaningful, but she didn't have time to ask. She pulled up in front of Sigrid's and turned off the engine. Hands on the steering wheel, she made no move to get out. "Nervous?" Erich asked when he heard her take a deep breath.

"I suppose I am. This is a first for me. Before now, I've never brought a man home to meet my aunt."

"Then this is a new experience for both of us. I've never been taken home by a lady."

"I guess there's no time like the present." Inge opened the door. "Shall we go?"

As they walked up the path, Sigrid came out to greet them. She hugged her niece as if she'd been gone for months rather than hours. "Inge," she said. "I was both surprised and pleased to hear from you. This must be the young man you've been talking about. I'm Inge's Aunt Sigrid." Though Sigrid smiled, Inge noticed an unfamiliar reserve on her aunt's face and in her voice.

"I'm Erich Riedl. Inge has told me a lot about you too."

"All good things, I'm sure," Sigrid said.

"Your niece said you could do no wrong."

"Of course she was right." Sigrid smiled, but half-heartedly. "Come into the house," she said. "There's no need to stand in the cold when there's a warm fire and hot tea inside."

Inge took her aunt's hand and they went inside. "I thought we drank the last of the tea. Have you been holding out on me?"

"I bought more at Herr Ott's this morning." With the reference to Ott, Inge's spirits dampened, but she quickly recovered. *This is our enjoyable day and I will not let Dachau ruin it,* she thought, as she forced the Otts and the camp from her mind.

"Tea sounds great," Erich said. "I'm sick of that barley-filled excuse for coffee they're serving nowadays."

The fire did its job, and when Sigrid served the warm bread and tea, Inge was no longer chilled. After thirty-minutes of tea and conversation about insignificant subjects, the women went to wash the dishes, leaving Erich alone in the parlor. Glad for the opportunity to stretch his legs, he got up and wandered around the room, stopping to look at the pictures scattered about. When he got to the mantle, his eyes rested on a group of photographs of Inge, her aunt, and another young woman, a brunette, who bore no resemblance to the other two. *Obviously she's someone important enough to have her picture included among the family treasures,* he reflected as he picked up what looked like a recently taken photo. When Inge returned, he held the picture out for her to see. "Who's this with you and your aunt?" he asked.

"Just a family friend," Inge said a little too hastily.

Erich put the photograph back up on the mantle and picked up another. "She must be a good friend. She's included in quite a few pictures."

"I said she's a friend, nothing more." Inge crossed the room, took the frame from Erich and put it back on the mantle.

"I was admiring your photographs," Erich said when, minutes later, Sigrid returned with a fresh pot of tea. "Who's the woman standing with you and Inge?"

Erich saw the silent exchange between Inge and her aunt. "She's a neighbor's daughter," Sigrid said. "She and Inge were good friends until the family moved away."

"Where is she now?" Erich asked.

"We lost track of her," Sigrid said. Without elaborating, she put the tray on the table, sat down, and picked up the teapot. "Will you have more tea, Erich? Or if you prefer, I have some very old brandy."

"Tea please," Erich said. He walked over and sat beside Sigrid on the couch as she poured. He figured it wasn't a good time to push for more information about the obviously significant woman Sigrid and Inge quickly dismissed as being insignificant.

Clearly Inge didn't want to talk about her, and he didn't want to alienate Sigrid when they'd just met, so during the rest of the pleasant afternoon no one mentioned the photographs again. As Erich listened to Sigrid talk about Inge's childhood, he sensed she was leaving something out of her story. He wondered if it might have to do with the mysterious woman.

When it was time to leave, Erich excused himself to freshen up. "I like your young man," Sigrid said to Inge when she heard the bathroom door close. "And frankly, I'm surprised I do."

"He's not my young man, Aunt Sigrid. He's merely a means to an end."

"Well whatever you choose to call him, I gather he doesn't know about Rosel or our concern that she's being detained at Dachau?"

"Not yet. I'm trying to trust him, but in the back of my mind is your comment that all SS officers are fanatical in their support for the Fuhrer and party principles."

"That's what I said, but in Erich's case, I *may* have been wrong. It's too soon for me to make a definitive judgment, but it's obvious how he feels about you."

"And how does he feel, Aunt Sigrid?"

"The man's in love with you, Inge. The question is how do you feel about him?"

"I guess the best word to describe my feelings is 'conflicted.' Erich *is* different from other SS officers I've met. I care about him, but I can't disclose our secret, at least not now. There's too much at stake."

"In view of the times, that would still be my advice." Sigrid took Inge's hand. "But then you're the only one who can decide what to do. I believe in time you'll figure it out."

"I hope so, but whatever my decision, it helps to know you're not adamantly declaring he can't be trusted."

Erich returned to the parlor, bringing the conversation to an end. "I hate for the afternoon to end," he said. "But it's time to go, Inge."

"Give me a minute." Inge stood up and walked toward the parlor door. "I need to get a heavier coat. I can't believe how cold it is so early in the season."

When she left the room, Sigrid patted the seat beside her on the couch. "Come sit with me for a minute," she said to Erich.

"Of course." Erich crossed the room and sat down. "What's on your mind?"

"There's not much time before Inge returns, so I'll get right to the point. You obviously care about my niece. I'm asking you to be patient with her. She's struggling."

"I know that, Sigrid. I'd have to be blind not to realize something's bothering both you and Inge. Whatever it is, I know it's important. If Inge won't tell me what it is, will you?"

Sigrid nodded no. "It's Inge's choice whether or not to explain, not mine. Give her time. I think she'll eventually share what's on her mind."

Before Erich could respond, Inge returned, coat in hand. "I'm ready," she said cheerfully.

Sigrid walked them to the door. "You'll come back soon," she said.

"The first chance we get," said Inge.

"We'll definitely see you soon," Erich said.

As she slid into the passenger seat, Inge watched her aunt go back inside and close the door. *At least Sigrid likes him,* she thought as Erich walked to the driver side of the car. *That's encouraging.*

There was no time for the car to heat up during the short drive to the Hofbrauhaus. Despite her heavy coat, Inge was shivering when they pushed through the Schwemme doors. *Nothing changes,* Erich thought when he saw Joachim sitting with two women in the Stammtisch. He guided Inge through the raucous crowd. When they neared the table, Joachim looked up to see who was standing beside him. Erich laughed. "That surprised look on your face makes my day," he said.

"You sly dog!" Joachim stood and slapped Erich on the back. "Good evening, Fraulein Friedrich," he said.

"Please call me Inge. We got off to a bad start the first few times we met. Since then I've heard so much about you from Erich. I feel we're already friends."

"Inge it is, and call me Joachim, though if you've been listening to this big hulk, you've probably come up with a few less-than-pleasant names."

Inge laughed. "Not at all. Erich's stories have made me want to know you better. I've never met a perfect person before."

"Do you think we might take time out from this love fest and have a beer?" Erich said.

Joachim winked at Inge. "Coming right up." He waved his hand and Gretchen, who was obviously watching her quarry's every move, came right over. "She can't resist my charms," Joachim joked as he put his arm around the barmaid's waist. As Gretchen blushed and grinned, Erich unwittingly contrasted the healthy, smiling girl with the Jewish woman who served the officers in the dining hall at Dachau. Unlike Gretchen, there was no smile on the lips that hid that woman's jagged broken teeth.

"What's the matter?" Inge said when she saw Erich grimace.

"Something on your mind, old buddy?" Joachim asked.

"Nothing worth discussing in such great company."

"So you admit you're in the presence of the wittiest gentleman and the loveliest ladies in all of Munich," Joachim quipped. He turned to Gretchen. "We'll take three of those dark beers off your hands, my love, and how about an order of weisswurste."

Gretchen put three steins on the table, and leaned toward Joachim, her ample breasts tauntingly close to his face. "I'll be right back with the weisswurste," she murmured.

"She's madly in love with me." Joachim chuckled. "But then they all are. You find me irresistible, don't you fair lady?"

"Absolutely," Inge joked.

"This fair lady, as you call her, is off limits," Erich said, his eyes shining.

Feigning dejection, Joachim turned to Inge, "Is he right, fair lady?"

"I'm afraid so, but if Erich ever decides to get rid of me, you'll be the first person I call."

Joachim rolled his eyes. "Second best!" He pointed to Erich. "And to him. I'm so offended."

"Cut the crap!" Erich said. "For you one more woman, even if she is the most beautiful woman in Germany, would be one too many. You can't keep track of all the girls you're juggling at the moment." On cue, Gretchen came back with the sausage. "And here comes one of them now."

Gretchen placed a serving platter in the middle of the table and gave Inge, Erich, and Joachim individual plates. "Thank you, love." Joachim winked. "I'll see you later."

"You certainly will," Gretchen said, promise in her voice.

Erich shook his head. "So you're still giving the poor girl a tumble. Apparently she hasn't realized she doesn't stand a chance in hell with you."

"I would hardly call it a tumble, and who knows, I could be serious about her. She's a sensitive, charming lady."

"Are you two ever serious?" Inge said.

"Only when we have to be," said Erich.

"Only when *he* has to be," Joachim said. "I'm not serious unless it's absolutely necessary."

The hours that followed benefitted both Erich and Inge. For him it was a welcome chance to relax and forget what he would face the following day. For her, it was an opportunity to learn more about the man in a relaxed and informal setting. She liked his light side and approved of his friend. Though she didn't truly understand the deep bond the two men shared, throughout the evening she marveled at their closeness.

At about eight o'clock Erich stood up. He slapped Joachim on the shoulder. "I think you've been on stage enough for one evening," he said. "Inge's ears are tired from all the noise you've made."

"But I've only begun," Joachim protested. "I promised to tell Inge about the day—"

"Another time," said Erich. "We're leaving. You'll have to find a new audience for your stories." He looked around the room. "I'm sure it won't be too difficult."

"Probably not, but this audience is so lovely." Joachim took Inge's hand. "Seriously, though—"

"Serious isn't a word in your vocabulary, remember?" Inge joked.

"It is now."

Still holding Inge's hand, Joachim turned to Erich. "Something's bothering you, my friend. I'm not sure what it is, but I know you well enough to know that all's not right. If you need help or a sympathetic ear, you know where to reach me."

"I might take you up on both offers in the near future," Erich said. "In the meantime, stay in touch."

"You know I will." He smiled at Inge. "And take care of this fair lady, my friend. She's not the ice queen I once thought she was."

Erich clutched his chest and sat back down. "I'm shocked," he groaned. "After all these years we finally agree on something."

"I appreciate the flattery, gentlemen," Inge said, smiling.

"Not flattery, just the truth." Joachim released Inge's hand. He put one arm around her and the other around Erich and walked them to the door. "Take care of each other," he said.

Erich raised an eyebrow. "Such seriousness. You'll have me crying in a moment. We're leaving before I make a fool of myself."

The warmth of the room they just left and the high from beers they consumed helped keep Inge and Erich warm while they waited for the car's heater to do its job. During the drive to Dachau, both were lost in personal recollections of the pleasant day they'd shared. Erich parked the car in front of the hotel and turned off the engine. "What a great day," he said.

"It was, and I hate for it to end."

"It doesn't have to." Erich took Inge's hand. "Will you stay with me?" He waited, and when Inge didn't immediately respond, he said: "Your hesitation is my answer. I want you to be sure. We'll have other nights."

"Please don't misunderstand," Inge said. "I have so much on my mind. When I stay with you, I don't want to be thinking of anything but us."

Erich grinned. "I like the word 'when.' I have to be at the office tomorrow morning at nine. Would you join me for breakfast and then drive me to camp?"

"I'd like that," Inge said, "but instead of eating in the dining room, let's order room service. I want to tell you something, and I'd rather our discussion take place where no one can overhear."

"What time?

"If you have to be at work at nine, I'll come at seven. Is that too early?"

"Seven's perfect."

Erich felt a rush. Was Inge finally going to trust him with her secret? He leaned over and kissed her tenderly on the mouth. "I don't know if I can wait so long to see you again," he whispered.

"I'm sure you'll be fine, though I admit, I don't like the thought of being away from you either."

"I know a way to solve our problem."

"I'll see you in the morning, Hauptsturmfuhrer," Inge kissed him again and slid over to the driver's seat. "At seven sharp."

# CHAPTER 17

When Inge arrived at the Wagner, Erich was waiting in the lobby. He rose to greet her, kissed her on the cheek, and led her toward the elevator. Appreciating her nervousness, he said little during the ride to the fifth floor or during the short walk down the hall to the room. He unlocked the door and pointed to the sofa by the window. "Shall we sit?" he said.

Inge made herself comfortable while Erich poured coffee from the pot he'd ordered before he went downstairs. He handed Inge a cup, took a few sips, put his cup down on the table, and took her hand. "I see no reason to make small talk," he said. "I want to know why you're so damn determined to report on the Luftwaffe tests."

The moment Inge had agonized about for so long was at hand, but the resolve she'd felt as she drove to the hotel evaporated as the moment of truth approached. Despite feeling she should trust the man sitting beside her, she couldn't say the words that could put her, Rosel, and, after yesterday, Sigrid at risk. She wanted absolute proof before revealing the reasons she needed to work at Dachau. She was sure Erich cared for her, but was that enough? She took another sip of coffee and began, tentatively at first. "I came here ready to explain," she said. "But before I do, I need to ask you a question."

"Ask me anything," Erich said. "I've said before and I'm saying again. Please trust me, Inge."

"I suppose I have no choice," Inge said, her tone a blend of nervousness and frustration. "But first I need to know why you're a part of the Dachau experiments. Did you volunteer for the assignment?"

*Honesty begets honesty*, Erich thought. "No," he said. "Though, in all honesty, when Muller first mentioned my new assignment I was excited. For months I'd been frustrated with my mind-numbing supply job as, day after day, I struggled to solve nearly insoluble problems. Then all of a sudden I was given a chance to do something meaningful and, I figured, less tedious."

"You had no doubts about what you were being asked to do?"

"Yes and no. It's hard to explain. While I was energized, I was also apprehensive."

"Had you heard anything about the camp prior to your meeting with Mueller?"

"Not directly. Dachau isn't often-discussed among the SS officers, which, as I think back, should have been my first clue that these tests weren't for me, but you asked if I knew about the camp. Several months before, I delivered papers to the Schulzstaffel next door. Though I didn't know what was occurring in the detention camp, I returned to Munich feeling unsettled. That said, as Mueller talked about the tests, I put my qualms aside and decided to think of my assignment as a chance to do something meaningful for our fighting men."

"And you still feel that way?"

*I've said too much to turn back now,* Erich thought. He took another swallow of coffee. "Quite the opposite," he said. "The moment I saw the Jourhaus gate with its ironic message, 'Arbeit Macht Frei,' I was concerned. Within five minutes my concern changed to disgust. Neither the years of intense indoctrination nor my SS training prepared me for what I witnessed in Roll Call Square."

"I don't understand," Inge said. "What could be so distressing that you'd have an abrupt change of heart?"

"I can't say, at least not specifically."

"Because of Article Eleven?"

"Yes, and to ensure your safety as well. After Rascher described the testing methods, I knew too much. I had to take part in the tests or, as Rascher put it, be eliminated."

"What are you saying?"

"That I won't be allowed to walk around knowing what I already know, and that's not much."

"You'd be killed?"

"Without a doubt."

"So you're working because you must. You don't actually approve of the experiments?"

"It's not that simple, Inge. I'd like to do my part to save our downed pilots—"

"But—"

"It's becoming increasingly difficult for me to support the Fuhrer and our cause as I witness the atrocities being committed at Dachau, and, I'm sure, throughout Germany. I'm beginning to think we'd be better off if Germany lost the war. What's going on is inhumane, and if Hitler and his henchmen are victorious, it won't stop. For me these are new and disconcerting thoughts. For years I wholeheartedly embraced the party's Jewish policy. Now I'm finding I can't accept that innocent people, regardless of their religion and despite the credible reason for the experiments, will be murdered to try to save a few of our pilots."

"But they're Jews," Inge probed. "Doesn't that make a difference?"

"Maybe a few years ago it would have. During my years in the Hitler Youth and throughout my SS training, whether to fit in, or because I couldn't think for myself, I paid little attention when the beleaguered Berlin Jews were tormented and persecuted. I ignored the yellow stars they were forced to wear, the filthy words scribbled on their property, and the ceaseless harassment they had to endure. Though I didn't actively participate, I admit I laughed as I watched members of the Hitler Youth, and later, SS officers engage in Jew baiting." Erich paused.

"What?" Inge said. "You were going to add a 'but.'"

Erich shook his head. "I was. There was one instance with a Jew that affected me personally and changed my life."

"Will you tell me about it?"

*I've gone this far,* Erich thought, *Why stop now?* "Alright," he said. "But what I'm going to say not only involves me, it also puts Joachim in jeopardy should you decide to go to the authorities." He didn't wait for Inge to respond. Instead, he spent the next few minutes telling her how Joachim rescued the Jewish girl who accidently bumped into their drunken companion, though he fell short of telling her how he saved Joachim's career and likely his life. He only said that Joachim was lucky Ernst hadn't pressed charges.

"Have you had any other experiences with Jews since the incident with Joachim?" Inge asked.

"Not personally, at least until now, when I'm forced to participate in a project that involves more than harassment. Every day it becomes more difficult to watch the abuse inflicted on the tortured, beleaguered men at Dachau."

"It's that bad?"

"Worse, Inge, but that's really all I can say, and it may be imprudent of me to be sharing this information with you since you haven't said how you feel. In the BDM you were subjected to intense indoctrination, and your dedication to the Fuhrer and the party must be indisputable, or you wouldn't be working for the *Völkischer Beobachter* or be permitted to report on a subject as sensitive as the Dachau experiments. Since I've opened up, I expect as much from you. I know something's driving you to report on these tests, and I don't think it's merely your journalistic nose for the news or the excitement you must feel because you're not being asked to write yet another inane article. I need to know why you're so damned determined to risk your life to report this story."

Inge swallowed hard. She had no choice but to lay it all out, so she began. "Yesterday morning you picked up a picture from my aunt's mantle. You wanted to know about the girl in the photo with Aunt Sigrid and me."

"I admit it seemed unusual that such a casual friend, as you called her, had pictures displayed so prominently around the room, and you and your aunt's disparate responses made me even more suspicious."

"Rosel isn't the casual acquaintance Aunt Sigrid and I made her out to be."

"Then you're close friends?"

"More than that. She's like a sister and a best friend rolled into one, and I'd do anything for her."

"Then why pass her off as the daughter of a neighbor who moved away? Obviously you've lost track of her, but not the way Sigrid suggested. Where is she?"

"I don't know," Inge said uneasily. "But I believe she's incarcerated at Dachau."

"You're kidding," Erich said. "Why would she be at Dachau? She doesn't appear to be a criminal or asocial type."

Inge took a deep breath and choked out the dreaded words. "Rosel's a Mischling, Erich. Her father was Christian, but her mother was a Jew. Her real name is Rosel Dollman. That's why we think she's at Dachau."

"Oh my God!" Erich exclaimed. In an instant he realized why Inge felt she had to cover the Luftwaffe experiences.

Inge continued. "After Rosel's parents were killed, Aunt Sigrid took her into our home and raised her as my sister. Johann, Rosel's father, and my aunt were childhood friends. I had no idea her mother was Jewish until after she was taken from us."

"*Taken* from you?"

"We think so. She simply disappeared."

"When was that?"

"A little over three months ago. She went out one morning and never returned. We have no idea where she is, but we know she'd never go anywhere for any length of time without telling us where she'd be. Furthermore she was scheduled to give a violin concert at the conservatory, so why would she leave Munich? The only rational explanation is the SS or the Gestapo discovered she was half Jewish and took her away."

"What have you and Sigrid done to find her?"

"At first I requested a leave of absence, but when we hit a dead end, I asked for and was given a transfer to the Munich office."

"So that's why you left Berlin. I wondered why a young, talented, obviously-ambitious reporter would want to leave such a prestigious position."

"And now you know."

"When you moved back to Munich, what did you do?"

"We questioned our neighbors."

"And?"

"No one saw anything suspicious, or, if they did, they wouldn't share what they knew. We think Rosel was taken while she shopped in town. Since Dachau's the nearest SS facility, we assume that's where she's being held. She's not important enough to be incarcerated at Gestapo Headquarters."

Erich held Inge's hand. "What I'm about to say may help, but it may raise even more questions," he said.

"Tell me."

"I haven't seen many women at Dachau, so if Rosel was initially transported to the camp, I doubt she's still there. The question then becomes, 'where is she and why hasn't the Gestapo come for you and Sigrid'?"

"We've wondered the same thing," Inge said. "We think it may be due to Berlin's failure to resolve the Mischlinge question; that and my position at the paper. I may be sounding overly optimistic, but I figure if we haven't been arrested yet, we're probably safe for the moment. However, if Berlin chooses to deal with the Mischlinge as they do the full-blooded Jews, we may be in jeopardy."

"Then we'll have to figure this out before Berlin acts."

"But where do we begin?" Inge's voice echoed her frustration "I've exhausted every avenue."

"If you're so determined to go forward with your search, let me help," Erich said. "At the moment I'm not sure how to proceed. Even if you get past the camp gates, you'll never find out what happened to Rosel, and you may be putting yourself in harm's way if you ask too many questions. When you come to camp, you'll be driven from the Jourhaus gate to the office and back again. That's it. Give me a few days to make discreet inquiries. Maybe I can find out where the Jewish women are taken without making anyone suspicious."

"Then you're willing to help me?"

"Of course I am. Even if I wholeheartedly approved of what's happening at Dachau, I would still try to help you find Rosel. I love you, and if you have a problem, so do I, regardless of the party, the SS, or whatever I may have been taught to believe."

"You love me?" Inge whispered. "I thought you cared, but—"

Erich took Inge's face in his hands and kissed her softly. "I think I began to love you when you first came into the Hofbrauhaus and rejected me so decisively."

Inge laughed. "I didn't know I loved you until I was jealous when I heard you were in town with Fraulein Hambro."

"Fraulein Hambro?" Erich chuckled. "You certainly have nothing to worry about in her regard, but that's a discussion for another time. Let's talk about our immediate problem. Being the liaison between you and the newspaper will make it easy for us to meet without being suspect, but you *must* let me do the investigating. The first experiments will begin in a few hours. If Rascher holds to his original plan, I'll complete my work during the day, so I'll be able to update you in the evening; that is if I can find a way to get to town after dinner."

"You can't leave with Fraulein Hambro at 4:30?"

"If I'm going to figure out what happened to Rosel, I'll have to spend time in the dining hall."

"It sounds like you already have a plan."

"A preliminary and hastily thought-out one at best. I'll eat with some of the officers who've been stationed at the camp for a while. In the relaxed atmosphere, I might be able to find out where the Mischlinge are taken. I'll try to cultivate Heinrich Wolfers, Weiss's general flunky. For some reason, he isn't popular with the other officers, so he'll probably be thrilled when I join him for dinner."

"Does he have access to the commandant's files?"

"I hope so. My problem is to find a way to make him search for information about Rosel without making him wonder why I'm asking."

"Any idea how you'll do that?"

"What I'm going to say won't be easy to hear."

"I didn't expect it would be."

"I just wanted to warn you."

"Erich—"

"Alright. Since the SS officers are prohibited from going to Munich, some of the Jewish women are kept in the camp for, wont of a better word, 'entertainment.' I plan to ask Heinrich about a Jewish whore who gave me some pleasurable moments and see if he'll find out if she's one of the women being kept at the camp. He'll assume I'm looking for a diversion."

Inge winced as, little by little, she learned about the plight of the Jews at Dachau. Her fears for Rosel were exacerbated with every new morsel of information. Despite her concerns, she was encouraged. Her own strategy for finding Rosel had been vague. Her first challenge had been to get inside the camp, and she'd failed in that regard. Now she had an ally on the inside who might be able to help.

"Will you give me a week?" Erich said.

"If you'll keep me informed, whether the news is good or bad."

Erich smiled. "I'll have. I can't stand to be away from you, and I doubt you'll be too cooperative with me if I don't cooperate with you." He quickly became serious. "I'll find a way to reach you, Inge, but again, don't say anything over the phone, especially if I'm calling from the office. Your interest in me and the tests we're conducting has to seem purely professional."

"You don't have to tell me twice. I'll remember."

"Good. So now that we've discussed the serious matters, shall we begin our new phase of full cooperation?"

"You're impossible, you know."

"I'd love to show you how impossible I can be, but unfortunately, I have to be at the office by nine. Forty-five minutes wouldn't do for the first time we cooperate. On the way to camp, we'll talk about what you can do while I'm investigating at Dachau."

# CHAPTER 18

While Erich settled the account at the front desk, Inge moved the car to the front of the hotel. "It's freezing out here," he said as he settled into the passenger seat. "I don't think the car will warm up before we get to camp."

Inge wasted no time engaging in small talk. "What do you want me to do next week?" she said.

"I want you to go to Munich and—"

"Surely you don't expect me to stay with Aunt Sigrid and sit idly by while—"

"Would you let me finish? No, I want you to stay at Frau Heiden's, and I'm not saying that to appease you. Once the experiments are underway, you can't spend too much time in Munich without arousing Beck's suspicions. You have to pursue the assignment vigorously or your boss will begin to wonder why you asked to write the article in the first place. He could ask questions you can't or don't want to answer."

"Then why the trip to Munich?"

"Because I want you to talk to Joachim, but not at head-quarters. I have no idea what kind of spying devices are being used in the offices, though I'm sure all calls are monitored. Go to Joachim's office and pretend you're one of his beautiful women. Ask him to join you for lunch. You won't have to explain; he'll realize you have something important to say. Once you're out of the building, you can speak freely."

"What do you want me to tell him?"

"Everything you told me."

"You can't be serious."

"I assure you, I am. I trust Joachim with my life. I'd never ask you to talk with him if I didn't also trust him with yours. The Hofbrauhaus is Joachim's home-away-from home. He knows everyone who walks through the doors, so he may be able to help us find out what we need to know. We can't do this alone. To have even a chance of succeeding, we'll need an ally. Fortunately, no one in Munich takes Joachim seriously, so he's the perfect person to help."

Erich waited for Inge to digest what he'd said. He was about to reiterate his request when she spoke: "I'm not sure I agree with what you're asking me to do," she said. "But it seems you're in charge, and if you're convinced telling Joachim is the right—"

"I am, Inge. Tell him to ask around and find out about where the Mischlinge are incarcerated. Have him join us for dinner at the Wagner on Tuesday, November 3rd at seven o'clock."

"What if he asks me what you're doing?"

"Tell him everything he wants to know."

"Will I hear from you tonight so I can tell you what he said?"

"I can't promise, but I'll try to find a way to call. And one more time, though I'm sure you're tired of hearing me say it, absolutely no talk of Rosel, the tests, or for that matter, anything else of importance over the telephone. You'll have to find a creative way to tell me about your meeting."

*There's the paranoia again,* Inge thought, sad that her country had come to this point. "Article Eleven again?" she said.

Erich nodded. "Always Article Eleven."

When they arrived at the Jourhaus, Erich got out of the car and walked over to Inge's window. "I appreciate the ride, Fraulein," he said. "I'll contact you when there's something to report." With his back turned so the guard couldn't see him, he winked.

"I'll let the Propaganda Ministry and Herr Beck know we've met and the tests are underway," Inge said. She put the car in gear and drove away as Erich was presenting his papers to the guard.

The guard opened the gates. Erich hurried into the Jourhaus, raced up the stairs, deposited his suitcase on the floor, and looked at his watch. There wasn't enough time to unpack and get to the office on time, so he combed his hair, straightened his uniform, and left for work. For some unknown reason, the morning roll call was still in progress, so he skirted the perimeter and turned onto the main camp road toward Block Five. At exactly eight o'clock he entered the office. "Good morning, Hauptsturmfuhrer," Erna said, this time without the usual "Heil Hitler" he'd come to expect. "We've been expecting you."

Rascher looked up from the papers he was perusing. "Right on time, Hauptsturmfuhrer," he said. "We'll begin the first high-flight test in fifteen minutes. Staying on schedule is essential during all facets of the tests."

The warning words weren't lost on Erich as he hung his coat.

"The first prisoners are being brought in now," the doctor said. "I initially said you wouldn't be part of the actual tests, but I've revised your orders. The original plan was to conduct the tests at night and write our reports during the day. However, we'll conduct this first series of experiments over the next few mornings. I want you to watch what occurs in the Skyride Machine."

"The Skyride Machine?"

"In front of other SS officers and the prisoners, that's how we'll refer to the high-flight chamber. The fewer people who know the details of the experiments, the better off we'll be. The Jews have been docile until now, but we don't take chances. Berlin is watching, and we can't risk even the slightest uprising."

Erich sensed that Rascher expected a response. "I agree," he said a little too enthusiastically.

"For these first tests there will be three observers; you, Fraulein Hambro, and, of course, myself. When you're no longer needed, one of the male nurses will join us, if he's not otherwise involved with the tests being conducted in the infirmary."

Rascher handed Erma and Erich stopwatches and clipboards containing notepaper. "We'll work separately this time," he said. "Your job will be to record the reactions of the subjects while they're in the chamber. The pressure in the Skyride Machine simulates a cockpit at the altitude of 8,961 meters. Any questions before we begin?"

Erich was determined to present a resolute front to hide the profound horror he was feeling for the prisoners, and, much as he hated to admit it, for himself. "None, Sir," he said. "I'm ready."

"Then let's proceed." Rascher looked at his watch. "It's Monday, November 1, 1942, at 9:30 a.m. Please record the time and date on your pads."

From the glint in the doctor's eye, it was apparent that he was eager to begin. As they entered the observation room, he continued to explain the process. "We will initially observe one prisoner at a time. When we become adept at our research techniques, we should be able to put three men in the chamber at once. Each of us will concentrate on a different subject, thereby saving valuable time."

Rascher led Erna and Erich through the door to the right of the office. Almost immediately, a scrawny male wearing a prisoner's striped uniform emblazoned with a yellow Star of David was brought into the chamber. Erich gazed at the man's somber, apathetic face. Strangely, there wasn't a hint of the terror or apprehension he had expected to see. Instead he saw despair and hopelessness. As the man was placed in a single chair in the center of the chamber, Erich's heart raced, and he began to sweat profusely. He studied the Jew's face. *My God. He no longer cares whether he lives or dies,* he thought sadly. *He's resigned to his fate.*

Rascher began to present a short biography. When he saw that Erich wasn't writing, he grabbed his arm. "You're not taking notes," Hauptsturmfuhrer," he said crossly.

"I apologize, Herr Doctor."

"See that it doesn't happen again. I repeat. The subject is thirty-seven years old. He was selected because he's in good general condition."

*Good condition for a walking skeleton*, Erich pondered as he kept taking notes.

The living cadaver sat staring blankly at the observers, as the sturman locked the door behind him. "We're ready to begin," Rascher said. "The test should last about thirty-minutes." He looked at Erich. "It's imperative that you accurately record any changes in the prisoner's behavior, Hauptsturmfuhrer. When the test is over, we will compare notes to see if we agree on what occurred."

As the scrutiny began, Erich sat motionless, his pen poised over his pad. He was thankful he hadn't eaten much breakfast. He doubted he'd be able to keep the food down.

For the first four minutes there was no change in the bewildered Jew, who dropped his head to his chest rather than look at the observers. Erich fervently hoped that nothing would happen, but realistically he knew he had no reason to be optimistic.

At the five-minute mark, the Jew began to perspire and roll his head. On his pad, Erich noted the prisoner's response. In five minutes and thirty seconds, the prisoner began to suffer spasms. His eyes were wide with a mixture of fear and disbelief as he tore violently at his head and face. Ten seconds later he stood and repeatedly beat the walls with his head and hands. Erich felt hopeless. He wanted to turn away, but he knew he had no choice but to maintain a calm facade.

"The man is screaming to relieve the pressure on his eardrums," the doctor explained. Erich recalled the interviews with the Berlin pilots who had complained of extreme pressure in their ears. They found flying at a lower altitude helped relieve the pain. There was nothing this man could do to alleviate his suffering.

"Now things are happening," the doctor said, grinning. "Be sure to watch carefully."

Erich wondered how the doctor conducting this cursed test could remain calm, even happy, while he watched another human being, Jew or not, suffer so greatly. *What a paradox*, he thought with disgust. *A doctor's job is to alleviate pain, not inflict it, yet Rascher seems to be relishing the prisoner's agony.*

Between six and ten minutes, a look of dread crossed the prisoner's tortured face. His respiration increased and he began to lose consciousness. The wretched man in the chamber of death was no longer suffering.

Between eleven and thirteen-minutes, Erich noted the prisoner's respiration dropped to three inhalations per minute. At fourteen-minutes, Rascher pronounced the first test case dead and announced the results of the autopsy would be available in several hours. He looked at his watch as the sturman removed the dead man from the chamber. "That took less time than I thought it would," he said. "Shall we go into the office and compare our data?"

Erich tried to remain erect as he felt his knees buckle. He recollected the sick Jew during the roll call the week before. He too had struggled to stand tall so as not to call attention to himself and suffer the consequences of being weak.

Erna noticed Erich's distress and whispered so the doctor could not hear; "Is this your first experience of this kind?"

"Yes," Erich said softly.

"It does get easier," she whispered, but Erich doubted he would ever be complacent while watching people suffer great pain and die.

"One hundred-ninety-nine to go." Rascher laughed. Erich felt he should offer a positive response, but, under the circumstance, he couldn't find suitable words, so he remained silent.

Rascher was pleased the three separate reports compared favorably, and he seemed eager to continue. "You'll write a letter describing our initial findings to your friend Sievers in the morning, Hauptsturmfuhrer."

"Very good, Sir," Erich said, struggling to sound enthusiastic.

"Our next volunteer should be in the chamber. Shall we go?"

The three observers reported similar data for the next victim, as they did for the following four cases of the morning. Besides the raw data, Erich recorded his observations of the men's emotions. Instead of writing in paragraph form, he numbered his findings:

1. The expression on the prisoner's face is one of torment.
2. There's a deep melancholy in the prisoner's sunken eyes.
3. His face is a picture of shock and grief.
4. His eyes are wide, almost as if he's in a demonic trance.

Contrary to Erna's assurance, it failed to get easier for Erich to watch men die. It grew more repulsive, and he struggled to keep from showing the horror he was feeling.

When the group was ready to break for lunch, Rascher announced that, since the morning results had been so consistent, further tests during the afternoon would be unnecessary. Erich was relieved until he heard the next part of the announcement. Instead of testing, they'd spend their time adding autopsy results to the already logged information. Eager to begin the inquiries that would give him an idea about where Rosel was being held, he had planned to eat in the dining room, but after the morning activities, he knew he couldn't stand the smell of food, let alone the taste. Instead he crossed Roll Call Square to the Jourhaus. His phantom roommate had put the suitcase on the bed. Exhausted from the events of the morning and eager to find a way to wipe the pictures of the suffering Jews from his mind, without unpacking, Erich put his bag back on the floor and lay down. The eyes of dying prisoners filled his thoughts, preventing sleep.

---

As she drove to Munich, Inge was conflicted. She had made the right decision trusting Erich, but she was skeptical about talking about Rosel with Joachim. She liked the jovial, carefree man who was so entertaining, *but is there a serious side to him?* She quickly answered her own question: *There has to be. There's no way Erich could be so fond of such a superficial person.*

She parked the car on Arcisstrasse near SS headquarters, turned off the engine, and sat for a few minutes contemplating her next move. *Is it possible two SS men could be trustworthy,* she wondered. *Will Joachim astonish his friend and report the plan to the commandant? Could it be I've misjudged him? After all, like Erich, he's been rigidly indoctrinated.* Several times she reached for the key in the ignition to turn on the car and leave, but each time she remembered Erich's words: "Trust him like you trust me." She figured she had no choice if she wanted Erich's help.

She got out of the car, locked the door, and slowly climbed the steps to the main door. At the duty desk she produced her Propaganda Ministry Identification card. The guard studied it carefully and waved her in. She had just reached the bottom of the stairs when she realized she had no idea how to find Joachim. She walked back to the desk. "Scharfuhrer," she said. "Could you direct me to Obersturmfuhrer Joachim Forester's office?"

The guard grinned, and Inge realized he'd probably heard the same question before. "Go up the stairs to the second floor," he said. "The obersturmfuhrer's office is the fifth door on your left."

Still conflicted, Inge climbed the stairs. Outside Joachim's closed door, she hesitated. *Well,* she reasoned, *I've come this far.* She took a deep breath, exhaled deeply, and knocked, half hoping Joachim would be out so she could tell Erich she'd tried but failed to reach him. *No such luck,* she mused when, from behind the door, she heard a friendly voice calling: "Come in, whoever you are."

"Good morning," Inge said as she entered the room, grinning at Joachim's surprised expression.

Joachim quickly recovered and stood. "Tell me Erich already tossed you aside, and you've come here to take me up on the offer I made last evening," he said, grinning. "Before you say anything, I accept!"

"I've come to ask if you'll take a lady to lunch. However, looking at the time, it appears I'm rather early."

Joachim looked behind him at the clock on the wall. It was only 9:45. "It may be too soon for lunch, but it's a great time for a late breakfast, and how could I refuse such a lovely lady?"

"What about your work?"

"Pleasure before work has always been my motto. Shall we go, fair lady?" Without hesitation, he removed his hat and coat from the rack, took Inge by the arm, and escorted her from the office.

As they left the building, Inge was sure the scharfuhrer who'd given her directions to Joachim's office was grinning. "Any particular place you'd like to go?" Joachim asked as they reached the street.

"Somewhere quiet and private."

"Evenings are much better for a tryst, my dear, but what the heck; any time's the right time."

"Be serious," Inge said. "Because what I have to tell you is crucial."

"Okay, fair lady. You clearly want to talk business. I'm heartbroken, but my time is yours, and I'm ready to listen. Why don't we go to the Cafe Feldherrenhalle on Theatinerstrasse? Since it's between breakfast and lunch, there shouldn't be many people around."

"Perfect," Inge said as Joachim took her arm.

The sidewalks were slippery as they turned onto Theatinerstrasse and approached Feldherrenhalle. As Joachim predicted, the cafe was nearly empty. Inge led the way to a table in the most remote corner of the room. They had just sat down when the waitress came over. "Coffee, Obersturmfuhrer? Fraulein?"

"Please," Joachim said. "Inge?"

"Anything, as long as it's hot."

"Then coffee will have to do. We don't have any tea." She frowned. "It's the war. What else could I bring you?"

"Nothing for me," Inge said.

"How about some real black coffee with clotted cream, a rich Danish pastry with an excessive amount of butter, and an order of sausage and eggs."

"Obersturmfuhrer, you know we can't—"

Joachim laughed at the waitress's reaction. "Teasing," he said. "I'll have toasted brown bread."

"That I can bring you."

The waitress left to fill the order. When she could no longer hear their conversation, Joachim leaned across the table. "Now tell me," he said; no longer joking. "What's this all about?"

"Before I begin, I want you to know I'm not entirely sure being here with you is the right thing to do, but Erich told me to trust you, and I'll do as he asked. I have no reservations in his regard."

"But you have doubts about me."

"Not really. Possibly. Oh, I don't know. Once I tell you everything, my life may depend on your discretion."

"That sounds serious."

"It is, Joachim. In fact Erich's life could be in danger because of what I have to say, and yours too if you do what he asks."

Inge waited until the waitress had served the coffee and Joachim's bread.

"So no more stalling," Joachim urged. "Talk to me,"

During the next half hour, Inge related the story of Rosel, Dachau, Article Eleven, and Erich's plan, including the request they all meet for dinner on November 3rd. She paused in her monologue only long enough for the waitress to refill Joachim's coffee cup.

Joachim listened intently. Though he was tempted, he didn't interrupt the woman who was obviously having difficulty trusting a near stranger. When she finished her explanation, he took her hand in both of his. "Have you told me everything, Inge?" he asked.

"All but what Erich wants you to do here in Munich; that is if you agree to help us."

"That goes without saying. I realize that revealing your secret was difficult, so let me ease your mind. You told me about your sisterly relationship with Rosel. You should know that Erich and I are as close as brothers. There's nothing I wouldn't do for him, including give my life. If Erich needs help, I'll be there. There's not enough time now, nor is there any need for me to relate specific reasons for my loyalty and friendship, but believe me, I owe him everything. When I watched him last night, I saw something I'd never seen before. For the first time in his life, the man's in love. If you're as important to him as I believe you are then, if for no other reason, of course I'll help you. So what does Erich need for me to do here in Munich?"

"At this early stage in the investigation, he'd like for you to ask discreet questions and keep your ears open while you're at the Hofbrauhaus. You know a lot of people, and Erich thought you might be able to discover where the SS sends the Jewish women who are arrested in the area."

"I can do that, and I'll find a way to get into the files in Sturmbannfuhrer Mueller's office. As commandant of the Munich SS, he should have records of where the women in his jurisdiction are taken."

"Won't searching his files be dangerous?"

Joachim leaned in. "Let me tell you a secret, fair lady," he whispered. "One I expect you to keep to yourself, because if Erich should find out, my reputation will be ruined."

"Your deepest, darkest secrets are safe with me," Inge whispered back.

"I hope so, because—"

"Get to the point, please, Joachim. I know all about your reputation."

"Well if I must. I sometimes work at night."

Inge's eyes widened. "I don't believe it," she said. "The ultimate party man doesn't party every night?"

"You don't believe it because it's impossible to believe, or because you think it's crazy?"

"The former." Inge paused. "But truthfully, a little bit of both. So this is your deep, dark secret?"

"It is, and if Erich knew, I'd never hear the end of it. He believes all my evenings are filled with fun and frauleins.

Mind you, most are, but once in a while, even I must work. Since I'm a regular fixture in the headquarters building at night, no one would be suspicious if I hung around after-hours."

"I see," Inge said. She thought for a moment and then said: "Since I involved you in this mess, I plan to help. Have you ever taken a woman to the office at night?"

Joachim feigned astonishment. "Me, mix pleasure with business?" he said. "How could you ask such a question?"

"Be serious, will you?"

"There's that horrible word again. Every time someone uses it, I'm in trouble, but, to be *serious* as you suggest, I've been known to take a fraulein to my office from time to time."

"From time to time?" Inge grinned, remembering the reaction of the guard on duty when she asked directions to Joachim's office.

"Well maybe often would be closer to the truth."

"In that case, it wouldn't look suspicious if I went to headquarters with you some evening. I could keep watch while you're searching the commandant's files for information."

"Absolutely not," Joachim said adamantly. "It's too dangerous, and Erich would never forgive me if I let anything happen to you. For that matter, I'd never forgive myself."

"I see you need to be convinced, so let me be clear. There's no way you and Erich are going to fight my battle without me. I *will* be a part of whatever you plan to do. In this matter there's no room for negotiation."

Joachim weighed Inge's words. "Alright, fair lady," he said. "I guess it makes sense. Tell Erich I'll begin my inquiries at the Hofbrauhaus tonight and meet you both at the Wagner on the 3rd. If he gives us his blessing, we'll search the commandant's files the following night. We have to accomplish our task before November 9ᵗʰ. Because the Nazi bigwigs will be around for the celebration, Mueller will be adding additional men to the security detail, which could be a problem."

"What are the chances Erich will give us his blessing?"

"He'll put up a fight, but if he realizes how insistent you are, and if I tell him I can't succeed without you, he should go along with what we want to do."

Inge reached for Joachim's hand. "It's rare to find one, let alone two such extraordinary friends," she said.

"There's been enough serious talk for one morning, fair lady." He paid the bill and walked Inge back to her car. "See you at the Wagner," he said.

"You will, and thank you, Joachim."

"Thank me when we've actually accomplished something."

# CHAPTER 19

Wondering if Inge had talked to Joachim, Erich lay sleeplessly on his bunk. He looked at the clock on the wall. He was about to get up when a tall, fair-complexioned man entered the room. "Finally," the man said. He walked over toward Erich's bunk and extended his hand. "I'm Hans Speer, your bunk mate. Our different duty schedule has kept me from introducing myself sooner."

"Glad to meet you, Hans," Erich said. "I thought about waking you up to say hello the other night, but I figured you needed your rest more than you needed to meet me."

"I managed to draw the night duty lately, and you haven't been around much since you got here. Heinrich said you're working with Doctor Rascher."

"The tests began this morning. I had a short break before we begin the next session, so I decided to take a nap. I was about to head back to the office."

"Then I won't keep you. Actually, I'm leaving shortly. I'm the duty officer at the crematorium this afternoon. Because of your experiments, we'll have several additional bodies to burn."

"The crematorium?" All at once the continually smoking chimney, the fetid odor emanating from the rear of the camp and polluting the air, and the thin layer of dust covering the windows and the walls of the buildings made sense. Erich couldn't believe he'd been so stupid and naïve. *Or have I been walking around with my head bowed because I didn't want to see what was happening all about me*, he reflected. "I wasn't taken to the crematorium during my modified tour," he said.

"You wouldn't be unless you have a legitimate reason for being there. The buildings are hidden away in the northwest corner of the campground. I imagine you were taken as far as the bridge over the Wurm before you turned back. If you'd gone a fifty-meters further, you would have seen the ovens. We've recently added a second set of furnaces to help deal with the increased number of dying prisoners."

"Do the SS men do the cremating?" Erich asked, thankful there was no way he could be assigned that duty.

"We only supervise. Prisoners fuel the fires and clean up afterwards. A capo, or prisoner's foreman, directs the crews. Next time you have a long lunch I'll be happy to show you around the facility."

Erich had no desire to see bodies burned, but he also knew he'd be expected to respond positively. "Thanks," he said. "I look forward to seeing more of the camp than I did on the modified tour."

Obviously Hans didn't see anything unusual in Erich's reply. He didn't look at him quizzically, nor was there a change in his tone when he responded. "Then for now, I'll leave you to get ready for work. Perhaps I'll see you in the dining hall this evening."

"I hope so." Erich shook Hans's outstretched hand.

The conversation with his roommate had taken the time Erich had set aside to shower, so he splashed water on his face, brushed his teeth, and combed his hair. As he stared at his reflection in the mirror, he noticed dark circles under his eyes. *At least I won't have to watch any more wretched men die this afternoon,* he thought, *so maybe I'll be able to rest tonight.*

As he walked up the main camp road, a gruff scharfuhrer was shouting at a cowering prisoner. "Work and your life will be spared."

Erich watched the guard brutally bring his stick down across the man's shoulders. "My God, can't I escape suffering anywhere in this place?" he whispered. This time he looked away. The scene was no longer mesmerizing.

The guard overheard and paused. "Excuse me," he said, apparently surprised that Erich would be addressing him. "Did you say something, Hauptsturmfuhrer?"

"Only that I'd better hurry or I'll be late to work, scharfuhrer. Carry on."

Erich picked up the pace. Again he thought about his earlier visit to the Schulzstaffel. He'd asked several officers to explain the rancid smell coming from the detention area, but no one would give him a straight answer. To a man, they'd dropped their eyes and refused to discuss what he now knew was occurring so close to them. He then reflected on his brief experience at Dachau. Somehow the SS officers who worked in the camp were able to ignore the brutalities taking place in Roll Call Square—case in point, the innocuous dining room conversations that had nothing to do with anything going on. With catch-phrases like the "Final Solution" and the "Final Act," the men were avoiding reality, and all on the pretext of obeying orders.

Erich's head was spinning. *My God, what are we all coming to?* He shook his head. *If the Fuhrer's words "conscience is a disease" apply to me, I'm incurably ill.* According to Nazi ideology, his conscience had become his weakness. Surprisingly he wasn't sure he wanted Inge to find Rosel, not if the girl was suffering like the Jews at Dachau.

When he entered the office, Erna and Doctor Rascher were at their desks. "Good afternoon, Herr Doctor, Fraulein," Erich said as he hung his cap and coat on the hat rack.

"Good afternoon, Hauptsturmfuhrer," Erna responded.

As Erich crossed the room to his desk, Rascher handed him a file. "These are the results of the autopsies," he said. "Two of our morning test cases died of ruptured lungs, and one had air bubbles in his brain."

Erich perused the results, glad he could concentrate on the reading material and hoping his bowed head would hide the revulsion he was feeling. He sat down, and, using the notes the three had taken, he wrote a detailed report of the first experiments.

Little discussion occurred in the office as the afternoon progressed. At four o'clock the doctor interrupted Erich's concentration. "I believe it's your dinner time, Hauptsturmfuhrer; that is if you plan to remain in camp tonight."

"That was my intention, Herr Doctor."

"I have a meeting in Munich, so I'll be leaving. We'll begin again at precisely nine o'clock tomorrow morning."

"Then you don't need a ride to town tonight?" Erna asked.

"No, but thank you for asking," Erich said. "I'll eat and return to the office. I have at least another hour of work, and I don't want to begin tomorrow's tests before completing today's reports."

Rascher seemed pleased. "Very good," he said and turned to Erna. "I'll walk you to your car," Fraulein.

"I'll be ready as soon as I let the commandant know we're leaving," she said eagerly, as Erich thought; *she's crazy about the man.*

"I did that a few minutes ago," Rascher said. He turned to Erich. "We'll see you tomorrow, Hauptsturmfuhrer."

When Erna and Rascher left the office, Erich placed his reports in a folder, straightened his desk, and left for dinner. At the corner of the block street and the main camp road, he glanced off to his right into the trees beyond the Amper. Smoke was rising from the smokestacks. He wondered if Hans was still on duty and if the stench in the air was due to the extra bodies from the morning tests. He turned left, and with the ominous building behind him, walked toward the dining hall. *I too am keeping my head down to avoid reality,* he reflected as he entered the cheery haven.

He wound his way around the almost-full tables to join Heinrich, who was sitting alone at a table by the far wall. The fact that the other officers avoided the man was still puzzling. "Busy day?" he asked as Erich sat down at the table.

"Busy and long."

The same pitiful woman who served dinner the night before brought his food and a cup of coffee. Erich decided to use her to begin his investigation. "Last night you said there were girls available for entertainment," he said to Heinrich. "Is our server one of them?"

"She is," Heinrich said, smirking, "From personal experience, I can report she's not bad."

"I prefer my women with a little more flesh on their bones," Erich said, trying to hide his disgust. "But she'll do if the selection is limited."

"Why would you require the services of the likes of her?" Heinrich said. "You're not restricted to camp. Aren't there enough women to satisfy your needs in Munich?"

"Actually, there are." Erich leaned in conspiratorially. "But I'm looking for a particular woman. About three months ago one of my buddies at headquarters took me to meet a Jewish slut who gave me quite a ride. The next day I went back for more, but she'd disappeared. I figured the Gestapo arrested her, so when you mentioned the women who service the officers here at the camp, I thought she might be one of them."

"They come and they go," Heinrich said, seemingly pleased with his pun. "There are very few women currently incarcerated at Dachau. Most of the females brought here are quickly shipped out to Ravensbruck, a frauenlager camp in Mecklenburg."

"Where's Mecklenburg?"

"The town's near Lake Furstenberg, about eighty-kilometers north of Berlin. I haven't been there, but I've been told about twelve thousand women are currently detained in the facility." Heinrich cocked his head. "But why all the interest?"

"I was just thinking how enjoyable it would be to work in a camp full of women, even if they are Jews."

"I know what you mean. I get tired of looking at men. It would be great to see a few females even if, as you suggested, they're Jewish."

Figuring he'd probed enough, Erich dropped the subject. He'd begun the process; he had his first clue to Rosel's whereabouts.

After dinner Heinrich left for roll call, and Erich returned to the office to call Inge. A guard standing outside the door snapped to attention. "Your papers please, Hauptsturmfuhrer. Merely a procedural requirement you understand. This office is off limits to regular camp personnel."

Erich presented his papers and went inside. Without pausing to hang his coat, he picked up the phone on Erna's desk and asked the camp operator to dial Inge's number. As before, Frau Heiden answered. This time she didn't ask questions. Several minutes later Inge answered. "This is Inge Friedrich, Heil Hitler."

"Heil Hitler and good evening, Fraulein," Erich said. "This is Hauptsturmfuhrer Riedl. I called to see if your meeting was successful."

"It was," Inge said. "I ran into an acquaintance of yours, Hauptsturmfuhrer. You remember Joachim Forester."

"How is Joachim?"

"He's well. In fact, he wondered if you'd have time to join him for dinner tomorrow evening."

"I'm sure I can rearrange my schedule. I also have preliminary test results. Since I know you're eager to write your article, why don't you join Obersturmfuhrer Forester and me?"

"Thank you, I will," Inge said.

"I was thinking," Erich said pensively. "If you're available earlier, perhaps we could meet to go over the tests and then enjoy our dinner. Would five o'clock work for you?"

Inge hesitated, and Erich waited. "I asked if five would be suitable," he finally said.

"I was looking at my schedule, Hauptsturmfuhrer. Five o'clock will be fine. I look forward to our discussion."

"So do I, Fraulein. Oh, and by the way, I'll most likely remain at the hotel tomorrow night. With the blackout in effect, reporting back to camp after dark can be a problem. It would be easier to find a ride in the morning."

"I'd be happy to provide transportation to camp."

"I was hoping you'd offer. Until tomorrow, Fraulein."

"Good night," Inge said wistfully; wishing she didn't have to wait another night to be with Erich.

---

All was quiet in the camp as Erich walked through the compound with its crisscrossing searchlights and parading guards. Taking two at a time, he dashed up the Jourhaus stairs. He took a shower and went to bed, concentrating on Inge and the day ahead rather than on the horrors of Dachau. For the first night in many, he slept soundly.

# CHAPTER 20

Erich's morning progressed much like the previous one, except two of the six test cases survived the ordeal in the chamber. "They're suffering from anoxia and the bends, so I doubt they'll live for long," Rascher said. As he spoke, Erich remembered what Hans had said about the need to burn a few additional bodies. He visualized the smoke pouring from the crematorium area and thought again about the putrid smell pervading the camp.

When the last test was over, Rascher left for a meeting and Erna ordered lunch so work could continue without a lengthy interruption. Bothered as he was, Erich knew he had to keep up the charade, so he forced himself to eat. When the sturman had cleared the last trays and left the office, he got back to work, spending the early afternoon documenting the morning results.

At 3:30 Erna stood up, locked the files in the cabinet, and began to straighten her desk. "How long before you'll be ready to leave, Hauptsturmfuhrer?" she said.

"I'm almost ready. I was about to ask if you'd drop me at the Wagner on your way home. I'm meeting with Fraulein Friedrich to discuss her article. For one reason or another, I've had to cancel the appointments we've made over the past week or so. Now I finally have enough data to brief her on our initial findings."

"I'll be happy to take you to town," Erna said. "Can you be ready to leave in twenty minutes?"

"Absolutely!" said Erich. "I'll check out with the commandant and meet you at your car."

"I'll tell them you'll be away when I let them know I'm leaving."

"Thanks." Erich put his files in his desk drawer, walked toward the door and turned back. "I'll see you in a few minutes."

There was nothing unusual happening in Roll Call Square, so he walked directly to the Jourhaus. He packed an overnight bag and went downstairs to meet Erma, who was waiting by the car. They presented their papers to the guard on duty, who waved them through.

"I appreciate the ride, Fraulein," Erich said as they crossed the bridge over the Wurm.

"Anytime." Erna flashed her attractive smile. "My apartment's not too far from the hotel, so it's not inconvenient for me to drop you off. Do you need a ride back to camp in the morning? I'll be happy to pick you up on the way in."

"Not this time, but thanks for offering. I left my replacement with a difficult problem to solve and we're meeting for breakfast to work through the issue; two heads and all. He's driving a motor-pool car to town, so I'm sure he'll drop me off at camp before he returns to Munich."

Erna stopped in front of the hotel. "Then I'll see you tomorrow," she said.

"You will." Erich, as he reached for the door handle. "Have a good evening."

---

Knowing she had to be prepared if anyone at Luftwaffe headquarters or the Propaganda Ministry should ask to see her article, Inge spent the morning trying to come up with some way to present the information Erich had provided. Frustrated with her lack of progress, she decided to drive to the camp to take a look around."

The trip didn't help. In fact, seeing the facility made things worse. She quickly realized there was no way she'd be able to put an optimistic spin on the high walls, the imposing guard towers, the rolls of barbed wire, and the putrid smells emanating from the facility.

*There's nothing positive to report,* she reflected as she drove by the Schulzstaffel. *I should have asked Beck's permission to write a piece about this place instead.* She imagined her boss's reaction had she made the request. Stories praising the glorious SS were old hat, and the *Völkischer Beobachter* wasn't going to put another inane piece on page one. *Anyway, an article about a training facility wouldn't get me into the camp, and that's where I need to be if I'm going to find Rosel,* she thought as she headed back the way she came.

With hours to go before dinner, she stopped at the Schloss Café for a quick bite of lunch. While she ate, she kept trying to come up with a way to present the experiments in a positive light. She still had no idea how to begin. If she wrote about anything she'd observed, the information would be redacted. There was no way the powers-that-be would allow her to present such an ominous, dreary picture to the public. Frustrated, she paid the bill and drove back to her apartment house.

Before going upstairs she called Joachim to confirm their dinner meeting. Encouraged when he hinted he had news from the Hofbrauhaus, she went to her room and again tried to work. Thirty-minutes later she still was still at a loss about what to write, but if Beck asked, at least she could tell him something.

When 4:30 finally arrived, she put her work aside and dressed for dinner. It was too cold to walk, so she drove to the hotel. At precisely five o'clock she went inside; her eyes scanning the lobby. Erich, who'd already checked in and come back down to wait, rose from the chair to greet her. "You're a beautiful sight," he said. He kissed her on the cheek.

"Why, Hauptsturmfuhrer," Inge joked to hide her nervousness. "What a strange way to greet someone who's here for a business meeting."

"Excuse me, Fraulein Friedrich," he teased. "I'm very excited to be conferring with you about the test results, but I'm afraid I left the statistics in my room. Would you mind joining me upstairs for the briefing?"

"Not at all, Hauptsturmfuhrer." Inge smiled. "I'm ready, and I must say, I'm excited too."

Erich guided her to the elevator and pressed the button for the fifth floor. When the door closed, he took her in his arms. As he nuzzled her neck, she moaned with pleasure. "Hauptsturmfuhrer, are you always this friendly with business associates?" she murmured.

"Only beautiful, desirable blondes I'm crazy about." ·

Not sure if there would be people in the hallway, he pulled away when they reached the fifth floor. Neither spoke as they walked toward Erich's room. He unlocked the door, moved aside so she could her enter, stepped in behind her, and flipped the security lock. Not wanting to appear too eager, he walked to the chest of drawers, put his cap on the shining wood, removed his jacket, and hung it in the closet. "Have I told you how gorgeous you are?" he said as he walked to her and slipped his arm around her waist.

Inge put her hand on the back of his neck and pulled his face down to hers. As they kissed, she felt a warm, tingling sensation rising from deep within. Erich's caressed the line of her cheekbone, nuzzled her neck, and kissed the hollow of her throat. "I love you," he whispered.

"I love you too," Inge said softly. "Though I didn't know how much until the day we spent with Aunt Sigrid."

Erich took Inge's hand, led her to the bed, and lay down beside her on the silky spread. She moaned as he reached for the top button of her blouse. His mouth moved hungrily over hers as, button by button, he moved downward, releasing the remaining obstacles. He dropped the straps to her slip and stroked her milk-white skin, now bare beneath his hands.

Inge felt a warm rush surge through her. With her help, Erich removed her skirt, nylons, and panties. Leaning up on his elbow, he looked longingly at the gorgeous body lying alluringly beside him. Loath to leave her for even a minute, he reluctantly got up to remove his clothes. As he did, Inge gazed with both admiration and more than a little apprehension at his masculinity. There was no softness anywhere on his body. He was solid; all hardness. His muscular chest bristled with curling blond hair. As her eyes traveled downward from his rock-hard stomach, she felt warm and flushed.

Erich lay back down. He kissed her again, softly, and then with increasing passion. His hands and lips moved over her body, leaving burning trails wherever he touched. Marveling at her warm, silky skin, he kissed the nape of her neck, the pale roundness of her breasts and her flat stomach. As he did, Inge gasped with pleasure, experiencing new and thrilling sensations as he explored her most private places.

As Erich loomed above her, Inge shyly ran her fingers through the hair on his chest, feeling the hard muscles of his body tense against her own. She took a deep breath as he lowered his body to hers. When he entered her, she gasped. He slowed down until she began to respond to his movements, wrapping her arms around him as she felt the play of the muscles in his back and legs. As his thrusts grew stronger, she heard an involuntary sound emerge from deep in her throat and a moan broke from her lips. She grasped at Erich's shoulders and dug her nails into his flesh as she cried out sharply, feeling a sensation like an explosion of a million stars sending waves of ecstasy surging through her. Erich couldn't hold back any longer. He cried out her name as he felt his release.

Fearing she'd be crushed by his weight, Erich rolled off and drew Inge to him. Her head rested on his chest as their breathing slowly returned to normal. He pushed her damp hair from her forehead and listened to her breathe as she drifted off to sleep. Suddenly the fiery passion he'd felt only moments before gave way to an overwhelming need to protect the woman he loved.

Inge napped, but with so much on his mind, Erich couldn't drift off. At 6:15 p.m. he caressed her face and kissed her lips. "You're so beautiful," he whispered as she opened her eyes.

"You're not so bad yourself," she murmured as she snuggled sleepily into him.

"I'd like to resume our discussion, but I think we'd better get up."

"Our conversation was so wonderful," Inge purred. "I really want to talk some more."

"I'd like that, but I think we should do a little legitimate work before we meet Joachim. Tell me about your trip to Munich."

During the next ten minutes Inge recounted the details of the previous day and her discussion with Joachim, explaining his eagerness to help, but not mentioning their tentative plans to go through Mueller's files. When she finished her spiel, Erich looked at his watch. "You said Joachim's meeting us at seven?" he said.

"That's the plan."

"I've never known the man to be late. It's 6:45—"

Inge threw back the covers, jumped up, and walked quickly across the room. She looked in the mirror. "Lord," she groaned. "I'll never be presentable in fifteen-minutes." Erich came over and put his arms around her waist. She moaned and said: "And if you keep this up we'll never get to the dining room by seven."

Fifteen minutes later they entered the lobby. Erich grinned at Joachim's shocked expression as they emerged from the elevator.

"Well, well, am I too early?" he teased. He shook Erich's hand and kissed Inge on the cheek.

"Absolutely not," Erich said. "We've been sitting around upstairs waiting for you to get here."

"Of course you have," said Joachim. "Frankly I'd be shocked if you thought about me at all, but enough about your tryst. I'm starving and I imagine you're both hungry." He winked at Inge.

The trio crossed the lobby to the dining room and were seated by the maître d. The waiter took their order and quickly brought beer for the men and wine for Inge. When he was out of earshot, Erich turned to Joachim. "Inge said she told you about Rosel. Will you help us?"

"Need you ask, old buddy? I've already begun. I asked around at the Hofbrauhaus last night."

"I hope you weren't too obvious," Inge said.

"Please, fair lady. Give me a little credit. I was very shrewd."

"So what did you find out, sly one?" Erich asked.

"Admittedly not a great deal as yet. Most of the men I spoke with are either unaware or are closed mouthed about the deportation of the Jews from Munich, but I did learn that most of the Jewish men from the area are being held at Dachau, and the majority of the women are imprisoned in a frauenlager called Ravensbruck. I'm not sure exactly where the camp is located. I didn't have a legitimate reason to probe. That said, I managed to discover a few things about the camp activities from one of the men at my table. What he had to say isn't pleasant, and it cost me a fortune to get him to open up."

"Cost you?" Inge said. "I don't understand."

"As I said, most of the men are tight-lipped, but I met one who harbors a real hatred for all Jews. He seemed to enjoy telling macabre tales of the camps, and his tongue loosened with every stein Gretchen brought to the table. I was more than a little disturbed by what he said." He turned to Erich. "And you know what it takes to shock me."

"What did he say?" Inge insisted, though she wasn't sure she wanted to hear Joachim's news.

"The particulars are far from pleasant, fair lady, so let me preface what I'm going to tell you by saying that from what I could discern, at the moment the Mischlinge are, relatively speaking, faring better than the full-blooded Jews. That's because no decision has been made about what to do with them."

"I know that," Inge said.

"What did the man say about Ravensbruck," Erich asked.

"Among other things, that the women are forced to take part in medical tests, 'for the good of the Reich,' of course."

"I've heard that line before." Erich looked at Inge and then back at Joachim. "Why don't we talk about the tests another time."

Inge nodded no. "You both know how I feel. Neither of you will keep anything from me no matter how unpleasant." She turned to Erich. "I appreciate that you want to spare me the gruesome details, but I won't allow you to conceal the truth."

"Tell this obstinate woman everything you learned," Erich said. "I'm sure she won't give up until you do, and she should know what we're facing."

Joachim paused while the waiter served their meals. When the man left the table, he began again: "I'll tell you what I learned," he said. "But it's not a pleasant dinner topic."

"I don't care," Inge said. "Tell me, Joachim."

"You heard the lady," said Erich. "What did your drunken, sadistic friend have to say?"

"I told you the medical staff at Ravensbruck is currently conducting a variety of medical experiments. For the most part, they're being performed on the Polish women called 'rabbit girls.' The tests include amputations and infecting leg bones with pieces of wood or glass to simulate wounds the soldiers suffer on the battlefields. They're also testing ways of transplanting bones from one individual to another."

Inge paled and reached out to Erich. He took her hand and squeezed. "Go on, Joachim," she said. "I told you I want to know everything."

Erich nodded, and Joachim resumed his narrative. "Apparently these 'rabbit girls' are also given gas-gangrene wounds, and chemical irritants are inserted in their uteri to make them sterile. If they don't die from these experiments, they're gassed."

Inge dug her nails into Erich's hand. "What else, Joachim?" she asked anxiously.

"That's it. I assume the guy realized he was revealing too much, and I couldn't push him anymore or he would have been suspicious. Anyway, I found it hard to be enthusiastic about the experiments he was taking so lightly, so I changed the subject." He turned to Erich. "Is this kind of testing going on at Dachau?"

"I've been told of medical experiments, but the infirmary wasn't on the modified tour I received when I first arrived at the camp."

"What about the Luftwaffe tests you're involved with, Erich?" Inge asked uneasily. "Are they anything like the tests being conducted on these so-called rabbit girls at Ravensbruck?"

"Inge, I've told you time and again. For your safety, I can only give you statistical data."

"But things are different now," Inge said. "I already know a great deal. Why don't you tell me everything?"

"Because if you're questioned about the tests, you have to be able to answer truthfully. If you're privy to what's occurring at Dachau, whoever's interrogating you would realize you're hiding something."

"But, Erich—"

"He's right, Inge," Joachim said. "It's unlikely that anyone would ask you about Ravensbruck, but you may be asked about Dachau. It would be better if you could answer truthfully instead of trying to hide what you really know. Remember, the SS and Gestapo are very good at extracting information."

"Alright," Inge said grudgingly. "I can't fight you both, so I won't argue with you anymore, at least about this particular subject. Joachim, tell Erich about our plan to get specific information about the Mischlinge. It's even more important now that I know about Ravensbruck. If Rosel's there, we have to get her out before she becomes an unwilling participant in one of those medical experiments."

"What have you two cooked up, or should I be afraid to ask?" Erich said warily.

"We plan to do a little night work," Joachim said. "Though you realize working at night isn't something I do regularly."

"Day or night, work has never been one of your priorities," Erich teased.

"Be serious, Erich," Inge said. "Tomorrow night Joachim and I are searching Sturmbannfuhrer Mueller's files to see if we can discover where Rosel was taken."

"You're joking, right?" Erich said incredulously.

"She's not," said Joachim.

"You can do whatever you want," Erich said to Joachim. "But Inge's not going near Mueller's office."

"You're wrong," Inge persisted. "Joachim needs a lookout, and since you'll be otherwise occupied at Dachau, I'm the only one who's available."

"What the hell are you thinking?" Erich glared at Joachim. "There's no way I'm letting Inge stand guard in the hall while you rifle through Muller's files. It's too dangerous."

"Actually it's not," Joachim said. "And Inge's right. I need a lookout. From the beginning, she made it clear this is her fight. I have no misgivings about letting her be part of whatever we do, as long as we're cautious and protect her."

Erich saw the resolve on Inge's face. She looked at him with a steady gaze, willing herself to maintain eye contact; to show him she wouldn't be deterred. He looked back at Joachim and saw the same stubborn determination in his friend's eyes. "I can't fight you both," he said. "So tell me about your crazy scheme, though I'm not sure I want to know."

For the next few minutes, Joachim explained how he hoped to find a list of Munich Jews arrested by the Gestapo in Muller's files. He would look for information about both Rosel Dollman and Rosel Friedrich to see if either was among those taken. If he could confirm their suspicions that she was, it would be up to Erich to find out if she was transported to Ravensbruck.

"What if we can confirm that Rosel's at Ravensbruck?" Inge asked. "How could we possibly get her out of there?"

"There may be a way," Erich said. "When I was in Berlin, Gruppenfuhrer Hippke said that women from Ravensbruck will be used during phase three of the tests. If Rosel *is* there, I'll try to convince Rascher that we, not the Ravensbruck staff should select the appropriate 'specimens' as he calls the women. If I win him over to my way of thinking, I'll go to Ravensbruck and, if I find her, choose Rosel, and bring her to Dachau."

"Then what?" Inge asked.

Erich shook his head. "I have no idea. I'm already getting ahead of myself. At this point we don't know if Rosel's at Ravensbruck, but assuming she is, tomorrow I'll begin laying the groundwork with Rascher. In the meantime, I'll continue to press Heinrich for information, and you two, if you must, see what you can find out in Muller's files. When we know something

specific, we'll make definitive plans, but even if I'm given permission to select the women, I won't leave for Ravensbruck for
several weeks. We have to complete at phase one before phase two
begins, and I believe Rascher wants to complete at least half of
them before we bring in the women."

"But what about Rosel, Erich?" Inge asked anxiously. "We
can't wait much longer. It's possible that three more weeks or a
month will be too late."

"If she's made it this long, several more weeks probably won't
matter," said Joachim.

"Joachim's right," Erich said. "Until a decision is handed
down, we have reason to be optimistic."

"Why don't we meet here for dinner day after tomorrow at
seven o'clock?" Joachim said. "Hopefully by then we'll have more
to discuss."

"That sounds good to me," said Erich.

"I'll be here." Inge pointed to the uneaten food. "And next
time I hope we get our money's worth. Maybe we should eat first
and talk after. My appetite vanished as soon as we got down to
business."

"Mine too." Joachim took a bite of his chicken, the specialty
of the house. "The food's too cold to eat," he said. "Shall we order
something else?"

"I really couldn't eat anything," Inge said.

Joachim glanced at his watch. "That's probably for the best.
It's getting late, and I have to return the car."

Erich paid the bill. They assured the waiter who cleared their
plates that, though the food was good, they weren't hungry.

At the front door of the hotel, Joachim turned to Inge. "We
need to firm-up our plans for tomorrow night, fair lady. Why
don't I meet you at our cafe tomorrow evening at seven o'clock?"

Erich frowned. "Your cafe?"

"Don't pay any attention to him, Joachim. Seven works for me, and so you know, I'll be spending the afternoon at my aunt's if either of you needs me."

"Maybe you should stay with Sigrid tomorrow night," Erich said. "It may be late when you and Joachim finish searching the files. I'd feel better knowing you weren't driving back to Dachau alone after dark. If I can get to the office before Erna arrives in the morning, I'll call you."

"Then if we all know what we're doing, I should be on my way." Joachim slapped Erich on the shoulder. "I'm sure you two want to discuss the test results without me."

"Like you, always work before pleasure, or is it pleasure before work?" Erich teased.

"Whichever works at the time. Inge, see you at the café tomorrow night."

"Plan on it." Inge kissed Joachim on the cheek.

"Shall we go upstairs and discuss those test results?" Erich said as Joachim left the lobby.

"Absolutely." Inge smiled and took his hand.

# CHAPTER 21

This time there was no hesitation. As soon as the door closed, Erich took Inge in his arms. She responded, surrendering to his kisses and returning them with equal ardor. The initial reserve she'd felt earlier vanished, and she eagerly welcomed his caresses as he guided her hands to his own body, teaching her where to give him pleasure and learning from her responses and sounds what pleased her.

The night was idyllic. They slept, woke, made love, slept, woke and made love again. Toward morning Inge stirred from a deep sleep and snuggled close to Erich, rubbing her fingernails gently through the hair on his chest. "I love you," she whispered.

Erich took her in his arms. He felt the wet tears fall on his chest and he rose up on his elbow. "What's the matter?" he said tentatively.

"I don't know. I'm fine. No, I'm wonderful. I suppose I don't want our night to end. If we get out from under this warm comforter, we'll have to face cold reality."

"Does it help to know we'll have many more wonderful nights?"

"But how can we plan beyond today? There are so many problems—"

"I thought we agreed to take this one day at a time. I know you're frightened, and I realize it's a lot to ask, but will you trust me to make things right?"

"I will, but—"

"What do you say we start the day with breakfast? We didn't eat much at dinner, and after our nighttime romp, I'm starving. We can talk about the tests while we eat."

"If food's the only thing on your mind, of course I'll go to breakfast with you."

Erich groaned. "I can think of other things—"As he reached out, Inge bounced out of bed.

"Actually, breakfast sounds great," she said. "I can hear my stomach growling. I'll be ready in thirty-minutes."

During the meal Erich reported on the initial test results while specifically avoiding details of the testing methods. When Inge pressed for explicit information, he repeatedly refused to reveal specifics. The conversation became frustrating for both, as Inge met a dead end with every question she asked. When the meal was over, the atmosphere at the table was more than a little strained.

During the ride to camp, the friction intensified. At 8:40 p.m. Inge pulled the car up to the Jourhaus gate, and the necessary formality began again. "Thank you for the ride, Fraulein," Erich said.

Suddenly Inge realized how ridiculous she was acting in view of the intimacy they shared and what they'd be facing that day and in the weeks ahead. "Good luck, Hauptsturmfuhrer darling, she whispered. "I'll see you soon. As she drove away, she was thankful there was no longer tension between them.

---

Once again, Erich's morning began much like those before, except, this time, Rascher, after voicing his pleasure with the recording procedures and similar statistics the three had produced the previous two days, decided to use three prisoners at once in order to utilize their time and the facility more efficiently.

At 9:15 the sturman led the first group of bewildered men into the chamber. Erich felt the same dread, but this time in triplicate. Within fifteen minutes, all three prisoners had slumped unconscious to the ground. When they were removed, two were dead, and the one Erich observed most closely was barely alive.

Three young men cleaned up the blood that had accumulated from a violent nosebleed experienced by one of the victims who, in his agony, pounded his head against the wall. When the room was ready, the sturman brought three more prisoners into the chamber. All died, as did the three who followed.

Erich was distressed when three more prisoners were led in. One died, and two lived. *To meet what fate*, he wondered. He knew the guinea pigs who survived would never be allowed back into the community of prisoners to talk about their experiences. The march through the chamber doors was a death sentence. Erich shuddered at the realization. Twelve men had lost their lives that morning so the observers could record almost identical statistics. He feared that many more would meet the same fate before Rascher could justify his results and pronounce them conclusive.

"That went well," Rascher said smugly as the last casualties of the day were removed from the chamber.

"Yes it did," Erich said, forcing a smile. As he returned to his desk to prepare the reports from the morning tests, he was anxious and uneasy, but not for the test victims. He was worried about Inge. Why couldn't he find a way to dissuade her from going to headquarters with Joachim? She was so stubborn, so determined to be involved and make a contribution. He shook his head. *I should have insisted Joachim handle the investigation alone,* he thought. *I should have found a way to keep Inge out of this.*

He attempted to concentrate on the reports he was writing, but his mind wandered as he thought about Inge and Joachim and the risks they'd be taking at headquarters. When the lengthy afternoon was finally over and four o'clock arrived, he realized his meditations had put him behind schedule. In order to be ready for the next morning's tests, he would need to remain in the office well into the evening. For a moment he thought about skipping dinner, but he quickly changed his mind. He had to work on Heinrich in a timely manner, so he reluctantly left the office and headed for the dining hall.

Roll Call Square was unusually quiet for that time of the afternoon. There were no prisoners on the main road or in the compound, but there was definitely something unusual going on. Compared to the previous evening, the dining hall was relatively empty. Heinrich wasn't around, so Erich approached Wilhelm Reiss. "May I join you?" he asked.

Wilhelm hardly looked up from his food. "I'm nearly finished," he said. "But please sit down."

"Where is everyone?" Erich asked. "I didn't see any prisoners in the square or on the main camp road."

"That's because Commandant Weiss is expecting important guests from Berlin in the morning," Reiss said. "The lockers have to be neat and the parade prisoners must be put in the barracks up front for inspection."

"Parade prisoners?"

The ones who are the most presentable. The rest of the prisoners will remain in their blocks."

"I see," Erich said, thinking the wretched men were probably thankful for a change in the routine. "Say," he asked, "is Heinrich Wolfers on duty tonight?"

A voice came from behind him. "Heinrich Wolfers is standing right beside you."

Erich turned to see the subject of his inquiry. "I didn't see you come in," he said.

"That's because I just arrived. I took Commandant Weiss to SS Headquarters for a meeting with Commandant Mueller. They're having dinner before returning to headquarters."

Erich could barely hide his shock. Would the two men see Inge standing outside the door and enter the office to find Joachim rummaging through Muller's files? He wanted to ask Heinrich more about the commandant's plans, but there was no reason for him to be interested in Weiss's activities, so he kept quiet.

His stomach was in a knot as he tried to think. Here was Heinrich who, with Weiss away, might be able to find out something about Rosel, but he couldn't take the time to ask the man for help. He had no choice. He'd have other opportunities to work on Heinrich. He had to keep Inge and Joachim from going to Mueller's office. Fearing it would look suspicious if he left his barely touched food in front of him, he ate quickly.

"What's the hurry?" Heinrich said as he watched Erich shovel the food into his mouth. "You have a hot date or something?"

Erich forced a smile. "Unfortunately, nothing that pleasurable. I have work to do and very little time for conversation."

"No time for pleasure? What about our tour of the ladies of the camp? I thought that might be why you were asking about me and swallowing your food so quickly."

Though he needed to get back to the office as quickly as possible and call Joachim, Erich realized Heinrich had given him the perfect opportunity to lay the groundwork for his project. "Since our discussion the other night, I've thought a lot about the Jewish whore I told you about. I'd like to find her again. You've been here for a while, so I thought you might be able to help with the search."

"She's that good?"

"It didn't take long for me to persuade her to be obliging. If we can find her, I don't mind sharing, but unfortunately I don't have time to talk now." He finished the last bite of his meal and pushed the plate away. "We'll talk again tomorrow," he said. Hoping he'd peaked Heinrich's interest, he put on his coat and left the room.

No one was in the office, so, once again, he had to present his papers to the guard on duty. Once inside he quickly reached for the phone. "Heil Hitler. SS Headquarters, Munich," said the operator.

"Heil Hitler," said Erich. "Please ring Obersturmfuhrer Joachim Forester."

"I believe he left the building a while ago, but it's possible he returned while I was on a break. I'll see if he's in his office." Minutes later he came back on the line. "I'm afraid Obersturmfuhrer Forester has gone for the day. Would you care to leave a message? I'll see that he receives it when he comes in tomorrow."

"No thank you," Erich said. "Heil Hitler."

Erich wished Joachim *had* gone for the day. "Maybe I can reach Inge before she and Joachim leave for headquarters," he whispered. He remembered they were meeting at a café at seven o'clock. *Why didn't I find out which one?* He answered his own question. *Because I didn't expect complications.* He dialed the camp operator again and gave her Sigrid's number.

"Hello." Erich noted that Sigrid omitted the official "Heil Hitler."

"Is Inge there?" he asked.

"Erich. Is that you?"

"It is," Erich said, realizing he'd been too abrupt. "How's my favorite lady?"

Sigrid chuckled. "Wait until my niece hears this. She has competition from the likes of me."

"Did you doubt it for a minute?"

"You're quite a flatterer, young man, but I see right through you. Inge's not at home."

"Do you know where I might reach her?"

"She went to see Herr Beck. After that she was meeting someone. I assumed it was you."

"Do you think she'll come home before her meeting?"

"I don't believe so, but if she does, should I ask her to call you?"

"No need. All of a sudden I'm in the mood to come to Munich. Would you like company?"

"I told you you're welcome anytime."

"Then, if I can catch a ride to town, I'll see you and Inge later."

Erich hung up the phone. He left the office and jogged across Roll Call Square to the dining hall. Out of breath, he approached the table where Heinrich was still sitting." What brings you back here?" Heinrich asked.

"Something's come up regarding a supply problem I was laboring to resolve before my transfer, Erich said. "Could I catch a ride when you go for Commandant Weiss?"

"Of course," Heinrich said. "But I hope your appointment's not too pressing. I'm not leaving until around 8:30."

Erich's heart pounded in his chest. How could he reach Joachim or Inge? If they were on schedule, they'd likely be in the commandant's office when Mueller and Weiss returned from dinner. "No chance you could go earlier and spend some time at the Hofbrauhaus with those beautiful frauleins?" he asked.

"It's tempting," Heinrich said. "But I'd have difficulty changing plans. Orders, you know. I don't have the freedom to come and go as you do."

Erich noticed the sarcasm in Heinrich's voice. He was disappointed, but he had no choice. He had to get to Munich. "Eight-thirty will be fine," he said. "Where should I meet you?"

"I'll pick you up in front of the Jourhaus."

"I'll be there. In the meantime, I'll be in the office. If you decide to leave earlier, you know where to reach me."

Attempting to work, but with little success, Erich tried Joachim again. He hadn't returned to the office, so Erich called the newspaper. Another disappointment; Beck and his staff had left for the day. He picked up the phone to call Sigrid, but he hung up before the operator had time to answer. *Another call might make her worry*, he thought as he tried to concentrate on the reports in front of him. As before, he failed miserably. It was agonizing knowing the two people he loved most in the world were in danger. What would he find when he reached Munich? He hoped for the best but dreaded the worst.

# CHAPTER 22

After a brief meeting with Beck, Inge drove to the Café Feldherrenhalle, parked, and went inside. Joachim wasn't there, so she found an empty table near the back and ordered coffee. At precisely seven, she heard whistling behind her and turned to see Joachim striding across the room. "You look cheerful," she said, smiling at the perpetually jovial man.

"After an hour or two with the lovely ladies at the Hofbrauhaus, how could I be anything else? The only thing that would make me happier would be to lure you away from Erich."

"Do you ever stop?"

"I'm always trying."

"That you are," Inge said, grinning.

Joachim scowled. "Ouch!" he said.

"Stop frowning. Sit down, and tell me about the plans for the rest of the evening."

"Well, fair lady, I managed to leave early today, reporting loudly that I had a late appointment, but would be back to work this evening."

"That sounds good. What else?"

"Before we go upstairs, we'll go to my office and pick up several files I borrowed from Mueller's secretary earlier today. Under the guise of procuring some additional information for the project I inherited from Erich, I spent about thirty-minutes in his office. He has eight four-drawer file cabinets. The folders

I have are from the two that contain information about supplies and staff organization, so we can skip them during our search."

"So that leaves six cabinets to go through."

"Exactly. I figure one of those will contain the records about the transportation of local Jews to the camps."

Inge thought about the daunting Gestapo Headquarters building she walked by on her way to work every day. "We haven't discussed the possibility the data on the Mischlinge has been transferred to the Gestapo," she said. "If a decision is about to come down, it's entirely possible the SS has relinquished authority."

Joachim grimaced. "That horrible thought hadn't even crossed my mind," he said. "If that's the case, let's hope the SS kept duplicate copies."

"Why would they?"

"Because Himmler's an obsessive record-keeper. You can't imagine the number of copies I have to make. I make copies of the copies of the copies."

"Let's hope you're right. So on to my next concern. What if someone should find us rummaging through Muller's files?"

"It's unlikely anyone will be on the third floor at that hour. Besides Mueller, Erich, and several other senior officers, secretaries occupy the other offices during the day. They won't be working at night, but in case we run into a problem, you'll warn me. If someone comes up the stairs, knock, and then walk quickly toward the stairs at the other end of the hall. Mueller's office is in the middle of a long corridor, so I should have ample time to open the appropriate cabinet and pretend to be returning the files. If anyone asks, we have a date, and you're looking for me."

"But would it be appropriate for you to be in the commandant's office after hours? I doubt many people would be authorized to rifle through those files, even in the daytime. From what

Erich told me about Mueller, he wouldn't be pleased to find you in his private domain."

"You're probably right, but we're worrying about a problem we won't encounter. Mueller left the building, and he's a stickler for routine. I can't remember the last time he came back after leaving for the day."

"But what if he does?"

"If that happens, I'll have some quick explaining to do, but you know me, I always have an answer for everything."

"Will you be serious?"

"I'm deadly serious."

"And if you don't mind, could you not use the word 'deadly'? At the moment it hardly generates positive images."

"I apologize, fair lady, but as I said, this will be easy."

"I wish I could be as optimistic as you sound."

"You know there's still time for you to back out. I'm sure Erich would be thrilled if you decided not to stand guard."

"Did you hear from him today?" Inge said, ignoring Joachim's suggestion.

"No, but I didn't expect to. He was involved with the testing this morning and said he'd be spending the afternoon writing reports. We'll meet him tomorrow evening at the Wagner to recount our glorious successes."

The waitress returned to the table before Inge had a chance to respond. Joachim paid the bill and glanced at his watch. "Well, fair lady," he said. "The time has come. Shall we go to work?" He helped her with her coat, took her arm and led her from the cafe into a lightly falling snow.

"The first of the season," Inge said. "I love the fresh, clean white of virgin snow."

Joachim gripped her arm more firmly to keep her from slipping on the slick sidewalk. "Everything is pure at first," he said as he opened Inge's car door. "It only becomes dirty and slushy after it's been around for a while."

"What a profound statement for Joachim Forester. If I didn't know you better, I'd believe you were comparing the snow with what's going on in Germany today."

"Ah, but you do know me, fair lady. I'm not that deep."

"I'm not so sure."

"Well, I am, and I'm also ready to change the subject."

Inge found a place to park on Arcisstrasse just beyond the headquarters building. Joachim held her arm to keep her from slipping as they climbed the stairs to door. The guard on duty grinned as they approached the desk. "Working late again tonight, Obersturmfuhrer?" he said.

"Shh, Ritter," said Joachim. "Do you want to ruin my reputation? I can't have the lady think I take my work seriously."

"Of course not," Ritter sputtered. "What I meant to say, Obersturmfuhrer, is it's highly unusual for you to be at headquarters so late in the evening."

Joachim laughed at the sturman's efforts to cover his faux pas. "Right, Ritter," he said. "The fraulein will be with me during my brief stay. Is anyone in tonight?"

"Only a few of the radio staff and the regular night guards." He turned to Inge and held out his hand. "Your papers, fraulein." Inge handed him her personal identification card, avoiding, as Joachim and Erich had suggested, the presentation of her official cards from the ministry and the newspaper. For the night she was merely one of Joachim's many ladies.

The guard declared the papers were in order and returned the card. "I hope your evening duty isn't too unpleasant," he said to Joachim.

"I'm certain it will be terrible," Joachim said, smirking.

Knowing the guard was watching, Joachim held Inge's hand as they climbed the stairs. When they were safely inside his office, he picked up the two decoy files from his desk drawer. He motioned for her to sit in the chair opposite his. "So you're clear, let's go over the plan one more time," he said.

Inge frowned. "I really don't think it's necessary."

"I beg to differ. What's your assignment?"

"You can't really think I've forgotten something so simple."

"Humor me."

"I'm to stand in the hall and keep watch. If someone comes, I have the difficult task of knocking on the door to warn you."

"Then what?"

"I walk down the hall to the stairs away from the sound and come back to your office."

"Exactly, and move quickly."

"No, I'm going to stroll," Inge said sarcastically. "I know the drill."

"Good. Then it's time to go."

Joachim paused at the door. "This is your last chance to back out, fair lady. There's no turning back once we leave this office."

"Not a chance. Anyway, you were right. It's quiet out there. This should be easy."

They climbed the stairs to the third floor. As they passed the secretaries' offices that lined the corridor, once or twice Joachim looked back to see if a guard was patrolling the area. When they reached Mueller's door, he tentatively pushed it open and peeked inside. The office was empty, but for some reason, the lights were on. *I wonder if that's the usual practice,* he reflected, but despite his doubts, he stepped inside, and turned back to Inge. "Okay, fair lady, stay out here," he said. "Remember what to do if anyone comes down the hall. Knock and get the hell out of here."

Joachim closed the door, and Inge began her guard duty. Minutes passed, each seeming like an hour as she nervously waited for Joachim to finish his search. The creaking and settling of the building unnerved her. The stillness and quiet of the deserted hallway closed in around her, and she felt her heart pounding in her chest. It hadn't been more than five minutes when, feeling spooked, she decided to go into the office to help. She reasoned that with her assistance, they could find the file more quickly and get back to the relative safety of Joachim's office. Her hand was on the doorknob when she changed her mind. Joachim's safety as well as her own depended on her following the plan. She had to stay outside and watch the hall.

Ten minutes passed, then five more. Inge's uneasiness quickly gave way to panic. She heard the sound of the telephone ringing in the commandant's office. Without thinking, she pushed open the door and rushed in to see Joachim staring at the phone on Muller's desk. Her voice reflected the alarm she was feeling. "What now?" she said. "Do we answer?"

"Certainly not," Joachim said irritably. "But I wonder why anyone would call the commandant at this hour. Surely the operator would know he'd left the building."

Inge stared at the ringing phone. "Maybe Muller's coming back," she said. "We need to get out of here."

"I've only been through three files. If we give up now, we may not have an opportunity to look again. Go back outside and listen for footsteps."

"Please, Joachim."

"Go on," Joachim urged. "I won't be long."

Inge reluctantly complied. Five more minutes dragged by as she stood at her post. Each time she glanced at her watch, sure a lengthy period of time had passed and Joachim would soon be finished, she was amazed to see it was only minutes later. She began to fidget. *How long can Joachim continue to search,* she wondered, feeling increased anxiety. There wasn't time to find out. Her worst fears were quickly realized. In the silence of the hallway she heard the thundering of feet on the stairs. As the footsteps grew louder and closer, she stood frozen to the floor. The sound of voices pierced the silence of the hall. She panicked, and instead of knocking and walking away, she opened the office door to warn Joachim.

"Trouble?" he asked as he saw the frenzied look on Inge's face.

"Coming up the stairs," Inge stammered. She felt a chill as she watched Joachim try to close the drawer, kept open by a protruding file. As precious seconds ticked away and he struggled to dislodge the jammed folder, Inge's dread increased. Finally after what seemed like an eternity, he was able to push the file back down. He quickly closed the drawer, grabbed Inge's arm, and dragged her into the nearby closet. Seconds later the outer office door opened, and at least two men entered the room.

From the reflection of the light under the door, Joachim could barely make out the features of the terrified woman who clung tightly to him. She looked as if she was on the verge of nervous collapse; her eyes wide with terror and dread. As she heard a chair being pulled across the office floor, she flinched and dug her nails into his coat sleeve.

The conversation outside was muffled, so the two in the closet could only understand an occasional word. Wedged in the tight space, Inge could barely breathe. *God, don't let the men need anything from the closet*, she prayed silently as she gripped Joachim's arm and buried her head in his chest.

When he heard the file drawer being pulled open, Joachim's apprehension intensified. *Did I push the stuck folder down enough*, he worried. *Will the always-meticulous major realize someone's been looking through his papers?* After several moments the drawer was slammed shut, and outside the confines of the closet, the conversation began again. An occasional laugh penetrated the closet wall, but thankfully, no one approached their hiding place.

When Inge heard a chair being pushed back and then footsteps near the closet door, she held her breath, fearing that Mueller and his guest were close enough to hear any sound she might make. As the footsteps moved away from their hiding place, she relaxed; even more so when the office door opened and the room was engulfed in darkness. Several seconds later she heard the door slam. She exhaled deeply. Joachim quickly covered her mouth with his hand; silently telling her to be cautious until they were certain there was no one there to hear.

As they listened for telling sounds, Inge felt she was suffocating in the small space. "We have to get out of here, Joachim," she whispered anxiously. "I can't stand it any longer."

"Just a minute more," Joachim mouthed. "We have to be sure Muller doesn't come back for something he forgot."

"Inge took several deep breaths. "Please," she pleaded.

"Alright," Joachim said. "I think we're okay." When he let go of her arm, Inge's knees buckled. He reached out and grasped her around the waist. "I've got you," he whispered, as they stood locked together, hearing only their breathing and, Inge was sure, the beating of her heart. Hearing nothing, Joachim opened the door and peered into the darkness.

"What do you see?" Inge asked.

"Thankfully nothing, so let's go."

As they entered the office, Inge took several deep breaths. "Thank God we're out in the open," she said, feeling a little less claustrophobic.

"Think you can stand on your own?" Joachim whispered.

Inge inhaled and exhaled deeply. "I think so," she said.

Joachim slowly released his hold on her waist and took her hand. "The door's on the other side of the room," he said.

"Before Mueller arrived, were you able to discover where the Mischlinge are being detained, or better yet, did you learn anything specific about Rosel?" Inge asked as they groped their way toward the office door.

"No, but I had another cabinet to search before we were so rudely interrupted."

"The lights are off, so I'm sure this time Muller has left for the night. Should we try again?"

"Not a chance, fair lady, at least not tonight. You can hardly stand up with me holding on to you. Your lookout career is over."

Still holding Inge's arm, Joachim moved toward the door and opened it enough to peek out. Breathing a sigh of relief, he looked back. "The corridor's empty," he said. He opened the door and led Inge down the hall past Erich's office to the stairs, steadying her as they descended.

Joachim's relief was short-lived. When they reached the second floor, he peeked around the corner. He had barely entered the hallway when a guard emerged from the office several doors away. He jerked Inge back into the stairwell and put his finger to his lips, cautioning her to be silent. The guard paused and listened intently for several seconds. Apparently hearing nothing, he walked toward the other end of the corridor, away from where Joachim and Inge were huddled.

As they heard another door open and close, Joachim began to worry. *My God, was he looking for us?* He wondered. *Did he look in my office and discover that Inge and I left the building without signing out?*

After a few minutes of uninterrupted silence, Joachim again peered around the corner. The hallway was empty, so he led Inge toward his office, opened the door, and helped her to a chair. "You can relax," he said to the trembling woman. "It's over. We'll stay here until you calm down and then get the hell out of the building."

Thankfully, there was no sign the guard had been in the room. Joachim was beginning to think the ordeal was over, when without warning, the door to the office opened, and the same guard who was patrolling the corridor stuck his head inside. Joachim's heart pounded. "Good evening, Sturman," he said cheerfully. "What brings you here, and without so much as a knock? You startled my friend."

"I apologize for intruding, Obersturmfuhrer," said the guard. "I'm on my nightly rounds. Are you and the fraulein cleared to be in the building?"

"We are." Joachim winked, hoping the young man would understand his implied message. "I needed to do a little extra night work."

"Then if everything's in order, and I can see it is, I'll check the third floor. It's probably my imagination, but I thought I heard footsteps and voices up there a few minutes ago."

Joachim put his arm around Inge's shoulder. "We didn't hear anything, did we, my love?" He looked back at the guard. "Please don't let us keep you from your rounds."

"Good evening, Obersturmfuhrer," the man said. "Heil Hitler."

"Heil Hitler, and carry on," Joachim responded. "I know I will."

"Do you think he suspects anything?" Inge asked as they heard him walk away from the door.

"I don't think so. I'm sure he routinely patrols the halls. He probably wasn't told I was cleared to work in the building. If he suspected we were in Muller's office, we wouldn't be standing here now. When he asks the guard at the main door, he'll learn that Muller and Weiss were meeting on the third floor, and he'll leave us alone."

Joachim's assurances help Inge relax. When her breathing returned to normal and her color came back, he asked the question that had been on his mind since Inge entered Mueller's office.

"When you heard the footsteps, Inge, why didn't you knock on the door and go the other way? You weren't supposed to come inside. I'd hate to think what would have happened if the file drawer hadn't closed or if Mueller had opened the closet door."

"I know. I panicked and thought I should warn you. When I entered the office, it was too late for us to leave. Muller would have seen us, and as good as you are, I don't think you could have talked us out of that jam."

"You're right about that. I might have been able to justify my being in his office, but I don't think I could have explained why you were there with me." Just as Joachim thought Inge was strong enough to leave the office, they heard footsteps coming from the direction of the left stairwell. "Don't worry," Joachim whispered. "I'll handle this."

"Why would the guard come back, Joachim?" Inge pleaded. "He knows I'm here, and he thinks we're having an affair. There's no reason for him to check on us again unless we're in trouble."

"It's possible he went to Mueller's office and found something amiss," Joachim said. He walked to his desk, opened the top drawer, removed the Lugar, and pointed it at the door."

"What are you thinking?" Inge said, looking horrified. "You can't think we'd be able to shoot our way out of SS Headquarters. Put the gun away."

"You're right" Joachim put the gun back in the drawer and went to stand by Inge's side, holding her arm as they waited. "Don't say a word," he whispered. "Most of the time I can talk my way out of messes. Let's hope this isn't an exception."

Whoever was in the hall paused outside the door, but didn't knock. Inge and Joachim watched the doorknob turn and waited for the door to open. Inge held her breath and Joachim clinched his fist, preparing for a fight. All of a sudden Inge pulled free from Joachim's grasp and raced toward the man who was coming through the door. "Erich," she cried. "Thank God!"

"What the hell's going on in here?" Erich growled as Joachim felt his body go limp.

"We're fine, old Buddy," Joachim said, trying to sound nonchalant. "You're the last person I expected to see walk through the door, but you're clearly the most pleasant sight I've seen in years."

Inge was trembling and, despite Joachim's obvious effort to seem cool and calm, he showed none of his usual lightheartedness. Confused, Erich addressed Joachim again. "I repeat," he insisted. "What's happening? Joachim?"

"Well, my friend, your lovely lady and I spent an exciting fifteen minutes together in a very small closet in the commandant's office." Joachim flashed a feeble grin. "If the circumstances had been different, it would have been quite an enjoyable experience."

Erich turned to Inge. "What the hell were you doing in Muller's office?" he growled. "You were supposed to stay in the hall and watch for trouble, nothing more."

"Two men came up the stairs, Inge said, her voice cracking. "I panicked and went inside to warn Joachim. It was too late for us to get away, so we hid in the closet."

"It was Mueller and Weiss," Erich said. "I rode in with Heinrich Wolfers. We arrived just as they were leaving the building. They stood outside and talked for several minutes, or I'd have been here sooner. I was terrified, though I felt better when Mueller and Weiss came out. I figured if you were in trouble, they'd still be inside trying to find out what you two were up to, or worse, calling the Gestapo. Thank God you're both safe, and you, Inge, have taken part in your last evening of sleuthing.

"But—"

"Don't start," Erich said.

"You two can argue about this later," said Joachim. "I suggest we get out of here as soon as possible." He paused. "Come to think of it, what brings you to Munich tonight? Weren't you staying in camp to work on Wolfers?"

"I had no choice. I've kept calling to let you know that Mueller and Weiss were returning to the office." He led Inge to a chair and turned back to Joachim, shooting him an angry look. "Where the hell were you? I tried at 4:30, but you'd already gone."

"I was doing my job," Joachim said irritably. "I went to the Hofbrauhaus. I figured it might look better if I had an afternoon appointment which necessitated my return in the evening to finish my work."

"Is that so?" Erich turned to Inge. "And you couldn't have stayed put at your aunt's house?"

Inge's anxiety gave way to displeasure at Erich's tone. "I do have a job," she said obstinately. "I can't be driving back and forth from Dachau to Munich without checking in with Herr Beck every once in a while. And you know I'm not a sitter. I have trouble staying in one place when I'm nervous."

"Well you both came close to giving me a full head of gray hair. I've been worried sick since four o'clock this afternoon, when Heinrich first told me about Mueller and Weiss's dinner meeting. I tried to find a way to come to town earlier, but I couldn't get a ride. I had to wait for him to return for Weiss and come in then."

Inge reached for Erich's hand. "Stop blaming Joachim," she said. "You know I'm a stubborn woman."

Erich rolled his eyes. "You don't need to remind me."

"Sure I do." Inge's smile instantly turned to a frown. "Unfortunately, the evening was trying and unproductive for all of us."

Erich smiled for the first time since entering the room. "Not entirely unproductive," he said. "I had a chance to talk to

Heinrich during the drive to Munich. He's eager to help me find the Jewish whore I keep raving about. I persuaded him to go through the camp files to see if Rosel Dollman is available for our entertainment."

"Why Rosel Dollman?" Inge asked. "Why not Friedrich?"

"I doubt the Gestapo would arrest Rosel Friedrich. She isn't a Mischling. Anyway if I mention the name Friedrich, it's possible that Heinrich will link you with the girl I want him to find. Same last name."

"In that case let's hope, if he manages to locate Rosel's file, there's no mention of the name Friedrich," Joachim said.

"Even if the last names are the same, I don't think Heinrich is astute enough to figure out the connection. While he's looking for information about Rosel, I intend to see what I can find out about him. When I was supposed to be finishing my work tonight I couldn't concentrate, so I got to thinking. As I told Inge, he's not popular with the other officers. He usually eats alone, and the men don't seem to appreciate it when he tries to join their discussions. It could be because he's the commandant's general flunky. It might be to my advantage to find out if that's the case. It could give me an idea about how far I can push him for information about Rosel. That's all I know, and I think we've all done as much as we can for one day."

"That's a good thing," Joachim said. "So now that all this unpleasantness is behind us, why don't we adjourn to the Hofbrauhaus for a little rest and relaxation?"

"Not this time," Inge said. "Erich's going to take me home. I'm sure my Aunt Sigrid is worried."

Joachim raised his eyebrows. "Are you trying to say that after fifteen minutes in a small closet with me, you still want to go home with him? Your close proximity to my sexy body has done nothing to change your mind?"

"I hate to hurt your feelings," Inge said. "But those were the most unpleasant fifteen minutes I've ever spent."

"What will it take to win you away?" Joachim said, feigning dejection. "Clearly my well-orchestrated plan failed miserably, even with the commandant's help."

Inge laughed. "I know I've said this once or twice before, but it bears repeating. You're incorrigible."

"I second that," Erich said. "Come on, Inge, let's get out of here. This building isn't the safest place to be at this moment."

"The sooner we leave, the better I'll feel." Inge opened the door and peaked out. "There's no one out there."

As Joachim switched off the light, he remembered the light in the commandant's office, and again, he chastised himself for not realizing there was trouble ahead. Suddenly beer and women at the Hofbrauhaus sounded even more appealing. He wanted to forget everything that had occurred over the past few hours.

# CHAPTER 23

"If your escapade had gone on much longer, we'd be shoveling our way out of here," Erich said as he held the car's passenger door open for Inge. He walked around to the driver's side and got behind the wheel. White flakes blanketed the front and back windows. "We're cut off from the world sitting here in this moving igloo," he said. "I can't even see the administration building and it's only eight-meters away."

"I wish the snow could block out the war, Dachau, the Gestapo—everything that's depressing and sinister," Inge said wistfully. "Wouldn't it be great if we could stay here locked away from reality forever?"

"Don't I wish?" Erich said. He took Inge's hand. "We haven't been outside long enough for your hands to be this cold. I don't think you've recovered from the scare in Mueller's office."

"I suppose I was stretching the truth a bit. When we were leaving, I half expected the guard at the door to take us into custody and turn us over to the Gestapo. They'd cart us to headquarters and use some horrible means of torture to force a confession out of us."

"Well at least you won't have to worry anymore. You've completed your one and only covert mission."

"I hardly think this is the time to decide what I will or won't be doing as we search for Rosel," Inge said stubbornly. "I admit, I don't relish the thought of hiding with Joachim in the closet only steps away from a man who, if he opened the door and found us—" She shuddered. "God, I don't even want to think about what would have happened to us. But you need to remember; this is still my fight. As I told you before, dangerous or not, I will be a part of any plan you and Joachim concoct."

"Why don't we talk about this if and when the need arises?"

"Erich—"

"A step at a time, remember? Shall we go see your aunt? I may have upset her when we talked earlier this evening. I told her I was at camp and didn't know who you were meeting tonight. I also said I'd try to come by this evening. It's late, and since neither of us is at the house, she's probably worried."

When the car was warm enough to drive, the windshield wipers did their job, opening their cozy igloo to the outside world. "So we're forced to face reality yet again," Inge said as he pulled away from the curb.

"We are, and I can't say I'm looking forward to the next hour or so. Sigrid's not going to be happy with either of us." He paused. "Maybe she won't ask where we've been."

"I can't believe you said that. Nothing gets by my aunt. Not only will she ask where I was, she'll also demand a full explanation, so be ready for anything. I can't remember a time when she let Rosel or me get away with anything. She could always tell if we were keeping something from her."

"I doubt she'll be happy with me when she realizes I okayed the escapade in SS Headquarters."

"That's putting it mildly. Sigrid's Article One—don't ever lie to me or try to deceive me. Believe me, that trumps Dachau's Article Eleven, and frankly, the consequences are just as daunting."

"Oh good. I can't wait," Erich said. "Maybe I'll drop you off and go back to Dachau. It might be safer and, I'm sure, a lot more pleasant."

"Forget it. You're going to stand beside me and experience the full extent of my aunt's wrath."

They had scarcely pulled up in front of the house when the front door opened. Though she couldn't see Sigrid's face, Inge saw the outline of her body against the light coming from the hallway. "God, it's worse than I thought," she said as she got out of the car. "We're going to be fighting our own world war in Sigrid's parlor."

"She's not happy is she?" Erich groaned.

"That's an understatement. See her hands on her hips? That's an 'I'm furious with you' stance." Inge reached over and pulled the keys out of the ignition. "Come on," she said. You promised to keep me out of danger. Now's the time to prove yourself."

"My image as a fearless member of the SS may be in jeopardy with this next suggestion, but I have a great idea."

"Unless it's how to make Sigrid feel better fast, I don't want to hear it."

"But it's a perfect solution to our problem."

"The only solution to *our* problem is to face the enemy head on."

"Would you listen? I could park around the corner. You can yell after you've finished telling your aunt about your exciting evening, and I'll come back to join you."

"No way," Inge declared. "Get out!"

"Even from out here, I can tell this isn't going to be pleasant."

Erich was right. Sigrid was clearly fuming. Not waiting for Inge and Erich to reach the door and without as much as a hello, the questions began to fly. "Why are you two together?" she said asked with fire in her eyes. "And, Inge, where have you been?" She turned to Erich. "When you called hours ago, you said Inge wasn't meeting you, yet here you are together. Were you lying to me? Couldn't one of you have taken a moment from whatever you were doing to call and let me know where you were; that you were alright? With things the way they are around here, did it cross your mind that I might be worried?"

"If you'll take a deep breath, step aside, and let us in, Aunt Sigrid, we'll tell you everything," Inge said calmly. "I'd much rather explained what happened in a warm house. I'm turning into a living snowman."

Inge's attempt at humor did little to placate her aunt. Sigrid took a deep breath and stepped aside. "Come in, both of you, and sit by the fire," she said sternly. "Erich, give me your coat. I'll make coffee and then—"

"We'll tell you everything," Inge said.

"You sure you want me to stick around?" Erich said as they stood by the fireplace waiting for Sigrid to join them.

"Stay where you are," Inge warned. "Sigrid's making coffee. She didn't offer to share her precious tea. This is definitely more dangerous than hiding in Muller's closet with Joachim, and you're not leaving me alone to deal with her. It's part of the deal."

"What deal?"

Inge didn't have time to answer. Sigrid came in with a tray containing three cups of coffee. She put it on the table in front of the couch and let Erich and Inge reach for their own cups. Without any pleasantries, she started again: "I asked you where you were, Inge. Now I demand an explanation. Normally I wouldn't pry into your business. You're an adult and your life's your own, but tonight's different. I know you were involved in something dangerous."

"Why would you think that, Aunt Sigrid?"

"Don't try to placate me. You know I have a sixth-sense when it comes to you. I always have. You may not be telling me an outright lie, but you're lying to me by omission."

Inge knew nothing short of full disclosure would satisfy her aunt. Sigrid would immediately know if she and Erich were hedging. She sighed and began. For the next fifteen minutes, Sigrid listened attentively as Inge explained what she and Joachim had tried to accomplish in Mueller's office. From time to time, Erich interrupted the narration, trying to make Sigrid believe that Inge had never been in danger; that he and Joachim had everything under control.

When they finished recounting the saga, Sigrid sat quietly. *The calm before the storm,* Inge mused as she watched her aunt nervously play with the edge of her apron. Appreciating that Sigrid had a great deal of information to process, Inge hoped, rather than expected, their explanation had been acceptable. When Sigrid looked up, it was clear the fight was far from over. She glared at her niece. "Inge," she said sternly, "did you know what you and Joachim planned to do before you left the house this afternoon?"

"I did, Aunt Sigrid. I didn't want you to worry, so I decided not to tell you about our plans. I couldn't have gone forward knowing you were sitting here scared to death. Anyway I expected the search would go more smoothly than it did. Had I been right, there wouldn't have been a need for you to know what Joachim and I had done."

"Inge's right, Sigrid," Erich said. "Commandant Mueller is a creature of habit. Once he leaves for the day he rarely returns to the office before nine o'clock the next morning."

"Rarely?" Sigrid said angrily. "You didn't say 'never.' Apparently you knew there was a chance the commandant could come back."

"There was always a chance, but I wouldn't have given my blessing to the project had I thought it would put Inge in harm's way. I mean I knew there was some risk, but—"

"I'll bet you didn't give more than a moment's considera-tion to what could have happened if Inge and Joachim had been discovered in the commandant's closet. I don't care how hard my stubborn niece tried to convince you she wouldn't be in any dan-ger, you had to know it wasn't true, and you should have found a way to stop her."

"I suppose—"

"Can you imagine how I'd feel if I learned the Gestapo was interrogating her? Most of the people who go into that building don't come out. I know what's going on. I have my sources."

"That wouldn't have happened, Sigrid. Maybe I didn't think this through, but it was merely an unfortunate coincidence that Commandant Mueller scheduled an evening meeting at headquarters."

Inge took Sigrid's hand. "What's important is the fiasco is over and we're fine. There's no need to worry anymore."

"Now, but what about next time?" Sigrid glared at Erich. "Will there be a next time, young man?"

"I assure you, Sigrid, if I have any say in the matter, Inge won't be involved in anything dangerous ever again."

"You may think you're correct in that regard, but I know this woman. Look at her face. Do you think she's listening to you? She's as stubborn and headstrong as I am. Without giving any thought to her safety, she'll do whatever she can to rescue Rosel."

"You're right," Erich said. "So let me say that in the future I'll do everything I can to keep Inge safe."

"And Inge, I want your word you'll leave the dangerous activ-ities to Erich and Joachim."

"I promise I won't get myself into a predicament like I did tonight."

"I won't accept a qualified promise. I need your absolute assurance—"

"Would you want me to lie, Aunt Sigrid? I can't guarantee I'll remain in the background while the men search for Rosel, but if it helps, I promise to listen to Erich."

"At least that's a beginning."

"Could we change the subject?" Inge said. "We all know where we stand on the matter and nothing more need be said. Tell me about your day, Aunt Sigrid."

It took a little while for Sigrid to relax, but she didn't mention the escapade again. Around eleven o'clock. Erich got up off the couch. "I think it's time for me to leave," he said. "Inge, you're yawning, and, Sigrid, you're struggling to keep your eyes open."

"Where will you go?" Inge asked. "Do you want me to drive you back to camp?"

"That wouldn't be wise. I've checked out for the night and there would be too many questions if I returned this late."

"What about the Wagner?" Inge said. "I could drop you there and then go back to Frau Heiden's."

"That's a tempting offer, but I promised Sigrid to take care of you, and she'd never forgive me if I let you drive in this terrible weather."

"You're right," Sigrid said. "You can stay on the couch in the parlor, Erich."

"I think it's best if I stay with Joachim, but I need to find him first. I imagine he's at the Hofbrauhaus."

"Will you join him for a beer?" Inge asked.

"Not if I can help it. I have to report to camp at nine-o'clock. I can't spend the whole night partying, and speaking of the office, would you drop me off at the camp in the morning?"

"She will, if you'll come to breakfast first," Sigrid said. "I can't send a man off to work on an empty stomach."

"I said you'd give your niece competition."

"What have the two of you been up to behind my back?" Inge teased, glad the evening was ending on a positive note and not the way it had begun.

"Let's say you'd be wise to stay on your toes." Erich put his arm around Sigrid's shoulders. "Your aunt's quite a woman."

"You'll get no argument from me in that regard."

"On that note, I'll retire for the night," said Sigrid. "Shall we say seven o'clock, Erich? That should give you plenty of time to eat and be at Dachau by nine."

"Seven it is. I'll see you in the morning, and thanks, Sigrid."

When she heard Sigrid's bedroom door close, Inge walked Erich to the door. "I wish you didn't have to leave," she said as she wrapped her arms around his neck.

"Are you sure we can't sneak into your room and—"

"It's tempting, but I'd hate to think what my modest, genteel aunt would say if she walked in on us."

"And I'm not willing to chance her displeasure again tonight. One ordeal like the one we just endured is unquestionably enough." He pulled Inge close. "Though standing here with you like this almost makes the risk worthwhile."

"I've been in enough perilous situations for one night. Muller's office and then Sigrid—"

"When you put it that way, how can I argue? I'll be on my way, though saying goodbye, when I know what pleasures await me, is sheer torture."

"For me too, though I don't show it like you do."

"No comment," Erich said. "I'll see you in the morning." He put on his coat and went to find Joachim.

---

Despite the hour and the dismal weather, the Schwemme was still full of revelers. Erich looked toward the back of the room where Joachim usually sat. As he figured, his friend was nestled amid a bevy of beauties. Stopping to speak with several friends along the way, Erich made his way through the throng. Joachim looked surprised when he turned around and saw who was standing behind him. "What brings you here, old buddy?" he said. "You're the last person I expected to see tonight."

"Decorum only, believe me. I didn't think Sigrid would approve of a man sleeping in her niece's bedroom. So, my friend, you have a roommate, though I know I'm not the person you'd like to take home with you."

Joachim glanced from girl to girl and then back at Erich. "Clearly you're cramping my style," he said. "But I suppose I can put up with your company for one night. Care to join the ladies and me for a few beers before we go?"

"No thanks. I hate to drag you away from such charming company, but I have an early appointment, and it's already late."

Joachim feigned shock. "Could it be you're getting old beyond your years? The night's still young, and these ladies will be miserable if we leave them unsatisfied."

"Joachim—"

"Okay, okay." He turned to the woman on his right. "It seems duty and friendship calls me away, my lovely, but don't despair. We'll have other nights." He leaned over and kissed her before getting up and following Erich toward the door.

"My God!" Erich said incredulously, as they walked through Marienplatz. "Do these women actually fall for that garbage?"

"The approach hasn't failed me yet, though lately I've given a great deal of thought to giving up this wild bachelor life. I'd do it in a minute if I could find a lady like Inge."

"As if I believed you, though I'm glad you approve. I imagine Inge would be pleased too, if she believed you any more than I do."

"It's a shame you both have so little faith in me."

Erich gave Joachim a friendly slap on the back. "Oh, we have faith, but sometimes it's difficult to separate the bull from the truth."

The snow was still falling and a brisk wind was blowing directly toward them as the men walked toward Joachim's apartment on Ledererstrasse. "If this is any indication, it's going to be a hard winter," Erich said as he exhaled and saw his frosty breath in the night air.

"Then I guess we'll have to spend more time indoors. Let me tell you from experience, an eiderdown-covered bed can be a hot place on a frigid night."

"I hate to admit I agree with you."

They were covered with snow when they pushed through the door into Joachim's building and climbed the steep stairs to Joachim's fourth-floor apartment. "You have to be in shape to make this trek," Erich said when they finally reached the top.

"Oh, I'm in shape, old buddy. I do my nightly exercises. Your being here is keeping me from my strict regimen."

"I'm sure you'll make it through one night. Besides I need to exercise your brain, and it won't be easy."

"Your insults don't affect me in the slightest. My brain is as well-tuned as my body."

"I'm not touching that one. Do you think we could discuss something important instead of talking about your favorite topic?"

Joachim grinned. "I can't promise, but I'll try," he said as he unlocked the door. Erich stepped in and looked around the comfortable, homey room. He walked to the desk and picked up a picture of him and Joachim taken at Unser Traum. *Those were the good days*, he reflected as he stared at the young boys smiling back at him from the frame. He put the photo down and looked back at the bed with its thick eiderdown comforter and pillows piled high against the headboard. A pillow-covered couch sat against the wall beside a five-drawer dresser that displayed mementos of Joachim's active social life as well as his collection of beer steins. "The couch will do," he said as hung his coat and hat on the rack by the door.

"It's been a long day," Joachim said. "Would you like to take a shower before we talk?"

"Think the hot water could get rid of my tension?"

"In your case cold might be better and that's a good thing, because there's no hot water in this building. In fact the shower's more a trickle than a torrent."

"Under the circumstances, any kind of shower will be welcome so, if you'll stop grinning and find a towel and robe for me—"

Joachim saluted. "Right away, Hauptsturmfuhrer."

The shower *was* bad, but when he returned to Joachim's room, Erich felt more refreshed and ready for a serious conversation. During the next hour, the two men strategized. Erich would press Heinrich for information, and, if necessary, Joachim would attempt to access Mueller's files, this time without Inge. They agreed to do whatever they could to keep her out of harm's-way, even if it meant hiding their activities from her. "I'm beginning to think we're fools for taking on this project in the first place," Joachim said. "What will we do if you find Rosel at Ravensbruck? Obviously you can't make your escape from there or from Berlin, and if we get her to Dachau, how do you get away from the camp? There are too many ifs."

"Of course you're right, but you know I can't turn back. You, on the other hand, can back out any time. You're under no obligation to help Inge and me."

"I suppose I'm a glutton for punishment," Joachim said. "In the last few days I've grown rather fond of your fair lady, and I'd like to help find her friend, not to mention that, as usual, you need me. Besides, I've been sitting behind a desk for too long. I need some excitement. So let's talk specifics."

"I have a few ideas, but as I've told Inge more than once, we have to take this one step at a time. Tomorrow I'll start working on Heinrich. In the meantime you keep asking questions, and, if the opportunity presents itself, try to get into Mueller's files, but be careful. We definitely don't need a repeat of tonight's fiasco. When and if we discover something definite, we'll discuss the next step."

"Sounds good to me. I never was one to plan too far into the future. Live and enjoy the moment. That's my philosophy."

"Well this particular moment calls for sleep. It's after two o'clock and I have to be at Sigrid's at seven. So set the alarm, will you?"

Joachim groaned. "You certainly keep boring hours. If this were a normal night, I'd barely be getting hot."

"I'm sure that's true, but since you're with your uninspiring friend, set the alarm and let's get some sleep."

Joachim reluctantly complied, and Erich settled down on the couch. His last thoughts before falling to sleep were about Inge and how to keep the incredibly stubborn woman safe.

----

The alarm sounded like someone was pounding a gong close to Erich's ear. He looked at the clock. It was six o'clock but it seemed that only minutes had passed since he shut his eyes. He waited for Joachim to push the button that would turn off the annoying sound. When the sleeping man made no move to do so,

Erich reluctantly threw back his blanket and got up to end the screeching himself.

He picked up his still-damp towel and Joachim's razor and headed to the bathroom. When he returned twenty-minutes later, Joachim was still lying in the same position. Erich dressed, left a note reminding his friend to meet him and Inge at the Wagner at seven, reset the alarm, and left for breakfast with Inge and Sigrid.

The driving wind had temporarily died down. As he walked toward Sigrid's, Erich looked up at the dark, foreboding sky. Though the snow had stopped falling, piles of white on the uncleared sidewalk hindered his progress. By the time he reached Odeonsplatz a little before seven, he was thoroughly chilled. Stomping his feet on the porch to rid his boots of excess snow, he knocked.

A warm blast of air greeted him when Sigrid opened the door. "Come in. Come in," she said as she motioned him inside. "You must be freezing. Take off your coat and go warm yourself by the fire."

Erich crossed the parlor to the mantle and picked up a picture of Rosel. "We're doing everything possible to find you," he whispered as Sigrid entered the room.

"Did you say something?" she asked.

"I was wondering why the other woman in my life isn't here to greet me."

"She'll join us soon. Be patient, though I've never known a man in love to be patient about anything."

"A man in love, am I? That's a sage observation."

"I'm not easily fooled. You love my niece?"

"You're right."

"And you want to protect her?"

"That goes without saying."

"Well I'm glad to hear that, because last night when you and Inge told me about your ridiculous scheme to go through the commandant's files, I wasn't so sure."

"Sigrid—"

"Let me finish. I had trouble falling asleep. As I tossed and turned, I thought about what you're risking for our family. You're putting your career and perhaps your life on the line for people you hardly know. I realize that in my anger and frustration I haven't thanked you properly. I'm sure Inge told you how much both my girls mean to me."

"You don't need to thank me, Sigrid. I'll do everything possible to find Rosel, and if it makes you feel any better, I learned my lesson last night. If I have any say in the matter, Inge won't be put in harm's way ever again."

"Did I hear my name?" Inge said as she entered the room. "Morning, Hauptsturmfuhrer. I hope you slept well."

"Joachim's couch was very comfortable."

"That's good. So what were you and my aunt talking about?"

"Erich wanted to know where you were," Sigrid said. "It seems I'm not good enough for him."

"Not so, Sigrid. I'm greedy. If I can have two gorgeous women around, why settle for just one?"

Sigrid threw her hands in the air. "I give up. I'll go make myself useful and finish cooking breakfast." She bustled out of the room, humming as she went.

Inge put her arms around Erich's neck. "How was your night?" she asked.

"Except for missing you, it was fine, though I don't think Joachim was happy about being dragged away from his bevy of beauties at the Hofbrauhaus. We went back to his place and talked before I forced him to go to bed."

"Did you come to any conclusions?"

"Only that we'll make definite plans as we go along."

"Where do I fit in?"

"Inge, what did I just say? We don't even know where Rosel's being held, or if the SS took her."

"But I will be able to help when you find her."

"We'll decide if and when the need arises."

Inge frowned. "It would be unwise for you to think about leaving me out," she said. "In fact it would be foolish. Of course I'd have a better chance to find Rosel if we work together, but if you won't keep me informed, I'll look for her by myself."

"And how are you going to do that? If I recall, you were at a dead end before you met me."

Inge raised an eyebrow. "My aren't we arrogant?" she said huffily. "Know this, Hauptsturmfuhrer. I have no idea how I'll proceed, but with or without you, I *will* find Rosel."

Eric quickly realized how his comment must have sounded. "Inge, this isn't worth arguing about," he said. "Until I find out something definite from Heinrich, we can't consider our next move."

When Inge spoke her anger had abated to some extent, though there was still a hint of irritation in her voice. "I suppose I have no choice but to accept that for now," she said. "But I'm serving notice. I expect to be a part of whatever you and Joachim decide to do."

"You've made that perfectly clear, so if you're finished reminding me, how about feeding a hungry man?"

"By all means, we can't let you starve."

Inge's sarcasm wasn't lost on Erich as he followed her to the kitchen. During breakfast her irritation persisted. Though she tried, Sigrid couldn't make her niece relax, so all three were relieved when it was time for Inge to drive Erich to camp. "Will you two be coming back to town soon?" she asked as she walked them to the door.

"As soon as we can," Inge said. "I'll be in touch, Aunt Sigrid."

"I hope so, darling. Please find a way to deal with whatever it is that's bothering you."

To avoid the snowdrifts making the road slick and hazardous, Inge concentrated on driving. She didn't feel much like making small talk anyway, and the topic she wanted to discuss was off limits, at least for the time being. As she drove, concern that Erich might try to keep information from her was foremost on her mind. On one hand she was afraid he'd exclude her, and on the other hand, she was glad he wanted to protect her. She couldn't reconcile the paradox.

When they reached the Jourhaus gates, Erich turned to face her. "I realize you're angry with me, Inge," he said. "But for no reason. I'm not leaving you out."

"Maybe not now, but I can't be sure you'll include me in your future plans."

"You don't trust me."

"I don't know, but in case you have thoughts of going ahead without me, I'm telling you one more time, I won't be put off."

"Then if there's nothing I can say to make you drop the attitude, I'll see you tonight. Maybe you'll be more reasonable by then. Have a good day."

"You too," Inge said with little enthusiasm.

Erich got out of the car, presented his papers to the guard at the gate, and, without looking back, entered the camp.

# CHAPTER 24

The tests continued throughout the morning. All twelve subjects died. When Erich was at a point where he didn't think he could stand to watch anymore suffering and death, Rascher announced a lunch break. *Finally a chance to get out of this chamber of death and work on Heinrich*, he thought as he crossed Roll Call Square.

Heinrich wasn't in the dining room. Erich had missed another opportunity to find out about the fate of the women who were originally transported to Dachau. So far the day had been a total disaster. Though the images of dying prisoners played like a movie in his mind, he managed to force down the food. *How quickly we tend to our own needs and forget the plight of others,* he reflected as he walked back through the empty square to the office.

Unfortunately the afternoon followed the morning blueprint. Erich completed the previous day's reports, but he'd only begun to transfer the data from the morning tests when Rascher came up behind him and interrupted his concentration. "Hauptsturmfuhrer, if you have nothing important scheduled for the evening I would like for you to accompany me to my office in the Fuhrerbau. When we're finished with our business, my driver will bring you back to camp. It's unusually cold for this time of year, so after consulting with Reichsfuhrer Himmler and Reichsmarshall Goring, I've decided to conduct the freezing experiments in the compound at the same time we're completing the high-flight tests in the Skyride Machine."

Rascher's news paradoxically excited and yet bothered Erich. Beginning the freezing tests would bring them one step closer to phase three, but Heinrich hadn't gone through Weiss's files to find out if Rosel was at Ravensbruck, nor had he and Joachim made any tentative plans in case she was being held there. *So much for taking this a step at a time,* he reflected. As Rascher cleared his throat, Erich realized his boss was waiting for a response. Trying to recover from his reflections, he spoke without thinking. "I realize the weather's cooperating, Herr Doctor, but I'm not sure Erna and I will be able to stay ahead of the enormous amount of paperwork necessary to report accurately on the test results if we're running two and perhaps three tests simultaneously."

Rascher's scowl didn't leave Erich in doubt about how he felt, and his tone mirrored his expression. "Schedules can be modified, Hauptsturmfuhrer," he said gruffly. "Berlin wants results now. It's cold enough to begin the tests in the compound, and we'll do so. Do I make myself clear?"

"Perfectly, Herr Doctor."

"Good. I assume you'll find a way to finish the reports on schedule?"

"I will."

"I'm glad to hear it. For a moment I wasn't sure I had the right man working for me."

"I apologize for giving you that impression," Erich said. "Of course I'll be ready to begin when you feel it's time."

"Excellent. After we've finished half of the freezing tests, we'll send for the women from Ravensbruck and begin phase three, the warming experiments."

"How soon do you expect we'll be able to begin the third phrase?" Erich asked, hoping to be given enough information to begin formulating tentative plans.

Rascher's vague response didn't help. "I have no idea," he said. "It depends on whether the cold weather persists and how far you get with the report-writing. We'll have to see, but my driver is waiting. Shall we continue our discussion at my office?"

Erich tried to come up with an excuse to phone Joachim before he and Rascher left for the evening. He was concerned about what Inge would think if he didn't show up at the hotel and worried she'd begin to search for information about Rosel on her own. His disappointment intensified when he thought about what he'd hoped to accomplish before going to the Wagner. Heinrich was primed and ready to help him find out where Rosel was being detained. Would he be as interested another day?

Rascher's words jarred him back to the moment at hand. "I'm waiting, Hauptsturmfuhrer."

Erich gave up all hope of contacting Joachim, put on his coat, and followed Rascher out the door.

On her ride to Frau Heiden's, Inge thought about her disagreement with Erich. She'd jumped to conclusions and chastised him before he'd actually done anything to shut her out. He was right. She was getting ahead of herself, and she was eager to make things right between them. Hoping to talk with him before he left for the Wagner, she stayed in her apartment waiting for the phone to ring. When he didn't call, she was disappointed with herself for sitting around.

As the long, tedious day finally came to an end, she showered and dressed. At 6:45 she checked her appearance one last time and left for the Wagner. Joachim was waiting just inside the lobby entrance. "Frankly, I'm surprised to see you come through the front door, fair lady," he said, smiling.

"You thought I'd be upstairs with Erich. Not this time. He's not with you?"

Though Joachim frowned, there was a twinkle in his eye as he spoke: "Always Erich," he said. "Apparently I'm not good enough for you?"

"Will you be serious, Joachim?"

"There's that horrible word yet again. I haven't seen him, but then it's not quite seven o'clock."

"But he's always early."

"Ah yes, I recall you two had a pre-meeting rendezvous the other night. That's why I'm surprised you're not together now."

Inge ignored Joachim's comment. "There's something wrong, Joachim," she said. "I feel it. Erich usually catches a ride to town with Fraulein Hambro, and she leaves camp by 4:30. He should have been here hours ago."

"He didn't ask you to pick him up or want you to meet him early?"

"No to both questions."

"He said he'd meet us here at seven. Maybe he checked into a room and fell asleep. Maybe he left a message. I'll check at the desk."

Inge watched Joachim briefly converse with the clerk. He was frowning when he returned. "Erich hasn't checked in and there are no messages for either of us, but that's no reason to jump to conclusions. He could have been held up for any number of reasons. Maybe the doctor asked him to work late. I'm sure he would have left word if he could."

As the two waited, Inge kept checking the time. At 8:15, her anxiety got the best of her. "Where could he be, Joachim?" she asked anxiously. "This isn't like him. Did you tell the clerk at the desk to let you know if he calls?"

"I did, but I'm sure Erich's okay. If the doctor isn't keeping him, maybe Obersturmfuhrer Wolfers asked him to help go through Commandant Weiss's files. That would be a valid reason to remain in camp."

"But he could have called from the office."

"Not if Erna was still there. Inge, you've got to stop speculating."

"There's something I haven't told you," Inge said sheepishly. "And it might change your mind. Erich and I had an argument this morning. I was stubborn and unreasonable. Maybe that's why he isn't here."

"I doubt it." Joachim thought for a moment. "How serious was the disagreement?"

"Let's just say we didn't part on good terms. Erich wanted me to promise I wouldn't do anything that would put me in danger, and, of course, I was angry and refused to tell him what he wanted to hear. I even threatened to look for Rosel on my own if the two of you try to do anything without including me."

"I can't understand why you'd be angry," Joachim said. "Erich's only trying to protect you. Our escapade at headquarters last night gave him quite a scare. We know too well the methods the Gestapo uses to loosen a person's tongue. If you and I were discovered in Mueller's office, we wouldn't be sitting here right now."

"I know that, but—"

"If it makes you feel any better, there's no way Erich would stand us up because of an inconsequential argument. If anything, he'd want to make things right between you."

"Then why isn't he here, and what happens now?"

"You go back to your apartment and stand by in case he tries to reach you. In the meantime, I'll see what I can find out, and don't worry about your argument, fair lady. Erich knows how lucky he is to have you." Joachim's eyes twinkled. "But I want to go on record. I'm always available if he doesn't appreciate your finer qualities."

"How comforting," Inge said sarcastically. "I apologize," she quickly said. "I was rude when you were just trying to make me feel better."

"No problem. We're both concerned. You go to Frau Heiden's and I'll head out to look for Erich."

---

The meeting in Munich was useless. Beyond what he'd discussed in Berlin and in the office, Rascher offered no new information. He reviewed general information about phase two, but didn't elaborate on the specifics. The highlight of the evening came when he mentioned the need to make preliminary plans for selecting suitable candidates to be used in the experiments. Erich tried to plant the seeds for a trip to Ravensbruck, suggesting they needed to choose women who best represented those the Luftwaffe would use if the test results warranted this type of resuscitation, women with a little flesh on their bones.

Throughout the evening Erich fought his impulse to look at the clock. At 9:45 Rascher finally brought the useless session to an end. In the time they spent together, they'd come to only one conclusion, and that had been decided before the trip to Munich. The second phase of the experiments would begin in two days and would run in conjunction with the high-flight tests.

When Rascher called for his driver, Erich realized there was no way he could stop at the Wagner, nor could he remain in Munich and try to contact Inge or Joachim. After a silent drive to the camp, he presented his papers at the Jourhaus gates, but instead of going upstairs to his room, he raced across the empty compound to Block Five. He flashed his papers at the guard, went inside, and, without removing his coat and hat, gave the operator Frau Heiden's number. "Damn," he said when he heard a busy signal. He hung up and rifled through papers on his desk. Five minutes later he tried the number again. The line was still busy. He waited another ten minutes and called once more, to no avail. Frustrated, he left the office and went to his room to catch a few hours of much-needed sleep.

---

When Inge was out of sight, Joachim went back into the hotel and phoned the camp from the public phone in the lobby. Grumbling that he was certain no one would be working at such a late hour, the operator reluctantly rang the office. When there was no answer, he brusquely informed Joachim there was no way to reach an officer in the barracks, but he could leave a message that would be delivered first thing in the morning.

Declining the offer, Joachim drove to the camp. After arguing with the guard, who adamantly refused to let him in, he reluctantly returned to the hotel. Thinking Erich might have registered while he was away, he checked with the desk clerk again. There was still no message for either him or Inge. He was aware his news or lack thereof would be upsetting to Inge, but he'd promised to keep her informed. Using the lobby phone, he dialed Frau Heiden's number.

"Heil Hitler. Joachim, is that you?" Inge said after half a ring.

"It is, fair lady. Have you been standing by the phone breathlessly waiting to hear my voice?"

"Of course, I didn't want to miss your call," she said. "I was afraid you'd given up. I think everyone in the apartment house needed the phone tonight. "Were you able to locate our friend?"

"No luck, fair lady. No one answered when I called the office, so I drove over to try to see him in person. I couldn't get past the big guys at gates. Apparently I don't have the appropriate papers."

"That's not a surprise. I couldn't get in and I have orders from Berlin. Did you find out anything?"

"Nothing. There's not much we can do tonight. I'll try to reach our friend in the morning. I'll call you if and when I get hold of him. There's not a phone in my apartment house, so I'll go back to my office and sleep at my desk. If you hear anything, call me there."

As Joachim spoke, Inge heard footsteps coming down the hall. Hoping it was Erich she turned around. She was disappointed to see another of Frau Heiden's tenants who was obviously waiting for her to finish talking. Because of the intruder, she cut the conversation short. "Thank you for your help," she said. "I'll talk with you tomorrow."

Fearing that Erich was in danger, Joachim left for Munich to wait for news.

# CHAPTER 25

Hoping to get to the office before Erna arrived, Erich set his alarm for 7:00 a.m. He hadn't slept well, his concern for Inge's feelings uppermost in his mind. As he passed through the square, the roll call was beginning. He shivered, pulled his heavy coat around him more tightly, and as usual, pitied the men who had to stand still in the freezing drizzle.

When he approached the office door, the night guard wasn't on duty. *Damn,* he thought as he opened the door. *Erna's already here.* His efficient secretary was sitting at her desk pouring over test results. "You're in early," he said as he removed his hat and coat.

"Since we're beginning phase two of the tests tomorrow, I have a great deal of work to do, Hauptsturmfuhrer." Erna looked at the clock. "You're early too. Is there a problem?"

"Nothing I know of. I came in to finish the report I was working on before I left for Munich with the doctor last evening." He opened one of the files on his desk and began to makes notes, but he couldn't concentrate. He knew Inge would be concerned, upset or both. He waited for Erna to take a break so he could call, but after thirty-minutes, she made no move to go, so he put his papers aside. "I'm going to breakfast, Fraulein," he said. "May I bring you something?"

Erna answered without looking up. "No thank you, Hauptsturmfuhrer. I ate before I came to camp."

Roll call had ended, apparently with no incidents, so Erich quickly crossed the square and entered the dining hall. Heinrich was sitting alone at a table near the back. Erich joined him and waited for the Jewish girl to bring coffee. "You weren't here for dinner last night," Heinrich said. "I was hoping we could get some information on the Jewish whore you've been raving about."

"I intended to be here, but I had a previously unscheduled meeting in Munich with Doctor Rascher."

Heinrich leaned in and whispered: "When you didn't show, I looked for information on my own."

Erich took a sip of coffee to conceal his anxiety. One way or another, he was about to learn something about Rosel. "Did you find out anything?" he asked hesitantly.

"I did, but I don't think you'll be happy. Unless you gave me the wrong name, I have bad news."

Wondering how he'd break the news to Inge and Sigrid, Erich waited to hear Heinrich say that Rosel was dead. "Tell me what you know," he said, trying not to mirror the concern he was feeling.

"Patience, my friend. Patience," said Heinrich.

Not wanting to seem too eager, Erich took another sip of coffee and waited. "So," Heinrich whispered, "I came in early this morning to go through Weiss's files."

"You weren't afraid of being discovered?"

"It wouldn't have mattered," Heinrich said smugly. "I have total access to the office. My initial purpose for being in the commandant's office this morning was to look for information on one of our guards who was recently accused of being too easy on the prisoners. When I found what I needed to know, I decided to look through the folders containing information about Jewish women who pass through Dachau."

Erich shook his head. *How stupid could I be,* he thought as he finally understood why the other men shunned Heinrich. He was

Weiss's informer as well as his flunky, and they all knew it. Erich was disgusted. In his eyes Heinrich's actions were more offensive than that of his often-brutal fellow officers. He wasn't killing so-called 'enemies of the Reich'; he was betraying his own. Erich was tempted to get up, walk away, and have nothing more to do with the disgusting snitch, but after Joachim and Inge's failure in Mueller's office, Heinrich was his only hope, and the man just said he had information. "Are you going to tell me what you learned?" he said. "Did you find the woman?"

"I did. Your Jewish whore is a Mischling, which means she was transported to Ravensbruck."

Erich knew he was risking a great deal by continuing to question, yet it was a chance he had to take. "Were her records kept up to date after she left Dachau?" she asked.

"I wouldn't know," Heinrich said. "The file said 'transported to Ravensbruck, July 14, 1942.' When she left here, the bitch became the responsibility of the Ravensbruck staff. But don't despair, my friend. We wouldn't be able to do much with her if she was standing in front of us begging to be raped. We haven't received final orders from Berlin regarding the Mischlinge."

Erich wanted to point out that Heinrich was not his friend, but he remained silent. He gulped down the rest of his coffee and got up to leave. "What no breakfast today?" Heinrich asked.

Erich shook his head. "No time. I have to get back to the office."

He put on his coat and was heading for the door when Heinrich called after him. "Will you be here for lunch? Maybe we could talk about finding another woman who's as appealing as your little Mischling."

"Yeah, sure," Erich called over his shoulder. Heinrich Wolfers had served his purpose. Erich would never join the snitch for a meal again. He had confirmed what he and Joachim already assumed. Now they just had to figure out a way to get Rosel out of Ravensbruck, bring her back to Dachau, and get her to safety. As he reached the door, Erich laughed. "Just," he whispered.

---

At seven o'clock, Inge shut off the blaring alarm, and pulled the covers over her head. She lay in bed thinking about the day ahead. She wasn't sure what she was going to do, but she knew she couldn't spend her time waiting for the phone to ring. She got up, dressed, and left for Munich. When she walked into the office, Beck had barely finished his briefing with Goebbels's representative "What's the news for today?" she asked, hoping to find out why her boss seemed so agitated.

"It's crazy around here," Beck said as he rifled through the papers on his desk. "Surely you remember what's happening tomorrow."

Inge looked at the calendar on the wall. "Oh Lord," she said. "Tomorrow's the holy day. I've been so involved with the Dachau story, the date slipped my mind. I can't believe next year will mark the twentieth anniversary of the Beer Hall Putsch. Time flies, doesn't it?"

Beck leaned closer to Inge and whispered: "If Hitler is still in power twelve months from now, we'll be celebrating."

"It's that bad?"

"Apparently so much so that the Fuhrer is skipping the event altogether." Beck's voice dripped with sarcasm. "He has pressing problems that will keep him in Berlin, and that's my dilemma. I have no idea who'll show up for the ceremony, and I have to come up with an explanation for why the party leaders won't be attending."

"I don't envy you. If Hitler isn't here—"

"Our readers look at what's occurring all around them and put two and two together."

"And you're the one who'll have to make them think that, despite the Fuhrer's absence, the war is going well. From the look on your face when the briefing ended, I assume the news wasn't too encouraging."

"You mean you could tell? I'm running out of ways to make the information we're given sound upbeat."

"You know that old saying, 'two heads are better than one.' Maybe I can help." Inge sat down opposite Beck. "Tell me about the briefing."

"It would take at least ten heads working overtime to make this news sound positive, but here goes." Beck looked at his notes. "The meeting focused on three subjects. First the Americans and British have landed on the coast of Northwest Africa. If that's not bad enough, the Soviets are staging a major counter-offensive at Stalingrad. Any idea how we present that information in a positive light?"

"Not off the top of my head. What's number three?"

"Actually, the third topic might interest you. There's a renewed push to move the Jews to Auschwitz."

"All of the Jews in Germany? Even the women being detained at Ravensbruck?"

Beck looked puzzled. "Yes," he said. "All the Jews in Germany as well as in the annexed countries, but why the interest in Ravensbruck?"

"No particular reason," Inge said, realizing she had to tread carefully. "Ravensbruck came to mind because I heard rumors of experiments being conducted there. I wondered if the directive included women as well as men."

"I don't know for sure, but I assume it covers all the Jews."

"Were you told when the transfers would begin?"

"Sometime in January." Beck looked at his notes. "The tentative date is January 20th. If those experiments you're currently writing about are finished, maybe you'd like to cover the transfer."

"I'd welcome the assignment." Inge said. "But who knows if I'll ever finish the Dachau article."

Beck looked at her quizzically. "I don't understand," he said.

"I have an outline, but that's as far as I've gotten. I'm surprised you're not irritated with me. I haven't produced anything substantial after all these weeks. My excuse is I've had little or no cooperation from anyone at the camp. Hauptsturmfuhrer Erich Riedl gave me a few preliminary test results, but for the most part, even that information is vague, and I can't get through the Jourhaus gates to investigate on my own."

"What do you mean you can't get through the gates?" Beck said incredulously. "You have your papers and the go-ahead from Berlin."

"That's true, but I quickly learned that, regardless of papers, the camp commandant has the final say about who is given access to the facility. Apparently Commandant Weiss has no intention of admitting me. This is my chance to do some worthwhile reporting, and I'm being thwarted at every level."

"Not every level, Inge," Beck said angrily. He picked up the telephone. "Connect me with Gauleiter Goebbels," he ordered.

As the operator on the other end put the call through, Beck put his hand over the mouthpiece of the telephone and turned to Inge. "Right to the top if you want action."

Inge only heard one side of the conversation, and after the initial discussion of the problem Inge was facing, Beck did more listening than speaking. When the conversation was over, he hung up and sighed. She wasn't sure how to interpret his response. "Any luck?" she asked tentatively.

"You'll be admitted to camp after noon today, and every afternoon between noon and four o'clock. That's the best I could do. Goebbels was furious that the SS treated one of his people so badly. While I was on hold, he contacted Reichsfuhrer Himmler. You'll have no further difficulties as long as you remain within the timeframe I just mentioned."

*How ironic,* Inge mused. *Beck thinks it's going to be smooth sailing for me from now on. Little does he know my problems are just beginning.* "Thank you." She stood. "Since you've managed to work miracles on my behalf, I should get to work and write this article."

# CHAPTER 26

There was only a minimum amount of time between the morning tests. Because both Rascher and Erna remained in the office during the breaks, Erich couldn't call either Joachim or Inge. The same held true during the lunch hour. Erna ordered in so no time would be wasted. While they ate, Rascher confirmed Erich's role in the next phase. He would write the reports for Berlin, though he'd be expected to observe the tests the first few nights to be sure he understood what he'd be writing about.

After the scharfuhrer cleared away the lunch plates, Erich settled in at his desk. He was deeply engrossed with testing statistics when, at 2:45, the phone on his desk rang. "Heil Hitler," he answered, hoping it was Inge.

"Heil Hitler," Joachim said with none of his usual cheerfulness. "You're a difficult man to reach."

"Work keeps me busy," Erich said. "How can I help you, Obersturmfuhrer?"

"I was hoping you could meet me in Dachau tonight, Hauptsturmfuhrer. I need to speak with you about the supply problem you left for me to solve."

"You're having difficulties?"

"Yes, and the secretary assisting me with the work on the project has numerous questions. She can't figure out what you were thinking."

"I'm sorry she's confused. Are you facing a deadline?"

"We are. Berlin is screaming for the final report."

"If I can get a ride to camp, I'll meet you this evening."

Erich put his hand over the receiver and turned to Erna. "Could you drop me at the Wagner on your way home this evening, Fraulein? I need to meet with the officer who inherited my supply project when I came here." He glanced at Rascher. That is unless you need me here, Herr Doctor."

"We won't be conducting any additional experiments this evening," Rascher said. "And I'm aware that Berlin is having difficulties getting supplies to the Eastern Front, so please feel free to go."

"In that case, with the doctor's permission, I'll be glad to drive you to town," Erna said. "I'll take my work home with me."

Erich took his hand off the receiver. "This evening will work for me, Obersturmfuhrer. Shall we say six o'clock?"

"Six it is. I'll be bringing my secretary. She has had a terrible headache for the past twenty-four hours, but I'm sure she'll rally when she hears we're getting together."

"I'll do what I can to help her figure things out. Please thank her for agreeing to accompany you. Hopefully our discussion will ease her concerns."

"Speaking with you should ease both our minds. I'll phone her right away and see you this evening."

Relieved, Erich hung up and went back to work.

---

Eager to ease Inge's mind, Joachim dialed Frau Heiden's number. "Damn," he whispered when the landlady said Inge hadn't returned from Munich. He left a message about dinner, hung up, and dialed the *Völkischer Beobachter* office. His frustration escalated when Werner said Inge had left for Dachau. *I hope he meant the town,* Joachim thought, but he knew the stubborn woman was headed for the camp to find Erich.

---

After leaving the office, Inge stopped by the administration building to speak with Joachim. When he wasn't in, she left a note asking him to call as soon as he returned. With time to kill, she went to see her aunt, but Sigrid too was out. She put several more logs on the fire and lay down to take a short nap.

In what seemed like only minutes, she felt a gentle hand on her shoulder. She woke to see her smiling aunt carrying a bag of groceries. "This is a pleasant surprise, darling," Sigrid said. "Had I known you were coming to town, I would have changed my plans and been here to greet you."

"I came to Munich to see Herr Beck and thought I'd stop by for a short visit. When you were out, I lay down. I feel like I've slept for hours. I have to leave for Dachau by one o'clock."

Sigrid looked at the clock. "Then you're very late," she said. "It's almost three."

Inge jumped off the couch. "Oh my God," she said frantically. "I can't believe I slept this long. I'd love to stay and talk, Aunt Sigrid, but I'm so late. If I don't get going, everyone in the office will be gone for the day."

"What office?"

"We'll talk when I have more time. Bottom line I'll be working in the camp every day from noon to four, but before you say anything, I'll only be going to the testing office. There's nothing dangerous about that."

"Can't you take a minute and tell me what you plan to do?"

"I wish I could, but there's no time. I have to catch Erich before he leaves." She kissed her protesting aunt and raced to the car.

Snow had fallen continually throughout the day leaving the roads icy and dangerous. When Inge finally reached the Jourhaus gates, it was 3:40, twenty minutes before she'd have to turn around and leave. The same guard stopped her again, but this time, after a brief discussion with the commandant's secretary, he cleared her for admission. "Please park to the right of the gate and wait," he said more politely than before. "Someone will arrive shortly to take you to the office."

Inge drove to the place the guard indicated, turned off the engine, and got out to wait for her ride. Moments later Heinrich pulled up to the gates in a staff car. When he introduced himself, Inge recognized the name and realized she was riding with unwitting ally. "I'll drive you to Block Five, Fraulein," he said. "Do you have an appointment with Doctor Rascher?"

"Actually I don't, Obersturmfuhrer," Inge said. "I hoped to arrive near the end of the day so I wouldn't disturb the doctor's work anymore than necessary."

Little else was said as they crossed the empty square and went up the tree-lined road toward Block Five. Heinrich pulled the car up to the office, leaped from the driver's seat, and opened Inge's door. "Follow me, Fraulein," he said.

Focusing intently on his work, Erich didn't look up when Inge entered. "Hauptsturmfuhrer Riedl and Fraulein Hambro, Fraulein Friedrich is here to see you," Heinrich announced.

If Erich was upset, he didn't show it. He rose and extended his hand. "Fraulein it's good to see you again," he said. "I don't believe you've met my secretary, Fraulein Hambro."

Smiling, Inge shook hands with Erna. "Fraulein, it's nice to meet you," she said.

"What brings you here so near to the end of the day, Fraulein?" Erich asked.

"I was given clearance from Gauleiter Goebbels and Reichsmarshall Goring, so I'll be here between noon and four o'clock every day, Hauptsturmfuhrer. I'm behind schedule, and my editor, Herr Beck, is eager for me to finish so I can begin a new assignment. I'll be covering the transfer of the Jews to Auschwitz, a camp in Poland."

Without comment, Erich looked at the clock. "Fraulein Hambro and I were preparing to leave for the day," he said. "I have a meeting with the officer who inherited my supply assignment. I believe you know him—Joachim Forester. He's bringing his secretary with him. Apparently she hasn't been feeling well of late. I'd like to start the meeting on time so she can get to bed, and, hopefully, feel better."

"I understand," Inge said. Erich saw a trace of a smile cross Inge's face, though he doubted Erna noticed.

Inge turned to Erma. "It's four o'clock," she said. "That's the time I have to leave camp. If you'd like to keep working, I'll be happy to drive Hauptsturmfuhrer Riedl to town." She looked at Erich. "We could discuss the testing data during the drive."

"Actually, that's better for me," Erna said. "I'll have my dinner delivered and continue to work on the reports."

"In that case, Fraulein Friedrich, I'll finish what I'm doing and we'll go." Erich turned to Erna. "When you check out, would you please let the commandant know I'll be away from camp for the night?"

"Of course, Hauptsturmfuhrer. I'm going to the office right now. Enjoy your evening." She smiled at Inge. "It was a pleasure to meet you, Fraulein Friedrich."

"You too," Inge said, *though you have no idea why.*

After Erna left, Erich kept filing papers in separate folders on his desk. Inge sat quietly, watching him work. She wondered if he was furious with her for coming to the camp, or even worse, still angry with her for their earlier argument. When he finished, he put on his coat. "Shall we go?" he said brusquely. "We have a great deal to discuss."

"Yes we do," Inge replied huffily.

Neither spoke again until Heinrich pulled up at the Jourhaus gate. "If you'll wait in your car, Fraulein, I need to pick up a few things from my room," Erich said, irritation evident in his tone and in his expression.

Inge presented her papers to the guard on duty and went to the car. When Erich slid into the passenger seat ten minutes later, the engine and the car were warm. The first few minutes of the drive passed in continuing silence, as neither she nor Erich, she judged by his aloofness, were eager to begin the conversation.

Inge stared out at the snow-covered road ahead as the hostility she felt in the office changed to concern. *Maybe my unannounced arrival at the camp angered Erich after all,* she reflected. When the silence became too uncomfortable, she gave in. "I'm sorry I didn't let you know I'd be coming to camp today, Erich," she said. "I didn't know until this morning when Herr Beck received clearance from Berlin. I tried to reach you. I even went to Joachim's office to ask him to let you know, but he was in a meeting. I fell asleep on Aunt Sigrid's couch, and when I woke up, I had to leave immediately or be denied entry."

When Erich finally responded, his anger had clearly abated. "I was surprised to see you, Inge," he said. "And that's putting it mildly. God knows how Herr Beck managed to pull the necessary strings to allow you access to Block Five, but somehow he did, and in you came. Now we have no choice but to make the best of it. Maybe we can use your visits to our advantage, but I want to be perfectly clear. You're going to have to be cautious and alert at

all times. Everything I told you before still applies. It's dangerous for you to be at Dachau, and if you see too much, you'll be
eliminated. Let me put it another way; by walking through the
Jourhaus gates you put your life at risk."

"You don't need to remind me again."

"But I do. Apparently you still don't understand."

For a few minutes Inge was quiet. When Erich didn't say
anything else about her trip to the camp, she took a deep breath
and asked the question that had plagued her since he hadn't
come to the Wagner. "Was there a reason you didn't show up last
evening?"

All at once Erich realized that Inge hadn't come to Dachau to
begin work on the article. She was there because he had stood her
up the night before, and she was worried because they had parted
on less-than-friendly terms. He smiled and put his hand on her
leg. "I'm sorry I missed our meeting, Inge" he said. "When I
learned I couldn't come to town, I tried to find a way to contact
you, but Erna and Rascher were in the office, and I didn't have
an opportunity. I considered using the article you're writing as an
excuse to call, but I decided it wasn't worth the risk. If Rascher
suspected you and I have a personal relationship, our plans, and
though it may sound melodramatic, our lives could be in jeopardy. At best, I'd be transferred and you'd be reassigned."

"So the cold shoulder you gave me in the office was only
pretense?"

"In a manner of speaking." Erich hesitated. "At least to some
extent; entirely after I got over the initial shock of seeing you
standing there."

"I assumed you were furious with me because of my attitude
the other morning."

"And you decided I was punishing you by not coming to the
hotel."

"I admit the possibility crossed my mind, actually, more than once. I assumed you'd given up on me."

Erich shook his head. "Inge, no matter how furious I am, and that's your word, not mine. I'd never stand you up without a damn good reason."

"Then what happened? Joachim and I were so worried. Though he didn't show it, I think he believed something happened to you."

Erich told her about his hastily arranged meeting with Rascher in Munich and reiterated his frustration that he didn't have an opportunity to let her and Joachim know about his change of plans. He mentioned the busy signal at Frau Heiden's, and how discouraged he was when Erna was already at work when he got to the office. "So there you have it," he said. "And if I can't make a prearranged meeting at some point in the future, and that's a real possibility, trust that business is keeping me away."

"I'll try to think rather than react," Inge said. "But you can't blame me for worrying."

"Now you understand how I felt when you and Joachim were involved in your fiasco the other night."

"Point made," Inge said. "What time do we meet Joachim?"

"Not until six. Can you think of anything we could do in the meantime, merely to pass the time, of course? We have almost two hours."

"I didn't sleep much last night, so maybe we should get a room and rest. We want to be bright and alert for our important discussion."

"Of course we do," Erich said. "I have a lot to tell you, and we have to make tentative plans."

"You have news about Rosel?"

"We'll discuss everything when Joachim joins us. There's no need to repeat the information. Right now it's time for us to clear up any doubts you have about how I feel."

# CHAPTER 27

Joachim was waiting in the lobby when, hand in hand, Erich and Inge left the elevator. "Somehow I thought I'd see you coming from this direction," he said. He slapped Erich on the shoulder. "And though I'm jealous as hell, I'm relieved. We were worried about you, old buddy."

"He was meeting with Doctor Rascher in Munich and couldn't call," Inge explained.

"I figured it was something like that, but when you try to convince a woman who's using her imagination, reality gets a little muddled."

Erich laughed at Inge's obvious displeasure. "Shall we eat before you two declare war on each other?" he said.

The waiter led them to a table near the back corner of the room and handed them menus. "I hope your appetites are better tonight," he said.

"I'm sure my friends are starving," said Joachim. While the waiter went for water, they perused the menu. When he returned they ordered and waited until he left the table. "We haven't talked in a few days, so tell us what's going on." Joachim said.

"Rosel is at Ravensbruck," Erich said. "At least she was there on July 14$^{th}$, and since Berlin hasn't decided what to do with the Mischlinge, we can assume she's still there. Heinrich Wolfers went through Weiss's files and found a record of the transfer. He was eager to tell me what he learned."

"I don't like the man," Inge said. "There's something about him, but I can't put my finger on what it is. During the short drive from the camp gates to your office I felt very uncomfortable."

"You're a good judge of character," said Erich. "Heinrich is Weiss's snitch. His primary role is to keep his eye on the other officers and report any sign of aberrant behavior."

"Then you both need to be extra cautious around him," Joachim warned.

"I plan to avoid him like the plague," Erich said. "And Inge, if he continues to drive you to the office, don't say anything. Trust me, he *will* ask questions."

"Did you actually get into camp," Joachim asked.

"I did. When Beck heard the SS wasn't cooperating, he called Goebbels's private number. Though he gave no reason for the time restraint, I'll be allowed to work in the camp office from noon to four o'clock."

"The tests will be conducted in the morning, and, beginning tomorrow, at night," Erich explained. "During the afternoons we'll be writing reports, so there won't be anything noteworthy for you to see."

"It figures," Inge said. "I can't write about what's really happening in the camp, so I'll watch you generate more paperwork."

"It's for your own good. As I've told you before, there's no way you'll be able to put a positive spin on what's happening at Dachau."

"I'm amazed you got beyond the Jourhaus gates," Joachim said. He looked at Erich. "I tried to get in to see you last night when you didn't show up at the Wagner. I was stopped at the gates, and that's with an SS ID."

"Waffen SS papers," Erich said. "You may have had a chance had you been a member of the Death's Head Unit, but even then, without the commandant's approval, you'd be denied entry. If I had my way, neither of you would go anywhere near the camp. In this case, ignorance is truly bliss."

Inge didn't have a comeback, so she changed the subject. "Speaking of what's going on, you haven't said anything about night tests," she said. "I thought you were conducting the high-flight tests early in the day."

"Right now that's true, but my Munich meeting with Rascher was to discuss the freezing tests which will get underway tomorrow night."

"Will you be directly involved?" Joachim asked. "Originally your job was to write reports for Berlin."

"That's true, but Rascher thinks I should observe for several nights. That means I won't be around for at least two or three days."

"Maybe Joachim won't see you, but I intend to be in the office keeping my eye on you every day," Inge said.

"Don't tell me you're still jealous of Fraulein Hambro?"

Joachim cocked his head. "Did I hear the mention of another woman who works in the office?"

"This one wouldn't interest you in the slightest, my friend," said Erich.

"Until today I thought she might," Inge said. "Her voice is sexy, but when I saw her, I realized she's not flashy enough for you."

"She does have her good points," Erich said. "Her smile is nice, and, as Inge said, she has a deep, breathy, sexy voice. She could be attractive if she'd let her hair down and take off the combat boots."

Joachim's eyes widened. "She wears combat boots?"

"If you two don't mind, I've heard enough about Fraulein Hambro," Inge said. "We agree she's no one's type, at least no one at this table. Shall we get back to the important issues?"

"Of course, fair lady." Joachim teased. "I'd much rather talk about business than the attributes of a beautiful woman." He turned to Erich. "How long do you expect phase two to last before you begin the warming phase?"

"I couldn't pin Rascher down, but I suggested I should hand-select the women we'll use for the tests."

"Did he agree?" Inge asked.

"He didn't say no, so it's possible he thought it was a good idea. I figured if I push too hard, he might wonder why I'm so eager to do the selecting, so I left it at that."

"We're going to have to move as quickly as possible," Inge said. "That's one of the reasons I came to the camp. When I met with Herr Beck yesterday, he told me about a directive to transfer all of the Jews to Auschwitz."

"You mentioned that in the office," Erich said. "Any idea when the process is scheduled to begin?"

"Beck thinks around January 20$^{th}$, though he wasn't certain, and I don't know if the deportation directive includes the Mischlinge. I didn't dare ask."

"That gives us a little over two months," Joachim said. "Do you think you'll complete the first and second phases by then?"

"I certainly hope so. I'm thinking weeks rather than months."

"What happens when you're ready to begin the warming tests?" Inge asked.

"If everything goes as planned, I'll travel to Ravensbruck, select the women and bring them back to Dachau. When Rascher hears about the deportation directive, he may want to move quickly. I'll try to find a way to mention it to him."

"Be careful, my friend," Joachim said. "Rascher may want to know where you got your information."

"I'll tell him you're my source. It makes perfect sense."

"Yes throw me to the dogs." Joachim paused, waiting for Erich to say he was joking. "You're serious, aren't you?" he said when Erich didn't respond.

"Absolutely. Rascher knows you and I are meeting tonight. Supposedly, I'm helping you solve a supply problem, so he wouldn't find it unusual if you mentioned the movement of the Jews. With additional transfers of prisoners and SS personnel to Auschwitz, you'd be expected to have concerns about sending additional supplies to the camp."

"It makes sense, Joachim," Inge said. "And actually, it makes me feel better."

"Making you feel good is my dream," Joachim teased. "But frankly—"

"What Inge's trying to say is, by having you tell me about the directive, we won't be involving her and Beck. I agree. Rascher can't think Inge knows anything beyond the statistics I'll be providing."

"Oh," Joachim said sullenly. "That's what you meant, Inge?"

"Enough!" Erich said with a twinkle in his eye. "Back to business, and not monkey business. If I get permission to go to Ravensbruck, I'd like for you to go with me, Joachim, at least as far as Berlin. Think you could arrange a short leave?"

"I doubt it, but I could use the supply problems to my advantage. I'm sure Mueller would send me to Panzer headquarters if he thought it would help resolve the issue. A solution would be good for his career."

"You realize I'm going too," Inge said defiantly.

Erich had no intention of letting Inge go, but this wasn't the time to argue. "Maybe you could go in conjunction with the article you're writing for the *Völkischer Beobachter*," he said thoughtfully. "We'll have to see."

"Find a way, gentlemen."

"We'll figure things out as we go along," Erich said. "At least we have a tentative plan. We'll find Rosel, select her for the experiment, and get her to Dachau. We can make our final escape from there. I don't think it's too early to start making plans that include Sigrid. When the Gestapo finds out what we've done—"

"Say no more," Joachim said. "What's my assignment? Surely I can do something while we're waiting for news."

"You, my friend, have to figure out a way to get the five of us out of the country. I was thinking Switzerland, but it won't be easy to cross the border."

"It may be difficult, but have no fear. How many times do I have to say you're working with a genius?"

"Then, genius, let's meet here Sunday night at seven o'clock. If one of us, most likely me, isn't here, we'll meet the following night. I picked Sunday because there's less going on in the camp."

"We're only meeting once a week?" Inge asked.

"I said definitely every Sunday. There will be meetings in-between, but if we can't make contact for some unforeseen reason, Sunday's meeting will stand."

Joachim winked at Inge. "I'd like to be included in some of those in-between meetings if you don't mind."

"That goes without saying," Inge said. "You'll be included in some of them but certainly not all."

When dinner was over, they lingered in the lobby. They made plans to meet after Erich finished watching the first few nights of the phase-two experiments. Because she was working in the office, Inge would coordinate the plans with Joachim when the meeting was imminent. Adding levity to the conversation, Joachim promised to look into tours departing Munich for Switzerland. After shaking Erich's hand and kissing Inge on the cheek, he left for Munich while Inge and Erich went up the elevator to a warm bed.

———————————

After making love, Erich and Inge slept soundly, wrapped tightly in each other's arms. It seemed like only minutes when she heard the alarm. She reached over and turned it off so Erich could rest as long as possible. She showered and dressed. It was 7:30 when she sat on the edge of the bed, leaned over and lightly kissed his lips. He opened his eyes, and seeing Inge ready to go, looked at the clock. "I set the alarm for six," he said groggily.

"I turned it off so you could sleep a little longer. You said you'd likely be up all night."

Erich pulled her down beside him. "I'd much rather have you than sleep."

"Would you give me a little credit for being a martyr? After all, I put your well-being before my pleasure this time."

"You're paradoxically a kind but cruel woman." He reluctantly climbed out of bed. Fifteen minutes later he emerged from the bathroom looking alert and refreshed.

"Do you have time for coffee?" Inge asked.

Erich glanced at his watch. "I'm afraid not. I need to get the office early. The next twenty-four hours will be grueling."

Inge put her hand on Erich's arm. "Will you be alright?" she asked.

"The tests won't be pleasant to watch, but they can't be any worse than what I've been watching during the past few weeks."

"Would it help to talk about what you're going through? Can't we forget Article Eleven even for a few minutes?"

"Never," Erich said firmly. "I hate that you're working in the office, Inge, and I know it's important for you to be part of the plans to rescue Rosel, but there's no way I'll pass on information that could put you in jeopardy."

Inge opened her mouth to protest. "Nothing you say could change my mind," Erich said. "So no use trying. Perhaps we'll talk about Dachau when we're all safe in Switzerland, but until then, a discussion about what's happening in the camp isn't going to happen." He thought for a moment. "I'm sure you won't like what I'm about to say, but I don't think it's wise for you to come to camp today. Tomorrow would be better. I can't give you anything but basic statistics in front of Erna and the doctor, and it may be difficult for us to remain impersonal."

"Erich," Inge said, her voice and expression mirroring the exasperation she was feeling. "I have to start writing this article. Now that Beck has done his magic, I have no excuse to procrastinate. He could ask for an update at any time."

"Then I'll fill you in on some of the phase-one details while we drive, and when you come to the office tomorrow, I'll provide the preliminary results for the second phase."

"Are you sure you aren't just tired of me and need a day off?" Inge teased.

Erich laughed. That's it. I hoped you wouldn't discover my secret. Erna and I are having a torrid affair. Every time I want her, I throw her on the floor and we make wild, passionate love."

Inge playfully slapped Erich's hand that was resting on her leg. "I knew it all the time," she said. "Okay I'll give you some alone time with your daytime partner this afternoon, but I'll be there at noon tomorrow. Don't let me catch you in a compromising position."

I'll be waiting," Erich said. "But choosing between you and Erna will be a difficult task. I'll need to give my options a great deal of thought. I should probably make love to you again so I can compare and decide which one of you I like best."

"You're as bad as Joachim, and I thought between the two of you, you were the more serious. Now help me with my coat so you can get to Erna. I know she's waiting breathlessly for you to come."

Inge blushed, and Erich laughed. "I can't wait," he said. He pulled her toward him for one more hug.

"I'll miss you," she said.

"We'll be back here in a few days, and I'll see you tomorrow. You sound like we'll be apart forever."

"Don't even suggest such a thing," Inge put her scarf around her neck and looked around the room one last time.

She waited by the lobby door while Erich paid the bill. As she drove to the camp, Erich supplied statistics about the tests. Though he didn't go into graphic detail, he described the reactions of the 'volunteers' as they went from unconsciousness to, in most cases, death. He talked about the autopsy results, which revealed the prisoners had died from ruptured lungs or air bubbles in the brain.

As he talked, Inge felt sick to her stomach. "You said in most cases," she said. "What happens to the survivors?"

Erich decided it would be unwise to mention the ovens that waited ominously at the far end of the camp. "I don't know for sure," he said. "But they probably don't live for long. Rascher wouldn't want them back in the general population spreading the word about what we're doing."

"How can I possibly make any of this information sound positive?" Inge sighed. "Do you really believe any reasonably sane person would believe 'volunteers' are participating in these tests?"

"You're the one who was trained to manipulate the news and present horrible things in a positive light, Inge, but to answer your question, I have no idea how you'll be able to write this article. I wanted you out of the picture, but given that you showed up in camp yesterday, it's too late to turn back. You're going to have to stick with your original plan."

"I will, though now I understand why you've been worried. I promise to be careful." She smiled. "I have too many good things in my life and I won't let these tests change that."

A kilometer from the Jourhaus gate, Inge stopped the car. She leaned over and kissed Erich lightly on the lips. "Be in touch when you can," she said. "If it's easier for you, call Joachim with an answer to his supply problem. Even if I see you at the office, I won't know how you're doing, and we both need to be sure you're alright.

"I'll try," Erich said. "But if I can't find a way to phone, don't worry. I can't take any unnecessary chances."

When Inge pulled up to the gate, Erich got out and walked around to her side of the car. She rolled down the window. "Thank you for the ride to camp, Fraulein," he said. "I'll call when I have more information for your article."

"Thank you, Hauptsturmfuhrer," Inge said. "I appreciate your cooperation."

Erich smiled, turned, and presented his papers to the guard. He entered the Jourhaus, went upstairs, put his bag in his room, and, without unpacking, walked back downstairs and through Roll Call Square to Block Five. A scharfuhrer was standing by the office door. "Is Fraulein Hambro in?" Erich asked.

"Neither she nor the doctor is here yet," the guard said, "though I believe they're expected later this morning.

"Then I'll get something to eat before I go to work." Erich turned and walked back across the square to the dining hall. He entered and looked around for a familiar face. Pretending not to notice Heinrich, who, as usual, was sitting by himself, Erich joined Curt Rath. Though momentarily dissuaded by the appearance of the Jew who served the meal, he ate a hearty breakfast while talking with Curt about trivialities having nothing to do with the camp. After a third cup of coffee, he returned to Block Five. "No one's here yet?" he asked the scharfuhrer.

"No Sir, though Obersturmfuhrer Wolfers came by and left a message. Will you be staying, or shall I remain on duty?"

"Give me a minute to see what Wolfers had to say. I'll let you know." Erich entered the office, went directly to the desk, and read a note from Rascher, who was cancelling the morning observations in order to prepare for the upcoming night. Erich hung his coat and hat on the rack by the door, dismissed the guard, removed the folders from his desk, and began to work. Now all he could do was wait to put the next part of the plan into operation.

It was close to noon when Rascher and Erna arrived to make last-minute preparations for phase two. With two enlisted men to assist the doctor, Erich was able to continue writing his report. At two o'clock Rascher came in from the test compound and suggested they all rest up for the evening ahead.

As he walked back to the Jourhaus, Erich stopped and stared in horror at the Snow Commandos clearing Roll Call Square. Using shovels and boards nailed to wooden planks, the sorry lot piled the snow in heaps on waiting wagons. When the wagons were full, they shoveled the heavy snow onto tables that four men carried on their shoulders to the edge of the square. Even the younger men buckled under the burden of the piles; their faces contorted in anguish as they struggled to tolerate the weight. "Tempo, Tempo," the SS guards barked as they walked behind the struggling prisoners prodding them with sticks or beating them with rubber truncheons.

Unable to watch anymore, Erich lowered his head and walked quickly toward his room.

# CHAPTER 28

Throughout the day Inge agonized over how best to present the data Erich had given her during the ride to the camp. As he said, there would be no easy way to report the test statistics. *In fact*, she thought, *it may be impossible.* Her problem; she had to make the story sound valid, but at the same time she couldn't reveal any of the actual research methods. Her first welcome break came when Sigrid called. She spent several minutes assuring her aunt that all was well and listened to her describe the events of the Beer Hall celebration in Munich.

The second interruption came about thirty-minutes later. Inge answered the knock. "There's a man on the phone," Frau Heiden said. "But it's not Hauptsturmfuhrer Riedl."

*She thinks I have a new boyfriend,* Inge reflected as she picked up the phone. "Heil Hitler," she said. "This is Inge Friedrich."

"Heil Hitler, fair lady. It's Joachim."

Inge shook her head. *Could anyone really have such a ceaselessly cheerful nature?* "What a greeting," she said. She put her hand over the mouthpiece and turned to her hovering landlady. "It's a colleague from the office."

Frau Heiden nodded and waddled off. "How are you?" Inge asked when her landlady was out of earshot.

Inge could almost hear Joachim grin. "Perfect, fair lady," he said.

She laughed. "Of course you are. Why did I bother to ask?"

"Could it be that at last you believe?" Joachim didn't wait for Inge to answer. "Any chance you're meeting our friend today?"

"Unfortunately, no. Evidently he doesn't want me around anymore. Can you believe it?"

"Maybe you underestimated the fraulein in the office."

"Not a chance. I reiterate; our friend's secretary is nobody's type." Inge smiled. Her conversations with Joachim were beginning to sound like the banter between him and Erich. She marveled she could feel so relaxed with both SS officers in such a short time.

"Are you there, fair lady?" Joachim was saying. "You haven't hung up on me."

"I'm here. I was daydreaming. You've interrupted my work, so I hope your reason for calling is important."

"About me, of course."

"About me what?"

"You were day-dreaming. I assumed I was the object of your fantasies."

"Joachim—"

"Okay. Okay. Did you hear anything I said?"

"No, tell me again."

"I repeat. Since our friend is tied up for the evening, maybe you'll have dinner with the other man in your life."

"And that would be you?"

"Of course. There isn't another man is there?"

"Joachim—"

"You keep saying that."

"For good reason, so enough. Anything to report?"

"I'm crushed. Must I have something to report before you agree to see me? Are you using me?"

Inge laughed. "Of course I'll have dinner with you, if only to shut you up, and I *will* use you, but only as an excuse to quit working on this ridiculous article I'm struggling to write."

"So now I've become an excuse. I'm not sure how to react—"

"Joachim—"

"There you go again with the 'Joachim's', but no need to explain. I'll eventually get over the myriad of insults you've been throwing my way, but even though you've advised me of your true feelings, I still want to see you. Why don't I come to Dachau? I don't want you to drive to Munich in this weather, but I'm sick of the food at the Wagner. Is there another place that serves a decent meal in your area?"

"I discovered a great local cafe." Inge gave Joachim directions to the Café Bieglebrau. "The food is wonderful, but the place closes early, so could you meet me at five o'clock?"

"You mean the hour when you had a business meeting with your friend before meeting me for dinner?"

"Will you stop?"

"Five o'clock works for me."

"I'll see you then." Inge hung up, hoping Joachim had good news.

Throughout the afternoon, as she wrote and rewrote the introduction to her article, thoughts of Erich and Rosel made it hard for her to concentrate. They were so near to the end of their quest, yet still so far away. If she was still alive, Rosel was at Ravensbruck. Nothing remained but to bring her home. Inge frowned. *Nothing remains? How ridiculous. What remains is the actual escape and the uncertainty of what's ahead for all of us as we begin a new phase of our lives; that is, if we're able to get away.*

She finally gave up and put her pad aside. She could say nothing beyond explaining the predicament of the Luftwaffe pilots shot down over the North Sea. When it came to presenting specific information about the experiments, she was at a total loss. The meeting with Joachim would be a welcome respite from the drudgery of propaganda-oriented journalism.

---

After napping and washing-up, Erich went to the dining hall for dinner. It was almost two hours past the usual 4:30 p.m. meal time, so there were only a few officers lingering over coffee. *Thank God there's still food available,* he thought as he heard his stomach growl, *and thank God I don't have to deal with Heinrich Wolfers.*

After a light supper he reported to the office, where final preparations for phase two were already underway. "Where's the doctor?" he asked Erna, as he hung his coat and hat on the rack.

"He's in the compound," Erna said.

Erich went out the back door to join Rascher just as a scharfuhrer was placing the last of five naked prisoners on stretchers in the test area. The doctor momentarily glanced up and saw Erich. "As you can see, we're almost ready to begin," he said. "Shall we get our coats? I asked the scharfuhrer to put a portable heater in the observation area, but it's still going to be cold. While we observe the first test, I'll explain the procedure." As they walked back to the office, Erich felt an unexpected chill, but it wasn't coming from the bitter cold air.

When they returned to the observation area, Rascher began. "As you can see, the scharfuhrer is pouring cold water over each of our volunteers—"

*There's that word again,* Erich thought to himself as the doctor droned on. *Rascher knows the prisoners didn't volunteer to die a terrible death for the good of the Reich.* Suddenly he had an epiphany. *But maybe they did. Perhaps death would be preferable to the living hell of Dachau.* He thought about all he'd seen and learned about the

Jews since coming to Dachau. Every day, all day, they suffered torture, degradation, and humiliation inflicted on them by their tormenters; actions intended to break them down and rob them of their dignity and their will to live to the point where they became desensitized to the acts of violence that threatened their very existence. They witnessed so many beatings and murders that little surprised them anymore. To a man they had lost their self-respect, while the lack of food made them walking skeletons. They were, Erich thought, like animals always on alert for danger. *Yes,* he thought again; *Death might be preferable to this kind of life.* He shuddered and turned to Rascher who was pointing to two men standing on the far side of the room. "The medical technicians from the infirmary will take rectal temperatures every hour," he said. "We'll get our first read now." He paused while the two burly men made less-than-gentle trusts of thermometers into each man's rectum. When they were through, Rascher continued. "Over the next few days some of the prisoners will be covered, while others will remain naked. Shall we see what happens?"

After watching the bewildered, shivering victims for thirty-minutes, Rascher led Erich and Erna back into to the warm office. He appeared eager as he motioned for his cohorts to sit. "This is going well," he said enthusiastically. "It's a dream come true."

*It isn't a dream, it's a nightmare,* Erich reflected. Forcing a smile, he nodded in agreement.

"I spoke with Gruppenfuhrer Hippke this morning," Rascher said. "We are making preliminary preparations to implement the second part of phase two. As you know, our original plan was to wait until we completed the first component of the test before beginning the second, but Berlin is becoming restless. Hippke and I believe we can logistically combine the two elements of the experiment. That way we'll finish sooner than we originally anticipated and perhaps save more Luftwaffe flyers. You're clear on the methods we will employ in the next phase, Hauptsturmfuhrer?"

"Only what you and Gruppenfuhrer Hippke told me at breakfast in Berlin," Erich said.

"Then I'll elaborate. Over the next few days a large vat filled with water will be moved to the compound. We will use snow and ice to reduce the temperature. Hippke is sending flying uniforms that should arrive tomorrow. We'll dress some of the volunteers in the Luftwaffe clothing, add life jackets the pilots would be wearing, and submerge them in the vat, some with the backs of their heads and their brain stems above the water, and others in the water with the backs of their necks and their cerebellums beneath the surface. As we're doing tonight, a medic will regularly take their temperatures. The three of us will watch to see how long it takes for each one to die."

Appalled, Erich listened to the doctor gleefully introduce the next part of his scientific project "It's obvious we're going to be ahead of schedule," he said. "So there's no need to put off the warming phase of the tests."

At last the moment Erich had been waiting for—the opportunity to talk about the process for selecting the women who would warm the survivors. "And how will the women be used?" he asked.

"We'll put each man between two of them." The doctor smirked. "But I'll be more specific when we actually begin that phase of the testing."

Erich analyzed Rascher's words. He had stressed the word "our." Did that mean they would personally select the women? Once again he was grateful for the seemingly worthless Munich meeting which had allowed him to make his point about the selection of the females for the tests. Though he was eager to learn more, he knew it would do no good to press for additional information; in fact it might hurt his cause. He would continue to be vaguely interested until another appropriate opportunity presented itself.

The night dragged on, and with it, the horror. As the grisly cries of the sufferers disturbed the quiet of the camp, Erich wondered what the other prisoners housed nearby were feeling. Did they wonder if they would soon be the ones screaming in pain? Were they able to block out the sounds and sleep? Many times throughout the night he closed his eyes. *If only I could plug my ears too,* he thought. He wanted to break down the barrier, race into the room, and set the suffering prisoners free. Instead of watching the dying men, he imagined himself rallying other SS officers, opening the camp gates, and freeing all the pitiful Jews. *How many of the outwardly cold, brutal SS men would follow me? Not many,* he quickly decided.

During one of the warming sessions, Rascher, who had originally forbade the tests to take place under anesthesia, decided drugs would have to be used in the future "to prevent such a racket," he said, and Erich hoped the next victims would be spared the agony these men were obviously experiencing.

Near morning, the interior temperatures of the victims reached twenty-five degrees Celsius, and they showed signs of peripheral frostbite. As they slowly died, Rascher, Erich, and Erna recorded heart action, respiration, and other bodily functions presented to them by the medical personnel.

When the sun finally began to rise, Erich was exhausted. He knew he couldn't stand to watch the suffering any longer, so he tried to escape the macabre scenes by thinking of Inge. *If I can't single-handedly rescue the Jews, perhaps she could write an article exposing the atrocities being committed at Dachau,* he thought. *To hell with Article Eleven.* Quickly, reality set in again. *But even if she wrote an expose, it would never be printed, and if, by chance, it were, would the German people believe what they were reading? I doubt it,* he thought. *How could they begin to comprehend something as horrible as Dachau?* "I've got to stop thinking," he said under his breath as he watched men die.

———

The snow was no longer falling, but it was bitterly cold when Joachim arrived at Cafe Bieglebrau. He spent a few minutes warming his hands by the fire and then joined Inge at a table. When the smiling waitress came to take their order, Joachim turned down a cold beer and, instead, opted for coffee. "To take off the chill," he said as he sipped the hot brew.

The conversation was limited to the weather and other trivialities until the woman served the meal. When she returned to the kitchen, Joachim whispered so he wouldn't be overheard: "I want you to let Erich know I think I've found a way for us to leave Germany if it becomes necessary."

"All five of us? So soon?"

"Yes, I'm a miracle worker, remember?"

Inge opened her mouth to respond but Joachim put up his hand to stop her. "I'll pass on the 'Joachims' for now if you don't mind, and remember, nothing's definite at this point."

"So tell me," Inge urged.

"I've been struggling with the assignment. First I considered that desertion might be the way to go. Then I realized that Erich and I could probably disappear, but not with you, your aunt, and Rosel. Next I thought about ways to get the five of us into Austria or Czechoslovakia, but what good would that do? We'd only be going from one Nazi-controlled area to another and we'd still be dodging the Gestapo. Of course I considered crossing into Switzerland, but I had no idea how or where to cross the now heavily-guarded border. When I was running out of ideas, a miracle happened. I remembered that one of the men I drink with at the Hofbrauhaus mentioned a cabin his family owns near the Swiss border. Before the war they used the place for cross-country skiing in the winter and hunting in the summer."

"So we'll go there and cross the border into Switzerland?"

"Patience, fair lady, let me finish. I had lunch at the Hofbrauhaus today, and who should come in, but Obersturmfuhrer Wrieden."

"The man who owns the cabin?"

"Yes. I suggested it would be a great spot for me to escape the pressures of the war." Joachim chuckled. "I even mentioned the possibility of taking a few lovely frauleins with me."

"And Wrieden agreed?'

"Will you let me finish explaining?"

"I'll try to curb my enthusiasm until you're through."

"Because of the war and transportation difficulties, the family has no plans to use the cabin anytime soon. Wrieden says I can take my frauleins whenever I can arrange leave. I thanked him and said I'd ask for time off and get back to him with specific dates. This cabin could be our answer."

"Where is it?"

"I don't know specifically, but somewhere in the Black Forest near Lorrach and the Swiss border."

"But won't the border will be heavily guarded? That could be a problem, especially with Aunt Sigrid."

"Hopefully Erich and I will figure out the border guards' routines so we can all get across without too much difficulty. In any event, the cabin's our best hope, at least for now."

"I hate to think of running, but I know we don't have a choice. I'm not looking forward to telling Aunt Sigrid she has to leave her home."

"You think she'll put up a fight?"

"Initially, but if Rosel is free and leaving Munich is the only chance we have to be together, she'll acquiesce, though I'm sure it will be difficult. She's lived in that house all her life."

"Clearly nothing's definite at this point, but I wanted you both to know at least we have an option."

"I'll tell Erich about the cabin the first chance I get, unless you see him when I do. Then you can tell him yourself. I have no idea how long he'll be tied up in that horrible place."

"That place is obviously upsetting you. Why don't you tell me what it was you wanted to share?"

Inge spent the next half-hour quietly relating the information Erich had given her in the car during the morning ride and explaining her difficulties with the presentation of the test results in an article acceptable for print. Joachim offered no suggestions, but he promised to try to come up with an idea for her article before they met again. Inge gladly accepted his offer to help.

When they left the warm room, it was too cold to stand outside and talk, so after repeating their promise to stay in touch and call one another immediately if anything new developed, they said goodbye. Joachim waved as she drove toward Frau Heiden's.

# CHAPTER 29

The cold sun was rising in the sky when the guards assigned to the experiment removed the frozen prisoners from the yard. Rascher announced a breakfast break before the high-flight tests he'd suspended the previous day would begin. "At precisely nine o'clock," he said, making it clear he expected to start on time. He spent a few minutes on the telephone before announcing he had to attend a noon meeting in Munich and was cancelling the afternoon writing session so Erich and Erna could rest after the morning tests, before another long night. Erich was glad he'd have time away from the office, but he wondered if he'd be able to rest after what he'd witnessed throughout the night and knew he'd observe during the rest of the morning.

When Rascher and Erna left the office, he leaned back in his chair and closed his eyes. All of a sudden he remembered Inge planned to come to the camp that afternoon. He knew she'd be disappointed, or worse, angry, he wouldn't be there to meet her. Apprehensive about delivering the news, he picked up the phone and asked the camp operator to connect him to Inge's apartment house. After several rings, Frau Heiden answered, said Inge was upstairs, and went to get her.

"This is Inge Friedrich, Heil Hitler," Inge said a few minutes later.

"I hope I didn't wake you, Fraulein," Erich said. "I need to cancel our afternoon appointment. No one will be in the office between noon and four o'clock, so a trip here would be a waste of your time."

"I see," Inge said, afraid if she commented further, her irritation would show. "So when do you think we might meet, Hauptsturmfuhrer? I have to write my article, and, more importantly, I have some news from Munich, which I believe you'll find interesting."

"Hopefully things will settle down around here in a day or so," Erich said. I'll call you then and we'll figure out a convenient time to meet."

"Of course I'm disappointed, but I look forward to your call, Hauptsturmfuhrer. Is everything alright with you?" she asked a little too softly.

"Of course it is. I'm simply busy," Erich said gruffly. "I'll contact you very soon, Fraulein." As he hung up, he realized he'd been abrupt, but he had no choice. He put on his coat and cap, left the office, and walked toward the Jourhaus.

---

Inge stood by the telephone wondering what to do next. Despite her efforts to come up with an acceptable angle for her article, she had no fresh ideas. There was no way she could write the piece without Erich's help, and now that he'd canceled their meeting, her task seemed impossible.

With no options open, she decided to use her time constructively. "I'll go to Munich," she said. *Maybe it's time to tell Aunt Sigrid what's happening, and, if the time seems right, begin to prepare her for the possibility we might have to leave Germany.*

---

Erich hoped a shower would wash away thoughts of what he'd witnessed and make him feel better, but he was far from refreshed when left the bathroom. His body-clock was off, and he wasn't responding well to the new routine. He dressed, and, without turning to look at the hordes of humanity standing in the square, walked directly to the dining hall. He couldn't stomach the thought of breakfast, so he drank a cup of coffee in the almost-deserted room. Just before nine o'clock, he left for the office.

The morning experiments were a repeat of the day before. With increasing revulsion, Erich grappled with the knowledge that he was becoming used to watching prisoners die in the chamber. Though the revelation disturbed him, he could at last see how the other officers could go about their lives so nonchalantly in the face of the misery and death in the camp.

Nine of the twelve prisoners died before Rascher called the morning tests a success. When the scharfuhrer removed the last prisoner from the chamber, the doctor dismissed his staff; "We'll begin at eight o'clock tonight," he said. "I suggest you get some sleep between now and then."

"We're beginning at a different time this evening," Erich said.

The doctor nodded. "The freezing tests we performed last night required that the volunteers be out in the cold for ten to twelve hours. Each of tonight's tests should last two hours at most. If we're lucky, including preparation and cleanup time, we'll be able to do three experiments before morning, and incidentally, our first two volunteers will be Russian officers."

Erich was surprised, but remembering no one at Dachau asked questions, he didn't ask the doctor to explain why Russians rather than Jews had "volunteered" for the test. Confirming he'd be back at the office by eight o'clock, he went to his room, hoping exhaustion would keep him from dreaming about the gruesome tests he'd just witnessed.

———————

When the leisurely lunch with Sigrid was over and the dishes had been washed and put away, Inge joined her aunt in the parlor. "It looks like we're about to have a serious discussion," Sigrid said as Inge sat beside her on the couch.

"I suppose we are," Inge said. "I'm keeping you informed. I'm surprised you haven't asked for information about Rosel or our plans lately."

"That's because when I ask, you refuse to answer my questions. I decided you'd tell me what you want me to know when you're ready."

"Well, I'm ready."

"And I'm eager to hear what you have to say. Put a log on the fire and let's talk."

When the fire was blazing, Inge rejoined her aunt on the couch. "Aunt Sigrid," she said. "I hope you know I never wanted to keep anything from you. I thought it would be best if you were kept in the dark. If anyone questioned you about Rosel—"

"By 'anyone,' you mean the Gestapo. I assume there's a reason you're willing to share now. Have circumstances changed since we last talked?"

"Not really, but there are some things you need to know."

"You mean you're finally going to let me help?"

"Not yet, but we have to start thinking about the future, so just listen. When I'm finished I'll try to answer all of your questions."

The two women sat in front of the roaring fire while Inge told her aunt about Joachim and his friendship with Erich. She talked about their strategy to find Rosel and transport her to Dachau. For the most part, Sigrid listened intently, though she interrupted from time to time, asking Inge for clarification. "What are we going to do if you're able to get Rosel out of Dachau?" she asked when Inge was finished.

Inge had been waiting for the question. Deciding she had to be honest and direct, she took her aunt's hand. "We have to leave Germany, Aunt Sigrid; all of us."

"Leave our home?" Sigrid said, looking shocked. "For how long?"

"Until the end of the war. If the Fuhrer is successful, perhaps forever."

Sigrid let go of Inge's hand, got up, and walked over to the mantle. "Oh my," she said as she picked up Rosel's picture. "I want nothing more than to have Rosel home, but I'm too old to start over, Inge."

Inge went to the fireplace and put her arm around her aunt. "You're not old, Aunt Sigrid, and you'll have me, Rosel, and Erich. Joachim too. I'm sure you'll like him."

Sigrid didn't seem to be listening. She was talking to herself as much as she was asking Inge for information. "Where would we go? How would we get away?" The questions flew. "What about our home? Will the Nazis seize it when they discover we've gone?"

"We're getting ahead of ourselves," Inge said calmly, hoping to assuage her aunt's fears, but realizing it would be an almost impossible task. "We haven't made any specific arrangements, but Joachim is working on a way for us to cross the border into Switzerland."

Again Sigrid ignored Inge's explanation. "When will this happen, and what will I be able to take with me?" she said anxiously.

"I don't know when we'll have to go. It depends on the progress Erich makes at Dachau. As far as what we'll be able to take with us, that is if we have to go, I'm afraid not much. We'll only be able to take the clothes we have on and a few personal possessions."

Inge expected her aunt to cry, but she wasn't surprised when Sigrid again showed her spunk. She straightened her back and when she spoke, she sounded determined. "Then I'll have to start making plans," she said. "At least we don't have to worry about how we'll live. Thank God we transferred Rosel's and my money into Swiss accounts before the war got underway."

Inge squeezed Sigrid's shoulders. "I for one am thankful you did. I only wish I'd done the same thing with the money I earned when I started working."

"I should have advised you—"

"I wouldn't have listened, and speaking of listening, leaving the country isn't a topic we discuss with anyone; not with Frau Ott, with no one."

"I may be old, but I'm not foolish, Inge. Of course I won't say anything."

"Good. I'll let you know when we make specific plans, and I'll be bringing Joachim by to meet you very soon. He'll let you know what's going on if neither Erich nor I can get to Munich. Never forget we have to communicate in person. Don't say anything important over the phone."

Sigrid sat back down on the couch. "I have so much to think about," she said. "But in some ways, despite my apprehension, I'm excited. It will be wonderful when we're all together, and maybe, if I'm interpreting the signs correctly, we'll also be planning a wedding."

"Now we *are* getting ahead of ourselves." Inge smiled. "But I can't rule out the possibility."

The two women spent the rest of the afternoon together. Sigrid wanted to go through the house and select personal items to take with her if they should have to leave Munich. While Inge helped with the task, the two reminisced about the seemingly carefree days of the past when Rosel had been with them; before the "Pied Piper" had come to power. As they talked, Inge could picture Rosel in the house. She remembered the music lessons and the violin recitals Rosel gave for them in front of the fireplace in the parlor. She smiled as she recalled the cooking lessons held in Sigrid's kitchen. She had barely been able to boil water, but Rosel cooked like a chef, sometimes preparing hendl, grilled chicken marinated with pepper and spices, cabbage rolls, and her favorite, sauerbraten. Rosel even mastered the art of baking schwarzwälder kirschtorte, a rich Black Forest cake, and wiener apflestrudel. Inge vividly recalled the day when she was relegated to the role of dishwasher for Rosel, the chef.

Late in the afternoon, Inge phoned Joachim. With nothing new to discuss, they agreed a meeting wasn't necessary. Although Sigrid wanted her to spend the night in Munich, she declined, explaining she had to return to Frau Heiden's. She wanted to be close by in case Erich needed her.

---

Throughout the afternoon, Erich slept the sleep of a drunk. When he finally dragged himself out of bed, it was 6:30, well past the dinner hour. He shaved the stubble from his face, dressed, and went to see if he could get something to eat.

Coffee was brewing, but besides brown bread, there was nothing else available. Erich filled his cup and sat down; surprised he was actually enjoying the bitter ersatz coffee served in the dining hall. *It's amazing what we learn to accept,* he reflected, thinking not only of the coffee, but also of the experiments going on in Block Five.

With ten minutes to spare he arrived at the office compound and joined Rascher and Erna in an observation area near a large water-filled vat that waited ominously in the yard.

After receiving instructions from the doctor, the scharfuhrer brought the two Russian officers from the barracks, dressed them in flight uniforms and life vests, and dumped them in the icy water with their brain stems barely above the waterline. An hour passed, during which the doctor repeatedly expressed his surprise at the passage of time. In the briefing he'd predicted unconsciousness would occur within an hour, but the two men still responded two and a half hours after being submerged.

One of the freezing men begged the scharfuhrer standing guard to shoot him. The guard looked at Rascher for direction. The doctor refused and the man continued to suffer. The release of death didn't come until the Russian officers had been in the vat for five hours, three hours longer than Rascher had originally predicted.

After a short break in the warm office, Rascher seemed eager to begin the second tests of the evening. "Shall we begin?" he said as he put on his coat. "Maybe this time the men will die sooner. I realize the first deaths took longer than expected, but we learned something. Hopefully this next test will confirm our findings."

Erich wondered what they'd learned. He was about to ask when Rascher answered his question. "I don't know if I mentioned the reasoning behind our use of the Russian volunteers during the first test," he said. "We wanted to find individuals who would best mirror the conditions of our pilots. That meant we needed men who aren't all flesh and bones. The fact that the officers lasted so long is encouraging. It gives us a better idea how much time we'll have to get our aviators out of the water before they succumb to the freezing temperatures, as well as what kind of equipment we'll want to provide to ensure they'll make it until our rescue teams arrive. In this case, we've learned keeping their necks out of the water will be important."

"Of course," Erich said. "If the pilots can keep their shoulders above water, they have a better chance—"

"My point exactly," Rascher said.

"And yet we're using Jewish volunteers for our next tests," Erich said, wondering at his ability to echo the ludicrous term.

"We have no choice," said Rascher. "There are no other men in the camp who meet our criteria. Of course we can still learn a great deal by watching the Jews, so shall we begin?"

Erich wanted to say he was through and walk out, but of course that wasn't an option. *If I did, I'd likely take the place of the next man in line to die,* he thought. As he left the warm office, he pulled his coat collar around his neck to keep out the night's chill, and, he hoped, to hide the disgusted expression he knew would be obvious if Rascher looked closely.

Even though they were dressed in hooded flying uniforms, it was obvious the two Jews being escorted into the yard were already in bad shape. They looked pale and emaciated; their eyes were sunken into their sockets. "No life jackets?" Erich asked.

"Not this time," Rascher replied. "The jackets would keep their heads and necks above the water. We want these men to be submerged up to their chins. Note we've chosen volunteers of approximately the same height and adjusted the water level accordingly."

The scharfuhrer measured the water temperature at four-degrees Celsius and positioned the men in the vat with their feet on the bottom of the tub, their brain stems just above the icy water. He placed a metal collar on each man and tied their outstretched arms to metal hooks on the sides of the vat. "So they can't dip their heads in the water and intentionally drown," the doctor said, looking pleased he'd thought of everything.

After several hours of suffering, the Jews were still alive. "Enough of this," Rascher said. He ordered the guard to remove the unconscious men from the tub. The medic took their temperatures and reported the readings were twenty-six and twenty-eight degrees Celsius, respectively.

"These would be good candidates for our warming test," said Rascher. "We might have to get those Ravensbruck women to Dachau sooner than we originally projected."

This was the first positive news Erich had heard in days. He wanted to pin the doctor down to a specific schedule, but, once again, he knew it wasn't the time. *Too much too soon, and I could blow everything,* he thought, and he remained quiet.

When Erich next looked at his watch, it was four o'clock a.m. He hoped Rascher would call it quits for the night, but the enthusiastic doctor declared there would be one more test. Erich felt the same foreboding, exacerbated this time by exhaustion, hunger, and tension.

The next test cases were also fully clothed Jews. They too were chained and submerged so the backs of their necks and their cerebellums were below the surface of the icy water. It took two hours for the "volunteers" to die. "I'm glad that didn't take as long," the doctor said matter-of-factly. "We should have the autopsy reports by tomorrow afternoon." He looked at his watch. "That's it for tonight."

Erich could barely hide his relief. There would be no more deaths to witness that night, or rather that morning. Rascher turned to the young enlisted man who was about to remove the bodies from the vat. "See that the remains are taken to the infirmary for autopsy, scharfuhrer," he said. "He looked back at Erich and Erna. "Shall we go into the office and get warm?"

Once inside, Rascher noticed the dark circles under Erna's eyes. He cancelled the morning tests and the report writing scheduled to follow during the afternoon. In another act of generosity he canceled the tests scheduled for that night. "We'll meet back here and begin again tomorrow morning at nine o'clock," he said. "That should give the medics adequate time to complete the autopsy reports on tonight's cases, including the men who survived the vat. Then we'll be able to do some significant analysis. Fraulein, you and Hauptsturmfuhrer Riedl will be involved in that aspect of the work from now on. I see no reason for either of you to watch any more of the actual tests. The statistics are piling up, and Berlin is demanding results."

"Does that include observations of the high-altitude chamber experiments, Herr Doctor?" Erich asked.

"It includes all of the tests currently underway. I'll train several officers to observe. You will work from nine to four completing the final reports for Gruppenfuhrer Hippke and Reichsmarshall Goering."

"What about the warming tests, Doctor?" Erich asked cautiously. "You previously suggested we might want to transport the Ravensbruck women earlier than originally anticipated."

The doctor didn't respond right away, and Erich waited nervously. "You're right," he finally said. "It may be time to begin thinking about phase three. I've been thinking about the suggestion you made in Munich, Hauptsturmfuhrer. We will need to select suitable women. They can't be too bony; they need some fat on their bodies if they're going to warm freezing men."

Rosel's fate hung on what Rascher would say next. Erich could almost see the doctor's brain working. After what seemed like an eternity, he finally spoke. "Perhaps you *should* be the one to travel to Ravensbruck, Hauptsturmfuhrer. Since you know what we require for phase three, you're the one who should select the appropriate guinea pigs."

Erich made a concerted effort to prevent an audible sigh of relief from escaping his lips. "I assure you, I will make suitable choices, Herr Doctor," he said, struggling to appear impassive. "I'm prepared to go to Ravensbruck whenever you think the time is right."

Rascher seemed to be pondering Erich's words. *Come on,* Erich thought, s*ay something.* Unfortunately, Rascher didn't say what Erich wanted to hear. "I'm not sure when that will be," he said.

Erich was frustrated. With no guidance from Rascher, he and Joachim couldn't make specific plans. *Don't let him see you're disappointed,* Erich told himself. *You're not supposed to have a personal stake in choosing the women.* "Whenever you think I should go, I'll be ready," he said.

As quickly as his hopes were dashed, his spirits rose again. "I don't believe it's too early to make preliminary plans," said Rascher. "After all, preparations will need to be made, and some of them may take time."

Erich wanted to scream, "*Yes!*" but he only nodded. "You and Erna work on those reports over the next four or five days," Rascher said. "After that we'll evaluate our progress and make more definitive plans. If the report writing goes as we expect it will, and if the experiments continue to go well, we should be able to begin the warming phase in two or three weeks. That will give you a week to travel to Ravensbruck, select the women, and transport them to Dachau." He turned to Erna. "We will need to make arrangements for special housing. Perhaps the women could be held in the Strafblocke."

"The Strafblocke?" Erich said. "That building wasn't part of the modified tour I received when I first arrived."

"The Strafblocke is the lock-up behind the administration building," Rascher said. "The facility is primarily used for severe punishments as well as for prisoners who are returned to the camp after they have been released, but I believe the commandant could make space for our test women." He turned back to Erna. "Will you please make the arrangements, Fraulein?"

"Certainly, Herr Doctor," Erna said, as she noted the task on her tablet.

"If, as I said, these phases of the experiment can be completed in two or three weeks, we'll use the high-flight chamber for the warming tests. We'll continue to use the compound for the exposure and vat tests." He paused again. When he finally spoke, he was grinning. "I admit I'm looking forward to watching some of those women work. We'll have to devise countless ways for them to make those ice-men hot."

Erich looked at Erna, wondering how she'd react. Surprisingly she didn't flinch.

Indicating he wanted everyone to leave the office at the same time, the doctor waited for Erich and Erna to straighten their desks. Erich was annoyed. He'd hoped to call Inge and arrange a meeting with her and Joachim. Now he'd have to come back and try later.

When the guard secured the office and took his post outside the door, Rascher walked Erich and Erna across Roll Call Square. He left Erna at her car and said goodbye to Erich at the Jourhaus gate.

Erich wearily climbed the stairs to his room, set his alarm for noon, and without undressing, plopped down on his bunk.

———————————

Throughout the morning, Inge tried to call the camp office, but she was repeatedly told there was no answer and to try again later. Frustrated, she phoned Joachim. He hadn't heard anything either, but he promised to be in touch as soon as he got a call.

Both to pass the time and because she hadn't kept current on the news of the day, she spent part of the morning reading the paper. Coincidentally, Josef's article on the Munich Art Show ran in the morning's edition. Well aware of his actual feelings about the garbage on display, she smiled at the lavish praise her colleague had heaped on the art of the Reich.

The longer she waited to hear from Erich, the more agitated she became. She went outside and took a walk to pass the time, but the cold, coupled with her concern that she might miss his call, forced her back into the apartment building. At 12:30, as, once again, she began her futile efforts to make progress with her article, the call finally came. Frau Heiden knocked on her door. "Your young man is on the telephone," she said.

"Thank you," Inge said eagerly. She sped past the woman and raced down the stairs. "This is Inge Friedrich, Heil Hitler," she answered.

"Heil Hitler, Fraulein. This is Hauptsturmfuhrer Riedl. I find myself with some free time. Since I know you're eager to work on your article, I thought we might meet."

"Of course, Hauptsturmfuhrer," Inge said. "Should I come to your office?"

"I would prefer to meet in town, Fraulein. I'm tired of camp food. Perhaps we could have dinner at the Hotel Wagner, or some other place if that doesn't suit you."

"I know of a quiet cafe where we can talk undisturbed. I had dinner there last night with a friend."

"Wherever you'd like to meet is fine, but I do have a problem. Fraulein Hambro isn't in camp and I don't have a way to get to town."

"I'll be glad to pick you up, Hauptsturmfuhrer. What time would be convenient?"

"We worked all night, so I'm exhausted. I'd like to sleep for a few hours. How about four o'clock?'

"I'll be there," Inge said, trying to suppress her excitement. "Do I need to do anything or make any calls before our meeting?"

"Perhaps you should call your colleague in Munich and inform him of your plans. You know he's been asking if you've made progress. Reassure him that I'll be providing pertinent information."

"I'll do that," Inge said. "I'm sure he'll be pleased to know you're doing your part. Would you like for me to tell him anything specific?"

"Let's see." Erich paused. "Instead of having you act as a go-between, why don't you ask him to join us for dinner? It might be better if he hears what I have to say firsthand."

"I don't know if he'll be available, but I'll certainly ask. If he is, what time should he be here?"

"I'd say 4:15, unless you think we should reserve some private time to confer beforehand."

Inge stifled a laugh. "Actually I think that would be an excellent idea," she said. "But then I wouldn't want to inconvenience our guest. It's cold out there, and I imagine he'll need to get back to Munich as soon as we're finished."

"I'm sure he will. I plan to remain in town until tomorrow morning should you and I find the need to continue our discussion after dinner."

"I'll keep that in mind. In the meantime, I'll meet you at the Jourhaus gates at four o'clock."

Inge waited until the line went dead and excitedly dialed SS Headquarters in Munich. As the central number rang, she waited, hoping Joachim wouldn't be out for one of his long lunches. When there was no answer after three rings, she feared he was, but she let the phone ring two more times. She was about to give up, when Joachim answered. "Heil Hitler," he said, clearly out of breath.

"Heil Hitler. Where were you?" Inge said brusquely.

"My, aren't we irritable. I was in the hall with Anna from the mailroom."

"I hope you didn't plan to see her this evening."

"Actually I did, but if you're propositioning me, I'd be glad to cancel."

"I wouldn't call it a proposition, but I would like to see you."

"Alone?"

"I'll have a friend with me."

"In that case, I'll keep my date—"

"I don't think that's a good idea. I miss you, and I am sure our friend would be very disappointed if he couldn't see you."

"Then how could I refuse? When and where?"

"How about the Café Bieglebrau? Can you be there at 4:15?"

"Are you insinuating work might keep me from arriving on time?"

"Not at all. I know you too well to think that."

"Then 4:15 it is. I'm surprised you want me there so early. Aren't you usually busy for several hours before I arrive?"

"I don't think your comment merits a response. Be on time."

Joachim laughed. "I wouldn't miss our meeting for the world, fair lady."

# CHAPTER 30

Erich was waiting just outside the Jourhaus gate when Inge arrived. "You're a welcome sight," he said as he slid into the passenger seat. "I missed you."

"I missed you too. Are you alright?"

"I'm fine."

Inge could tell Erich was anything but fine. She sensed something was eating at him. "You're sure?" she said.

"When I called, I'd been up all night and needed a nap." He smiled with his mouth, but his eyes were still troubled. "But I rested all day, just for you, so to the Wagner, Fraulein."

"Are you sure you're not sleepwalking, because you're obviously dreaming," Inge said. "Weren't you the one who insisted we meet with Joachim before we begin our private discussion?"

"Business before pleasure?" Erich shook his head. "How could I be so stupid?"

"Now you're sounding like Joachim, and you're both impossible."

"Where you're concerned, my love, pleasure is foremost on my mind. It's going to be hard to control myself across a table. How's Joachim? Has he had any luck with his assignment?"

"Why don't I let him tell you?"

"If that's what you want, but remember, two can play that game. If you're not going to cooperate with me, you'll have to wait to hear my news."

"What news?"

"I said you'll have to wait. In the meantime, tell me how you spent your day. Thinking of me, no doubt."

"No doubt."

"Seriously how's the article coming? From the look on your face I'd say you're not making much progress."

"I can't think of anything positive to say about your gruesome tests."

"So it was a wasted day."

"Not entirely. In terms of my article, yes, but I was able to accomplish something unrelated to work. Aunt Sigrid and I talked about leaving Germany. I'm eager for you and Joachim to sit down with her. I did as much as I could to address her concerns, but I think you two could do a great deal more to make her feel better about what she'll be facing in the days and weeks ahead."

"How much did you tell her?"

"Exactly what Joachim suggested." Inge grinned. "But you'll have to wait until we're all together to learn what that was."

When Inge and Erich got to the Café Bieglebrau, Joachim hadn't arrived. "Would you like to wait for your friend before ordering?" the waitress asked as she delivered menus to the table.

"Maybe a cup of chicken soup would warm me from the inside out," Inge said.

The waitress looked flustered. "I'm sorry, Fraulein," she said. "We're limited by increased rationing and there were no chickens available at the market."

"Then how about onion soup?"

"A bowl for me too," Erich said.

While they waited for Joachim, Erich presented the preliminary results from phase two. Inge knew not to ask for more details than he offered, but she sensed the tests were affecting him more than he was willing to admit. *He's trying to protect me,* she reflected as Erich spoke in broad terms, stressing what they'd learned from the experiment rather than how they ascertained the information.

At 4:35 p.m. Joachim arrived. "Sorry I'm late," he said. "Before I could leave the office the Proud Prussian called one of his last-minute meetings."

Erich greeted his friend with an extended hand and a grin. "And meeting with him was more important than joining us?" he said.

"Believe it or not, this time it was, but then this isn't where I expected to find the two you at this early hour. If I'm late, you're early."

"Touché," Erich said. "Will you ever run out of comebacks?"

"My great wit hasn't failed me yet. I imagine when it does I'll be dead."

Inge felt a chill as she thought of what lay ahead of them. "I'd rather avoid that gruesome topic altogether if you don't mind," she said. "I've grown rather fond of you, and your demise isn't something I want to discuss, even in jest."

Joachim sipped coffee while Inge and Erich ate their soup. When the time came to order dinner, the waitress apologized several more times for not having items on the menu. "It's the war," she complained, as she scurried off to put in the order, leaving her diners in the nearly deserted room.

"Inge tells me you have news," Erich said to Joachim.

"I do." Joachim described his conversation with Wrieden and the cabin near the Swiss border.

"Good job," said Erich. "With the cabin as an option, we can begin to make more specific plans. We may be moving more quickly than I'd originally anticipated. I've been given the go-ahead to travel to Ravensbruck and hand-select the women for the warming phase of the experiments."

Joachim slapped Erich on the shoulder. "That's great news. When are you going and how do I fit in?"

"To answer your first question, probably within the next two or three weeks. Rascher thinks it will be the latter, but I believe I can push the date ahead."

"How?" Inge asked.

"I'll tell you in a minute, but first, I have more good news. Last night marked my final involvement in the actual testing. From now on I'll only be writing reports.

"So you'll be coming to town more often," Inge said.

"Probably not. I can see that's not what you wanted to hear, but it's why I expect I'll be able to go to Ravensbruck earlier than Rascher anticipates. I'm going to put in a lot of overtime. Rascher expects Erna and me to work from nine to four every day, but I doubt we can accomplish all we need to do by maintaining a seven-hour day. If I work every night, I should be able to push my date of departure ahead. There's a mountain of paperwork, and I know Rascher won't give the go-ahead for the next phase of the tests until it's cleared away."

"I can't say I'm pleased," Inge said. "But if it's for Rosel—"

"It is. You know I'd rather come to town and spend my nights with you."

"I'm serious," she said. "I understand why you're working late, but I need material for the article that probably won't run. I can't sit around doing nothing. Herr Beck is already pressing me for more than an outline."

"Then come to the office; every afternoon if you'd like. You're expected to be there, so no one would be suspicious. Actually it would arouse more suspicion if you didn't come. I'll give you copies of my notes and answer any questions you may have, as long as they're within the limits we've set."

"What if I need to contact you?" Joachim said.

"I didn't say I'd be a hermit. I'll be available whenever you need me, and I definitely want to be kept up to date with what's going on. If you find a need to meet, call and tell me you want to discuss a supply issue." He thought for a moment. "But maybe that would be something we could discuss on the phone, so I wouldn't be able to race out of the office to meet you. Better yet, invite me to a party at the Hofbrauhaus. Say the event's for an old friend who's being transferred. That will let me know we need to meet in a timely manner. Inge will let you know when and where we can get together."

"So we don't have to discuss where to meet each time there's a need, why don't we use Aunt Sigrid's house?" Inge said. "That way it will only be a matter of the day and time."

"Sigrid's it is," said Erich. "Shall we plan to hold our first meeting this Friday at 4:30? Does that work for you, Joachim?'

"It does, though you realize I'll be breaking Gretchen's heart."

Erich rolled his eyes. "I'm sure she'll survive. So we're all set. Friday I'll give you an update, though I still won't have specific dates, and, Joachim, you should be ready to meet me in Berlin sometime within the next two or three weeks."

"I doubt Mueller will give me leave time, so I'll have to come up with a work-related issue that necessitates a visit to Panzer headquarters."

"What do you want me to do?" Inge said. "You realize I'm coming to Berlin with you."

Erich nodded no. "I realize that's what you want, Inge, but we need to be realistic. If your being in Berlin jeopardizes our plans, you'll have to remain in Munich. Think about it. I'll only be in the city one or possibly two nights. The rest of the time I'll be at Ravensbruck. You can't go with me, and even if you could get permission to make the trip, it wouldn't be wise. You can't see Rosel. Her reaction to you would give us away. For her safety and ours, it's best she know nothing about our plans until the last minute."

Inge frowned and started to protest, but Joachim cut her off. "You know Erich's right, fair lady."

"But I think—"

"Come on, Inge," Joachim urged. "I understand how you feel, but listen to reason. You're covering a story in Dachau. Why would you need to go to Berlin? Even the mention of a trip would make Beck suspicious. And if you could come up with a valid reason for going, you're adding the newspaper and the Propaganda Ministry to the mix. That could cause problems we can't handle. Erich's trip has to seem like nothing more than the selection and transportation of nameless women to Dachau for the experiments."

"Besides that, you need to help Sigrid," Erich said. "I'm sure she'd be frantic if all of us were away at the same time. She needs to be ready to leave immediately after we get Rosel to Dachau, and she can't do it alone. I figure we'll only have a day between the arrival of the women and the beginning of the warming experiments. We can't let Rosel be a part of the tests. Of course there are still quite a few ifs, but bottom line, if we do find Rosel, we'll have to leave Germany without delay."

Inge sighed. "I can't fight you both. So if I'm going to be forced to stay in Munich—"

"Inge—"

"I hate it, but I know it's the right thing to do. As I was saying. If I'm going to be staying here, I think we should all go see Aunt Sigrid tonight. If you have to leave sooner than anticipated, could you be sure you'd recognize Rosel from a few pictures you saw on the mantle? Aunt Sigrid and I can give you more information to help you identify her, and we can show you other photographs."

"The lady's right, my friend." Joachim said.

"Don't tell me you're also advocating business before pleasure."

"Me put work first? You're kidding, right? I just happen to agree with Inge. Anyway you know you'd have much more fun bunking with me tonight."

"I wish I'd kept everything to myself." Erich looked at Inge with pleading eyes. "Are you absolutely positive you wouldn't rather spend the evening with me at the Wagner? Remember our private discussion?"

Inge laughed at the forlorn look on Erich's face. "Of course I want to be with you, but there's work to be done."

Erich threw his hands in the air. "Alright, I give up. Inge, call Sigrid and let her know we're coming."

Inge looked around the room, but she didn't see a phone. "I guess we'll have to take our chances," she said. "That's unless you want to stop at the Wagner."

Erich grinned. "Oh, I do."

"To use the phone in the lobby; nothing more."

"In that case, let's not waste the time. Are you sure Sigrid won't be upset if we drop in on her unannounced?"

"She'll be overjoyed, and I'm equally certain she'll be home. She does all her visiting during the day."

"Then let's be off." Erich stood up and held the chair for Inge. He grinned at Joachim. "I assume you're treating us to this lovely dinner."

"It kind of looks that way, doesn't it?" Joachim threw the money on the table, and, with Erich and Inge following closely behind, he drove toward Munich.

Twenty-five minutes later, they pulled up in front of Sigrid's house. When he joined Erich and Inge on the front walk, Joachim was shivering. "I wonder if these damn motor-pool cars will ever have heaters that work properly," he said. "I feel like a living, breathing snowman."

"Then let's get inside," said Inge. "The fire will take off the chill, and if you're lucky, Aunt Sigrid will brew some of her precious tea."

Deciding not to startle her aunt by using her key, Inge knocked. Several minutes later, Sigrid opened the door a crack and peered out into the night. When she saw who was standing on the porch, she opened it all the way. "Inge, Erich," she said excitedly. "I didn't expect you. "Come inside. It's so cold." She spotted the man standing behind her niece. "You must be Joachim. Come in! Come in!" She ushered the three into the warm entry hall. "Take off your coats and go in by the fire while I put on some water for tea."

"This is Joachim, Aunt Sigrid," Inge said. "Joachim, this is my aunt."

Appraising Joachim, Sigrid extended her hand. "You are welcome, young man. My niece speaks highly of you."

Joachim patted Sigrid's small hand that rested in his. "She's told me wonderful things about you, too," he said. "It's a pleasure to meet you, Aunt Sigrid."

"Sigrid, please. Your hands are cold, Joachim." She looked at her niece. "Inge, take this man to the fire and let him warm up. I'll be right back."

As she bustled off to the kitchen, Inge, Erich, and Joachim hung their coats and left their boots by the door. "If you two will excuse me, I'm going to help my aunt," Inge said as the men walked toward the blazing fire.

"Hurry back," Erich called. "I may not be able to spend the night with you, but I can—"

"Shh," Inge said. "Do you want my aunt to know everything?"

"She probably already has an idea, but I promise to be more discreet if it makes you feel better."

While they warmed their hands in front of the crackling fire, Joachim studied the pictures on the mantle. He selected one and held it out to Erich. "Is this the lady we hope to rescue?"

"That's Rosel."

"She's nothing like Inge, but she's attractive in her own way." Joachim studied the other photographs. "It shouldn't be too hard to spot her at Ravensbruck."

"I doubt she looks like this anymore. That's why I'm hoping Sigrid will be willing to part with a few of her pictures. I'd like to cut the hair off one of them. It's likely that Rosel's head has been shaved or her hair is very short. If I could familiarize myself with her face minus the locks, it might be easier for me to identify her."

"With Inge around, I haven't dared ask, but what makes you think Rosel will be one of the women the Ravensbruck staff makes available for selection?" Joachim asked.

"Good question, and to be honest, I'm not sure she will be. I'm hoping because she's a Mischling, she'll have been treated better than the other prisoners."

"Why's that important?"

"She'll probably be plumper."

Joachim looked at the picture again. "She's not exactly plump to begin with. She's as thin as Inge."

"But compared to the serving girls in the officer's dining hall, she's obese. Those women are walking skeletons, and to answer your question, I plan to give the camp commandant a list of our requirements. At the top will be those with a little fat on their bones."

Before Joachim could respond, Inge returned with a tray that held a teapot and four cups. She placed the tea set on the table in front of the fire, and Sigrid poured the steaming liquid. Joachim took a sip and smiled at his hostess. "This is worth braving the cold weather," he said.

The four sat quietly, enjoying the warmth from the hot tea and the blazing fire. It was Sigrid who finally spoke. "Would you all like to tell me why I'm enjoying the pleasure of your company tonight?" she asked.

Inge looked at Erich. "Why don't you do the honors?"

"It's simple, Sigrid," Erich said. "We decided it was time for you to meet Joachim."

"And in keeping with my promise to tell you everything, we want to share what we're planning and address your concerns," Inge added.

Sigrid's eyes were wary. "Then you have news."

"We do," said Erich.

"So tell me," Sigrid insisted. "Inge told me a little of what's ahead for all of us. I admit I was shocked when she said we might have to leave Munich, but since I've had time to think, I realize, if you are able to get Rosel out of Dachau, we'll have to leave the country."

Inge squeezed her aunt's hand. "That's true," she said, "but at least we'll all be together."

"I'm not complaining, Inge. I'll manage. I always have."

Erich, Joachim, and Inge spent the next hour telling Sigrid what they were planning, answering her questions, and trying to alleviate her concerns. When the conversation was over, Inge pleased everyone by announcing that she'd remain in Munich while the men went to Berlin. "I know how hard it was for you to make that decision, fair lady," Joachim said. "But I still believe staying here is best for everyone, including you."

That decision made, Sigrid excused herself and went to her room. A few minutes later she returned and handed Erich a box of photographs. Erich examined each picture while Sigrid and Inge pointed out characteristics they thought might help him identify Rosel.

With Sigrid's permission, Erich cut Rosel's hair from several of the pictures. When he finished, he studied her features with dark hair closely cropped around her face and with no hair at all. After a sufficient amount of time, her face was indelibly drawn in his mind, and he was relatively sure he would be able to recognize her no matter how her looks might have changed during the months of incarceration. Nevertheless, at Sigrid's urging, he put the pictures in his pocket, promising to look at them again just before he went to Ravensbruck.

Despite the unspoken doubts and fears, everyone tried to enjoy the evening, and when Erich and Joachim stood to go, they were all reluctant to say goodbye. As the two men stepped out into the cold, snowy night, Sigrid took Erich's arm. "Thank you," she said.

"You're welcome. With any luck, I'll bring Rosel home to you and Inge."

Tears fell down Sigrid's cheek as she responded. "Whether you do or not, and, of course, I pray you're successful, I'll always be grateful for your—"

"I know," Erich said. He bent down and kissed Sigrid's cheek and then embraced Inge. "I'll see you soon," he whispered in her ear. "I love you."

Sigrid and Inge stood on the porch until car's tail-lights disappeared in the distance. The two women linked arms and went in by the fire. "You have two wonderful friends," Sigrid said. "I once thought we could find Rosel on our own, but now I realize that, without Erich and Joachim, we wouldn't know where she was taken, much less have a chance of bringing her home."

"We *will* bring her home, Aunt Sigrid. You heard Erich."

"I did, but I really wonder if he believes he can fulfill such a seemingly impossible task."

"I'm sure he does or he wouldn't be going to Ravensbruck, but we've talked enough for one night. It's time for bed."

"You go on, darling," Sigrid said. "I'm going to sit here a few more minutes."

"Don't be too long." Inge kissed her aunt on the cheek and left her to her private thoughts. As she closed her bedroom door, for the first time she dared to hope her dream might become a reality after all.

———————————

Joachim and Erich left the car at the motor pool and trudged through the snow to Joachim's apartment. Glad to be out of the icy cold, they hurried up the stairs. "It's freezing out there," Erich said as he rubbed his hands together over the warm radiator. "I'm glad Inge decided to stay with Sigrid. I wouldn't want her out on the icy roads."

"That's quite a family you've adopted, old buddy," Joachim said. "For all our sakes, I hope this turns out well in the end."

"So do I. You know how much I appreciate your help? Even locating Rosel, let alone getting her out of Ravensbruck, is a long shot at best, but if we *are* able to find her, I could never pull off the escape without you."

"You're giving me too much credit. But we've had enough serious talk for one night. I'm ready for some upbeat conversation."

"Not yet. I still have a few questions, beginning with one that's been hanging in the air for some time. How do you really feel about leaving Germany? You may try to make all of us believe you're fine, but I'm not so sure."

"Is it easy for you to go?"

"No, but what I've experienced lately is excuse enough for leaving, and because I love Inge and her aunt, it will be less difficult. Now answer my question."

Joachim began as if he were answering the question for Erich and for himself at the same time: "When we first joined the Hitler Youth, we were so enthusiastic," he said. "And though I don't feel the zeal I once felt, I don't have any complaints. I like my life, but I'm not stupid. From what I've read, and taking into account what those in the know are saying, my way of life will drastically change in the near future. Though no one is willing to say it out loud, the war is all but lost."

Erich started to speak, but Joachim nodded no. "Let me finish so we can put this discussion behind us once and for all. Don't misunderstand. I have no problem fighting for my country or for a cause I feel is important, but when it comes down to it, I'd rather do something meaningful for a friend. I know you believe in what you're doing, and I'm ready to support you. We both know our friendship goes beyond the evenings we've spent in beer halls. I will, as I've said before, do whatever's necessary to help you and the two women you love."

"Wow," Erich said. "That's the longest and most solemn speech I've heard you give since our early days in the party—maybe forever."

Joachim didn't react as Erich expected he might. "I'm being serious because I want you to know this wasn't a decision I made easily," he said. "When Inge first told me about Rosel, I considered what my future would be like if I helped you. I decided then and there that I'd do what I could, and after getting to know your fair lady and meeting her aunt, I'm ready to follow through on my commitment to whatever end."

"Then let's hope it's a good outcome for all of us. If I had a beer, I'd toast you."

"Normally I'd challenge you to go with me to the Hofbrauhaus and raise a stein or two, but this philosophical discussion has been exhausting. I'm going to bed."

Erich raised an eyebrow. "At this hour?"

"At this hour. What time would you like to get up? I'll get up with you and we can continue to plan. There's no room for failure. All of our lives are at stake."

"You're right," Erich said soberly. "Inge's picking me up at eight. Shall we get up at six?"

"Six o'clock it is."

Joachim set the alarm, and he and Erich headed for the shower. When they returned, Joachim fell into bed and turned his face to the wall. Erich realized his friend needed quiet time to consider the enormous changes taking place in his life. He respected his wishes and without saying goodnight, he stretched out on the couch.

# CHAPTER 31

Joachim was dressed and ready to go when the alarm went off at six o'clock. "Am I looking at a new Joachim?" Erich asked as he dragged himself out of bed.

"If you mean am I up early because I can't wait to get to work, then the answer is a definite no."

"That's the Joachim I know and love, but the Hofbrauhaus isn't open this early."

"There you go again," Joachim said. "You think beer and barmaids are the only things on my mind?"

"You're telling me they're not?"

Without waiting for Joachim to counter, Erich grabbed his towel and headed for the bathroom. When he returned, Joachim handed him a cup of coffee. "I only have an old coffee pot," he said. "So this crap is probably worse than what you're used to drinking."

"At least it's hot. I'll get dressed and we'll talk."

Apparently a good night's sleep had done the trick, because Joachim was his old self. He occasionally made Erich laugh as they made plans that would radically change their lives. They decided Joachim would tell Wrieden he'd like to use the cabin for a getaway if and when he could take a break from pressing business in Munich. At Erich's urging, Joachim promised to visit Sigrid often. By keeping her informed, they could address her fears and concerns and be sure she'd be emotionally and physically prepared to leave Munich at a moment's notice.

With Erich's help, Joachim concocted a supply problem which would necessitate a trip to Panzer Division Headquarters on or around the twenty-third. You know that's pushing it," Erich said. "Rascher still believes it will take us three weeks to complete the current tests and write the reports."

"But you believe you'll be able to reduce the time by about seven days."

"I do. We're not going to learn anything new. There's no reason to watch more men suffer and die."

"Apparently Rascher disagrees with you."

"You're right, but why? He either wants to be sure all the data we send to Berlin is accurate, or he's a sadistic son of a bitch. I tend to think it's the latter."

"So he's killing people for the hell of it?"

"That's my take, and I don't know how much more I can tolerate. If I hadn't met Inge, it's likely I probably would have deserted the first day of the damn tests. I can't count the number of times I've wanted to walk out of Block Five and never return. Be sure I'm going to work my butt off to finish the reports in two weeks."

"Should I start complaining about the supply issue now?"

"Not yet. If for some reason we're behind schedule, maybe because Rascher wants to kill a few more *volunteers*, you'll have to delay your departure date or go to Berlin and spend more time in the city."

"I'm not sure Mueller will approve a lengthy stay. We're already understaffed as more and more men are being sent to the front, depleting us even further."

"Then wait at least a week before you start mentioning a possible need to meet with the Panzer people. You don't want Muller to get irritated and order you to fly out too soon simply to shut you up. I'll keep you up to date as we go along. A few days should give you sufficient lead-time to make final arrangements for your trip."

Eight o'clock arrived too quickly. When they said goodbye, both men felt confident, at least for the moment, that they'd done all they could. Thinking their original plan to take things a step at a time still seemed the best way to proceed, they hadn't discussed specific strategies for the final escape. Instead they focused their attention on the difficult task of finding Rosel and then getting her out of Ravensbruck before they could begin to think about what they'd do when she got to Dachau.

---

On the first half of the drive back to Dachau, Erich told Inge about the plans he and Joachim had made. When they neared the outskirts of the town, he was unusually quiet. "Is anything the matter?" Inge asked. "You're not having second thoughts?"

"No second thoughts," he said. "Though until yesterday I hadn't considered the momentous changes we're all facing. Before we only talked about leaving Germany. Now our departure is becoming a reality."

"Are you upset about leaving?"

"I'd say I'm concerned, but not for myself. Joachim and I had an enlightening conversation last night before we went to bed, though I'm not sure it was actually a conversation because Joachim did most of the talking while I listened. He was so different from the Joachim I know, or, for that matter, have ever known. He was serious. It was like I wasn't talking to the man who's been my best friend for so many years."

"Is he reconsidering?"

"Definitely not. He talked to me about the Fuhrer, the party, and his own personal philosophy. He's prepared to sacrifice everything for our friendship, for what he believes he owes me, and for his newly-formed relationship with you."

Inge reached over and put her hand on Erich's leg. "And you're worried you're asking too much of him."

"I don't know. I guess that's part of it. Joachim and I have been friends for so long. By now I should know he only does what he wants to do."

"Then what is it?"

"I can't explain. Suffice to say, over the past three or four weeks everything I've been taught for the last five or six years has become a sham."

"Because of me?"

"Partially, but chiefly because of what I've seen and been a part of at Dachau. I'm upset because, until now, I've kept my head down and paid little attention to the atrocities taking place all around me. Until I was selected to be a part of these gruesome experiments, I accepted that everything Hitler and the party expounded was the truth, with slight deviations here and there of course."

"I can relate," Inge said. "Remember I write for a newspaper whose primary purpose is to see that the public embraces the party line. It's what I've been trying to do for years; report only what I'm told to write, while ignoring the truth."

"So you understand what I'm trying to say."

"Of course. It's ironic, but Aunt Sigrid was right all along. She once called the Fuhrer the 'Pied Piper of Hamelin.' Maybe we've all been rats following behind him without thinking or reasoning for ourselves."

"So you think it's possible to make profound changes in our way of thinking over such a short period of time?"

"I'm not so sure it's been that brief, Erich. I believe we've both been ambivalent for a while. Maybe it took disgusting and extremely personal circumstances to bring both of us to our senses. For me, it was the Gestapo abducting Rosel. For you it's your aversion to Rascher's experiments. I'm convinced we've always been astute individuals, but for whatever reason, the truth was temporarily lost on us. Now we can finally see the reality behind the years of indoctrination."

Erich pulled the car to the side of the road and turned to look at Inge. "Have I told you how much easier my life is with you around?" he said.

"I'd think knowing me has made your life far more complicated. I got you into this predicament."

"In some ways it is, but it's easier because I finally understand myself. I'm looking forward to our future, and before you break my train of thought, I want you to know I'm thoroughly convinced that leaving Germany is right for me and for all of us."

"Even for Joachim?"

"Even for him. He was never a true believer. I think he embraced the party because of me. For a long time I've worried that his *laissez-faire* attitude would eventually get him killed. At least by going with us he'll be free to live as he chooses."

"Speaking of the future, do you *really* think we have a chance to find Rosel and escape to Switzerland?"

"I can't lie to you. It won't be easy, but I do think it's a possibility. That said, whether we locate her or not, I've made a decision."

"I don't understand."

"I'll explain, but before you respond, I want you to give a great deal of thought to what I'm about to say. We may not find Rosel, but even if we fail, I'm leaving Germany."

"Even if there's no need to go?"

"That need, as you put it, existed for me the moment I walked through the Jourhaus gates, though I didn't fully realize it until last night. I can't be a part of those offensive tests any longer. I'll persevere until we've exhaust all possibilities of finding Rosel, or until we actually help her escape, but that's the only reason I'm going back today."

"And the decision I have to make?"

"I'd like for you, your aunt, and Joachim to leave with me, but each of you has to decide whether to stay or go. I won't try to influence you."

"The decision's easy for me to make," Inge said without hesitation. "Regardless of what happens, I'm going with you. I imagine Aunt Sigrid will feel the same way, especially if I'm leaving, and I hope Joachim will want to come along, but for now, I want us to think positively. We *will* find Rosel."

Erich squeezed Inge's hand and pulled back on to the highway. "I hope so," he said quietly. "I really hope so."

---

The following eight days were routine and almost identical in nature. There were no opportunities for Erich and Inge to meet outside the office, including the prearranged Friday night meeting, which had to be cancelled because Erich had too much to do.

Inge went to Block Five almost daily. Each afternoon she and Erich held business-related discussions concerning the tests that were continuing day and night. During her hours in the Dachau facility, she didn't encounter any unusual or potentially upsetting incidents. Each day after clearing her papers with the now-familiar guards on duty, she waited until Heinrich picked her up in the staff car and drove her to the office. He was waiting outside Block Five to take her back to her car when she was finished.

Erich spent most of his workday compiling statistics and writing reports for Berlin. Once or twice he considered including

an "I love you" among the notes he gave to Inge, but he thought
better of it. He'd have a problem if either Erna or Rascher asked
to see Inge's article and found the message.

Mentally and emotionally exhausted, he collapsed onto his
cot each night. He fell asleep thinking about Inge, and she was
his first thought when he woke up in the morning. Somehow
imaging their future together made the grim business of recording deaths a little easier.

---

Inge spent her mornings working on the article she was glad
she would never submit, meeting with Sigrid or Joachim, or seeing Beck so he wouldn't suspect anything out of the ordinary. For
all of them the waiting was difficult. There was nothing more
to do until Erich received word he could travel to Ravensbruck.
Even Joachim had to put his planning on hold. He had begun
to grumble about his supply problem, and Wrieden had said he
could use the hunting cabin sometime at the end of the month,
though Joachim was unable to specify a date. Beyond that he was
limited in what he could accomplish.

Finally on November 21ˢᵗ, their waiting came to an end. The
tests were progressing well, and Erich felt he had the best of the
paperwork and not the reverse. He'd completed the summaries of
the morning tests, straightened his desk, and was about to leave
for dinner when Rascher stopped him. "I'm very pleased with the
way your reports are progressing," he said. "You're doing a fine
job, Erich. I can see why your former bosses were impressed with
your work ethic."

The doctor's newfound familiarity didn't go unnoticed. Erich
guessed he had officially become a member of the trio of death.
"Thank you, Doctor," he said.

"You're up to date with your reports, and we're finding that our data remains uniform, so I believe we're ready to begin the final phase of our work."

Erich struggled to hide his excitement. These were the words he'd been waiting to hear. "So you're ready for me to travel to Ravensbruck," he said calmly.

"I've made arrangements for you to leave on a military transport tomorrow morning at 7:15. You'll fly to Berlin and stay overnight in the city. On Monday the 23rd you'll be driven to Ravensbruck. I'm sure you'll agree we can't waste time. Berlin continues to call for results, and we can't deliver the final report without completing the warming tests."

As Rascher droned on, it was difficult for Erich to concentrate on what he was saying. He had so many questions. Among them: *Was Joachim still aiming for the 23rd? Had he been able to convince Mueller the problem with Panzer supplies merits a trip to Berlin?*

"You will, of course, stay at the Aldon," Rascher said. "I assume you'll be able to drive to Ravensbruck, select the women, and return them to Dachau in four days. What do you think?"

"If all goes well, that sounds about right," Erich said.

"I told the Ravensbruck commandant you'd provide him with a list of our requirements when you arrive. You do know what we're looking for."

"I do."

"Good. Plan to spend one or two nights at the camp. "There's no reason to return to Berlin every night. When you've finished the selection process, notify Luftwaffe Headquarters. You'll return to the city and meet the women at Tempelhof at eight the morning of the 26th. Unfortunately you'll have to fly together. There aren't too many spare aircraft right now, and a separate plane to transport Jewish women would most likely be deemed extravagant, even if it was for a special Luftwaffe project. I hate to subject you or any other passengers to a flight with Jews, but we all must make sacrifices for the good of the Reich."

As he responded Erich wondered what sacrifices the doctor had made lately. "I imagine I can stand the ride for a few hours, Doctor," he said. "I'll be in the front of the plane so the smell won't get to me."

Rascher nodded approvingly. "Excellent," he said. "And while you're gone, Erna and I will complete the high-flight tests and see that the chamber is prepared for the next phase."

"When will we actually begin the warming tests?" he asked.

"If the women arrive on the afternoon of the 26th, we'll begin on the 27th. If it takes more time for you to make the selections, we'll plan accordingly."

"The next day?" Erich said incredulously.

"You seem surprised. I see no reason to delay."

Erich's mind jumped from one uncertainty to another. *Would Joachim have time to make arrangements to join him? Could he arrange for the hunting cabin before he had to leave? If not, would he be able to accomplish the task from Berlin?*

Everything was happening too quickly. *Why in the hell did I insist we take things a step at a time?* Erich wondered. *We haven't even come up with a tentative plan to get Rosel out of Dachau.*

He had no idea what the doctor had said while he was lost in thought. He snapped back to reality in time to hear the doctor tell him to take the rest of evening to prepare for the flight and report back to the office for his papers and final instructions at 6:30 the next morning.

Rascher finally left for the day. At the doctor's insistence, Erna had gone home earlier, so Erich was finally alone in the office. Rather than track Inge down, he decided to call Joachim; hoping to catch him before he left for the day. The camp operator connected him with Munich headquarters. He asked to be connected to Joachim's office and held his breath. "For once, be there," he pleaded silently.

On the fourth ring, Joachim answered. "Heil Hitler," he said jovially.

"Heil Hitler. It's Erich."

"This is a surprise, old buddy. I haven't heard from you in days."

"I've been rather busy, but I have a night off tonight and wondered if we could meet to discuss the supply snafu you told me about. I'll be leaving the Munich area tomorrow and should be gone for about five nights. Could we get together for a beer?"

Erich could hear surprise in his friend's voice. "That could be arranged," Joachim said.

"I've been cooped up here for over a week now and I'd really like to come to Munich. Do you think you or someone else might be able to pick me up at camp?"

"Someone will be there, Hauptsturmfuhrer. What time is good for you?"

"I need an hour to finish here in the office and then pack."

"How about six o'clock?"

"Six should be fine. I'll meet you or whomever at the Jourhaus gate."

―――――――――

Joachim sat at his desk wondering what to do next. He hadn't expected Erich to call, and even though they'd planned with November 23$^{rd}$ in mind, the news that Erich would be leaving on the 22$^{nd}$ and travel to Ravensbruck on the 23$^{rd}$ was surprising. He had a great deal to accomplish in a short time. He'd already made Mueller aware of his supply problem and the possibility he'd have to go to Berlin, but he hadn't mentioned a specific day. *Maybe I can make some headway before the meeting, if Inge will meet Erich,* he thought. He looked at his watch. *First things first, though.* He dialed an extension number in the building, hoping he wasn't too late.

"Heil Hitler," came the curt response from the other end of the line.

Joachim stifled his sigh of relief. "Sturmbannfuhrer, this is Obersturmfuhrer Forester. Do you have time to see me for a moment before you leave?"

Mueller paused. "I was preparing to go, Forester," he finally said. "But if it's necessary, I could delay my departure for a few more minutes."

"Thank you," Joachim said; stifling a sigh of relief. "I'll be right there. Heil Hitler." *Step one accomplished,* he mused. *Hopefully step two will be as easy.* He picked up the phone again, and this time asked the operator to dial Inge's number in Dachau. When they'd talked earlier, she hadn't mentioned coming to Munich, so he imagined she was still at the apartment. Frau Heiden answered, but she hadn't seen Inge all afternoon. "Would you check to see if she's there?" Joachim asked.

"Of course." The landlady put down the phone, and, minutes later, Inge answered.

Joachim sighed. "Fair lady, I'm glad to hear your voice!"

"This is a surprise, Obersturmfuhrer. It's late. Shouldn't you be at the Hofbrauhaus flirting with Gretchen?"

"I'm about to head over there now. I'm hoping to meet with a friend. I'm leaving for Berlin tomorrow and I need his advice."

"Tomorrow?"

"If Commandant Mueller gives me the okay, that's the plan."

"Do you have time to see me before you go?"

"That's why I called. How could I leave without seeing my fair lady? How about tonight?"

"Tonight works for me. When and where?"

"Our own little hideaway?"

"Perfect. Should I bring anything with me?"

"Why don't you go by and get our usual."

"What time do you want to meet?"

"If you leave Dachau at six o'clock you should be here by 6:30, weather permitting."

"I'll be counting the minutes."

"So will I." Joachim hung up. If anyone was listening, it would have been a relatively normal conversation for him. Glad he had a reputation for liking the ladies, he left his office and raced upstairs to see Mueller.

"I thought you said right away," Mueller roared, as Joachim knocked and opened the door.

"Heil Hitler! I apologize for the delay, Commandant."

"Now what can I do for you that can't wait until tomorrow?" Mueller said, still irritated.

Joachim prayed the anxiety he was feeling wasn't apparent to Mueller. "As I told you earlier this week, I have a problem with the final report that outlines the means of supplying our troops on the Eastern Front. I believe the only way to work through the dilemma is to go to Berlin and meet with the Panzer Division leaders."

"When would you need to leave?"

"I'm at a total impasse, and the matter is pressing. The Panzer people want me there as soon as possible. I was hoping to leave tomorrow morning, with your permission, of course."

Joachim waited nervously while Mueller pondered the request. "I don't see a problem," he said thoughtfully. "Is there anyone I can speak with in Berlin to make your task easier?"

"Not at the moment, but if I run into difficulties, I'll contact you for assistance."

"In that case stop by the radio room on your way out and tell the sturman to cut your orders. I'll sign them by noon tomorrow. How long do you expect to be away?"

"I have no idea, but I'll do my best to resolve the issue in a timely manner. I'll keep you informed."

"Do that," Mueller said. "I can't spare you indefinitely. You have a week at most."

Joachim wanted to scream with relief. He thanked Muller and left the room. After stopping by his office to pick up his coat and cap, he went to the radio room. He wasn't sure how he'd get to Berlin, but he imagined there would be a military transport leaving Reim the next afternoon. The first two obstacles had been relatively easy to overcome. There was only one more thing to deal with, and he prayed that too would fall into place. He left the building and walked toward the Hofbrauhaus.

---

When Inge reached the Jourhaus gate, Erich wasn't there. She parked the car and waited. Five minutes passed; then ten. She was beginning to feel uneasy when he strolled through the gates. "Sorry I'm late," he said as he got into the passenger side. "I worked until six o'clock, and then had to notify the commandant's office I'd be away tonight."

"I was beginning to wonder if I misunderstood Joachim. You're usually right on time."

Erich grinned. "Or early."

"On a good day, right. Do you want to drive?"

"Not unless you want me to. I'd rather make some notes on the way."

"Then I'll save my questions for later." She put the car in gear and headed for Munich and the meeting they had all waited to attend.

------------

Joachim looked around the crowded Schwemme, wondering if it might be for the last time. He knew he'd made the right decision, but memories of evenings at the Hofbrauhaus were, as other memories of his homeland, good ones, and he wasn't stupid enough to believe his departure would be easy.

He studied the faces at the bar and at the tables. Unfortunately, Wrieden wasn't among the throng. Frustrated, Joachim looked at his watch. *It's early,* he thought. *If it's a normal day, Wrieden just left work.* He stood near the oompah band and waited.

By 6:15 he'd about given up any hope of achieving his third objective. He was about to leave for his meeting at Sigrid's, when Wrieden pushed through the Schwemme door. Joachim made his way through the crowd to greet him. "Am I glad to see you," he said, inwardly chuckling to think how the man would feel if he knew why. "I thought we might talk a little business. I have a table. Will you join me?"

"Of course," Wrieden said. "Though I've never known you to be interested in anything that's business related."

"It's not that kind of business." Joachim grinned and led Wrieden toward the back of the room. "I'm leaving for Berlin tomorrow," he said when they were seated and the barmaid delivered steins of beer. "I thought I'd take you up on your offer to let me use the hunting cabin. I could use a little rest and relaxation."

"Couldn't we all," Wrieden said. "When do you need the place?"

"I have about a week before I have to be back in Munich. I'll be in Berlin for at least four days to meet with the Panzer Division leaders, and I thought I'd use the remaining time to get away from all these tedious supply problems; on the sly of course. If Mueller discovers I'm back in Munich, he'll find something for me to do, and my fair frauleins would be so disappointed. My plan is to come back long enough to get the proper clothes and leave right away."

"Then I'll make arrangements. An old man from the area looks in on the place from time to time. I'll let him know you're coming so he isn't surprised to find you there." He chuckled. "I'd hate for him to be shocked by your behavior."

Joachim grinned. "I'm sure he'd be horrified."

"That goes without saying. I'll wait to hear from you; that is, if you promise not to take all the lovelies away from Munich when you go."

"I'll leave one or two behind, and tonight you can have them all. I have to pack."

As he shook hands with several of the men at the bar, Joachim thought about the great times he'd had at the Hofbrauhaus. "I can't look back now," he said as stepped out into the cold wind and trudged through the snow toward Sigrid's house.

# CHAPTER 32

Joachim was the first to arrive for the meeting. Sigrid ushered him into the parlor to sit by the fire while she went to make tea. Instead of sitting, he walked to the fireplace to warm his hands. As he studied Sigrid's precious family photos lining the mantle, he spotted a picture of Inge and Rosel. He picked it up and studied the girl who smiled back at him from the photograph. "I pray your ordeal will be over soon," he whispered.

"Are you talking to yourself?" Sigrid asked as she came in and placed the tray on the table in front of the fire.

"Thank God I haven't resorted to that, at least not yet. I was looking at this picture." He held it out for Sigrid to see. "I told Rosel she'd soon be reunited with you and Inge."

Sigrid poured tea. "Is that the reason for this meeting?" she asked. "All Inge said was the three of you would be here around 6:30."

"Inge and I didn't talk for long, and because we had no idea who might be listening in, the conversation was cryptic. Erich will fill us in when he and Inge get here, but I can say that he and I are leaving for Berlin tomorrow."

"So soon? I had no idea."

"Neither did we."

"Are you going to Ravensbruck with Erich?"

"I don't think so, but I don't know anything more than what I've already told you. I've had minimal contact with Erich over the past ten days, and when Inge sees him, she's at the camp office, so they can't have a private conversation. That's why we're meeting here."

"But Inge's not going to Berlin with you," Sigrid said anxiously. "Erich hasn't changed his mind about that, has he? I know my niece is a stubborn woman, but I'm not sure I can be ready to leave if she's not here to help me."

"As far as I know, nothing's changed in Inge's regard, Sigrid. She'll stay here in Munich with you."

Before Sigrid could ask any more questions, the front door opened and Inge and Erich bustled into the entry hall. Erich peeked into the parlor. "It's cold out there," he said. "How's my favorite lady?"

"Can't you be satisfied with one beautiful woman?" Joachim said indignantly. "Do you have to be greedy?"

Sigrid laughed. "I'm flattered," she said. "It's been a long time since two men fought over me, even if it's all in jest. Is anybody hungry, or shall we talk first?"

"The food smells good," Joachim said. "I'd rather eat and then talk. I should boost my physical strength before I force my brain to work overtime."

Everyone laughed at Joachim's perpetual aversion to work before pleasure, but they agreed to eat first. Inge helped her aunt in the kitchen, and fifteen minutes later, they were sitting around the kitchen table enjoying wienerwurst, Sigrid's special fried potatoes, and home-baked bread.

When the dishes were washed and put away, they gathered in the parlor. "I wish we could put off the inevitable conversation a little longer," Inge said. "It's hard to face reality after such a pleasant meal."

"I can stall for a few more minutes," said Sigrid. "Would anyone care for tea or some very old brandy before we begin?"

The men chose brandy, and Inge opted for tea. When they were finally settled, Erich began. "Our wait is almost over," he said.

"So soon?" said Sigrid. "I had no idea."

"I wasn't informed until today. I figured I'd be writing reports for several more days before Rascher sent me to Ravensbruck. I also thought Rosel and I would have a couple of days to make our escape once I got her back to Dachau. As it stands now, I'll return on the afternoon of November 26th, and the tests will begin on the morning of the 27th."

"That's cutting it close, old buddy," Joachim said.

"That's an understatement. So assuming I get back to camp at four o'clock in the afternoon, Rosel and I will have five hours or so to get away. We should try to be at the cabin before the guards realize she's missing."

"When do you think that will happen?" Inge asked.

"By eight o'clock the next morning at the latest. The tests are scheduled to begin at nine, and Rascher's always punctual." He shook his head. "Another mistake on my part," he said. "I hadn't considered breakfast. Realistically, we'll only have until six. That's when the guards will feed the women, and we'll be discovered."

Sigrid grimaced and Erich took her hand. "Even with two fewer hours, we'll be fine," he said. "I have a plan, but before I give you the specifics, let me tell you my schedule as it stands now. Tomorrow morning at eight o'clock, I'll fly to Berlin. I'll stay at the Aldon tomorrow night, and the next morning at nine, I'll be driven to Ravensbruck. The selection process will begin after lunch and continue through the afternoon and the next day. On the morning of November 26th, I'll return to Berlin with the women and we'll fly to Munich."

"So you'll be on the plane with Rosel," Inge said.

"As far as I know, that's the plan."

"Can't you escape with Rosel before you come back to Dachau?" Sigrid asked. "Maybe you could get away before you board the plane."

"There won't be an opportunity, Sigrid. Guards will accompany the women from Ravensbruck to Tempelhof. They'll remain with them during the flight, turn them over to the Dachau guards in Munich, and return with the plane."

"So you don't have a choice. You have to come back here."

"We do, and for another reason. If Rosel and I try to get away in Berlin the Gestapo will take over the investigation. In a few hours they'll know Joachim and I are friends."

"How?" Sigrid asked.

"They'd access our records and realize we trained together."

"And remember, Joachim took over Erich's supply project," Inge said.

"The SS and the Gestapo are known for meticulous record-keeping," said Joachim. "They knew Rosel was a Mischling, and they knew where to find her."

"So they had to know she was living with Inge and me," Sigrid added.

Erich nodded. "I'm sure they did. Frankly, I'm still amazed you weren't arrested, especially in light of Inge's position with the paper."

"Maybe the fact that you write for the *Völkischer Beobachter* is the reason you're still free," Joachim said.

Inge recalled the article she'd recently read about the Abwehr Agent. "It would be a good story," she said. "I can see the headlines now—*Völkischer Beobachter* reporter arrested for harboring an enemy of the Reich."

"It's a story I wouldn't want to read," Erich said.

"Could we be in danger now?" Sigrid said.

"It's possible," Erich answered. "That's another reason we have to leave Germany. If Rosel and I weren't on the plane, I guarantee it wouldn't be long before a Gestapo agent knocks on your door."

"Or barge in without knocking," Joachim said. So, Sigrid, it's better if they take their chances at Dachau."

"I understand," Sigrid said. She turned to Erich. "But once you're back, how will you get Rosel out of that terrible place?"

"I'll explain what I'm thinking, but remember, this is just the preliminary plan. That's why we're all here. I'll talk; you'll ask questions, and we'll fine-tune. Feel free to interrupt if you have thoughts or concerns, and I'm sure you'll have plenty of the latter. So here goes. As soon as I get to the office, I'll ask Erna for an update."

"That is if she's still around when you arrive," Joachim said. "You said you'd be back around four. That's usually when Erna leaves for the day? What if she's already gone?"

"Good thought. I'll call from Berlin and say I need to be briefed before I see Rascher on the 27th."

"What if she's not convinced?" Sigrid asked.

"I'll go to Plan B. Erna lives to please Rascher, so she should agree to wait for me if she thinks it's in his best interest. If she's still reluctant, I'll call the doctor and tell him I need her. She would never refuse a direct request."

"Then what?" said Sigrid.

"I'll say hello to Erna and go get Rosel."

"You're kidding," Inge said. "I can hear it now. 'Rosel Dollman, meet Fraulein Erna Hambro. I know you two will get along well.'"

"And for that matter, how will you know where Rosel's being held?" Joachim said. "Or did you plan to search the entire camp in five hours?"

"You'll understand if you give me time to finish. First let me answer the question about where Rosel will be taken once we're back at the camp. Rascher plans to keep the Ravensbruck women apart from the Jewish girls who work in the camp."

"Why?" Sigrid asked.

"So they can't share information about the experiments. Rosel and the others will be housed in the Strafblocke, a section of the camp usually reserved for more hardened criminals and second offenders. Since I transported the women from Ravensbruck, it would be natural for me to take a look at their accommodations, so I'll go with the guards while they get them settled. That way I'll know exactly where to find Rosel when I return for her."

"You know the guards aren't going to leave the women to fend for themselves," Joachim said.

"Of course I know—"

"Then how—"

"Again if you'll give me a chance, I'll tell you. As I was saying, after I've talked with Erna, I'll go for Rosel."

"Care to explain how you're going to get her back to the office?" Joachim asked.

"Sure. I'll tell the guard I want one of the women for my own pleasure. Making whores of the women who serve in the dining room is a relatively common practice among the camp officers."

Erich saw the pained look on Sigrid's face. "I'm sorry I have to be so blunt, Sigrid," he said. "Y said you want to hear everything—"

"I do. But I didn't realize—"

"It's okay, Aunt Sigrid. I was shocked when I first heard about the atrocities being committed at Dachau. Do you want Erich to skip the specifics?"

"Of course not," Sigrid said adamantly. "I'm fine. Please go on, Erich."

"Before you do, I have yet another question," Joachim said. "Won't the guard want to know if you have the authority to remove Rosel from her cell? The serving girls are one thing, but—"

"I thought of that. I'm hoping my personal involvement in the experiments will justify my warming a woman before she's handed over to Rascher to warm the volunteers. It's the only thing I have at this point. I certainly can't shoot my way into and out of the Strafblocke."

"What happens if you succeed and the guard lets you take Rosel?" Inge asked.

"Here's where it gets tricky and why I need Erna. I'm going to use her car."

"So your plan is to get Erna's keys before you go for Rosel, take her directly to the car?"

"Unfortunately, it's not that easy."

"Because Erna leaves her car by the Jourhaus gate," Inge said.

"Exactly, and if I took Rosel from her cell to the gate, the guards would come out to investigate. If we were able to get her into the car before we were noticed, we we'd likely encounter another problem, two for that matter."

"Like what?" Joachim asked.

"First, Rosel would have to drive, and I'm sure she won't be in any shape to get behind the wheel."

"Nor would she know where to go," Inge said.

"Right again."

"You could drive," Sigrid said.

"That would immediately arouse suspicion. Erna always drives me to town."

"So we're in trouble before you begin," said Joachim.

"We are, and that brings us to the second problem. It's not unusual for the guards to search the cars at random."

"In which case they'd realize Erna wasn't driving," Inge said.

"Right, so I'll take Rosel to the office, switch her with Erna, and have her, that's Rosel, drive me out of the camp."

Joachim laughed. "You're not serious." He paused. "Oh my God, you are. You're going to take a skinny, possibly-bald woman in prisoner's clothes and have her coolly drive through the camp gates."

"I assure you, I'm perfectly serious, and with Inge's help, Rosel won't look like a prisoner. She'll look like Erna."

But even if she physically transformed, Erna's hardly going to say, 'Certainly Hauptsturmfuhrer, I'll be glad to switch places with a Jewish prisoner and warm the volunteers'"

"It won't be easy, but if you'll stop interrupting, I'll continue to explain. Inge, while Joachim and I are in Berlin, you're going to purchase a wig. Don't buy it in Dachau. The town's too small and you'd be remembered if the Gestapo starts asking questions. You know how Erna wears her hair. Buy a wig that's the same color and style it so a casual observer would think it's her."

"Okay," Inge said. "What else?"

You've also seen the coat Erna wears every day. The guards would expect her to be bundled up on a cold night, so that's the only clothing we'll have to worry about. I imagine we could use her coat, but in case she doesn't have her usual one with her, buy one that looks as much like the one she wears most days."

"And you think the guards would be suspicious if the woman driving the car had on a different-colored coat?"

"Maybe, maybe not, but why take a chance? I'll put the coat and wig on Rosel and wrap a scarf around her neck to cover her chin. As I said, the guards are used to seeing Erna drive me to town, so they'll most likely wave us on. They may stop us momentarily and take a cursory look in the back seat. Because of the cold, I doubt they'd bother with much else. They don't want to be out of the warm Jourhaus any more than they have to be. Once we're beyond the gate, I'll switch places with Rosel and we'll drive to meet you."

Joachim shook his head. "I don't know where to begin," he said. "There are so many ifs in your scheme."

"I know, but that's all we have; that is, unless any of you has come up with something while I've been stuck in the camp." He looked at Joachim and Inge. "Apparently you haven't or you'd be telling me what it is. So I've told you what I'm thinking. Start asking questions so we can fine-tune the plan and discuss the possible complications. You look skeptical, Joachim. Do you want to go first? What's on your mind?"

"Everything you're suggesting," Joachim said. "But I'll give it to you one thing at a time. First, you're forgetting I'll be in Berlin and can't tell Mueller I'm back in Munich. He'd never give me additional time-off for personal leave, and if I didn't show up for work—"

"So you won't let anyone know you're back."

"Okay, so if I'm supposedly still in Berlin, I won't be able to check out a motor-pool car in Munich."

"We'll use the Volkswagen," Inge said.

Erich nodded no. "The little car won't hold all of us, and I'm not sure it could survive the trip."

"Then what do we do?" Sigrid asked.

"We'll take Erna's car to the cabin and cross the border on foot. There's no chance we could make the final escape in a car. You three will drive the Volkswagen to our prearranged meeting place."

"Why can't we leave from here?" Sigrid asked. "I'm sure Rosel would like to see her home one more time before we go, perhaps for good."

"Because we'd use thirty precious minutes bringing Rosel here and another half hour driving back the way we came. With every minute we waste we're tempting fate and risking discovery."

"And if we leave from here, one of the neighbors might see us," Inge added. "It wouldn't take much for the Gestapo to find out we all left together. My little car's a regular feature in the neighborhood. If you and I leave home, even if Joachim's with us, no one will think twice. We'll pack the trunk a little at a time so all we'll be carrying when we walk out the door will be our pocketbooks. Anyone who sees us will think we're going out to dinner."

"Let's back up a minute," said Joachim. "We haven't finished talking about your insane plan to get Rosel out of Dachau. Won't the guard be suspicious when you don't bring the woman you took away back to her cell? And I'm not through talking about Erna. Of course I was being sarcastic when I said she'd wave goodbye and wish you luck, but she's not going to sit there while you and Rosel drive out of the camp in her car."

"I'll have to silence her before I go for Rosel."

Inge's eyes grew wide. "Surely you're not going to kill her, Erich," she said in disbelief.

"I hope it won't come to that. I've grown rather fond of Erna. She's efficient and totally dedicated to her work, and she's always been helpful and decent to me, especially at the beginning when I was having such personal difficulties."

"So if you're not going to kill her, what are you going to do with her?" Inge asked. "More than once you've mentioned her almost fanatical dedication to Rascher and his causes. You know she won't cooperate."

"I'm sure she'd scream bloody murder. So she'll have to take Rosel's place."

Joachim chuckled. "I hate to say this, my friend, but you are absolutely certifiable." When Erich started to respond, he put up his hand. "No, this time you let me finish. Even if you could work your magic and make Erna do as you ask, a lady who's well fed and has a full head of hair would look out of place among skinny, bald women. The guard would know something's not right."

"I'm counting on Rosel to be more than skin and bones. Remember, if what we've heard about the Mischlinge is true, she hasn't been treated as badly as the other prisoners. Erna is thin, and because the women will have just arrived, the guards won't be familiar with them."

"What about the hair?" Sigrid asked.

"Erna will go to the infirmary minus her locks."

"You're going to shave her head?"

"It may come to that, but, again, it depends on Rosel. If she's bald, then Erna will be bald when I take her to the barracks. If Rosel's hair is short—"

"We all get the picture," Joachim said. "You're expecting Erna will sit quietly while you shave her head, and when she takes Rosel's place, she'll go happily and never try to signal the guards."

"That's what I'm hoping."

"Erich," Inge began.

"Come on. Give me a little credit. Of course I know Erna won't be a willing participant."

Joachim scowled. "Then what the hell are you going to do?"

"I'll tell you, if you'll shut up and listen." He looked a Sigrid. "Please excuse my rudeness."

"Apology accepted," Sigrid said. "So what about Erna?"

"When I'm finished with her, she won't object to having her head shaved, nor will she warn the guards. I intend to knock her out."

Sigrid's eyes grew wide. "You're going to hit a woman?"

"Not if I can help it, Sigrid. I'm hoping to locate some sort of medication that will do the job, but if I absolutely have to, I *will* knock her out."

"But if she's sedated, she won't be able to walk back to her cell," Inge said.

"I know, so I'll drag her. When the guard asks me why, and I imagine he will, I'll tell him she wouldn't cooperate with me and I had to get a little rough. He won't think a thing of it. In fact he'll probably be amused."

"What about the other women in the barracks?" Sigrid asked. "Surely they'll realize the person who left isn't the one who's being returned."

"I'm counting on their fear to keep them quiet. The Dachau prisoners don't have much personal interaction. Every man realizes that drawing attention to himself could prove disastrous, so he tries to remain anonymous and in the background. These women have been incarcerated at Ravensbruck, and I imagine it's the same there. They won't say much, even to each other."

"Let's say everything goes as planned and you and Rosel make it through the Jourhaus gates," Inge said. "Rascher will realize something's wrong when you and Erma don't report to the office for the tests, and he'll start to investigate."

"They'll know about Erna well before Rascher arrives, and after they interrogate the guard who was on duty when I took Rosel from her cell, they'll discover my involvement. I told you it's likely the women will be fed breakfast at six o'clock. As soon as they deliver the food, the guards will know that Erna is in Rosel's place."

"Maybe earlier if she wakes up and starts yelling," Inge said.

"You're right, but I plan to give her a dose of medication strong enough to keep her unconscious until at least six."

Sigrid looked hopeful. "So maybe they won't figure out Rosel isn't there until much later."

"I wish that were true, but unfortunately, we're in just as much jeopardy if Erna is still sleeping soundly when her breakfast arrives."

"I don't understand," Sigrid said. "If Erna's unconscious, she won't be able to say anything."

"No, but at Dachau, prisoners are expected to obey the minute an SS guard issues an order. Not doing so could result in a beating, or worse. If Erna's still out cold, the guard will want to know why she isn't responding to his command to get out of bed. Even if he doesn't immediately recognize her, when she's revived and explains what happened, the search for me and Rosel will begin in earnest."

"So as you said, we only have until six o'clock in the morning," Inge said.

"Exactly, so you realize the importance of timing. I doubt the SS, or the Gestapo, if Weiss calls them in, will immediately make the connection among all of us, so until they actually begin to ask around, the three of you will be off their radar. That means, for a short while, the hunting cabin is safe territory, but once Rosel and I arrive at the meeting place, we're going to have to make good time."

"And once we're at the cabin?" Joachim said.

"You and I will try to figure out the guards' routines. As early as possible we'll cross the border. The nearest town of any size is Basel. Even in the cold and snow, we can and we *will*, make it. And before I forget, Inge, you'll need to buy some wire cutters when you shop for the coat and wig. We'll probably have to cut the wires that separate Germany from the neutral zone."

"I'll go to the local hardware store."

"And if Inge can't find the cutters, I'll try Herr Ott," Sigrid said.

"How long before we're able to cross into Switzerland?" Inge asked.

"Hopefully as soon as it's dark. It would be better to cross at night. Once the Gestapo discovers Joachim and I are connected, they'll call the border guards. It won't be long before they come looking for us."

Thinking ahead, Sigrid changed the subject. "What will I be able to take with me, Erich?" she asked.

Erich took Sigrid's hand. "Only one suitcase for all three of you, Sigrid, and I'm not sure we'll be able to take that across the border."

"Only one suitcase?"

"I realize deciding what to bring will difficult, but there will only be room for the five of us in the car, and the trunk isn't large enough to hold five suitcases. We need to pack it with supplies. Rosel won't have any belongings with her, so include a few personal mementos you think she might appreciate, a picture of her parents or something of that nature, and pack as many warm blankets as you can, and her heavy clothes. She won't be in the same physical condition as we are."

"What about food?" Sigrid asked.

"We'll take as much as you can prepare. Food and warm clothing are the primary needs. Anything else, though it might be personally important, is secondary. I'd love to be able to tell you we'll all return to this house someday, but—"

"I know you don't have any answers," Sigrid said.

"You're right, I don't."

"I understand, and I'll do as you ask. While you're in Berlin, Inge and I will go through Rosel's belongings. I'm sure we'll find a few keepsakes she'll want to have."

"The more I hear you talk, old buddy, the more I wonder if it's really necessary for me to go to Berlin," Joachim said. "It seems you have everything figured out."

"That may seem to be the case, but you've already made plans to go and Mueller would be suspicious if you miraculously found a solution to the supply problem you've been griping about for weeks. Besides we can go over the details of the plan and talk about potential issues we haven't considered."

"Okay, if you're sure you need me—"

"I do need you. Besides being my sounding-board, you're going to be the liaison between us and Inge. I'm sure calls going out of or coming into the Aldon are monitored, so you'll cryptically relay information and additional instructions." Erich slapped Joachim on the shoulder. "And frankly, I'd like to have you around for moral support."

"Then if you can't do without me, and I figured that would be the case, I'll catch a transport from Munich to Berlin tomorrow afternoon. I'll reserve a room at the Aldon, and we'll meet for dinner tomorrow evening."

"Under the circumstances it might be better if we order room service. We shouldn't be seen together."

"You mean I won't have one last opportunity to look at all of Berlin's beautiful sights?"

"You can do your carousing while I'm at Ravensbruck."

Inge looked at the clock on the mantle. "It's getting late," she said. "You two need to get some sleep. I know you have to get up early, Erich. And Joachim, if you're leaving for Berlin, you won't be able to be the leisurely soul you are most mornings."

"Insulted again," Joachim said. "I'm not sure I want to spend the next months and years of my life around people who have such little respect for me and my needs."

"Oh we respect you, but we also understand you," said Sigrid, her eyes twinkling.

Erich laughed. "You're very wise, Sigrid," he said. "And Inge's right. We have a great deal to accomplish over the next few days."

Erich had his hand on the doorknob when Inge took his arm. "We've forgotten something else," she said. "How will I get the wig and the other things to you?"

As he answered, Erich wondered how many other small but important details they'd overlooked. "When we get back to town, I'll call to say I have information for the article. Meet me at the Jourhaus gate. We'll drive until we're out of sight, and I'll put the things you brought under my topcoat. I'll be bundled up anyway, so the extra bulk won't be obvious when I walk back through the gate."

"That works, but I have another question."

"Ask away, though all these additional concerns aren't helping my confidence."

"I know, but we all want to make sure everything goes as planned. What will you tell Rosel? She'll be terrified when you select her for the tests."

"I'm sure that's true, but I can't say anything until the last minute. Any unusual reaction on her part could ruin everything."

"When will you tell her?" Sigrid asked.

"When we get to the office, but I won't say much. We'll have plenty of time to talk during the drive to the cabin."

"I hate to ask yet another question, especially when it seems everything's under control," Joachim said. "But we need to talk about something all you brilliant strategists seemed to have overlooked."

"Come on, Joachim," Erich said impatiently. "This is hardly the time for joking. What's on your mind?"

"It's this, my friends. Can Rosel drive?"

Erich looked at Joachim and then at Inge and Sigrid. "Joachim's right," he said. "A bumpy departure from the camp could ruin everything."

Inge thought for a moment. "I think she can drive, Joachim, but you know, I'm not sure. She used to have friends who had cars, but I never saw her drive one."

"Oh, my God," Erich moaned. "That one question has ruined my evening. Come on, Joachim. Let's go see if we can think of anything else that could go wrong."

# CHAPTER 33

When the plane left Reim at eight o'clock, Erich was thinking about the drive back to camp. Much of what they discussed was redundant, but they wanted to be sure they hadn't overlooked even the slightest detail. There was another reason he had opted to go with Joachim rather than spend more time with Inge. His friend was making an enormous sacrifice, and, for now, he had to be the priority.

As he flew above the snow-covered landscape, Erich wondered if they really had a chance to make their plan work. Since no one was sitting near him. He removed the picture of Rosel from his pocket. Her face was now firmly etched in his mind. He was sure he'd recognize her however much she'd changed. *But how many women can I reject to get to her,* he wondered, *and how far can I push the Ravensbruck administrators?*

Suddenly a troublesome thought crossed his mind; it was something, despite their careful planning, he and Joachim hadn't considered. What if Berlin's failure to decide the fate of the Mischlinge kept Rosel out of the mix? He put the pictures back in his pocket. Worried about what else they might have forgotten and eager to land in Berlin and put the plan in motion, he settled back in his seat and passed the time fine-tuning the plan.

"Isn't 6:30 a.m. a little early for you to be here, Obersturmfuhrer," the sturman said when Joachim presented his papers.

"Normally it would be, but I need to book a seat on the first plane to Berlin. I don't have a phone in my apartment house, so here I am." Joachim chuckled. "If I didn't have this difficult supply problem to solve, I'd be home like everyone else with any brains. I wasn't ready to oust that beautiful fraulein from my bed."

The sturman was grinning as Joachim raced up the stairs. He threw his coat on the chair, picked up the phone, and asked the operator to connect him with the Luftwaffe office at Reim. He was told there wasn't an afternoon flight from Munich to Berlin, but a Luftwaffe transport would be leaving at 10:30 a.m. and there was a seat available if his papers were in order. He reserved the seat, though he wondered whether he could be ready to travel before noon when Mueller said his orders would be ready. He doubted he could push the slow SS bureaucracy to act in a timelier manner. On top of that, he hadn't packed. Thinking he'd be leaving later in the day and have plenty of time to choose items he wanted to take to Switzerland, he'd gone right to bed after returning from Dachau.

Realizing he couldn't accomplish much before nine o'clock, he battled the wind and blowing snow as he trudged back to his apartment. He filled two suitcases, one for Berlin containing the clothes and personal items he'd need for the short stay, and because he wasn't sure how much time he'd have when he got back, a second bag for the drive filled with civilian clothes and a few personal keepsakes. He was uncharacteristically nostalgic as he went through the items that made up the record of his life. He packed pictures of his parents, the photo of him and Erich at Unser Traum, and mementos of his youth. When the bag was full, he gathered up additional blankets and a second coat, closed his Berlin bag and the suitcase of memories, and left the apartment for Sigrid's.

When he reached Sigrid's walkway, the snow was really coming down. He had just knocked when Inge, still in her robe, answered the door. "What an unexpected surprise." She paused. "Is there something wrong?"

"I hit a snag, but I'm sure I'll be able to work it out when I get back to headquarters. I hope I'm not disturbing you and your aunt, but I thought it might be a good idea to bring these things by today." He handed Inge the coat and blankets and put his suitcase by the door. "I have no idea what to expect when I get back from Berlin. These are a few mementos I'd like to take with me if we can find room."

"I'm sure we'll find a place for them. Will you stay and have coffee or breakfast with us? My aunt's in the kitchen cooking."

"I'd love to, fair lady, but there's no time. The problem I alluded to concerns my flight to Berlin. I hoped to leave this afternoon, but the only transport departs at 10:30 this morning. If I'm going to make the flight, I have to pick up my orders and be at Reim by 10:15, but I have to have Mueller's signature before I can board. Yesterday he told me my orders would be ready at noon."

"Surely if Mueller knows you have a plane to catch, he'll be obliging."

"I doubt it, but there's no hope if I keep standing here talking with you."

Inge took Joachim's arm as he turned to leave. "If you have one more minute, there's something I need to say before you leave for Berlin."

"Please tell me you're not going to deliver a serious speech," Fair lady.

"I imagine you could call it serious, so stop frowning and bear with me. I want you to know how much I've come to value your friendship. We wouldn't have the slightest chance of succeeding without your help and support. Please take care of yourself."

"You know I will." Joachim grinned. "In a month or so from now, I'll be driving you crazy in Switzerland."

———————

A staff car met Erich at Tempelhof. The young driver retrieved the bags, and once off the tarmac, they moved quickly through the sparse traffic toward the Aldon. "Would you like help with your luggage, Hauptsturmfuhrer?" he asked as they pulled up to the front of the hotel."

"I can manage," Erich said.

"I'll be driving you to Ravensbruck in the morning. You're expected for lunch at eleven o'clock, so we should leave Berlin by nine. Even with the snowy roads, two hours should give us ample time to get to the camp with a few minutes to spare."

The clerk at the front desk recognized Erich from his previous visit. Kurt carried Erich's bag to the room, placed it on the stand by the bed, and opened the blackout curtains to let in the bright sunlight.

With time to kill, Erich unpacked, sat at the desk and mentally reviewed the plan once again. "I can't imagine the outcome if we don't do this right," he whispered; his apprehension growing as he thought about the daunting task ahead of them.

———————

Feeling anxious, Joachim returned to his office. If he failed to make the early flight, he couldn't leave until the next morning, and when he landed in Berlin, Erich would already be at

Ravensbruck. He stopped at the radio room. "Any orders for me?" he asked the hauptscharfuhrer behind the desk.

"I'm working on them now, Obersturmfuhrer. Commandant Mueller said you wouldn't be picking them up until noon."

"Plans have changed," Joachim said. "The only flight to Berlin departs Reim at 10:30. Please try to expedite the process? I need to be on that plane."

"I'll do my best. Are you traveling on business or for pleasure?"

"A combination of the two." Joachim grinned. "I have to attend some tiresome meetings, but we all need to engage in another kind of business from time to time. Now I'll get out of here and let you cut those orders. I'd like to get them to Sturmbannfuhrer Mueller for his signature when he arrives at nine."

Figuring the trip to Berlin had to look legitimate, Joachim went to his office and put files related to the supply issue in his briefcase. He checked the clock. It was 8:45 and Mueller wouldn't be in for at least fifteen more minutes. Deciding it wouldn't do him any good to sit and worry, he picked up the phone and asked the operator to connect him with Wrieden's office.

Wrieden answered on the first ring. *Finally, something's going right*, Joachim mused. "Heil Hitler. Wrieden, this is Joachim Forester," he said.

"Joachim. What can I do for you?"

"Later this morning I'm flying to Berlin to meet with the Panzer leaders about that pesky supply issue. When I get back, I'd like to take you up on your offer to use the cabin."

"The place is all yours," Wrieden said. "I'm on my way to a meeting at the Fuhrerbau in five minutes. I'll jot down the directions and come by your office before I leave. When I get back this afternoon, I'll call old Ernst and let him know to expect you.

How many women are you taking?" He chuckled. "I hope you plan to leave a few in Munich for us poor unfortunates."

Joachim thought about the three women who'd be going with him. They wouldn't be what Wrieden envisioned. "I haven't decided on a number yet," he said. "Definitely two, but I hope three. It depends on how exhausted I am after sampling Berlin's nightlife. I can't be expected to work twenty-four hours a day, can I?"

Wrieden laughed again. "Of course not. What time are you leaving?"

"I hope to leave for Reim within the hour."

"Then I'll see you in a few minutes, and in case Ernst isn't available when you get there, I'll bring the spare key."

While he waited for Wrieden to arrive, Joachim went through his desk. He placed several personal items in his briefcase along with a map of Germany in case something went wrong and they had to figure out another escape route. As an afterthought he removed his gun from the drawer and packed it along with the papers and mementos. *You never know when this could come in handy,* he reflected.

In barely five minutes Wrieden knocked on the door. "Come in," Joachim called. He motioned to a chair opposite his desk. "Do you have time to sit?"

"I'm already running late," Wrieden said. These are the directions to the cabin." He spread out a map on Joachim's desk and pointed to a dark line. "The cabin is about two kilometers beyond the first house in town. He traced the route with his finger. "You'll come to this road exactly one and a half kilometers from the last house on the main road. Turn right and drive for about half a kilometer. You can't miss the place."

"Will the roads be passable with all the snow?"

"You never know. With fewer visitors and strict fuel rationing, the townspeople may not be sufficiently motivated to keep the roads clear."

"How close is the cabin to the border?"

"A little less than a kilometer. If you run out of things to do, you can make a little money playing cards with the border guards. They're not very good."

Joachim shook Wrieden's hand. "I imagine I'll be busy, but I'll keep it in mind should the frauleins need a break." He smiled. "Seriously, he said. "Thanks for letting me use the place. A few days off will do me a world of good."

"I'll eagerly await stories of your escapades."

Joachim grinned. "I hope to have many tales to tell."

When Wrieden left for his meeting, Joachim again checked his watch. *I'm running out of time*, he thought as he put on his hat and coat. He picked up his briefcase and looked around the room one last time before heading for the radio room to wait. When he opened the door, he literally bumped into the hauptscharfuhrer holding a manila envelope. "Your papers," said the young man. "I caught Sturmbannfuhrer Mueller as he was leaving for a meeting at the Fuhrerbau."

Joachim sighed in relief. "Thank you, Hauptscharfuhrer," he said. "Because of you I'll make the plane." Without looking back, he walked swiftly to the motor pool and ordered a sturman to drive him to Reim.

---

By seven o'clock, Erich was worried. He had no way to know if Joachim had left Munich, and he couldn't call to find out. He was pacing when the phone finally rang a little after eight. "Heil Hitler. How are you?" Joachim said cheerfully."

"Better now. Where are you?"

"Several floors above you. Are you hungry, because I'm starved."

"Five minutes ago I wasn't, but now I am. Order dinner and I'll join you."

Seconds after Erich knocked, Joachim opened the door. "Welcome to ultimate luxury," he said. "I can see why the Aldon is the headquarters for the European elite. I could never afford to stay here if we weren't fighting a war."

"Ironic, isn't it?" Erich hugged Joachim. "Damn I'm glad to see you. I was beginning to think you might be stuck in Munich."

"I'd like to say getting here was easy, but truthfully, I wasn't sure I'd make it before you left for Ravensbruck in the morning. There was only one flight out and I had to get Muller's signature on my orders before I could board. I'd have been at the hotel much earlier, but the damn transport stopped in every town from Munich to Berlin."

"But you're here now. Anything new in Munich?"

"Not much. Everything seems to be under control. I saw Inge early this morning. Since I have no idea what kind of time we'll have when we get back, I left some of my things at Sigrid's. I also took over a few extra blankets and a heavy coat. The women are busy cooking and packing. As far as I could tell, both of them are coping well."

"Did you have time to talk with Wrieden about the cabin?"

"We're all set. He gave me a map and a key. The place is about a half-kilometer from the Swiss border. He even suggested I join the guards in a game of cards."

"We'll have to keep that idea in the back of our minds. If all else fails, it might be a way to find out what we need to know if we have time before they're alerted to watch for us of if we can't figure it out by observing."

"Wrieden's arranging for the caretaker to have the place ready. Since he believes I'm taking several women along, I imagine he'll tell the old man to keep his distance."

Erich grinned. "I always knew your reputation would serve us well, though I can't say this is how I envisioned it happening."

As they began to review the plans one final time, there was a knock on the door. Not wanting to be seen, Erich waited in the bathroom while Joachim answered. Kurt brought in a tray. Joachim signed the receipt and, after Kurt left, locked the door.

When he heard the door close, Erich returned to the room. "The food smells delicious," he said as he removed the lids from the plates. "You ordered a feast. Who would have thought there's a food shortage in Germany or that rationing is in effect everywhere in the country?"

"I figured we might as well live it up. We may not have a chance in the days to come."

Erich raised his glass of beer. "How right you are. Let's drink to a successful completion of this project and more good meals with Inge, Rosel, and Sigrid in Switzerland."

Joachim lifted his stein. "To that, and to friendship."

"To friendship."

The two men ate slowly, spending more time discussing the days ahead than enjoying the food. When they finally finished the meal, all had been said that needed to be. They were ready. Erich got up to leave. "There probably won't be an opportunity for me to call you over the next few days," he said. "And I don't have any idea when I'll be back."

"You're thinking day after tomorrow?"

"Yes, but I can't believe the selection process will take that long, so stand by and wait for my call. If I've found Rosel, we'll make specific plans. If not, we'll figure out a way to give Inge and Sigrid the bad news."

"I don't relish that task."

"Believe me, neither do I."

Erich returned to his room. He took off his clothes and called the desk, asking for a 7:30 a.m. wake-up call.

Joachim sat quietly, trying to decide whether or not to go to bed. After several minutes of arguing with himself and knowing he should go through the material for his meeting the next morning, he got up, put on his jacket, and left the room to enjoy his favorite cabarets for what he imagined would be the last time.

# CHAPTER 34

Erich pushed through the hotel door a little before nine. The same young man who drove him from Tempelhof to the Aldon waited by the Mercedes. "There's a folder for you on the backseat," he said as Erich slid in. He nodded toward the man sitting in the passenger seat. "This is Sturman Schmid. He's attached to Commandant Suhren's staff at Ravensbruck. The commandant thought you might have questions about the camp, so rather than waste your valuable time discussing generalities when you arrive, Sturman Schmid will brief you during the drive."

"Good morning, Hauptsturmfuhrer," Schmid said. "Commandant Suhren said to tell you the procedures are in place to be sure the selection process runs smoothly."

"Thank you, Sturman," Erich said. "Did you drive from Ravensbruck to Berlin this morning?"

"I did, Sir. "I came to town with the driver who's picking up supplies for the commandant."

"I'm glad you did, and I do have a few questions, but before we talk, give me a few minutes to look through this folder."

It was misty, and the air was cold, but the heater in the car was working well. Erich removed his coat and opened the file. On top was a telegram from Doctor Rascher reminding him about lunch with Commandant Fritz Suhren at eleven. *Which I already knew,* Erich thought as he continued to read. A second telegram was for Suhren. It listed specific qualities Rascher was looking for in the women, including a request that only those who "possessed some fat" should be made available for selection.

Erich closed the folder. As he thought about the hundreds, perhaps thousands of women he'd soon be viewing, he was suddenly unnerved. Up to then, he didn't think he'd have a problem recognizing Rosel, but the closer he got to the camp, the more his confidence began to wane. The possibility she might be standing in front of him and he wouldn't know it began to haunt him. He put the folder in his briefcase. "Tell me about Ravensbruck, Sturman," he said.

"Do you know anything about our facility, Hauptsturmfuhrer?" Schmid asked. "I don't want to bore you with redundant information."

"I know very little, so that shouldn't be a problem," Erich said.

"Then I'll begin with the camp's geographical location. Ravensbruck is situated in a swampy area alongside Lake Schwedt, which is about eighty-kilometers north of Berlin. When the facility first opened in 1939, it was designed to accommodate about six thousand prisoners. Now we're the largest frauenlager in Germany."

"How many women are you currently holding?" Erich asked.

"Approximately eleven thousand."

Erich smothered a gasp. *Oh my God,* he thought. *With this vast number, chances of my identifying Rosel are diminished.*

"Hauptsturmfuhrer?" Schmid said.

"I'm sorry, sturman. I was thinking about the enormous amount of work involved in guarding all those women."

"The prisoners are guarded by the Aufseherinnen, the female civilian employees of the SS many of whom are recruited from the ranks of the Bund Deutscher Madel." At the mention of the girl's organization, Erich thought of Inge. *Had the SS tried to recruit her for detention camp guard duty?* He smiled at the prospect.

"Let me tell you about the camp itself," Schmid was saying. "Since it was first built, the layout has changed very little. We've been unable to build additional barracks because of swampland surrounding the facility, so we've had to make do with what we have. There are currently eighteen barracks. Two are the prisoners' sickbay where the ill are treated and experiments are conducted. Two are warehouses, and one is a penal block. The remaining buildings house the prisoners. The barracks were originally designed to hold 250 women, but now each one of them accommodates at least a thousand."

"That's 750 more than you're equipped to take," Erich said. "How do you manage?"

"The women sleep in three-tiered wooden bunks, but because we can fit additional bunks into the rooms, some of the newly incarcerated have to sleep on the floor. Of course we lose quite a few women every day."

"Lose them?"

"They die," Schmid said impassively.

"Of course," Erich said, sorry he'd asked the question and feeling very stupid.

Schmid continued without comment. "At Ravensbruck each barrack has one washroom and a door-less, windowless room containing three toilets. The prisoners are awakened for roll call at four a.m. I've seen as many as five-hundred women standing in the latrine waiting for a free toilet." He laughed. "Believe me, it isn't a pretty picture, and the smell is wretched."

*How degrading,* Erich thought. *If I manage to find Rosel, will she ever recover from the horrors of her incarceration?*

"Hauptsturmfuhrer?" Schmid said again.

Erich realized he had paused for too long before responding. "I was thinking that your situation at Ravensbruck is much like ours at Dachau," he said. "More and more Jews are being herded in as the Fuhrer implements the Final Solution."

"Exactly," said Schmid. "Would you like to hear more about the camp layout?"

"I've heard enough about the design," Erich said. "But I do have another question. Several days ago I was having a beer at the Hofbrauhaus in Munich. I happened to sit by an officer who had recently delivered medical supplies to Ravensbruck. He described an exciting program designed to help the men fighting on the Eastern Front. Since that's the kind of work I'm doing at Dachau, though our tests are being conducted to assist Luftwaffe pilots downed in the North Sea or suffering at high altitudes, I'd like to hear about your successes at Ravensbruck. I believe you call the women 'rabbit girls.'"

Schmid nodded. "The volunteers are helping our doctors learn how to heal our brave Wehrmacht foot soldiers who are wounded at the front."

*There's that word "volunteer" yet again.* Erich wondered if Schmid really believed the women were sacrificing themselves for the good of the Reich.

"The doctors treat wounds with various chemical substances to discover ways to prevent infections," Schmid was saying. They also transplant bones in hopes of learning how to assist soldiers who lose their limbs in battle."

"A noble cause," Erich said, feeling intense disgust, not about the intent of the experiments, but about the methods being utilized.

"Would you like to hear more, Hauptsturmfuhrer?" Schmid asked.

"I've heard enough for now," Erich said. "If you don't mind I'll close my eyes for a few minutes. I spent yesterday traveling, and I didn't sleep well last night."

"Very good," Schmid said. "I'll wake you when we get to the camp."

Erich didn't wake up until the driver slowed the car at the Ravensbruck gate. "Your papers, Hauptsturmfuhrer," said the guard on duty. Erich removed his orders from the briefcase and put them in the guard's outstretched hand. The man perused the documents, opened the gates, and waved the car into the compound.

The first thing Erich noticed were the Aufseherinnen Schmid had mentioned. Like their male counterparts at Dachau, they were armed, and some led barking German shepherd dogs. Erich examined the group as a whole. They were strong, stout, heavy, and not physically attractive. *They're not the epitome of femininity*, he thought as he looked at their tailored uniforms and masculine boots which resembled the ones Erna wore to work every day.

The driver proceeded slowly to the central offices located on the far side of the compound. As they drove, Erich watched a crew of prisoners carrying shovels. He guessed they were about to reclaim the surrounding swampland. Except that they were female, they could have passed for the same miserable examples of humanity incarcerated at Dachau.

He felt queasy as he watched the guards carrying dead women they'd just unloaded from dilapidated wagons. The corpses, in every state of decay, were so thin their bones were visible beneath the skin. Some had gash wounds, others were riddled with bullet holes, and still others were covered with terrible sores. He nearly gagged from the putrid smell coming from the open car window, and he wondered how the Aufseherinnen, who piled the dead on top of each other in the mountainous heaps, kept from being physically ill.

He swallowed hard and turned away, but his relief was short-lived. Schmid was staring at him. He wasn't supposed to be bothered by what he was seeing, so he looked back at the gruesome scene. As one group of Aufseherin unloaded and stacked the bodies, a second group of equally brawny women carried them from the piles into a structure from which emerged a tall, brick smokestack.

The driver pulled up in front of a sturdily constructed building with raised flowerbeds on either side of the door. The plants were seemingly lifeless. *How symbolic,* Erich thought. *The dormant plants are hanging on, waiting for the coming of spring when they can grow and bloom anew.* He mentally compared them with the prisoners he'd seen at Dachau and during the short time he'd been at Ravensbruck. What was keeping these wretched human beings alive? What hopes for a rebirth did they cling to in the dehumanizing camps? Did they still hope to bloom anew someday?

After thanking his driver and Schmid, Erich walked toward the camp administrative building. He had no sooner opened the door when a dark-haired, rail-thin, bird-like man got out of his seat to greet him. "Heil Hitler," he barked enthusiastically.

"Heil Hitler," Erich replied.

The man's voice was high pitched and raspy. "You must be Hauptsturmfuhrer Riedl," he said. "We've been expecting you, though you're early."

"My driver picked me up at nine," Erich said. "He wasn't sure how the weather would affect the road conditions and I didn't want to be late for my scheduled eleven o'clock luncheon meeting with Commandant Suhren."

"Don't misunderstand me, Hauptsturmfuhrer. I wasn't being critical, but Sturmbannfuhrer Suhren isn't available at the moment. He's inspecting the grounds. I'm Otto Feiling, the commandant's aide. Perhaps you would like to freshen up while you're waiting for him to return? The guest house behind the office has been prepared."

Feiling led Erich out of the front door and around to the side of the building where two identical houses stood side by side.

He pointed to the house on the right. Erich went inside and glanced around the room. The décor was charming; hardly the place one would expect to find in a detention facility. Ironically, the homey atmosphere reminded him of Sigrid's parlor. An overstuffed, flower-print couch rested against one wall and a mahogany table with two matching chairs sat by the window that was draped with plain but attractive curtains. The large bed was covered with a multi-colored quilt and goose-down pillows. Through a door that was slightly ajar, Erich could see a small bathroom, and beside it, another open door led into a closet.

"I hope this is acceptable, Hauptsturmfuhrer," Feiling said.

"It is, thank you."

"In that case I'll leave you to unpack. Please remain here until I come back for you. It shouldn't be too long, since the commandant expects you at eleven."

It took only minutes for Erich to put away the few items he'd brought with him. He stored the suitcase in the closet, washed his face, and brushed his teeth. With a few minutes to spare, he walked to the window and peered out. He saw nothing but the back of the administration building and a little open ground on either side. Relieved there were no camp activities within his view, he wondered if the placement of the houses had been intentional. *Perhaps the designers wanted to keep the camp administrators from having to face the horrors of camp life,* he thought as he heard a sharp rap on the door. "Come in," he called.

Otto opened the door, but he didn't enter the room. "If you're ready, Hauptsturmfuhrer, Sturmbannfuhrer Suhren is waiting in the office. It's awfully cold for this time of year," he said as they walked the short distance to the administration building.

"It is," said Erich. "Which is good for us. We need cold weather to begin the next phase of our tests."

Feiling opened the door and stepped aside allowing Erich to enter first. "That's the commandant's office," he said, pointing to a door across the room. "Knock and go in."

Erich rapped and immediately heard a gruff, "Enter."

He opened the door to face a man who appeared to be in his late forties or early fifties. He was huskily built, with a pale complexion, short-cropped graying hair, pale blue eyes, and thin lips. Erich snapped to attention. "Heil Hitler," he said with feigned enthusiasm.

Suhren glanced up. "Heil Hitler, Hauptsturmfuhrer Riedl?" he said. He pointed to a straight-backed chair opposite his desk. "Please sit down. I spoke with Doctor Rascher this morning. It was my first opportunity to speak with one of the Reich's most admired scientists. After our conversation I'm certain we'll be able to provide you with the specimens you require. The doctor said you would more specifically explain what you're looking for."

"I'd be glad to," Erich said. "Would you like to read the doctor's telegram, or shall I tell you what he said?"

"The latter," said Suhren. "Shall we talk over lunch?" He stood. "Here at Ravensbruck we have breakfast very early, so we eat lunch at 11:15."

"We keep the same schedule at Dachau, Sir."

"Ah yes, I'd almost forgotten. You're familiar with our camp routine. We'll eat in my quarters. I have my own cook, so I rarely dine with the Aufseherinnen."

They walked the short distance to Suhren's quarters. The commandant opened the door to his house and stood aside. Erich entered a room filled with heavy mahogany furniture, but it was the art that immediately caught his attention. Even with his limited knowledge, he realized the paintings hanging on the walls were museum quality. He remembered what Inge had said about the art exhibition at the Alte Pinakotek. *The works of art in here could well be the so-called decadent paintings that were removed from the museum in favor of the propaganda pieces,* he thought.

Erich realized that Suhren was waiting for a response. The man had said something, but Erich didn't know what. "This is very nice, Sir," he said, hoping his comment wouldn't be totally out of context.

"I'm glad you like it. Do you see the lamp on my desk?" He walked across the room and gestured to Erich to come nearer. "It's a gift from your own Commandant Weiss. He and I trained together at Sachsenhausen."

Erich went to the desk to take a closer look. "I don't believe I've seen anything like it," he said.

"Do you know what it's made of?"

Erich studied the shade with its strange blue design in one corner. He turned back to Suhren. "I'm afraid I have no idea," he said.

"The base is mahogany and the shade is made from the skin of some of those Jews you and Rascher have been eliminating at Dachau."

Erich tried to hide his shock and indignation as he stared at the lamp. Suhren seemed surprised. "You weren't aware of this unique craft?" he asked.

"No, Sir, I wasn't."

"The blue design is a tattoo, which makes the lamp even more valuable. Those with this particular mark are difficult to find. When you return to Dachau, please tell Weiss I'm proudly displaying his gift."

Erich couldn't believe the major could stare at the lamp day after day and be unconcerned that the shade had once been a living part of another human being. "I certainly will," he said, forcing a smile.

The commandant motioned toward a linen-covered table in an alcove adjoining the parlor. "Please join me, Hauptsturmfuhrer." Erich sat down and Suhren took his place at the end of the table. He rang a bell and a female prisoner entered with a tray of food.

Erich studied the girl. Tight curls surrounded her pale face, setting off her troubled, dark-brown eyes. He quickly realized she did more than serve Suhren's meals. She was servicing him in other ways to be in such excellent condition. She was nothing like the undernourished, scrawny women leaving the camp with their shovels to clear the swamplands, or the putrid skeletons piled high on the death cart.

"I usually don't discuss business during my meals," Suhren said as he began to eat. "But because there are time constraints, I'll make an exception this one time."

"Thank you," Erich said. "Doctor Rascher is eager to begin the next phase of the experiments and wants me to return to Dachau with the women as soon as possible."

"That's what he said when we spoke this morning. So while we eat, tell me more about your fascinating work and what I can do to help Doctor Rascher achieve his goals."

Erich was suddenly thankful that gruesome discussions were prohibited in the Dachau dining hall.

"I'd be glad to," he said, marshaling as much enthusiasm as possible.

Throughout the meal Erich talked about the first two phases of the tests, pausing only to answer the commandant's questions. When he finished with the broad overview, he began to focus on the reason for his visit to Ravensbruck. "For the warming tests the women need to be in relatively good shape," he said.

"Not walking skeletons," said Suhren.

"Exactly. Those who are just skin and bones won't provide accurate results."

"I see." Suhren smirked. "Will you be personally observing the tests, Hauptsturmfuhrer?"

"I will, as will Doctor Rascher and our secretary, Erna Hambro."

"It sounds amusing. I wish I could join you."

Erich managed a grin. "I'm looking forward to the experience," he said.

"So you need the healthiest women we have on hand," said Suhren. "Unfortunately we don't have too many who meet your specifications, at least not the ones who've been with us for any length of time."

The commandant had opened the door. It was time for Erich to walk through. His heart was pounding in his chest as he began. "We were told you are currently holding some of the Mischlinge," he said. "Because Berlin hasn't made a decision in their regard, we hoped they might be in better condition than the full-blooded Jews. Would you make them available?" *Come on, say something,* Erich silently implored while Suhren pondered his request.

"They probably are heartier," Suhren said pensively. "To date we've been required to keep the Mischlinge separate from the other prisoners, though I've always thought it was a shame to waste their talents. We haven't used even one of them to serve us." He leaned in conspiratorially. "I'm sure you understand."

*Only too well,* Erich thought. "I do," he said.

"We're expecting directives any day now. I was told the orders would be here weeks ago, but unfortunately they haven't arrived, and we're still in limbo. I've heard that one of the solutions currently being considered is forced sterilization, but that's only one option." Suhren scowled. "To be honest with you, Hauptsturmfuhrer, I don't understand the issue. A Jew is a Jew whether she's full blooded or not. It doesn't make sense. We should be treating all enemies of the Reich the same way. They need to be eliminated."

"I agree," Erich said with feigned zeal. "A Jew is a Jew."

Suhren shrugged. "Oh well," he said. "Our job is to follow orders whether we approve or not. It's what we do. Have you been given permission to use the Mischlinge in your tests?"

Erich knew he had to be careful. The project had top-level approval, but because he hadn't dared risk being denied access to the Mischlinge, he hadn't broached the subject with Rascher. "We've been given free reign by Reichsfuhrer Himmler and Reichsmarshall Goering," he said, hoping he'd exhibited enough surety to keep the commandant from seeking authorization from Berlin.

Suhren pursed his lips. "When I spoke with Doctor Rascher this morning, he asked me to give you every possible consideration with no restrictions," he said thoughtfully. "Though he didn't specifically mention the Mischlinge."

Erich continued to wait. The entire plan depended on the commandant's response. *If he says no, then what?* Erich thought. *What other argument can I make? There isn't one. We're finished!* When he didn't think he could stand the delay much longer, Suhren said: "Well, Rascher did tell me to allow you access to all of our women."

Erich stifled a sigh of relief. "Thank you, Commandant," he said.

"Will you do something for me in return?" Suhren asked.

"If I'm able, of course."

"Leave the girl who served our lunch." He grinned. "I'd hate to have her warm any body but mine."

"I'll be glad to," Erich said. "After all, you're making my job easy."

"Excellent," said Suhren. "Now shall we discuss the selection process? What plans do you have for viewing the women?"

Thankful he'd have a say in how the choices would be made, Erich said: "Here's what I'm thinking. Since you know what we're looking for, I'd like the Aufseherinnen to make preliminary selections this afternoon. Until Sturman Schmid told me you're currently housing eleven-thousand women, I thought I'd look at all of them—"

"The sturman was helpful?"

"He was. Your idea to have him answer my questions during the ride to camp was nothing short of genius."

Suhren nodded as Erich continued. "Please include all the Mischlinge in the initial group. In the morning, I'll look at all the women the Aufseherinnen have chosen. Though I am only taking six of your prisoners during this trip, I want to be certain I have the ones who best meet our needs. I'll initially select between thirty and forty candidates and scrutinize them more closely before deciding which ones I'll transport to Dachau."

"Great," the commandant said. "After lunch I have a meeting with Maria Mandel, the Oberaufseherin, or chief overseer of our female guards. I'll let her know how you wish to proceed. She'll then notify the Aufseherinnen who guard the Mischlinge that all of their prisoners are to be made available."

"How many Mischlinge are you currently holding?" Erich asked.

"About a hundred. We had about fifty more, but there was a dysentery outbreak a few months ago. Many died. We'll have all the survivors, whether they're thin or not, brought before you; along with those other prisoners the Aufseherinnen select. It should be quite a display. Even though I see hundreds of women every day, I never get tired of watching them march around in the nude. I hate for the show to end, if you know what I mean."

"I certainly do, Sir. It must be hard."

Suhren laughed at Erich's untended pun, and Erich joined in with a loud chuckle. Now he had an additional concern. Was Rosel one of the women who had succumbed to dysentery? *How ironic that would be when we're so close to our goal*, he thought. In addition, he'd also failed to consider that the women might be forced to appear naked. He could only imagine how humiliated and terrified they would feel. *God*, he prayed. *Let Rosel be among them, so I can select her and get her out of this hellish place.*

He quickly became aware of the commandant's stare and realized that, once again, he hadn't given the man his full attention. "I'm sorry, Commandant," he said. "I was daydreaming about all those naked women."

"And why wouldn't you be?" said Suhren. He pushed back from the table. "If you're through eating, Hauptsturmfuhrer, I'll attend to my business with Maria so she can brief the guards. I don't remember how long Doctor Rascher said you plan to remain with us."

"I'm to make the final selection by tomorrow afternoon and return with the women on the morning of November 26th. However, if we finish earlier, I wouldn't mind an extra night in Berlin's cabarets before returning to the activities at Dachau."

"Then I'll get busy so you'll have a chance to enjoy the little extra diversion. Will you join me for dinner this evening? Before we eat I'll brief you on the preliminary selections. I'm sure my guards know their women well enough to estimate how many might be suitable for your tests."

"I'd be pleased to join you," Erich said.

"I dine at 4:30. Come next door. In the meantime, would you like a tour of the camp this afternoon?"

Erich really didn't want to see more of the facility, but felt that he had to appear interested if not enthusiastic. "Yes," he said. "If I'm able to finish my report."

"If you have the time, go to the office and Otto will be your guide. If not, please remain in your quarters. Should you choose to go out, one of our staff members will accompany you."

"Of course. I understand." As Erich walked the short distance from the commandant's house to the guest cottage, he thought about Otto. Was the bird-like man performing the same duties for Suhren that Heinrich was carrying out for Weiss at Dachau? He had nothing but disdain for the two snitches.

Instead of going on a tour, Erich remained in the guest quarters. He wrote several paragraphs about his conversation with Suhren. *How ironic,* he thought as he put the paper in his folder. *I'm writing a report no one will ever see. What a waste of time.* It was hard to believe they were so close to the end of their quest, or, he thought, *is it just beginning?* He undressed and lay down on the bed to take a nap. There was nothing left to do but wait.

---

Erich was up and dressed when Suhren knocked on the door. Over wine, the commandant began his report. "I believe you'll have more than a hundred full-blooded Jews plus a hundred Mischlinge to select from tomorrow morning, Hauptsturmfuhrer," he said. "The <u>Aufseherinnen</u> will parade their healthiest specimens. I'm told they're holding a contest. Each one wants you to pick her charges."

"I appreciate their cooperation," Erich said. "I'm eager to begin the selection process." *If you only knew how anxious*, he thought.

"Roll call will begin at six o'clock. When it's over, the women pre-selected for your consideration will remain in the compound. At that time we will bring out the Mischlinge."

Erich acknowledged the commandant's plans with a nod. He thought of the misty cold rain that had fallen all day. There was no hope of a warm-up, so it was going to be grueling for the women who would be forced to stand naked in the compound.

"After you've chosen the women you want to look at more closely, we'll move the finalists to the officer's dining hall for further scrutiny," Suhren said.

"Thank you," Erich replied.

"I'm glad to assist you and Doctor Rascher, and, in return, you'll be helping us. The women you take will free up a little more space, and we won't have to dispose of the bodies. So now shall we talk about more pleasant matters?"

The commandant's cuisine was as good as that served at the Aldon. The prisoners were never mentioned, and Erich was thankful for the respite. *If I didn't know I was talking with a sadist, I'd think Suhren was a regular guy,* he reflected as the man shared stories of his family and patiently listened to Erich's humorous tales of his SS training. After dinner, Suhren indicated a desire to retire for the night. "I'm quite eager to see what new tricks our little Jew has to offer tonight," he said, grinning slyly. "You don't mind, Hauptsturmfuhrer?"

"Not at all." Erich watched the girl who was clearing the plates. He figured the experience would be less than pleasant for her, and he doubted she was a willing participant as the commandant suggested.

With Suhren's assurance that he'd be picked up for breakfast at 5:30 a.m., Erich put on his coat and cap and left for his quarters. After undressing and showering, he lay on his bed. Tomorrow was the day they'd all been waiting for. As he stared at the ceiling, he prayed he'd be successful.

After Joachim left Sigrid's, Inge dressed, said goodbye to her aunt, and navigated the slick roads to Dachau. She needed to pick up a few things for the trip to Switzerland and wanted to tell her landlady that work would keep her in Munich for at least a week.

At the apartment house, Inge went directly to her room to pack her warmest clothes and several blankets she'd brought with her to Dachau. When she reached the bottom of the stairs with her bundle, Frau Heiden had just come in with a bag of groceries. Inge thanked the kind woman for her hospitality and promised to return within the week. *A promise I'll have to break,* she thought as she loaded the car and left for Munich.

The heater wasn't working well, so Inge was cold when she arrived at Sigrid's. She took off her boots and hung her coat in the entry hall. "Burr, it's cold," she said, as she joined Sigrid in the parlor. "The fire feels great."

"Would you like tea, darling?" Sigrid asked.

"I would, but don't get up. I'll make it for myself. Would you like a refill?"

"Yes, thank you."

When Inge returned with the tea tray, she noticed several boxes on the floor in front of the couch. Sigrid was beginning the process of selecting the items she felt Rosel would want to keep. "Would you like for me to help you go through Rosel's things?" Inge said as she refilled Sigrid's cup.

"I would thank you."

The two women spent the next few hours choosing mementos from the boxes containing the record of Rosel's life. They put aside pictures of her parents, reports of her progress in school, and programs from the musical concerts she had given. While they chose the cherished items, they reminisced, as they had days before, about the years all three had spent together.

From time to time Sigrid cried, and Inge, knowing what a wrenching experience it was for the woman to leave behind everything she'd ever known, didn't try to stop her. Occasionally tears rolled down Inge's cheeks and, bittersweet as it was, she was glad she and Sigrid had this activity to occupy their time. She was worried about Erich, and she wondered what he would or wouldn't find at Ravensbruck. She hoped he would locate Rosel, not only for her friend's sake, but because she knew how difficult it would be for him to return and tell her and Sigrid he'd failed.

She also worried about the escape from Dachau. She had seen the barking dogs and knew about the strictly enforced rules. Even if everything went as they hoped it would, could Erich get away? So many things could go wrong and, quite possibly, cost him and Rosel their lives. She wanted to talk, but she kept her concerns to herself. She couldn't worry her aunt, and the two men with whom she could share her concerns were in Berlin.

After packing the last of Rosel's treasured things, Inge and Sigrid sat quietly and stared at the glowing embers in the fireplace. Inge sensed that Sigrid was thinking about Rosel and the two SS men who would be risking everything for them in the days to come. *Would Erich find her and did they have a chance to get away?* Inge shut her eyes and prayed they would.

# CHAPTER 35

At precisely 5:30 a.m. Otto Feiling knocked on Erich's door. He answered; his coat on and cap in hand.

"Good morning, Hauptsturmfuhrer," Feiling said. "The commandant asked me to take you to breakfast before you begin the selection process, so if you'll come with me. We will eat in the officers' mess and then go to the compound where the women will be waiting. The morning roll call should be over by the time we arrive."

Though he had no appetite, Erich knew his success would depend on his ability to convince Feiling and Suhren that the selection of the women for the Dachau tests was merely routine business for him. "Thank you, Obersturmfuhrer," he said. "I rarely eat breakfast, but I could use a cup of coffee."

With every step he took, Erich's nervousness increased. Everything they'd planned for depended on what would happen during the next few hours. He was paradoxically fearful, yet eager, to begin the process.

The officers' dining hall at Ravensbruck was not as large or cheery as the one at Dachau. The food smelled good, but Erich was too nervous to eat. When he finished his second cup of coffee, Feiling, who was obviously watching closely, immediately got up from the table. "If you're through, we'll go," he said. "I'm sure you're ready to see the women."

When they turned the corner into Roll Call Square, Erich took a deep breath. There, standing in rows, were at least two-hundred women. All were nude, and even from a distance, he could see that most of them were shivering in the dreary dampness. "Are your prisoners always naked during roll call?" he asked, trying to hide his astonishment with small-talk.

"We wouldn't be that cruel," Fielder said sarcastically. "The commandant wanted you to determine which ones are plumper, and he didn't think you could do that if they're dressed."

Erich nodded as he scrutinized the mass of humanity standing before him. Like their male counterparts at Dachau, these pathetic women stood erect, their eyes focused on the ground, for fear of standing out, he guessed, and, he assumed, from sheer embarrassment to be seen in this humiliating condition. As they approached the first row, Suhren joined them. "Shall we begin, gentlemen?" he said.

"I'm ready," Erich responded. His hands and feet were cold, and he knew it wasn't because of the weather.

"If you don't mind, Commandant," Otto said. "I see that Maria will accompany you. Since I'm not needed, I have a great deal of work to do before we can release the prisoners for transport to Dachau."

"Of course," Suhren said. "We wouldn't want paperwork to keep the hauptsturmfuhrer from enjoying one last night in Berlin."

"Thank you, Obersturmfuhrer," Erich said as the man headed for the office.

"We're ready for you, Hauptsturmfuhrer," Maria said proudly.

The two men and Maria followed closely by one of the heavily armed female guards leading a snarling German shepherd dog began the process. "Eyes front," she bellowed as they neared the middle of the first row. Her order gave Erich a chance to see the faces of the women who were now blankly staring at him rather than looking at the ground. As he examined the shivering bodies, he noticed there was very little fat remaining under the opaque flesh, and the outline of bones was apparent on most. From time to time, he selected a potential candidate, and the guard took the clearly terrified woman away.

After walking the length of four rows, he had only selected ten prospects. He'd yet to see one prisoner who vaguely resembled the woman in the picture on Sigrid's mantle. He thought about asking Maria if he was viewing the Mischlinge, but decided it would be best to keep quiet. He feared the commandant would question his preoccupation with the women of mixed blood and decide to call Berlin for approval, which, Erich knew, would be denied.

In the next three rows, he chose four more women. When they reached the end of the eighth row, there was still no sign of Rosel. Becoming more and more discouraged, he picked three more women from the ninth row. When he came to the last four rows, Maria uttered the words he'd been waiting to hear. "You are now viewing the Mischlinge, Hauptsturmfuhrer."

Erich breathed a silent sigh of relief. Maria had answered his unasked question. "On the whole they're plumper because they're given more food," she said. "I believe the commandant told you that many of them suffered from dysentery and, as a result, lost weight. However emaciated they are, I've included them in the lineup."

As she talked, Erich wondered how the almost-obese woman could be so indifferent to the nearly-starving prisoners she supervised.

"I can definitely see the difference," he said. "These women look like they'll serve our purposes better than those from the general population."

As they walked along the first row of Mischlinge, Erich slowed down. He wished he could compare the faces of the women with the picture Sigrid had given him. *That would be amusing,* he reflected, wondering what Suhren would say if he pulled out a photograph of Rosel from his pocket and held it up to each prisoner's face. *Perhaps 'deadly' rather than 'amusing' would be a better choice of words,* he thought.

Many of the Mischlinge had escaped the barber's razor, which further distinguished them from the women he'd already chosen. He quickly picked three more candidates. At the beginning of the second row, he paused in front of a woman who, at first glance, looked like Rosel. For a moment he thought his search was over, but his hopes were quickly dashed when, on closer inspection, he realized he was wrong.

Moving at a snail's pace, and feeling increased angst with each step, Erich studied each woman's face. When he was only four individuals from the end of the second to last row, he paused before a gaunt, pale woman, who, despite Maria's order, dropped her head to avoid his stare. Hardly able to breathe, he put his hand under her chin and lifted her face so he could get a better look at her features. Satisfied, he turned to Maria who trailed behind him. "I'll take this one," he said.

Struggling not to show his elation, Erich watched the despondent woman as the guard gripped her arm. He took a deep breath and turned away as weariness engulfed him in numbing waves. Though he selected several more candidates, they were irrelevant. He had completed his search: He had found Rosel.

While the preliminary choices were herded together and the remaining women returned to the barracks, Maria went to make arrangements for the next phase of the selection process. Within fifteen minutes the women Erich had chosen were ushered into the dining hall and arranged in three rows. He quickly surveyed the assembly, locating Rosel in the middle of the second row. His anxiety about recognizing her had been for nothing. She was thin, and her hair was much shorter than in the pictures on Sigrid's mantle, but despite her obvious emotional distress and the fear in her dull eyes, she looked basically the same.

Erich walked up and down the rows, scrutinizing each woman carefully, trying to present a semblance of legitimacy to the process. After twenty minutes, he had narrowed the field to eight. The guard removed the excluded women from the room, and Erich began again. He chose Rosel first. He wanted to tell the petrified woman that everything would be fine, but he knew he had to let her continue to fear the worst.

Over the next ten minutes he cut the number of women to six, all of them Mischlinge. When he was finished, the commandant addressed the final group. "Day after tomorrow, you will be transported from Ravensbruck to Dachau where you will be permitted to participate in a cause that will assist our glorious fighting men." Erich didn't see a hint of optimism or pride on the faces of the frightened women who were being "permitted" to participate in the project.

The guards led the six away. As he watched Rosel disappear out the door Erich could only imagine what she was feeling. He wanted to call out: "Help is here, Rosel. Hang on just a little longer." When the women were out of sight, he looked at his watch. It wasn't even ten o'clock. He couldn't figure out why Rascher had expected the selection process to last two days. "Thanks to you and your efficient staff, the selection went well," he said to Suhren. "I will speak with Doctor Rascher and Commandant Weiss about your extraordinary cooperation."

"Thank you," the commandant said smugly. "I did it for you. I told you we'd be finished in time for you to enjoy the cabarets."

"That you did," Erich said. "Though I didn't expect I'd also have a good part of the afternoon. With your permission, I'll use your outer office to make travel arrangements for the women, and then return to the city."

"When you get back to Dachau, please give Doctor Rascher my regards, and say hello to my friend Weiss. Don't forget to mention the lamp."

"When I see him, I'll let him know you're proudly displaying his gift."

"Thank you," said Suhren. "So back to business. I assume you want us to transport the women according to the original schedule."

"Yes," Erich said. "Though we finished early, adhering to our original plan would be better for the Dachau staff. The Strafblocke is being modified to accommodate the women, and I don't believe the changes will be complete much before we're scheduled to arrive."

"In that case, Hauptsturmfuhrer, you should leave here and enjoy the extra leisure time in the city. I'm sure you could use some real entertainment. Weiss tells me the town of Dachau has a dismal night life."

"The cafes close by seven o'clock, if that's any indication. When phase three is underway, there's no telling when I might have a free moment. I believe the doctor said we'll go directly from the completion of the warming tests to writing the final report for Berlin."

"Call him before you leave. Tell him it was my idea to send you back to Berlin today rather than tomorrow. Tell me when your plane is scheduled to depart, and I'll have the women there to meet you."

"I'm sure Doctor Rascher will be grateful," Erich said. "The Luftwaffe transport is scheduled to leave Tempelhof at 8:00 a.m. on November the 26th.

"The truck will be on the tarmac by 7:30."

Feiling jumped up as the two men entered the office. "Otto, Hauptsturmfuhrer Riedl will need to use your telephone," Suhren said. "Have the driver bring the car around. He'll be leaving for Berlin within the hour."

"Certainly, Sir. Right away," Feiling said.

*He's as eager to please as Heinrich,* Erich pondered with disdain.

After phoning Rascher and accepting the doctor's praise for a successful trip, Erich called Joachim. The major had told him to have a good time in Berlin, so it wouldn't be out of line for him to phone a friend to make plans.

When there was no answer in Joachim's room, Erich left a message saying he'd be returning that afternoon and hoped they could meet for dinner. He assumed if anyone was listening, the request would be reasonable, and the call wouldn't be suspicious. He shook his head. He was truly becoming paranoid. He reserved a room for the night, hung up, and after thanking Suhren yet again, he went to the guest house to pack.

During the drive back to the city, Erich's thoughts were different from those he'd experienced during the trip to Ravensbruck. He closed his eyes and pretended to sleep, as, over and over he went through the plan of escape from Dachau, trying to think of anything he and Joachim had forgotten. When they arrived at the hotel, he registered and tried Joachim again from the lobby. When there was still no answer, he left a message at the desk and followed Kurt to the room.

With nothing to do until Joachim arrived, he picked up a propaganda magazine from the dresser and began to read. Twenty minutes later, when he'd about had his fill of the ludicrous publication, there was a knock on the door. He raced across the room and pulled it open. Joachim strolled in. "What brings you back to Berlin today?" he said. "I thought you were staying at Ravensbruck tonight."

"I finished the selection in record time. I have no idea why Rascher thought it would take more than a few hours to choose the women. It was a relatively simple process."

Joachim sat on the couch. "I'm almost afraid to ask, but if you're not going to offer any information without being prodded, I'm forced to initiate the conversation. Did you find Rosel?"

Erich nodded yes. "I did, my friend."

Joachim jumped off the couch and grabbed Erich's hand. "Outstanding," he said excitedly. "I've been worried that all our planning would be for nothing. I didn't say anything before, but I didn't think you'd be successful."

"Since we're confessing, from the beginning I thought our search was a lost cause. So let me explain what happened." Erich spent the next fifteen minutes telling Joachim about Ravensbruck, the selection process, his fears the Mischlinge wouldn't be included among the women, and his relief when he finally recognized Rosel.

"Have you called Inge and Sigrid?" Joachim asked.

"I wanted to, but we agreed you should be the one to tell them, and from your room."

"Then let's give the women the good news. Come on."

On the first try, the hotel operator was unable to connect them to Sigrid. She said she'd try again and call back when she could link the two parties. "Why is it always possible to reach someone when you have something bad to report?" Joachim said. "When there's good news, something inevitably goes wrong."

"I felt that way when I called you from Ravensbruck. I wanted to tell you I'd found Rosel, but you weren't in your room. I assume you were in a meeting. I'd hate to think you were cavorting night and day."

Erich was surprised by Joachim's response. He had expected a casual retort, but Joachim was actually serious. "I don't want to disappoint you or tarnish my image, but I came to Berlin to meet with the Panzer bosses," he said crossly. "It would look suspicious if I skipped the meetings."

"So have you been spending all your time working?"

"Though I hate to admit it, yes. We've about solved the problems you and I already solved and then unsolved." Joachim laughed, but his eyes weren't smiling. "It's a shame no one will ever hear the solution from me. I might have received a little credit for a change. Who knows, I might have been promoted to hauptsturmfuhrer."

"Are you concerned you won't receive the praise and a promotion?"

Joachim quickly mellowed. "Of course not, old buddy," he said. "You know rank's not important to me. I was giving you a hard time. You're not as sharp as you usually are. I can't fool you very often."

"That's because I have a hundred other things on my mind."

"Like Inge Friedrich?"

"Like Inge, Sigrid, Rosel, you, Switzerland, the trip to Munich, the escape from Dachau." Erich was surprised when Joachim didn't react as he normally would. "What's the matter?" he asked. "You're so serious and that's not like you."

"You're not the only one with a lot on his mind. I didn't want to come charging in here yelling, punching, and spoiling your return to Berlin, though I admit, the thought of doing just that crossed my mind several times over the past few hours. At any rate the time has come for a discussion that's long overdue."

Erich looked at his friend quizzically. "The floor's all yours, Joachim," he said. "But I have no idea what you're talking about."

"Then let me enlighten you. Over the past two days I've been working—"

"Alright, but why's that so earth shattering, except that you worked for a change?"

Uncharacteristically, Joachim ignored Erich's teasing. "After yesterday's session, I had some free time. Knowing I'd be leaving Germany, possibly forever, and feeling sentimental, I went out to see Unser Traum." Joachim saw Erich flinch. "I see you're anticipating what I'm going to say next," he said.

"On the contrary, I don't have any idea what a few acres of land could possibly have to do with whatever it is you're trying to tell me."

"In a round-about way it has everything to do with it. If Germany loses the war, do you think you and I might come back from Switzerland and build a couple of houses on those acres?"

"I imagine we could. Why not?"

"Because, old buddy, you no longer own Unser Traum, and you've kept that information from me. Why'd you sell, Erich? Did you need money?"

"I don't know," Erich said nonchalantly. "With the war and all, I thought the land would lose value. It was time to let it go."

"Try again," Joachim said curtly. "In the first place, I heard you say if you had to eat out of garbage cans, you'd never sell Unser Traum. Secondly, the property was sold before the war really got underway. Would you like to give me another answer? And this time try the truth!"

"The property's gone, Joachim," Erich said somberly. "Why I got rid of it isn't important."

Despite the distress on Erich's face, Joachim persisted. "I think it's very important. In fact, what I inadvertently found out yesterday may have been the single most significant discovery of my life."

"Again, I have no idea what you're talking about."

"I'm sure you do. Are you going to tell *me*, or do I have to tell *you* what I learned?"

Erich stood up, walked to the window, and looked out. "There's nothing to tell," he said, without looking back.

"Then maybe this will jog your memory. When I went to look at the property, I met an old friend of ours. Does the name Ernst Halder bring back any memories?"

Erich inhaled deeply and turned to Joachim. "Halder?" he said. "Let me see. Wasn't he the bastard you fought with over the Jewish girl a few years ago?"

"The same. As I recall, he threatened to break me, or worse, have me shot over the incident. You said you could take care of Halder, but until yesterday, I had no idea how you accomplished the seemingly impossible. My God, Erich, you gave him your father's property in exchange for my clean record, and likely my life. Halder was wounded on the Eastern Front. He came home and is living on Unser Traum. That's what you meant when you said it was 'a fair exchange.' Those words have haunted me over the years, but the subject has always been off limits."

"I never intended for you to find out about Unser Traum," Erich said pensively. "You had your freedom. That was enough for me."

"But look what it cost you. I'm not worth the sacrifice. You traded your only legacy from your father and his father before him. I deserved to be punished for my actions, and I would have taken my lumps."

There were tears in Erich's eyes as he responded. "Joachim, not too long ago in Munich, you spoke about friendship; about why you were helping me look for Rosel. Have you ever stopped to think how important your friendship has been to me? I know you better than anyone could, and I've always seen beneath your happy-go-lucky facade. I appreciate the real Joachim, the sincere, honest, caring man. Inge sees it, and so does Sigrid, so you don't hide it as well as you'd like to think. Material possessions, no matter how dear, don't come near the gift you've given me over the years; your friendship. I didn't want you to know I bartered Unser Traum. Since you do, you need to know I've always believed I made the right decision."

"How can I ever repay you?" Joachim said, his voice shaking with emotion.

"I'm not, nor have I ever asked anything beyond what you've always given willingly, loyalty and friendship. Now this conversation is getting more than a little maudlin. I really see no reason to continue. If you really want to repay me, don't mention Unser Traum again."

Joachim nodded; his silence his consent.

"So," Erich said, "it's time to finish strategizing and make contingency plans." The two men talked, shared ideas, and planned for the days ahead. They were interrupted when the operator called to say she hadn't been able to reach Munich due to heavy traffic on the lines.

As dinnertime approached, they felt they were ready. They thought about going to the hotel dining room or to a nearby restaurant for a bite to eat, but decided that telling Inge and Sigrid the good news was more important than eating out, so they ordered room service. The meal was nearly finished when the phone rang. "I have your call on the line," the operator said to Joachim.

"Inge, is that you?" Joachim asked breathlessly.

"Joachim. Yes. How are you? I didn't expect to hear from you so soon."

"I'm having the time of my life. Berlin is a great place, even if I am here for meetings. Of course I miss you, fair lady."

"I miss you too. Anything new on your end?"

"I couldn't stand not hearing your sexy voice."

"You don't have to overdo it," Erich whispered.

Joachim laughed. "What's so amusing?" Inge asked. "Is someone with you?"

"No one to make you jealous. I'm sitting here with an old SS buddy who returned early from an excursion into the countryside."

Inge's heart went to her throat. She motioned for Sigrid to join her by the phone, took hold of her hand, and held her breath. "What are you and your friend doing?" she asked tentatively.

"We just finished dinner, and we're enjoying a brandy while he tells me about his productive trip." Joachim paused so Inge could consider his words.

Tears ran down Inge's cheeks and she hugged her aunt. "I see." She choked out her words. "I'm glad his trip was successful."

"My friend says, despite the cold, the countryside was beautiful. He was away on business, but in his spare time he got together with an old friend. He invited her to Munich, so you'll meet her very soon."

Inge put her hand over the mouthpiece and sobbed with relief. It took several moments for her to recover enough to respond. "Maybe she'd like to meet my aunt," she said.

"I'm sure she would. Anyway, fair lady, I called to see if I was still in your every waking thought and to let you know I'd be back in Munich on schedule. Perhaps we can have dinner if you're not otherwise occupied."

"I'd love to see you," Inge said. "And, Joachim, thank you for calling. You've made me very happy."

"Don't I always? I'll talk with you soon."

Erich spoke as Joachim hung up. "Did she understand what you were telling her?"

"I'm sure she did. You could hear the emotion in her voice, though she did a good job of covering. You've trained her well. Now after all this serious business, why don't we hit the night spots? It may be our last trip to Berlin for some time, if ever."

Erich didn't feel like partying, but it was the least he could do for his friend. He patted Joachim on the back, and they headed to the cabarets.

# CHAPTER 36

Inge hung up the phone. Her chin dropped to her chest and she sobbed. "He found her, Aunt Sigrid," she said. "Rosel was at Ravensbruck and Erich's bringing her home to us."

Sigrid gathered Inge in her arms and the two women held tightly to each other. Finding Rosel was more than either of them had dared hope for.

When they recovered from the initial shock and realized Rosel had a chance to be free, they began to prepare even more enthusiastically for the journey ahead. Sigrid baked bread while Inge sliced cheese and prepared sausage to take on the journey to Lorrach.

After exhausting Sigrid's supplies, they said goodnight. It was late, but, though she was tired, Inge couldn't fall asleep. Thoughts of Rosel, Erich, Joachim, and the dangers they'd all face the days ahead, kept her awake, fearful, and anxious.

---

Erich was sure that he and Joachim went to every cabaret in Berlin. It was a little after eight a.m. when he fell into bed. Before he turned out the light, he picked up the phone ask the hotel operator to hold all calls, but he remembered that Joachim would be calling to talk about his flight plans.

It seemed like only minutes had passed when the phone jolted him awake. He looked at the clock on the bedside table. "Heil Hitler," he droned.

"Still in bed, old buddy?" Joachim said cheerfully. "I thought you might be up and about."

"Not a chance. How the hell can you be so jovial? I feel like a truck ran over my head."

"You're obviously out of practice. I recall the days when you were the one who didn't want to go home."

"That was then; this is now. Did you arrange a flight to Munich?"

"I'll be leaving this magnificent city at two o'clock this afternoon. How about lunch before I go?"

"I'd rather sleep, but if you must, drop by my room around noon? We can spend a few minutes talking about your supply problem before you leave for Tempelhof."

"I'm on my way to a meeting that shouldn't last more than an hour. I've already packed, so I'll check out and come up."

"Fine." Erich hung up before Joachim could respond. He didn't stir again until he heard a knock on the door. "Oh God," he said as he looked at the clock. "It can't be noon." It took a concerted effort, but he threw back the warm covers, pulled on his pants, and plodded across the room. "How can you possibly be so wide awake?" he said when he saw his grinning friend standing in the doorway.

"Practice, my friend." Joachim crossed the room and plopped down on the couch. "You do look a little worse for wear. Too much beer?"

"Something like that. Thank God my bachelor days are over."

"You've proposed?"

"Not yet."

"When you do, be sure and tell Inge to think long and hard before she accepts second best."

"Joachim—"

"Why do you and Inge keep saying my name with such disdain?" Joachim held up his hand. "No, don't answer that. You're a lucky man, old buddy. And speaking of Inge, is there anything specific you want me to say when I see her later today?"

"Tell her that, under the circumstances, Rosel looks good. And one more thing; short of slugging Erna, I haven't been able to figure out a way to knock her out. Have Inge see if she can find something to do the job and bring it to camp along with the coat, wig, and wire cutters."

"Have you called Erna to be sure she waits if you're running late?'

"I'll call right after you leave. If she has other plans, this much advanced notice should give her enough time to cancel or reschedule."

"You think she'll do as you ask?"

"If it's for Rascher, I'm sure she will."

Joachim shook his head. "I hope so," he said. "Because our entire plan depends on her remaining at the office."

At the door, Erich shook Joachim's hand. "Thanks for coming to Berlin," he said. "Having you here made the trip easier."

"I'm not so sure I helped."

"Believe me, you did."

Joachim smiled. "Good," he said, and though I know the subject's off limits, I want you to know—"

"I do know, and you understand how much I appreciate your efforts on Inge's and Rosel's behalf, so enough; we're even. Let's discuss the escape. The next time we meet will be on the road to Lorrach, and don't worry if I'm a little late. Rosel and I *will* be there."

"What time should I be concerned?"

Erich hadn't considered a time limit. He thought for a moment. "Start worrying at midnight," he said. "If we're not there by one o'clock, you and the women leave for Lorrach. If I can't rescue Rosel and get to our rendezvous point before then, we won't be there. You'll have to get Inge and Sigrid over the border on your own."

"Such pessimism." Joachim frowned. "I only asked what you expect to be there."

"Seriously, Joachim, we have to consider every possibility. If I can't get Rosel out of Dachau, you, Inge, and Sigrid go on as planned."

"You know I can't leave you behind."

"You won't have a choice. It's no longer just about you. It won't be long before the Gestapo connects Sigrid and Rosel, and Inge has been coming to the office every day. You get the point. If you go back to Munich, you'll all be joining Rosel behind barbed wire; that is if she hasn't already been executed, and by the time you find out I've been caught helping a prisoner escape, I'll be beyond help. Don't even think of intervening. Get out of the country."

"You know if it comes to that, I'll take care of Inge and Sigrid, but let's think positively. We have everything figured to the last detail. We *will* succeed."

"I hope you're right." The two men embraced. As Joachim left to settle his account and catch the flight to Munich, Erich called Erna.

————————————————

When morning came, Inge dragged herself out of bed, showered, dressed, and built up the fire in the fireplace. "Couldn't you sleep either, darling?" Sigrid asked as she joined her niece by the fire.

"I'm too restless. I apologize for waking you. I tried to be quiet."

"I was getting up anyway. You're already dressed."

"I have to go shopping, remember?"

"I do, but the shops won't be open for several hours. Would you like a cup of tea?"

"I would." Inge followed Sigrid into the kitchen filled with pots, pans, and baskets ready to be packed. "It looks like we'll have plenty of food," she said.

"I hope so, but there's no telling how much those two big men will eat or how long we may be delayed at the cabin."

"I'm sure Erich and Joachim won't expect to eat royally, and as for the time we'll be spending in Lorrach, Erich said we'll most likely cross the border tomorrow night, so we'll have to move quickly."

When they'd finished the last of the tea, Sigrid began to pack the food while Inge went to her room to finish selecting the personal items she hoped to take with her. She chose photos of her parents as well as a few of her with Rosel and Sigrid taken over the years. When she had safely tucked her treasures in a small suitcase, she joined her aunt in the kitchen. "The stores should be open by now," she said. "I should be on my way."

"I don't think you'll have any trouble finding a coat or the wire cutters, but it may be difficult to locate a wig? With the wartime restrictions, luxury items aren't readily available."

"I have no idea where to begin, but I'll find one somewhere. What are your plans for the day?"

"I have an appointment at the bank. After Joachim phoned with the good news about Rosel, I called Herr Huber and told him I want to withdraw funds to help a friend whose son was wounded on the Eastern Front."

"Did he believe you?'

"He'd have no reason to doubt me. Who'd think an old lady would need money to facilitate an escape to Switzerland?"

"You're not old, Aunt Sigrid, but let's hope you're right and Herr Huber thinks your request is legitimate. Who knows if the Gestapo tracks bank withdrawals."

"I wondered that too, so I won't empty the account. We need just enough cash to get to Basel." Sigrid walked over to the table by the couch, opened the drawer, and removed a sheet of paper. "Take this," she said.

Inge crossed the room and took the paper from her. "What are these?" she asked.

"The numbers for the Swiss accounts. If I don't make it across the border—"

"You'll make it, Aunt Sigrid. We all will."

"But if I don't, you and Rosel will have the money. As you can see, there are two separate accounts. Put the paper with the things you're taking with you."

"I will, but I won't need it. Now I've got to go." She put on her coat and scarf and set out to do her part to facilitate the escape.

As Sigrid expected, a gray wool coat resembling Erna Hambro's wasn't a problem. Inge found one at her first stop at a shop on Leopoldstrasse. The hardware store carried wire cutters and she bought a heavy-duty pair. As the day progressed, she realized, as Sigrid had predicted, the wig was going to be a problem. She tried all the likely stores in the shopping areas from Odeonsplatz to Marienplatz. She went to the shops down on Tal and up on Stachus as well as on Sendlingerstrasse, Schelling/Turkenstrasse, and Franz-Josefstrasse; all to no avail.

Despite her warm boots, by early afternoon her feet began to ache from the cold and the endless walking from shop to shop. Her entire body was numb, and she was disheartened. By two o'clock she began to wonder if she would find any wig at all, let alone one that matched Erna's hair color. Because of the winter, rationing, and the blackout, many of the shops closed early, so if she wasn't successful within the next hour, she knew she'd have to begin again in the morning.

Her final destination for the day was on Hohenzollernstrasse. In the first shop, she found a wig, but the hair was blond, and Erna was a brunette. She thought about dying it to match Erna's color, but there was the problem of finding dye. She put the wig down. She'd come back if she couldn't find anything better.

She left the small shop and drove two blocks to what she resolved would be the last store she'd visit that afternoon. Fatigued and frustrated, she pulled up in front and parked. Suddenly, she was glad she hadn't given up. In the window on a fashionably-dressed mannequin's head, was a brown wig that, if styled differently, would definitely do. She parked the car, got out, and tried the door. The shop was locked, but hanging from the door-knob was a sign saying the proprietor would return in thirty-minutes. Rather than stand in the cold and battering wind, Inge returned to the car and turned on the heat. It wasn't long before a tall, middle-aged woman removed the sign and unlocked the door.

Inge turned off the car and went inside. The smiling shop-keeper finished hanging her coat and came over to greet her. "May I help you, Fraulein?" she said.

"I'd like to purchase the wig on the mannequin in the window," said Inge.

The woman nodded no. "I'm sorry, Fraulein," she said. "The wig isn't for sale. We would never be able to get another one for our display. Because of the war it's not possible to buy luxury items like wigs for mannequins."

"I'm willing to pay any reasonable price."

"As I said, Fraulein. I'm not selling the wig."

"Perhaps if you knew why I need it, you'd rethink your decision," Inge persisted. "My elderly aunt is recovering from a disease that caused her to lose her hair. As I'm sure you can imagine, she's very self-conscious. The doctors told her she has to get some fresh air if she expects to recover completely, but she refuses to go out because she's embarrassed. I've been searching for a wig for several days, and this is the first one I've seen. You understand how important it is. Her very life may depend on it."

"What about a scarf?" said the shopkeeper. "Wouldn't that do just as well?"

"I suggested a scarf or a hat, but my aunt refuses to go outside without a wig. I'm so worried about her. I'd about given up any hope when I saw the mannequin in your store window. Buying the wig is the most important purchase I'll ever make."

The woman was obviously rethinking her decision. She hesitated for a moment longer and then walked over to the mannequin. "Well I suppose we could lay the dresses out flat and sell the wig," she said. "I wouldn't want your aunt to die."

"I'd be so grateful," Inge said. She grasped the shopkeeper's hand and squeezed. "If you'd like, I could return the wig to you when my aunt's hair grows back. If you're using it on a mannequin, it shouldn't matter if it's been worn."

"That won't be necessary," the woman said as she removed the wig from the display. She charged more than Inge wanted to pay, but there was no time to search for another less-expensive wig, so Inge didn't argue and paid the asking price.

As she left the small shop, wig in hand, Inge looked back. Still smiling, the shopkeeper was already rearranging her window display. As Inge pulled away from the curb, she wondered why she hadn't chosen acting as a career.

---

Joachim slept soundly throughout most of the flight to Munich. Exhausted, he was only vaguely aware the plane made two stops en route. When the transport touched down at Reim, he retrieved his luggage and called a taxi. He hadn't had time to phone Inge and Sigrid to let them know when he'd be arriving, but he figured they'd be at home preparing to leave.

Worried about being discovered, he asked the cab driver to drop him at the Hofbrauhaus instead of at Sigrid's. He doubted the Gestapo would go so far as to locate and question the cabbie, but why take a chance? If nothing else, the infamous group was thorough. Who knew if they kept track of cabs going to and from Reim?

When they pulled up to the building, he thought about going inside for one last beer, but he knew there was no way he could. By eight the next morning, everyone at headquarters would know he was back. He paid the fare, and, when the cab was out of sight, walked toward Odeonsplatz.

The knock on the door startled Inge. It was after dark and too late for the neighbors to be visiting. *God, I wonder if something went wrong in Berlin,* she thought. *Could the Gestapo know Erich had a personal stake in the selection process? Could they have seen Rosel's name on the Ravensbruck papers, realized she lived with Sigrid and me, find out that Erich and I are acquainted, and arrest them both?*

She pulled her robe tightly around her and anxiously went to see who was calling. When she saw Joachim standing on the porch, she threw her arms around him. "What a surprise and, for that matter, a relief," she said. "I couldn't imagine who'd be visiting at this hour. I thought the Gestapo had discovered our— Oh, never mind. Come in! Come in! We didn't expect you until tomorrow."

"Slow down, fair lady, though I'm enjoying the warm reception. I didn't have a chance to call from Berlin. I'm here to help you and your aunt with final preparations."

"How's Erich?"

"Always Erich—"

"Joachim—"

"Okay, he couldn't be better, unless, of course, you were with him in Berlin."

"We'll all be together soon. Take off your coat and warm yourself by the fire. Can I get you something to drink? Unfortunately Sigrid and I drank the last of the tea last night, but there's hot coffee or brandy if you prefer."

"Coffee and food. I haven't eaten since this morning, and I'm not sure I ate then."

"It must have been some night."

"Oh, it was, but you have no reason to worry, fair lady. Your man behaved admirably. It didn't take long for me to realize the only reason he went along was because he felt I deserved a final night on the town. Every other word he uttered was your name."

"I'm not sure I believe you, but nonetheless, I'm flattered. Now let me get you something to eat."

In a few minutes she returned with several slices of bread, sausage, and a cup of hot coffee. "I hope I'm not eating up all our supplies," Joachim said.

"This won't make a dent. Aunt Sigrid cooked enough to feed the entire Munich SS for a week."

"Then I'll clean my plate without feeling guilty."

Sigrid came in just as Joachim finished the last bite of sausage. The two women listened to all the news from Berlin. Sigrid told Joachim about her preparations for the escape, and Inge related her anecdote about the wig.

"It sounds like you have *almost* everything Erich needs," Joachim said.

"Almost?" said Inge.

"We have one more obstacle to overcome. Remember when Erich explained his plans for Erna? We need to find something that will knock her out. I don't think he'd like to slug his secretary."

"I can help with that," Sigrid said excitedly. "I should have thought of it before. When Rosel disappeared, I couldn't sleep, so the doctor gave me a strong sedative. I took one and I was out for the entire night, so I imagine three or four would take care of Fraulein Hambro for quite a while."

"Excellent," said Joachim. "Let's put the pills with the other things so Inge has them when she meets Erich at Dachau."

When Sigrid returned with the bottle, she was beaming. "I never imagined the sedatives I was given to help me live through Rosel's disappearance would help bring her back to me." She handed the bottle to Joachim. "Here is my contribution, though it's not much."

"It's huge," Joachim said. "And while we're on the subject, I hope you know we couldn't have accomplished any of this without you. Look at all this fabulous food, and you gave us a place to meet and plan. From the beginning you've been critical to the success of this undertaking."

Sigrid basked in the appreciation, but after several moments, she was once again serious. "Now, Joachim," she said. "I'm not telling you what to do, but I don't think you should go back to your apartment tonight. You're not supposed to be in Munich, and we wouldn't want someone to see you and start asking questions. You can sleep in Rosel's room."

"I'll gratefully take you up on your offer," Joachim said.

"Good. I'm going to bed. It's early, but we have a long day and night ahead of us tomorrow."

Inge kissed her aunt on the cheek. "I'm proud of you," she said. "You're a real trooper. Sleep well knowing we're almost at the end of our ordeal."

---

As soon as Joachim left the Aldon, Erich called the camp and asked the operator to connect him to Block Five. After two rings Erna answered. "Heil Hitler, Fraulein," he said. "It's Erich."

"Yes, Hauptsturmfuhrer," Erna responded. "The doctor said your trip was successful. Do you still plan to return with the women tomorrow afternoon as scheduled?"

"I do, and it's tomorrow I'm calling about. I'll be back in camp around four o'clock, and I would like an immediate update on the tests that were conducted while I was away. It's important I be up to speed before we begin phase three."

"I see no need to work late," Erna said. All my reports are current. If you'd like, I'll leave them on your desk."

Erich was immediately uneasy. He'd made contingency plans to call Rascher if need be, but he hadn't expected Erna to give him any trouble about working overtime. "They may be up to date and yes, you could leave them for me to read on my own," he said. "But I may have questions. Ultimately I'm the one who's responsible for the final reports we send to Berlin, and the accuracy of what I write will do a great deal to determine the Luftwaffe's reaction to Doctor Rascher's recommendations. We both want to further our favorite doctor's career, don't we?"

Erna paused as Erich's breath caught in his throat. He hoped he'd exerted enough pressure without bringing Rascher into the mix, but if she still refused to stay, he would make the call.

When Erna finally spoke, he could tell she wasn't happy. "I planned to meet friends for a birthday dinner in town tomorrow evening, Hauptsturmfuhrer, but if you really believe it's necessary for me to work, I'll leave here at four o'clock, attend the celebration for a while, and return to the office by six. You know I'd do anything to enhance Doctor Rascher's reputation."

Erich stifled a sigh. "Excellent, Fraulein," he said. "I appreciate your sacrifice." All of a sudden he thought about something else he'd overlooked. His heart sank. *Damn. What if Rascher decides to stay and work with us? That could ruin everything.* "Will the doctor be in tomorrow?" he asked tentatively.

"No, Hauptsturmfuhrer. He's still in Berlin. He's dining with Obergruppenfuhrer Doctor Hippke at the Aldon this evening. Perhaps you'll see him there. Tomorrow he has a meeting that's expected to last all day. When it's over, a special plane will return him to Munich. He should arrive at Reim an hour before the phase three testing begins."

"Excellent," Erich said, grateful they'd dodged yet another bullet.

"Then if that's all, I'll see you tomorrow."

"And you'll wait if I'm running late."

"Of course," Erna said crossly. "I said I'd be here."

"Thank you." Erich hung up, glad that Joachim urged him to make plans with Erna before returning to Dachau. He wouldn't have been able to use her or her car if he'd procrastinated, and without both, the plan would have fallen apart.

He phoned Ravensbruck and checked to make sure the arrangements had been made for transporting the women. Feiling assured him that all was in order and the women would be at Tempelhof by seven a.m. Erich hung up, pleased that, so far, everything was on track.

# CHAPTER 37

Erich slept soundly. When the alarm sounded at six o'clock, he showered, dressed, and, suitcase in hand, went downstairs to settle his bill. He was waiting in front of the hotel when the driver arrived at 6:30.

He was surprised how sentimental he felt as the Mercedes made its way to Tempelhof, down well-known streets and past familiar sights he was seeing for perhaps the last time. As he passed the Chancellery Building that had played such an important role during his early days in the party, anger replaced nostalgia. His dreams of the great new order under Hitler were buried beneath the outrage and revulsion he'd felt from the first hours he'd spent in Dachau. The Nazi movement was not what he hoped it would be; *but had it ever been*, he wondered.

Berlin had also changed. The darkened, bomb-scarred city no longer held the excitement and promise it had during the Fuhrer's rise to power. The struggles and hardships of war were visible in the landscape as well as on the faces of the German people.

The driver stopped in front of the unusually quiet terminal. Tempelhof too bore signs of the conflict. Few people waited to travel and the only planes visible on the tarmac were military transports or civilian aircraft that had been converted for military use.

With so many disparate emotions racing through his head, Erich tried to concentrate on the business at hand. At the Luftwaffe transport desk, he spoke with a gruff civilian worker who was obviously too old for military service. The man looked through a stack of papers and reported that the truck from Ravensbruck hadn't arrived, though the plane was on the tarmac. Preferring to wait on board, Erich walked briskly to the rolling stairs attached to the aircraft.

At 7:30 a.m., a canvas-covered, open-backed military transport truck drove onto the tarmac and directly to the waiting plane. As soon as it came to a stop, Schmid jumped out. "Heil Hitler," he roared. "The women you selected are in the back of the truck, Hauptsturmfuhrer. Would you like me to supervise while they're put on the plane?"

"Please do," Erich said. "Will you be flying on to Munich with us, Schmid?"

"No, Sir. Scharfuhrer Heilmann and Sturman Baer will be guarding the women during the flight. Heilmann is in the terminal signing the forms necessary for the release of the women from Ravensbruck to the Dachau jurisdiction. Baer is with the women."

"Then let's get the women on board so we can take off as soon as the scharfuhrer arrives," Erich said.

Schmid opened the back of the truck and Erich peered inside. The six clearly terrified women were huddled together in the middle of the floor. *Because they're frightened or freezing,* he wondered, *or a combination of both.*

The sturman, whom Erich assumed was Baer, jerked them from their seats and pushed them roughly toward the open door and across the tarmac to the base of the steps leading up to the cabin. Making sure no mistakes had been made, and that Rosel was among the group, Erich walked up and down in front of the women lined up at the base of the stairs. "You may board," he said when he saw she was indeed there." He boarded the plane first and waited beside the door while, prodding them from behind, Baer pushed the women up the stairs.

As Rosel came through the door, she twisted her body in a last effort to break free. "Don't be a fool," Baer growled as he yanked her arm, pulled her down the aisle, and pushed her forcefully into a seat near the back of the aircraft.

"Thanks for delivering the prisoners on time," Erich said to Schmid.

"You're welcome, Hauptsturmfuhrer. Before I return to Ravensbruck I will introduce you to Baer." Erich followed Schmid to the back of the plane. "Hauptsturmfuhrer Riedl, this is Sturman Klaus Baer," he said.

"Heil Hitler, good morning, Hauptsturmfuhrer," Baer said, smiling.

*The name fits the bear-like man,* Erich thought. "Good morning, Baer," he said.

Erich walked back to the front of the plane, met Heilmann, who had just boarded, and found a seat that afforded him a clear view of Rosel. He watched her and the other women, all of whom were staring at the floor. All at once he remembered the flower beds beside Suhren's office, thinking that remaining inconspicuous was the only hope the women had to bloom again.

Near eight o'clock Heilmann presented the signed transfer papers to Erich and sat directly across the aisle from Baer. Erich wondered why the guards felt the need to watch his prisoners so closely. It was ludicrous to think the shrunken submissive women would try to escape.

As the plane left the ground, he noticed that Rosel was trembling. He wanted to walk over, sit beside her, and tell her the flight would bring her joy instead of the horror she expected, but of course that was out of the question.

The flight was uneventful. At each of the three stops, Baer parked his huge carcass in the aisle in front of the prisoners while Heilmann stood rigidly by the door to prevent them from escaping if they happened to get away from the first line of defense.

At three o'clock p.m. the plane finally approached the Reim runway. As the pilot taxied up to a spot opposite the Luftwaffe office, Erich looked out the window. Heinrich was standing by the usual staff car. Beside him was a canvas-covered truck similar to the one that transported the women from Ravensbruck to Berlin.

As the aircraft came to a halt and the rolling stairs were put in place, Heilmann moved quickly to the open door and Baer took up his usual position in the aisle. Erich picked up his briefcase and joined Heilmann near the cockpit. "I believe the Dachau guards are ready to take the prisoners," he said. "Please transfer them to the truck."

"Of course, Hauptsturmfuhrer." Heilmann went to get the women while Erich deplaned. Instead of going directly to the car, he stood on the tarmac and watched the two guards herd the group down the stairs.

Heinrich exited the Mercedes and approached Erich. "Would you like to supervise the loading of the Jews, Hauptsturmfuhrer, or would you prefer to leave for camp and meet the truck there?" he asked.

There was no way Erich was leaving for Dachau without making sure Rosel was safely in the transport. "I'll wait," he said curtly.

Baer shoved the women into the back of the truck, and he handcuffed them to each other and to iron rings set in the wooden seats. The two Dachau guards sat down on either side of the flap. Satisfied that all was progressing as planned, Erich turned to Heinrich. "We'll follow the truck," he said.

Heinrich seemed less than pleased at the prospect of being slowed down by the snail-like progress of the truck, but Erich had given him an order. "Yes Sir," he said, his expression exuding irritation.

Erich thanked Heilmann and Baer and watched them board the plane for a return flight to Berlin. He slid into the backseat of the Mercedes, opened his briefcase and took out some papers.

"How was your trip?" Heinrich asked as he pulled off the tarmac."

"Successful," Erich said brusquely. "I'd tell you about it, but I have paperwork to do before we get to camp, so if you don't mind."

"Not at all," Heinrich said, but Erich knew he did mind.

At the Jourhaus gate, Erich presented his papers and the transfer documents Feiling had prepared. The guard on duty opened the back of the truck, counted the women, and waved the truck and the Mercedes through. "Where would you like to go, Hauptsturmfuhrer?" Heinrich asked.

"Does the driver of the transport know where to take the women?"

"He does."

"Then follow him. I've brought them this far. I want to see they're safely housed in the Strafblocke. We wouldn't want anything to happen to them before they begin to do their duty for the Reich tomorrow night, would we?"

Heinrich chuckled. "I envy you," he said. "You get to watch the Jews warm the men who survive the vat."

Erich didn't respond, but he wondered how Heinrich managed to know the specifics of tests that were supposed to be classified. He quickly realized if Commandant Weiss knew what was going on in Block Five, Heinrich was also aware. He felt intense loathing for the man who spied on his fellow officers and reported their activities to Weiss.

The transport turned right at the gate and proceeded along the tree-lined lane opposite the administration building. The farther they drove from the Jourhaus, the more concerned Erich became. The Strafblocke was farther away than he expected. It would be difficult, if not impossible, to take Rosel from there and return with Erna without being discovered. He'd have to cross Roll Call Square, or at least skirt the area and go past the iron gate and along the back of the Jourhaus, if the guards at the camp entrance didn't spot them first. The searchlights would be crisscrossing the square, and the guards with dogs would be on patrol. If one of the men stopped him to ask why he was in the square, how could he explain why he was taking one of the prisoners from the Strafblocke to his office? Any reason he gave would be reported to Weiss. *God, I'll never make it,* he thought. *I'm dead before I get started.* He shuddered at his choice of words.

By the time Heinrich pulled up in front of the Strafblocke, Erich knew his entire plan would have to be rethought. He felt a knot in his stomach, and despite the cold, he was sweating. What if Rosel actually had to participate in the warming experiments? He had to find a way to get her out of Dachau before they started, but how? *What the hell am I going to do,* he asked himself. He didn't have an answer.

The truck and the Mercedes reached the entrance to the Strafblocke. As soon as they stopped, the sturman on duty held up his hand. "Hauptsturmfuhrer, Heil Hitler," he bellowed.

"Heil Hitler, Sturman. I'm Erich Riedl. These women are taking part in Doctor Rascher's Luftwaffe tests. They are being housed here in the Strafblocke."

"Plans have changed," the guard said. "Last night an unusually large number of second-time offenders were brought to the camp, so all of the cells in the Strafblocke are currently occupied. You're to take the women to the infirmary in Block E. When we've dealt with the issue here they will be transferred back here."

Erich tried to conceal his elation. The infirmary barrack was several rows away from Block Five, so logistically he'd have no problem switching Erna and Rosel. He wouldn't have to cross Roll Call Square or go anywhere near the Jourhaus, and even if the searchlights came close, he could duck into the darkness between the buildings. More importantly, when he and Rosel crossed the square to Erna's car, there would be no reason for the guards to stop them until they had to present their papers. He sighed and thought; *the gods are smiling on us.* "Follow the truck to Block E," Erich told Heinrich.

"Yes, Sir," Heinrich said, though his frown indicated his displeasure.

While Heinrich waited, Erich followed the women into the infirmary. He watched as Rosel lay down on a bed against the back of the right wall. He then dismissed Heinrich and walked the short distance to his office. The walk took less than three minutes, and again, Erich marveled at his good fortune.

When he reached Block Five, the usual guard stood by the door, which meant that Erna was still in town. "Heil Hitler, Scharfuhrer," he said. "I'll be working late, so there's no need for you to guard the office any longer. Fraulein Hambro will return to camp within the hour. Go have a hot cup of coffee and get warm."

"Thank you, Hauptsturmfuhrer," the young man said, clearly pleased for a break in a warm room.

Erich entered the office, hung up his coat, picked up Erna's phone, and gave the operator Sigrid's number. Inge answered on the second ring. "Heil Hitler," she said breathlessly. "This is Inge Friedrich speaking."

"Heil Hitler. Good afternoon, Fraulein. This is Hauptsturmfuhrer Riedl."

"Welcome back, Hauptsturmfuhrer. I understand you had a successful trip."

"That's why I'm calling. I have what I believe will be important data for your article. I'd like to discuss the progress you made while I was away. Would you meet me at the Jourhaus gate at 4:30? I realize that doesn't give you much time to drive from Munich to Dachau, but I'm pressed for time. I have a meeting with my secretary at six."

"I'll be there, Hauptsturmfuhrer," Inge said. "I'm at a standstill and would welcome additional information."

"I'm sure what I have to report will get you get back on track. I'll see you in about thirty- minutes, but please don't take any unnecessary risks. If you're running late, I'll wait inside the Jourhaus office."

Inge hung up and returned to her room. She picked up the bundle for Erich and put the pills in her purse. "Erich and Rosel are at Dachau," she said when she returned to the parlor.

And it sounds like we're on schedule. He said Erna would arrive at six, so apparently she agreed to work late."

"Do you have the pills and wire cutters?" Joachim asked.

Inge patted her purse. "Right here."

"Drive carefully," he said. "We'll see you back here about six. If you're with Erich longer than expected, stop at the Wagner and call so we won't worry."

"I will, though there probably won't be a need. Erich said he only has a few minutes, so I'll likely be back sooner than later." She stuck her head in the kitchen door. "I'm off, Aunt Sigrid. Joachim will fill you in."

"Be safe, darling, and give Erich my love."

"Mine too," Joachim teased.

The roads were clear, and Inge arrived at the Jourhaus a few minutes early. Bundled up to keep out the evening chill and to hide the coat from the guards, Erich was waiting. He spoke loudly enough for nosy guards to overhear. "Good evening, Fraulein. Have you brought your notes?"

"I have, Hauptsturmfuhrer," Inge said, continuing the charade.

"Then shall we drive a short distance in the warm car while we discuss the progress you've made during my absence? I have a few minutes before my secretary is scheduled to arrive."

"An excellent idea," Inge said. "I don't like to run the heater while the car is idling."

Erich got in and she pulled away from the gate. When she was certain they could no longer be seen, she pulled off the road. He leaned over and kissed her on the cheek. "I missed you."

"I missed you too. Thank God you're safe. How much time do you have?"

"Only a few minutes. No one is guarding the office, so I have to get back. Did you bring everything I need?"

"I did." Inge handed him the coat, the wig, the wire cutters, and the pills. "Would you rather I pack the wire-cutters with our things?"

Erich nodded no. "If Rosel and I have to break out of Dachau, we'll need them; that is if we can find a part of the fence that isn't electrified."

"But you don't think it will come to that."

"God I hope not. The wig looks great."

"Thanks, I styled it last night before I went to bed. When we have time, remind me to tell you how I got it."

Erich smiled. "It will be my first question when we get to Switzerland. Are you and Sigrid ready to leave?"

"We're counting the hours. How's Rosel, Erich?"

"Naturally she's terrified. From her expression when she catches me staring at her, I can see she's also angry. I wanted to explain that she'd be alright, but of course that wasn't an option."

"When she's safely out of Dachau, and we've told her everything, she'll understand why you had to be cautious."

Erich looked at his watch. "I wish I could stay, but I'd better get back."

"What happens next?"

"Erna should be back at the office anytime now, which is another reason we have to be on our way. I don't want her to see your car parked here and have to explain. As soon as she arrives I'll put our plan in motion. If all goes well, we should be out of the camp forty-five minutes after she falls asleep. She usually drinks coffee to stay alert, so I'll stop by the dining hall and pick up a cup for her before I return to Block Five."

"She won't think it's strange you have coffee waiting?"

"I'm hoping she'll see it as an apology of sorts. I insisted she change her plans for the evening, and she wasn't pleased."

Erich looked at his watch again. "I've got to go, Inge." He got out of the car, took off his coat, and tied the coat Inge brought around his waist. He stuffed the wig behind his belt, put the wire cutters and pills in his pocket, put his own coat back on, and got back in the car. Inge pulled off the shoulder and turned back toward the camp. "Please be careful," she said as they approached the gate.

"I will. Think positively. Rosel and I will see you later tonight."

"I love you," Inge whispered.

"And I love you. This is going to work. I'll see you soon."

Inge didn't turn back as she drove away from the Jourhaus gates for the last time.

# CHAPTER 38

When Erich reached the office, Erna had yet to arrive. He stashed the coat and wig in the bottom drawer of his desk and headed to pick up the coffee. He assumed Erna would be on time and wanted to be ready when she arrived.

Nothing was happening in Roll Call Square. "Thank God," he whispered. In all their planning sessions neither he nor Joachim had considered there might be an extended roll call. Had there been, he and Rosel couldn't have walked across the square without being stopped by an alert guard. He shook his head. *Damn, what else have we forgotten,* he wondered again.

Only a few men lingered in the dining hall. Erich poured two cups of coffee, and with his back to several officers who were playing cards, dropped five pills into one. When he got back to the office, Erna was hanging her coat. "Good evening, Fraulein," he said. "Thanks for coming back to work."

Erna's scowl mirrored her mood. "I was surprised there wasn't a guard on duty and the office was empty," she said irritably.

"My fault," Erich said. "After I let the guard take a break, I decided the least I could do was have a cup of hot coffee waiting. I figured I owe you something for making you cancel your plans for the evening." He handed Erna the steaming liquid, making sure he gave her the doctored cup, and thinking that, after all the planning, how ironic it would be if he were the one to consume the drugged brew. "I was only gone a few minutes."

Erna managed a weak smile. "Thank you, Hauptsturmfuhrer. That was considerate. When I walked through Roll Call Square, I felt a chill in my bones."

Erich waited nervously as Erna removed the lid from the cup and took a sip. Would she think the coffee tasted different? As he feared, she pursed her lips and put the coffee cup down on the desk. "This so-called coffee is worse than usual," she said. "I'll be glad when Germany finally wins the war so we can get the real thing."

"I know what you mean," Erich said, wondering if he'd have to hit the woman after all. "There's only one thing good about the stuff. It's hot, and that makes it acceptable, if not tasty, on a cold night." He took a sip of his coffee. *Please let her be cold enough to keep drinking,* he silently prayed.

"I guess so," Erna said. "If nothing else, it helps get rid of the chill. Shall we get to work?"

"Give me a minute to get my notes together, Fraulein. In the meantime, drink your coffee and I'll tell you about my trip to Ravensbruck."

Erna sipped the coffee as she listened to Erich describe his trip to Berlin and his selection of the women at Ravensbruck. When he saw her put the empty cup in the trash, he opened a folder. "Now that we're both warm, shall we begin the briefing?"

"I'm ready," Erna said groggily, "but I can't figure why I'm suddenly so tired."

Seconds later she slumped over her desk. Erich waited for a few minutes, but she didn't move. He walked to her desk and lifted her arm. She groaned, but showed no resistance.

He quickly returned to his desk and removed a pair of scissors. He propped Erna's body against the back of the chair. One by one he removed the pins that held her bun in place. As her lovely brown hair cascaded around her face, he leaned back and took a look. Though she hid it well, Rascher's secretary was a very attractive woman. The hair softened her usually dour and manly appearance. *I may be doing the woman a favor,* he thought as he began to snip her long locks.

In ten minutes Erna's hair was as short as Rosel's. Erich cleaned up all traces of his barbering, put the cut locks in a large envelope, and buried it beneath several discarded letters in the trash. He removed Erna's shoes and outer jacket and paused. He'd wait for Rosel to remove the rest of Erich's clothes.

The time had come. He took a deep breath and left the office. As he walked the short distance to the infirmary barracks, he was plagued with anxiety and foreboding. *God, let this go well,* he prayed as he approached Block E. *We've come this far. Please don't let us fail now.*

He was encouraged when the young sturman guarding the women snapped to attention as he approached. *He has to be new to camp,* Erich pondered. *An older and more seasoned guard would give me much more trouble. Once again the fates are smiling.* "Heil Hitler, Sturman," he said.

"Heil Hitler," the young man bellowed. "How may I help you, Hauptsturmfuhrer?"

"I'm Erich Riedl, Sturman. We haven't met. Are you new to Dachau?"

"I reported to camp earlier today. This is my first duty."

"Excellent," Erich said enthusiastically, and he meant what he said. "I'm Doctor Rascher's assistant in the Luftwaffe experiments being conducted in Block Five." He turned and pointed to the office. "The Jews you're guarding will be utilized in a series of tests beginning tomorrow morning. I've come to take one of them for a little while."

"I wasn't told any of the prisoners would be removed from the Infirmary Block tonight, Hauptsturmfuhrer. Your orders."

"If you're asking for written authorization—" Erich laughed. "Welcome to Dachau, Sturman. The Jews will be warming our test cases with their bodies tomorrow night. I think one of the bitches should warm mine first; simply to see if she meets our requirements, of course."

"Of course, Hauptsturmfuhrer. Since you're conducting the tests, I doubt anyone would object. My orders were to keep the enlisted men and officers out of here. I'm sure the directive doesn't include you."

"I'll have the Jew back in a flash." Erich laughed. "It shouldn't take very long for her to satisfy my needs. I haven't had a woman in quite a while—well, you understand."

The sturman obviously did understand, because he stood aside and allowed Erich to enter the room. It was clear the women overheard the conversation, because all of them lay on their cots with their faces to the wall. Erich didn't hesitate. He walked straight to Rosel and grabbed her by the shoulder. "Get up," he screeched. "It's time to do your duty for the Reich."

Rosel looked terrified as Erich jerked her off the cot. *If there were any other way, Rosel, but*—as he tugged the panicked women toward the door, he struggled to maintain his bravado. "Thanks for your cooperation, Sturman," he said loudly. "And because you're keeping my tryst a secret, I'll stand guard later on and let you have your way with the bitch."

The guard's eyes grew wide with anticipation. "Thank you, Hauptsturmfuhrer," he said. "Of course I'll tell no one." He was still smiling when Erich disappeared around the corner.

Erich was relieved when he saw Erna still slumped over her desk. He closed the office door and turned to Rosel. It was the moment he'd been waiting for. "Rosel Friedrich," he said.

"I'm not going to rape you. Do you hear me?"

Rosel looked bewildered as Erich took her by the shoulders and squared her body so she faced him. "Listen to me, Rosel," he said. "You're safe. I don't have time to explain, so you have to stop crying and listen to me. I brought you to Dachau from Ravensbruck. Now I'm going to take you to Inge and your Aunt Sigrid. Do you understand, Rosel?"

"To Inge and Aunt Sigrid?" Rosel choked out the words.

"Yes. Inge, your aunt, and I have been searching for you for months. You and I are going to leave here and meet them a short distance from the camp. They'll answer all of your questions. Right now I have to know how you are physically."

Erich could almost see the cobwebs disappear from Rosel's brain. Her eyes brightened and there was renewed strength in her voice when she spoke. "I'm not as strong as I was once was, but I believe I can do what you ask," she said.

"Good. First help me remove my secretary's clothes." Rosel flinched. "Come on, it's the only way," Erich urged. "We have to move quickly." Rosel nodded and helped Erich strip Erna to her underwear. "Now remove your clothes," he said.

Rosel recoiled. "My clothes?" she whimpered.

"Please. I'll respect your modesty and turn my back, but hurry. When you've taken off your prison uniform, put on Erna's blouse and skirt."

Erich heard Rosel struggle as she did what he asked. While she dressed, he removed the coat and wig from his desk drawer. "I'm dressed, er—"she said a few minutes later, not knowing what to call her rescuer.

"I'm sorry, Rosel," he said. "I'm Erich Riedl."

"Erich, I'm ready."

"Good. Now help me put your uniform on Fraulein Hambro. While I'm returning her to the infirmary, put on her shoes and coat along with this." He held out the wig. "Inge styled it to look like Erna's hair."

The two struggled, but they finally managed to get the striped prison uniform on Erna's unconscious body. Erich hoisted her up, supporting her weight with his arms under her armpits. "Finish dressing, Rosel," he said. "I won't be long. We'll leave as soon as I get back."

He headed toward the door and quickly turned back. "By the way, can you drive?"

Rosel's eyes narrowed. "I could," she said. "But it's been a long time. Why do you ask?"

"You'll know soon enough. Let's hope, once you learn, you don't forget."

Holding Erna upright, Erich carried her toward the infirmary. "What's the matter with the Jew, Hauptsturmfuhrer?" the sturman asked nervously.

"There's not a problem, Sturman. I was too much for her. She must have fainted from pleasure."

"But she'll recover? "I mean—"

"Of course she will, and I'm sure she'll give you a good ride later on. I'm going to put her back on her cot. If I can, I'll come back later and keep watch for you. If I don't make it, she's yours tomorrow night. That is if you're on duty."

"If I haven't been assigned the duty yet, but I'll trade to get it."

Erich smirked. "I thought you might."

He dragged Erna into the building and laid her on the cot with her face to the wall. "See that you leave her alone for the night or you'll satisfy my desires," he said to the woman, loudly enough so the sturman could hear. He paused at the door and kept up the farce. "If one of these bitches gets up to comfort the slut, Sturman, come get me. I'll take care of her."

"I will, Hauptsturmfuhrer."

*That should keep the women from looking too closely*, Erich reflected as he walked away. Before rounding the corner, he turned back to the guard and called out: "Remember, your turn will come later this evening or tomorrow night."

When Erich entered the office, Rosel was cowering against the wall. "It's Erich, Rosel. There isn't a problem. Erna's on your cot in Block E, and I've warned the other women to leave her alone. I doubt she'll be discovered until morning, which gives us plenty of time to get to the Swiss border." Rosel didn't look reassured. "You should be excited," he said. "You'll soon be with Inge and Sigrid."

"I am excited," Rosel said, her voice quivering, "but I'm also frightened. The phone kept ringing while you were gone. The caller must believe someone's here. He or she hung up and immediately called again."

"Oh God, there's something wrong," Erich said, pacing as he talked. "Erna probably told Rascher we're working late, and he's trying to reach one of us." He paused in front of Rosel. "Listen carefully," he said. "We have to leave immediately. I'm going to take your arm and lead you across the square to Erna's car. It's parked to the left of the main camp gates."

Erich picked up Erna's purse. He removed the car keys and walked back to Rosel. "When we get to the car, go directly to the driver's side and get behind the wheel. I'd drive, but since Erna always does, a change could make the guard suspicious. When you get in, reach over and unlock my door. I'll tell you what to do next." He handed her the keys and Erna's scarf. "Pull the scarf around your face as if you're trying to keep warm. Your hair looks like Erna's, and your coat is identical. I guess we didn't need to buy one after all."

"If this is like the coat Erna usually wears, I'm glad you did." Rosel pointed to the coat hanging on the rack by the door.

"Damn, it's red," Erich said. "Erna was going to a birthday party before she came back to work. I guess she came to camp in her dressy clothes." He considered having Rosel switch coats, but decided to take a chance on the usual attire, thinking the red coat could cause undue attention.

He continued to give instructions. "When you get to the Jourhaus gate, stop the car and bury your head in the scarf. I'll comment about the cold, and you nod in response. Don't say anything. The guards shouldn't look too closely. They're used to us leaving together by now, and I sometimes speak to them, so I doubt they'll give us a second thought. If anything, they'll shine their flashlights into the back seat. However, if I'm wrong, put the car in gear and head through those gates as fast as you can." Erich stifled a laugh. There was no way Erna's car could crash through the iron bars of the Jourhaus gate, but Rosel didn't have to know that.

Rosel looked anything but confident. "I'm so frightened," she moaned.

"I know, but you'll be fine," he said with as much certainty as he could muster. "Once the guard waves us through the gates, drive slowly until we're out of sight and I'll take over."

"Where exactly are Inge and Aunt Sigrid?"

"They and Joachim, a friend of mine, who played an important role in your rescue, will be waiting for us about twenty kilometers from here just off the main road. We'll change cars, drive to Lorrach, and cross into Switzerland, but as I said before, we'll have plenty of time to talk once we're safely out of Dachau. So shall we do this?"

Rosel managed a weak smile. "I guess so," she said, "but I'm still frightened."

"I know it's a lot to ask, but try to relax and think positively. We *will* make it."

Erich had his hand on the doorknob when he abruptly pulled back. Someone was coming toward the office. He pushed Rosel back into the room and put his finger over his lips, signaling her to keep quiet. He listened intently as the footsteps came closer to the door. When he heard the creaking wooden steps, he grabbed Rosel by the shoulders and pulled her toward him. "I'm going to kiss you, Rosel," he whispered. "We have to make it look like there's something going on between us." He squared her around so he could keep his eye on the door and kissed her firmly on the lips. *God, let anyone who's here to investigate get the idea we don't want to be disturbed,* he silently implored as he saw the doorknob turn. Heinrich burst into the room. Erich hid Rosel's face from view and looked up at the intruder.

"Working late?" Heinrich said snidely.

Erich pressed Rosel's face into his shoulder. "As you can see, I'm not exactly working. Could we talk tomorrow, Obersturmfuhrer? I'm rather busy and the lady is obviously embarrassed."

"It's the lady I've come to see. A little while ago a message came from Doctor Rascher. I saw Fraulein Hambro's car parked in its usual place. I can see why you didn't answer the phone. Fraulein, Doctor Rascher wants you to meet him in the office tomorrow morning at eight o'clock rather than nine. His meeting is over and he's returning to Munich earlier than he originally expected."

Rosel didn't move.

"Fraulein," Heinrich said again. "Did you hear me? I'm sure the doctor will be calling back. What should I tell him?"

Erich had no choice. He had to act or Heinrich would discover the deception and sound the alarm. He pushed Rosel aside, and in one quick move, he struck Heinrich, who staggered; stunned both from surprise and from Erich's blow to his chin.

Erich spun Heinrich around so his back was to him, put his arm around his neck in a death choke, and held on until the snitch went limp. He applied pressure until he was sure Heinrich was dead. "Come on, Rosel," he urged. "I need help."

"What will we do with him?" Rosel pleaded. "What if someone saw him come in?"

Erich thought of the sturman guarding the women in Block E. He would have seen Heinrich walk by. *Who else knew Heinrich was coming to find them? Could he have told the camp operator he was going to deliver Rascher's message? Could Weiss know where he'd gone?* For the first time, he was grateful the dead man was the camp snitch. No one would care if he was missing. His unpopularity would help him and Rosel. "We can't take him out of the office," he said, again thinking of the sturman guarding the infirmary. "Help me get him into my desk chair." When the body was in place, Erich folded Heinrich's arms and rested his head face down on his crossed hands. "We'll leave him here."

"But won't someone find him and come looking for us?"

"Not if I play it right, but you have to stay calm. We're going to do exactly what we planned, with one exception. I'm going to stop and talk to the young sturman who's been so cooperative all evening. Let's hope he continues to be obliging."

Erich took Rosel's arm to steady her and they left the office. She pulled the scarf around her face and stood quietly at the end of Block E while he walked to the door to talk to the guard. As Erich approached, the young man grinned. "Are you back to relieve me already?" he asked eagerly.

"Not yet, Sturman. I hate to disappoint you, but your rendezvous will have to wait until tomorrow night. I assure you, I won't forget. You've been a great help."

The sturman pointed toward Rosel. "Who's the woman, Hauptsturmfuhrer?" he asked. "Was she in the office when you had the Jew in there with you?"

Erich hadn't anticipated the question. Of course the young guard hadn't seen a female enter Block Five since he'd come on duty. Erna was already in the office "She was, Sturman." Erich smirked. "She enjoys watching, and now that you know, the lady's reputation rests in your hands. She's my secretary and a close associate of Doctor Rascher, who is Commandant Weiss's friend. It wouldn't do either of us any good to reveal her secret."

"I understand," the young man whispered conspiratorially. "I'll be sure to keep quiet."

"You're getting quite the indoctrination tonight, Sturman, and your education isn't finished. Did you see the officer who walked toward Block Five a few minutes ago?"

"I did, Sir, but I didn't recognize him."

"It was Commandant Weiss's aide. Unfortunately, he's been having problems with his woman. You know how that can be?" Erich doubted the young man had any idea, but he grinned and nodded as if he did. "Well, his problems finally got the best of him," Erich continued. "He got drunk tonight.

"On the camp grounds?" the guard asked incredulously.

"Yes, so you see how this indiscretion could damage his record. I put him to bed in the office. I would appreciate it if you'd leave him alone and let him sleep it off until morning. He should have a hell of a hangover, but he'll still have his clean record."

"I'll leave him alone," said the sturman.

"You can be sure word will get around. Your cooperation can't hurt your status around here. In fact, you could help yourself even more. When the usual man comes to guard the office at 11:30, see that he doesn't enter the office either. I'm going to go back, lock the door, and turn off the lights before we leave. Tell him everything has been quiet. He'll have no need to go in and look for himself."

"I'll do that too, Hauptsturmfuhrer."

Erich could see the man mentally planning his glorious future. The reality that he'd suffer for helping him was rather ironic. He thanked the guard, whose career he'd destroyed, and returned to Rosel. "Everything's okay," he said calmly. "I'm going back to the office and lock the door, so wait here. The guard will leave you alone."

Erich turned out the lights, locked the door behind him, and joined Rosel, who was still shaking from fear and the cold. As they passed the infirmary, he waved to the sturman. Holding Rosel firmly by the elbow to keep her from stumbling, they walked up the camp road and through Roll Call Square toward Erna's car, which was parked about forty-five meters from the Jourhaus gate.

When they got to the far side of the open space, Erich felt slightly better. There were guards on patrol and searchlights crisscrossing the area, but there didn't appear to be anyone near the secretary's car. So far their luck was holding. They arrived at the parking space with no problems. "Open the door and get in like you have done it for years," he said to Rosel.

The shaking woman complied and slid behind the wheel. She leaned over to unlock the door, and Erich slid into the passenger seat. "I've never driven a car like this," she said nervously.

"It's like all the others," Erich responded, trying to hide the concern he was feeling. "Remember to ease the clutch out as you press down on the gas, but don't push too hard. We want to go slowly."

Rosel took a deep breath, pushed in the clutch, and turned on the engine. "You're doing fine," Erich said. "Let's let the engine warm up for a moment. We don't want to stall because the car's cold." They sat quietly, watching the gauge steadily climb. "Okay," Erich said. "Now release the hand brake. Put your foot on the gas, and, as you press down, let out the clutch."

Rosel obeyed, and the car crept ahead. "Keep doing what you're doing," he said, thankful the car wasn't jerking. He hoped if Rosel had a problem it would be there rather than at the gate where their lives could depend on a smooth start. Suddenly he imagined the worst. They would be discovered, and in a desperate attempt to escape, Rosel would let out the clutch too fast, and the car would die just inside the Jourhaus gate. He swallowed hard. "You're doing a great job, Rosel," he said again as the car rolled ahead smoothly. "Good. Now put the clutch back in and shift into second gear."

With another success, Rosel seemed to gain confidence. "Now turn toward the gates and keeping your foot on the clutch, stop a few meters from the guard. Pull your scarf around your face and let me do the talking. When he opens the gates, do exactly what you just did so well. Work for a smooth, steady departure."

Rosel pulled up to the gate and stopped without killing the engine. As the guard approached her door, Erich was immediately alarmed. He had removed the keys from Erna's purse, but he'd left her papers behind. He prayed the guard would be a regular who knew them too well to ask for proof of identity. "Good evening, Fraulein, Hauptsturmfuhrer," he said. "You worked late this evening."

Erich leaned across and spoke for Rosel. "We had a great deal to do before we resume the testing tomorrow morning."

Despite the cold that rushed into the car through the open window, Erich's hands and body were sweating. The tension made him want to scream. He worried about Rosel. Remembering how frightened she was during the episode in the office, he prayed her renewed angst wouldn't affect her driving.

The guard shined his flashlight in the backseat. "Everything appears to be in order, Hauptsturmfuhrer," he said.

"Thank you," said Erich, his heart in his throat.

"Goodnight, Fraulein." Rosel nodded, but she didn't speak. Erich held his breath. The guard apparently accepted the nod as a typical response, because he returned to the Jourhaus and opened the gates.

As Rosel rolled up the window, Erich realized the entire escape depended on the next few minutes. "Okay," he whispered. "Now do as I said."

Rosel put one foot on the clutch and the other on the gas. Erich could see the intense concentration on her face as she eased up the clutch while applying pressure to the gas pedal. The car began to move slowly. "Excellent," he said. "Go a little faster and then shift."

When the car built up enough velocity, Rosel shifted. As they smoothly advanced, she grew more self-assured and looked less terrified. She shifted again and the two passed out of the guard's sight.

"Not much farther," Erich said. "You've done a great job." They traveled another kilometer. "Okay," he said. "You can pull over now."

Rosel pulled off the road and braked without putting in the clutch. The car jerked and died. Erich grinned. "If you had to kill the engine, now is definitely the time to do it," he said.

When Rosel was seated in the passenger's seat, Erich turned and put his hand over hers. "It's over," he said. "We made it. Your aunt and Inge will be so proud of you."

Tears of relief streamed down Rosel's face. "Thank you," she cried.

"You're very welcome," Erich said as tears pooled in his eyes. Realizing it was unlikely he'd ever experience the intense emotions he knew Rosel was feeling, he remained quiet and let her cry as he put the car in gear and headed for the rendezvous point.

# CHAPTER 39

When Inge got home, supper was on the table. During the unusually quiet meal she did most of the talking, telling Sigrid and Joachim about her meeting with Erich.

When the last of the food was gone, Sigrid stood and began to clear the table. "It's getting late," she said. "I'm going to wash the dishes and put them away before we leave. That way, when we return home at the end of the war, the kitchen will be neat and tidy."

"Would you like some help?" Inge asked.

"No, darling," Sigrid said quietly. "If you don't mind, I'd like to be by myself for a few minutes."

Inge smiled, but she was anything but cheerful. She felt edgy, anxious, and worried about Erich, but for Sigrid's sake she hid her angst. Though he too kept his thoughts to himself, she knew Joachim was more than a little concerned for his friend. She could see it in his eyes, and he wasn't engaging in his usual banter.

It was close to seven when Sigrid finally finished in the kitchen and returned to the parlor. Joachim stood as she entered the room. "It's time to leave," he said. "I'd like to be at the rendezvous site early in case Erich and Rosel get out of Dachau ahead of schedule. I've been figuring that if Erna got to the office on time, and from what Erich told me about her, that's a given, and if she drinks the coffee right away—"

"It would take no more than ten or fifteen minutes for the pills to work," Sigrid said. "I know from experience."

"Good," said Joachim. "Once she passes out, Erich will go for Rosel. Let's say he leaves the office at 6:30 and returns fifteen minutes later—"

Inge chimed in. "He'll switch Rosel and Erna's clothes. It shouldn't take more than twenty minutes from start to finish, especially since the Ravensbruck women are being housed in the infirmary block, which is close to the office."

"So that takes us to 7:00 or 7:15," Sigrid said.

"Right, and allowing fifteen minutes to cross Roll Call Square, talk with the guard at the Jourhaus gate and drive away—"

Sigrid's face lit up. "They could be leaving any time now."

"Exactly, so the two of you should finish any last-minute tasks. I'll put the rest of the food in the car and wait for you there." He put on his coat and gloves, picked up the packages piled by the front door, and left Sigrid and Inge to share a private moment together before leaving their home.

Five minutes later, Sigrid and Inge exited the house. Inge waited on the porch while Sigrid closed and locked the door. She linked arms with her aunt, and they walked briskly up the path toward the car. Joachim got out and opened the doors. "Are you alright?" he asked.

"We're ready to go, young man," Sigrid said resolutely. "We've cried our last tears."

Sigrid climbed into the small space left for her in the back seat. As he pulled away from the curb, Joachim noticed that neither woman looked back.

---

As they neared the rendezvous site, Erich held his watch up to the dashboard light. It was 8:30. The extra time it had taken to deal with Heinrich had put them behind schedule. He'd told

Joachim to start worrying at midnight, but he knew if his friend had calculated the time it would take to escape, he would already be concerned, if not frightened.

Rosel was quiet during the drive. Erich realized she was just now beginning to understand what had happened to her, so he let her be. Even though the two of them had been through a great deal together, he was still a stranger.

"We're almost there," he said as they neared the turnoff. "We'll switch everything from Inge's car to Erna's and be on our way to Switzerland."

Searching for the obscure side road, Erich crept slowly through the darkness. Several times he stopped the car, thinking he'd found the turn-off, but each time he was wrong. He wondered if he might miss the exit altogether. Finally he spotted what he believed was the designated road and he turned off the highway. Clouds covered the moon and only the outline of trees was visible on either side of the narrow lane. He proceeded slowly and cautiously for three kilometers without seeing any sign of Inge's car.

Another half kilometer and he began to think he'd taken the wrong turn after all. He was about to give up, turn around, and try the next turnoff, when his headlights lit up the Volkswagen blocking the road ahead. As he pulled up behind the smaller car, Inge jumped out and raced toward them. Joachim got out and helped Sigrid from the back seat.

Erich watched Rosel's face as Inge and Sigrid neared Erna's car. "Oh my," she cried, as, in an instant, all her doubts and fears visibly disappeared. "Thank you," she mouthed to Erich, as she opened the door and rushed toward her family. Tears again welled up in Erich's eyes as he got out of the car to watch the meeting.

"I'm glad to see you, old buddy," Joachim said, enveloping Erich in a bear hug. "I was beginning to worry."

"With good reason. Let the ladies enjoy their reunion for a few more minutes. I have something to tell you before we join them."

"From the look on your face, it's bad news."

"You could say that. Rosel and I had a problem. As a result, Heinrich Wolfers is no longer with us."

"What do you mean 'no longer with us'?"

"I mean when Rosel and I were about to leave the office, Heinrich barged in looking for Erna. I couldn't let him raise the alarm."

"You killed him?"

"I didn't have a choice. It was the only way we could get out of the camp alive."

"You couldn't have knocked him out?"

"Think about what you said, Joachim. Yes, I could have knocked him out. Rosel and I would have likely gotten away, but how long before he'd wake up and report the escape? An hour? Two?"

"I get the point, but frankly I'm surprised he didn't see Rosel and sound the alarm before you had a chance to grab him."

"He probably would have, but he thought she was Erna. If he'd respected our privacy and left, he'd still be alive, but he wouldn't give up. He kept asking questions, and while he did, he moved closer to us and away from the door."

"Your privacy?"

"I tried to make Heinrich think Erna and I were having an affair and she was embarrassed because he'd found out."

"You're kidding."

"I'm not. I had to keep him from realizing Erna was really Rosel. When Heinrich pushed open the office door, I grabbed Rosel and kissed her. When I was sure Heinrich knew what we were doing, I pressed her face into my shoulder. I wanted him to think she was too self-conscious to look at him."

"Rosel must have been terrified," Joachim said. "And I don't mean because Heinrich walked in on you."

Erich realized that for the first time in days, if for only an instant, they were engaging in carefree banter. "You're probably right," he said, grinning. "When we get to Switzerland you'll have to ask her how she was feeling."

Joachim didn't comment. The lighthearted moment was over, and once again, he was all business. "So as a result of the incident with Heinrich, if you could call it that, the efficient SS could figure out what transpired much earlier than we originally anticipated. We need get out of here."

"I agree, but I don't think we're in imminent danger. I covered my tracks; at least I hope I did. Fortunately, the sturman guarding the infirmary is new to the camp. He saw Heinrich enter the office, so I had to tell him something. I said Heinrich was having problems with his woman and got drunk."

"Did he believe you?"

"He did. He's young and impressionable. I convinced him we were saving Heinrich's career by leaving him in the office to sleep off his drunken stupor." Erich smiled. "It's ironic, isn't it? He believes he's furthering his career by keeping Heinrich's secret, when, in fact, he'll likely be disciplined."

"Or worse, shot."

"It's possible. I made it clear the man he's protecting is Weiss's favorite."

"Which would give him reason to believe he could benefit from his silence."

"That was the idea. So I trust we're in the clear, at least until six o'clock, when the guards bring breakfast to the women. If by chance they leave the food by the cots without awakening the women, they won't figure out Rosel is really Erna."

"Unless Erna is already awake. Why didn't we buy tape and rope?"

"Even if we had, I couldn't have taped Erna's mouth or tied her hands. I had to make the sturman believe she fainted from rough sex. So assuming Erna is still unconscious, it won't be long before the general alarm is sounded. Ditto if she's awake. Heinrich came to the office to tell Erna that Rascher is coming back to Munich in the morning rather than tomorrow night as originally planned. He asked her to come in at eight o'clock rather than nine, and he's obsessively punctual. So at eight he'll find Heinrich slumped over the desk and no Erna in sight, so worst-case scenario, I'm thinking we have ten or so hours to get out of Germany—at best, twelve."

"Then let's get the hell out of here," Joachim said. "The women can continue with their reunion on the way to Lorrach."

As Erich neared the car, Inge hurried to him and wrapped her arms around his neck. "Thank you for what you did for our family," she said.

"Seeing the three of you together is thanks enough for me," Erich said. "But Inge, we have to leave right away. Rosel and I had a problem when we were about to leave the office. I think we're okay for now, but we won't be for long."

Before Inge could ask Erich to explain, Sigrid, holding Rosel's hand, approached Joachim and Erich. Her eyes were bright and wet with tears as Erich opened his arms and hugged her. "You've made me a happy woman," she said. "I thank you with all my heart."

"We'll have plenty of time for thanks later," Erich said. "Now we're going to load the car and get underway."

"In a minute," said Sigrid. She took Rosel's hand again and walked toward Joachim. "I want you two to meet," she said. "Joachim, this is Rosel. Rosel, this wonderful man is one of the reasons we're all together."

Joachim smiled. "I'm happy to meet another fair lady."

"It's a privilege to meet the man who has given me back my life and done so much for my family." Rosel extended her hand and Joachim took it in his. "I'll never be able to repay you, Joachim," she said as tears fell down her cheeks.

"No need to talk about repayment," Joachim said with uncharacteristic bashfulness.

Erich rescued his self-conscious friend. "Unfortunately, this reunion will have to be put on hold for now," he said. "We need to unload the Volkswagen and load Erna's car."

Everyone pitched in, and in only a few minutes, the transfer was complete. Erich slid behind the wheel of Erna's car. Inge moved next to him, and Joachim sat beside her. Sigrid and Rosel shared the back seat with the food. As they approached the main road, Erich suddenly remembered he'd forgotten to pick up Erna's papers. He glanced back at Sigrid. "By chance, did you bring Rosel's identification card with you?" he asked.

"I didn't," Sigrid said. "It never occurred to me that anything with Rosel's real name on it would be of use to her now. Will there be a problem?"

"I hope not, but we'd better make a contingency plan just in case. If there's a roadblock, Rosel, you'll have to hide under a blanket on the floor. We can't have a passenger without proper papers. There would be too many questions, and we wouldn't have the answers."

"Do you think the roadblock would be for us?" Inge asked uneasily.

"I doubt it, at least not this early, but like I told Joachim, Rosel and I had a setback as we were leaving the office, so all bets are off the table."

"What could go wrong?" Sigrid asked. "You and Joachim thought of everything."

"Unfortunately we didn't," Erich said. "To name a few issues we could be facing, the sturman guarding the women could ignore my orders, or Erna could wake up earlier than we expected and start yelling, but at least we don't have to worry about Rascher coming to the office. He's in Berlin and won't be back until early tomorrow morning. Bottom line, we can't take any chances."

"You said you and Rosel had a setback," Inge said. "What happened in the office?" Skipping the graphic details, Erich described his encounter with Heinrich. "Wolfers is dead?" Inge said, shock on her face and in her voice.

"Erich had to kill him," Rosel said. "There was no other way. He refused to leave."

"I'm sure what Erich did was necessary," Sigrid said.

"I'm sure it was," said Inge. "I was just surprised. Do you think we could have problems at this early hour?" she asked Erich.

"Possibly. The sturman guarding Block E is a curious young man. He all but interrogated me when I went to get Rosel. In the middle of the night, there's no one keeping an eye on the guards, so out of sheer boredom, why wouldn't he strike up a conversation with his counterpart outside Block Five. He's new to camp. Maybe he figures he could make a few points by revealing the scandalous news that Weiss's assistant is passed out in a drunken stupor in Block Five."

"But I saw you lock the door," Rosel said. "How would he get in?"

"At Rascher's insistence, our guards carry keys to the office," Erich said.

And we can't hope for two novices in one night. When he hears the words 'Weiss's assistant,' the sturman guarding Block Five will realize who's in there. Assuming he knows Heinrich is the camp snitch, and it seems to be common knowledge, why wouldn't he go in, take a look for himself, and spread the word? No doubt the man who brings down the informant will instantly become the camp hero."

Rosel's eyes narrowed into a squint. "Then we really don't have much of a chance to get away," she said.

Erich quickly realized he'd said too much. "Of course we do, Rosel," he said. "I didn't mean to upset any of you. I was presenting worse-case scenarios. Whenever Heinrich and Erna are discovered, and we're hoping it won't be until tomorrow morning, it will take several hours for the SS to put the puzzle together. That's good news for us, and here I go being negative again. They will eventually connect every piece and come after us with a vengeance. I imagine they'll alert everyone from here to Lorrach."

"If everybody's looking for us, how will we be able to stop for gas?" Inge asked. "We can't make it to the Swiss border on one tank. Did you look at the gauge? Is Erna's tank full?"

"See what I mean about forgetting details?" Erich groaned. "No I didn't check the gas gauge. I'm looking now. We have about half a tank, so we'll have to stop, probably twice."

"Could there be Gestapo agents waiting for us?" Sigrid asked. "Do you think maybe they've alerted gas-station attendants?"

"It's possible," Erich said. "It won't take long for our efficient secret police to find and interrogate Joachim's friend Wrieden. He'll tell them we're on the road to Lorrach, and they'll assume our destination is the Swiss border, so when we have to fuel up, Joachim and Inge will go to the station, while Rosel, Sigrid, and I wait nearby. If by chance the station owners have been alerted to watch for us, they'll be looking for a car carrying four or five passengers. If they're questioned—"

"They'll remember a couple," Inge said.

"Exactly."

"Maybe it won't be an issue," said Sigrid. "The SS might not think we're important enough to alert anyone. It's winter. Why would anyone want to brave the elements for five ordinary people?"

"I know I'm not usually the voice of reason," Joachim said. "But we're hardly ordinary, Sigrid. Erich is an SS hauptsturm-fuhrer who helped a Jew escape from Dachau, and not just any Jew, a woman he brought from Ravensbruck to be a part of a series of tests ordered by the Luftwaffe brass. If that's not enough, Inge is a reporter for the most important newspaper in the Reich, and I'm a member of Mueller's staff. Believe me, the commandant won't be happy when he learns I'm escaping the country, leaving him embarrassed and with no solution to the supply problem I went to Berlin to solve."

"I realize this is probably a silly question, Joachim," Rosel said. "But please bear with me. I don't know very much about what's happened in Munich while I was at Ravensbruck. Apparently, you think the Gestapo will realize you're friends with Inge and Erich."

"In minutes," Erich said. "Joachim and Inge have been seen together at the Hofbrauhaus recently. I'd hoped his reputation with the ladies would keep him off the radar, but—"

"Must you tell Rosel my deepest and darkest secrets before she gets to know me?" Joachim said, frowning.

"Absolutely," said Erich. "And to answer your question, Rosel, Joachim made the arrangements for the cabin. He loudly boasted about taking two or three women with him."

"Really? And people believed you, Joachim?" Rosel said seriously.

"Of course they did," said Inge. "They'd believe anything about Joachim when it comes to women."

"I can't believe we're talking about this with important matters to discuss," Joachim said. "Shouldn't Rosel have an opportunity to know the real me before she thinks I'm beyond redemption."

Sigrid joined in. "Oh, I think she already has you figured out. They all laughed; the interlude momentarily allaying the mounting tension brought on by Heinrich's death, Rosel's missing papers, and the fear of premature discovery.

At the town of Memmingen, while Erich, Sigrid, and Rosel waited off the road several kilometers back, Joachim and Inge roused a sleeping gasoline attendant, who filled the tank. Despite the hour of the morning, the man didn't ask questions.

"Is anyone hungry?" Erich asked when he and the ladies were back in the warm car. "I haven't eaten since I had room service at the Aldon last night, and I'm sure Rosel is ready for some real food."

"I can't believe we didn't think of that earlier," Sigrid said. "You must be starving, darling."

"I'm used to surviving on very little, Aunt Sigrid, so don't stop because of me."

"We're not stopping only because you're hungry," Sigrid said. "I didn't eat much today, and I don't think Inge had much dinner."

Instead of pulling onto the road, they ate bread and sausage. The others watched with pleasure as Rosel savored the food, which, to her, must have seemed like a feast. After a few pleasant moments, Erich put his food aside. "You all can keep eating, but it's time to go," he said. "So far the weather hasn't been an issue, but it's beginning to snow. At the moment it's falling lightly, but that could change and the roads could eventually become impassable."

Erich was right. Within fifteen minutes the snow was really coming down, and he was forced to slow down to a crawl. While he and Joachim watched the road, Sigrid and Inge brought Rosel up to date; telling her about how they managed to locate her at Ravensbruck and the efforts Joachim and Erich had made to save her.

As they talked, Sigrid held Rosel's hand, watching her emotions change with each new anecdote. She laughed when they talked about Joachim's escapades, and she cried when she realized how much he and Erich were giving up for her.

Instead of asking probing questions, Inge and Sigrid let Rosel decide how much she wanted to share about her experiences. She offered a rudimentary account of her capture in Munich. As Inge suspected, she was shopping when the Gestapo grabbed her, calling her Mischling, Jewish pig, and other names that it seemed from the look on her face, were too painful to mention.

As Rosel talked about the abusive SS guards, Sigrid began to cry. "All of this is my fault, darling," she said. "I should have told you and Inge about your parents and your background years ago. Because she was a reporter, Inge would have known Hitler was arresting the Mischlinge, and we could have protected you."

"I don't understand—"

"I'll explain," Sigrid said. "But I hate to upset you." As she had with Inge only months before, Sigrid recounted the story of Rosel's family. As her aunt talked, Rosel cried quietly, not from distress, but with empathy and understanding.

With the story of her background out in the open, Rosel shared snippets about her ordeal. At Dachau her hair was cut short and her personal possessions were taken from her. At first she thought the camp was her final destination, but after two days, she and fifteen other women were loaded into the back of a transport and driven to Ravensbruck. She didn't offer specifics of the long, arduous journey and no one asked questions. There would be time for her to fill in the particulars when she was ready. Realizing Sigrid was distressed, she tried to allay her concerns by talking about the special treatment she'd been given by the SS guards at Ravensbruck. When Joachim explained why she hadn't met the same fate as the other women in the camp, Rosel finally understood.

As they neared Schopfheim, their last planned stop before arriving in Lorrach, Erich, Rosel, and Sigrid once again got out of the car to wait for Inge and Joachim to purchase gas. The snow had stopped falling, but the white flakes covered the ground and Erich sank up to his ankles as he led the women off the road to hide in the trees. He looked at his watch. It was 6:30 a.m. and the sky was beginning to brighten. He'd hoped to reach the turnoff to the cabin while it was still dark, but because of the snow, they hadn't made good time.

"Don't be too long," he called to Joachim as he drove away. "We'll freeze to death out here, and we don't have extra time to spare."

The decision he and Joachim made to purchase the fuel in Schopfheim rather than in Lorrach was pragmatic. If the Gestapo notified the border guards, they would begin their search there. He didn't want anyone in the vicinity of the cabin to remember them. If the guards didn't get answers from the attendant, they'd likely go back to Schopfheim, but the delay would buy extra time.

Joachim pulled up to the pump. A scowling attendant trudged out of the station and up to the window. "What can I do for you?" he growled.

Joachim stifled the urge to say, "What the hell do you think we'd be doing here?" He smiled at the grouch. "We need gasoline," he said.

"We don't have very much on hand," he man said sourly. "What with the additional activity in the area, our supply is limited. Do you have a ration card?"

Joachim ignored the question. He had a ration card, but he didn't want to use it in the vicinity of the cabin. "What activity?" he asked.

"With the war going badly and more and more Germans trying to cross the border, additional guards have been transferred to the area. Of course they need gas for their patrol vehicles."

Joachim realized that they had to get back to Erich and the others as soon as possible. With more guards on patrol, there would be more men on hand to search for them. "We'll take any gas you can spare," he said.

"No gas without your ration card," the attendant muttered.

Joachim reluctantly produced his card, and the man began to fill the tank. He talked as he cleaned the snow off the back window. "And where would you two be going this early in the morning?" he said. "There aren't many strangers coming around here lately, especially in the early hours and with it snowing and all."

Joachim wondered at that contradictory statement. If there weren't too many strangers, why would there be a need to increase the guards to prevent border crossings? He considered asking the attendant to explain, but thought better of it. "We got married last night," he said, thinking fast. "Our wedding dinner lasted late into the evening, and we haven't enjoyed our wedding night." He took Inge's hand. "I have a friend with a cabin nearby. He tells me it's private and cozy."

He thought he detected a smile on the grumpy attendant's face. "I see," he said.

"Thanks for the gas," said Joachim. "We'll stop by on our way back. Hopefully, you'll have more on hand. We'll only be here a few days, and as you might imagine, I'm eager to get to the cabin." Inge lowered her eyes, pretending to be embarrassed and shy.

The grumpy attendant wasn't through. "I thought every able-bodied young man was in the army fighting for the Fuhrer," he said.

"I'm in the army," Joachim said impatiently. "I was granted leave to get married and enjoy my honeymoon."

"What branch?"

"I serve with the Afrika Korps."

"Then you're not doing too well, are you? I'm surprised Rommel let you go."

"We're all given leave from time to time," Joachim said. "Particularly if it's to get married and have children for the Reich. If my wife and I could get to the cabin, I might produce more members of the future Hitler Youth." He turned on the engine. "Now if you'll excuse us, the snow is really coming down. Maybe if my luck holds out, we'll be snowed in and I won't have to go back to the front."

The attendant finally seemed satisfied. "I guess I'll be seeing you when you come back through here again," he said. He took Joachim's money and stepped back from the car window.

"That man would make a great Gestapo agent," Joachim said as they headed back toward the trio waiting for them. "He has a knack for interrogation."

"Are you sure he isn't an agent? He asked so many questions. What if he knows about us and is waiting until we pick up the others before he makes an arrest?"

"Your imagination's on overdrive, Inge. If the Gestapo is using men like that attendant, we have nothing to worry about." He paused in thought. "Still, we can't be too careful. We'll drive past Erich and the others and then double back. I realize our three companions will hardly appreciate being left standing in the elements, but I'm sure when we tell them the story, they'll forgive us."

Joachim drove several kilometers beyond the pick-up spot. He thought he saw Erich wave as he passed by, but he kept on driving. When he was certain no one was following, he turned back.

"It took you long enough," Erich said crossly. "Despite my frantic waving, you drove right by. How could you have missed us? We're freezing to death."

"Look at it this way," Joachim said. "You're lucky we're here at all."

"We thought you might have forgotten us," Sigrid said.

"We decided it was best to be safe rather than sorry," said Inge.

"What do you mean?" Erich asked. "Was there a problem?"

"If you'll give me a chance, I'll tell you." Erich nodded, and Joachim quickly explained the episode at the gas station.

"You're certain no one followed you?" Erich asked.

"As sure as I can be. We didn't see anyone behind us. Did anyone pass by here?"

"No, so I guess we're okay for now. Joachim, you drive and I'll sit up front with you. If there is increased border activity, we may have a problem."

After moving a few packages to the front between Erich and Joachim, Inge joined her aunt and Rosel in the back seat. As they passed the station, they were glad to see the gasoline attendant had gone inside. "Thank God," Joachim said. "The man was already suspicious. Imagine what he'd think when he saw us heading in the opposite direction with three more passengers."

The town was still asleep as they drove through. Joachim took out Wrieden's map and gave it to Erich. After they reached the last house on the outskirts of town, they all began to concentrate.

No one wanted to miss the turnoff, so there was little conversation. When they saw the narrow street and turned off the main road, Inge brought up the subject she'd been worrying about for hours. "Do you think the SS is on to us yet?" she asked. "Could the guards be waiting when we arrive at the cabin?"

Erich looked at his watch. "It's 7:30. If they haven't already discovered Erna, all hell will break out in about thirty-minutes."

"What will happen when they find Wolfers?" Inge asked.

"The security detail will interrogate the man on duty at the office, as well as the sturman who guarded the women last night. It won't be long before they find out I took Rosel from Block E, supposedly for my personal pleasure. When the story is pieced together, they'll realize I incapacitated Erna, killed Heinrich, and helped Rosel escape. We've already talked about what will happen next. I'd say we have three or four hours with any real certainty of not being discovered. The Munich Gestapo agents won't actually come after us. They'll radio ahead to the guards who will begin to search for the cabin."

"Then we won't have much time to study the movement of the guards," Joachim said.

"Very little. When we get to the cabin, the women can freshen up. While they fix something to eat, you and I will scout around. I hate to think of crossing into Switzerland during the daylight hours, but the more we talk, the more I realize we'll never make it until dark. We have to assume the worst is happening in Dachau and hope for the best."

# CHAPTER 40

The short trip from the main road to the cabin took more time than Erich had anticipated. The wind velocity increased considerably with the sunrise. It howled and whipped the flakes in their faces as Erich and Joachim got out to remove the accumulating snow from the windows so the wipers would work.

When they finally reached the small A-frame chalet, drifts of white powder covered the entire front of the house. Joachim got out, cleared the snow from the cabin door with the shovel propped nearby and opened it with the key Wrieden had provided. He led the others inside. Inge lit the lamps placed strategically about the main room and looked around. The blowing wind caused the door to creak and the windows to rattle, but the building had been securely built to keep out the winter cold.

Using wood piled on the hearth, Erich built a fire. "Won't the guards see the smoke coming from the chimney?" Inge asked as he lit the kindling.

"The snow-sky and the strong wind should prevent them from noticing," Erich said. "Joachim, you and I will unload the car while the women look around to see if there's anything we might find useful when we cross the border."

The men accomplished their task in several trips. When they finished, Inge held out her discovery. "Knapsacks," she said. "They must be used for hunting or hiking."

Erich reached for one of the canvas packs. "We can put food and personal items in these. That way we won't have to struggle with bulky packages or suitcases when we cross the border. How many are there?"

"I could only find three," Inge said.

"Then pack them tightly." The women began to unpack the suitcases while Erich warmed himself by the fire. After several minutes he turned to Joachim. "Shall we head out and have a look around?"

"I'm with you," Joachim said as he reached for his gloves.

Sigrid took Joachim's arm. "You will be careful?"

"Absolutely! When two men have three of the most beautiful women in Germany waiting for them, they tend to be cautious." He was teasing, but only to ease Sigrid's mind. He wasn't feeling jovial.

"You three stay here until we get back," Erich said. "Don't go outside for any reason. If there's a knock on the door—I'd tell you to hide, but I don't know where you'd go. Finish transferring the food and mementos to the backpacks. We shouldn't be gone for long."

As he and Joachim left the warm cabin, a blustery wind impeded their progress. Joachim looked up at the threatening sky. "We could be battling a powerful storm that's more dangerous than the German border guards."

"Or the weather could work to our advantage," Erich said. "The swirling snow will make it more difficult for the guards to locate the cabin, and if we're lucky, the wind will knock down the telephone lines."

"I doubt if it's that strong," Joachim said. "But you gave me an idea. What if we cut the lines? The guards will probably think the outage is due to the storm."

"Good idea. Let's see if we can find the main line to the guardhouse."

The two men walked parallel to the main road that crossed the border. After battling the wind for fifteen minutes, they spotted a barbed-wire fence in the distance. The land around the barricade had been cleared so observing the border would be easier for the patrolling guards. "How far would you say we have to travel from the woods to get to that fence?" Erich asked.

"At least fifty-meters and then fifty on the other side before we get to the trees. It could be tough in daylight, especially with the added patrols and the increased alert status."

"And with the women. The only thing we have going for us is the storm. Let's hope the wind keeps gusting and the skies get even darker. If the weather gets worse, the guards may stay inside the warm shelter for longer periods of time."

"Maybe, but I keep remembering the gas-station attendant's words. The increased attempts to escape might make them see the storm as a chance for more border crossings. In that case they would step up the patrols."

The two men trudged toward the main road, keeping to the trees as they neared the guardhouse. At one point they had to duck deeper into the forest to avoid being seen by two guards who patrolled the fence. They neared the guard-house, crouched, and watched. From time to time a sentry would enter the building, and another would take his place out in the cold.

After noting no definite pattern of rotation, Erich and Joachim left their observation point and hiked back through the snow toward the chalet. Warmth and the smell of tea and sausage greeted them. They removed their snow-covered coats and shoes, placed them by the fire to dry and joined the women at the table. "What did you learn?" Inge asked.

"The storm isn't keeping the guards inside." Erich said. "There are fifty-meter clearings on either side of the fence separating the two countries. It won't be easy to cross unseen, especially if we have to move during the daylight hours."

"What are we going to do?" Sigrid asked anxiously.

Erich paused before answering. "I don't know if you agree, Joachim, but there seems to be less activity in the vicinity of the guardhouse. I assume the patrols would have less reason to suspect someone would attempt a crossing so near the sentries. It also seems the distance we'd have to cross is narrower at that location."

"You can't be serious," Inge said with disbelief. "You're suggesting we cross near the main road?"

"I think it's our best bet," said Erich. "We'll take the same route Joachim and I took. After the guards change places we'll make our break."

"You mean we're going to try to cross in plain sight of the patrols?" Rosel asked.

"No, Rosel," Joachim said. "The guards won't be able to see us. We'll only be in the vicinity, and I agree with Erich. There are fewer men near the guardhouse and the ones who are patrolling go out individually instead of in pairs, as they do in the outlying areas."

"Are you sure we can't wait for dark?" Inge asked.

Erich sat down beside her on the couch and put his arm around her shoulders. "I don't think that's a good idea," he said. "If we wait that long, we'll be pushing our luck. Joachim and I are going to warm up for a few minutes and then cut the phone lines to the guardhouse. That should give us several more hours to rest before we make our escape. The guards will likely think the storm is responsible for the outage. I doubt they'll be disposed to find and repair the damage with the snow falling and the wind blowing as it is."

"Is it necessary to cut the lines?" Inge asked. "Why waste more time? When you two warm up, we should go. Aunt Sigrid and I are fine. The final decision is yours, Rosel."

Rosel nodded. "I agree. If we have to cross in the daylight, there's nothing to be gained by waiting. The storm might let up which would make our escape more difficult. I'm fine; at least as good as I could be in a few more hours. I don't think you should risk cutting the lines. Let's go before a call comes from Dachau."

"What do you think, Joachim?" Erich said.

"I believe the ladies have a good point. Why wait?"

"And you, Sigrid? How do you vote?"

"Inge's right. I don't need to spend a few more hours sitting around here worrying. Even if I tried, I couldn't sleep."

"In that case it's unanimous. We'll leave as soon as we finish packing."

Not everything would fit in the knapsacks. By mutual consent, they left most of the food behind. They'd just eaten, and they could eat again when they got to Basel. Their mementos were far more important. Erich wished he'd been able to retrieve his parents' picture, but he knew there was no reason to dwell on something that couldn't be changed, so he helped the others prepare to leave. Joachim put his Lugar in his pocket, and Erich made sure he had the wire cutters.

During the packing Erich noticed Joachim separate himself from the others for a short time. He called across the room. "Anything wrong, old buddy?"

"No," Joachim said, smiling. "I just need a few moments to collect my thoughts."

Erich let him be. After they stuffed the last of their treasures into the knapsacks and dressed to face the cold, Rosel took Erich's arm. "Could I have a minute before we leave?"

"Of course," Erich said.

"I don't know what will happen when we cross the border, but I want all of you to know how much I appreciate what you've done for me. You saved my life."

"This all began as something we were doing for you, Rosel," Erich said, but after a while, it became a lot more. Whether we found you at Ravensbruck or not, Inge and I were leaving Germany. Fortunately, we never had to try to persuade Sigrid and Joachim to join us. What I'm trying to say is that we're not giving anything up solely for you. We're leaving Germany; at least I am, to live a life that's not directly opposed to all I believe in and value."

"He's right, Rosel," Joachim said. "We've all given this escape a great deal of serious thought, even me, and as I imagine Erich and Inge will tell you, in my vocabulary, the word 'serious' is anathema. We're all ready to leave the country. The Fuhrer's Germany is not the Fatherland we know and cherish."

Inge hugged Rosel. "See, darling," she said. "You're just an excuse for us to leave, so be happy. This is a new beginning for all of us."

Joachim moved toward the door. "We'll have plenty of time to be sentimental and serious when we get to Switzerland," he said. "So let's get on with this."

Erich opened the door. When he was outside, Joachim took Inge's arm and held her back. "Do me a favor, will you, fair lady?" he said.

"Of course, Joachim. Anything."

Joachim handed her a folded piece of paper. "If something happens to me, give this note to Erich. If all goes well, please give it back to me when we reach Switzerland."

"If anything happens to you, it will happen to all of us. We're a team."

"That we are," Joachim said. "But nevertheless, will you promise to do what I ask?"

Inge took Joachim's hand. "Of course I will. Now let's get on with the new life we've talked about for so long."

As they trudged through the snow, they could see little except for the falling flakes that swirled in the gusting wind. Sigrid stumbled several times, and Joachim took her arm to steady her as she walked. Erich held on to Rosel, and from time to time, he assisted Inge with his free hand. After twenty minutes of braving the elements, they approached the road leading to the border.

Blowing snow obstructed the view from the trees, so Erich left the others and crossed the short distance to a clearing to take a closer look. He had gone about fifty-meters when, out of nowhere, a lone soldier appeared. For a split second, their eyes met. Every nerve in Erich's body tensed. With a single step, he approached the startled man and with a twisting motion, kneed him in the groin and planted a fist on his chin. As the injured man slumped to the ground, he pulled him up and hit him once again for good measure. He was about to drag him behind a snow bank when Joachim and the women came into view. "We started to worry." Joachim saw the unconscious guard. "What the hell happened?"

"The guy appeared from out of nowhere. I think he was as surprised to see me as I was to see him. Come on. Help me drag the body into the woods."

Joachim nodded no. "There isn't time. It won't be long before his buddies realize he's missing and come looking for him. Leave him where he is and let's get the hell out of here."

Keeping to the trees to avoid detection, the five moved toward the road. When they'd progressed as far as they could without being detected, Erich put up his hand. "I'm going to take a closer look," he said.

"Want me to go with you?" Joachim asked.

"Stay with the women. If I'm caught, use the distraction to get across the border."

"Erich—"Inge began.

"No, Inge. Promise me you'll go with Joachim."

"I—"

"Promise me."

"I promise; we'll all go."

Erich kissed her on the cheek and started toward the guard-house. He had gone ten-meters when he stopped dead in his tracks. The frosty air was filled with the sound of barking dogs. The guards weren't alone. He raced back to the group. "There's no way we can escape right now," he said. "The sentry I knocked out didn't check in and his buddies unleashed the dogs."

"What do we do now?" Sigrid asked, her brow puckered and fear in her eyes. "Will we be able to escape?

"Not now. We'll go back to the cabin and take our chances after dark."

Inge nodded no. "You know we can't do that. The patrols will discover the cabin before we could try another escape."

"Inge's right, Erich," Rosel said solemnly. "We've reached the end of our journey. We can't cross the border, and we can't go back."

"Give me a minute to think," Erich said brusquely. He turned to talk with Joachim, but he wasn't there. "Where's Joachim?" he asked.

Inge looked around. "He was right beside me a minute ago. I didn't see him leave."

"His knapsack's on the ground," Sigrid said.

Erich felt a chill, and it wasn't from the cold snow and gust-ing wind. His mind raced as fast as his heart was beating. He knew where his friend had gone. At the same moment Inge real-ized what was happening. "Oh my God!" she cried. "It can't be. Joachim didn't—"

Erich forced himself to move. "Come on," he said urgently. He picked up Joachim's discarded knapsack and shoved it toward Inge. "Take this."

He half-dragged the women to a place where they could see the road. As they peered through the swirling snow at the open space separating the two countries, Erich saw what he'd instinctively been dreading. He watched the spectacle that seemed to progress in slow motion. With the guards following close behind, Joachim was running toward the Swiss border at an angle away from the road. "Joachim," Erich yelled, but the gusting wind muffled his cry. "Joachim, stop." Without warning there was a volley of shots and Joachim fell.

"Erich!" Inge cried. "Oh my God! What's Joachim doing?"

Trying to make sense of what was happening, Erich didn't move. It took all he could to stay where he was. Every fiber of his being urged him to rush into the void and help the struggling man who was crawling toward the barbed wire. "Joachim," he cried, but this time his shout was a whisper.

As the guards raced toward the downed man, Joachim turned and fired his gun. The men returned fire, and Joachim lay still. Erich tried to make sense of something that didn't make any sense. All at once everything was clear. Joachim had died so the four of them could get away. His death would be for nothing if they failed to reach Switzerland, and Erich wasn't going to let him down. He removed the wire cutters from his coat pocket, and he grabbed Sigrid and Rosel, shocking them back into the reality with his voice and the pressure on their arms. As he dragged the two women behind him, he turned back to Inge. "We have to move now!"

The guards were gathering around Joachim's body. Erich pulled Rosel while Inge helped Sigrid to the fence. He cut the wire near the gate. As the guards watched Joachim die, the foursome took advantage of their inattention and crawled through the opening. At Erich's urging, they moved unobserved across the open space into Swiss territory.

Erich pulled the women into the trees on the other side of the clearing. Only when they were safely out of sight of the German guards, did he pause to allow them to rest. Staring back across the clearing, it was impossible to make out anything on the German side of the neutral zone. As he caught his breath and realized the full impact of what had happened, he began to cry. Never before, not even when his beloved mother died, had he felt such acute grief and intense frustration. They had been so close to success, yet a new life was now beyond Joachim's reach. As never before, Erich had a profound understanding of the meaning and finality of death.

Inge approached the tearful man whose entire being suggested immeasurable sorrow. She buried her head in his chest and the two clung tightly to one other. There were no words to express what each of them was feeling. The man who had nothing to gain by leaving Germany had given everything for them.

"We'd better go, Erich," she said between sobs. She removed her knapsack and took out the paper, which despite the cold, still seemed warm from Joachim's touch. She handed the note to Erich. "Joachim gave this to me as we were leaving the cabin."

"This must have been what he was doing while we were packing." Erich swallowed hard and unfolded the paper. He read the words and crumpled the note. His body bent at the waist as he put his hands on his knees and sobbed. Inge put her arm around him and rested her head on his shoulder. "What did Joachim say?" she said between sobs.

Without looking up, Erich reached out and handed her the wrinkled wad. Carefully, Inge straightened and smoothed the sheet of paper. On it were two phrases: "Unser Traum," and "a fair exchange."

Inge was about to ask Erich to explain what the phrase meant when they again heard the barking dogs. Erich stood up and wiped his eyes. "It's time to go," he said. "The patrol has probably discovered the severed barbed wire. I don't think they'll pursue us into a neutral country, but we're not taking any chances. There's more at stake now. We have to make it for Joachim. We owe him that much."

Erich managed to pull himself erect. He took Inge's hand. She, in turn, linked hers with Rosel, and Sigrid clasped Erich's other hand. The four set off across the snow-covered landscape to the Swiss border station and to a new life. Erich was sure the women were thinking of Joachim. He certainly was.

# EPILOGUE

The following April, Inge, Sigrid, and Rosel were settled in a small rented house on the outskirts of Zurich and Erich was living in an apartment nearby. After the escape, they had spent a week at a hotel in Basel. There were new papers to secure, bankers to see, and plans to be made for the move to Zurich.

After settling in their new homes, Erich began a long, often frustrating, search for a job. He'd recently begun to work in a bank, and though he often seemed sad, he was beginning to adjust to his new life. A week before, he had proposed to Inge. She accepted, and Sigrid, who had waited for so long for the day her niece would marry, was helping to plan the wedding.

Inge too had been applying for jobs. She was eager to continue her career, and was looking forward to reporting the news without a propagandist slant. That morning she had been asked to return for a second interview and was optimistic about securing a staff job at *Der Schweizerische Beobachter*, a publication for German-speaking Swiss.

Rosel had regained much of her strength. Her hair curled attractively around her face and she was beginning to look like her old self. She was talking about pursuing a musical career, and it was obvious to everyone that, for her, the healing process was underway.

Sigrid mothered everyone. The move from Munich hadn't affected her as negatively as Erich and Inge feared it would. She was making new friends in the neighborhood and getting into a routine not unlike the one she enjoyed in Munich. However she too was often quiet for no apparent reason. No one pushed her to talk, feeling she would eventually open up and share her feelings.

They rarely mentioned Joachim. Inge realized they all needed to talk about their friend and the sacrifice he'd made so they could get away. She missed him, and wanted to share her memories of the good times they'd spent together, but Erich seemed so miserable at the mere mention of his name that she, Rosel, and Sigrid remained silent and waited patiently for him to begin the conversation.

One evening, after another of Sigrid's delicious dinners, they gathered in the parlor, sipping tea and enjoying a quiet moment together around the fire that blazed below the mantle which held the precious pictures they'd safely carried across the border, including the ones of Joachim and his family. After a short period of quiet reflection, Erich finally started the discussion. "I miss Joachim," he murmured. "It doesn't seem right that he's not here sharing moments like these with us, especially since he's the reason we're all sitting here. I can't accept what happened. In fact I sometimes wonder if the constant sadness I feel will ever end."

"Tell me about Joachim, Erich," Inge urged, hoping that talking would help to assuage his pain. "I've wanted to talk for so long, but you seemed reluctant to share your thoughts and memories, so I've kept my questions to myself. Will you answer them now?"

"Perhaps Rosel and I should leave," Sigrid said.

Erich nodded no. "We were all a part of Joachim's life, and we've all suffered the loss. Please stay, both of you."

"The paper, Erich," Inge said. "What did Joachim mean by 'Unser Traum' and 'a fair exchange'?"

Erich closed his eyes. The phrases he'd refused to speak over the months once again caused him horrific pain as he said them aloud. "Unser Traum was a piece of property I owned on the outskirts of Berlin. It was my only legacy from my father. As children, Joachim and I built a lean-to in the middle of the land. We would sit there for hours talking and dreaming about our glorious futures. After Germany won the war, we planned to return to Unser Traum, build two houses, and raise our families together."

"And 'a fair exchange'?" Sigrid asked.

"'A fair exchange' meant that Joachim was exchanging his life for mine. He made the ultimate sacrifice so we could safely cross the border. We all know how much he loved life. He died because it was the only way for us to live."

"But what do the words mean?" Rosel asked.

"They go back to the week after we finished our SS training; when we were awaiting our first assignment." Erich spent the next fifteen minutes relating the story of Joachim, Halder, and the Jewish girl Joachim kept from being raped. He had mentioned the episode to Inge at the Wagner the morning she first told him about Rosel. Now, as he told the others, Inge finally grasped the depth of the friendship between the two very-different men.

When Erich finished his story, all four sat quietly, staring into the fire. It was Sigrid who spoke first. "He gave his life for you, Erich, because he felt that you saved his life."

"He did exactly that," Erich said pensively.

Inge knew the long-overdue conversation would finally let all of them begin to heal. "It was in keeping with his character," she said quietly.

"It was. On the night we made our final plans to rescue Rosel from Ravensbruck, Joachim told me he valued friendship above all else—that he would leave Germany for us. He certainly showed us the depth of his feelings."

"I'm not so sure he'd approve of this discussion," Sigrid said. "You know how he hated the word 'serious.'"

As they talked, they laughed and they cried, as each began to let go of the pain and guilt that had haunted them after Joachim died. Inge wasn't sure how the others felt, but for the first time since Joachim's death and their escape, she was focusing, not on what had been, but on the days to come.

# POSTSCRIPT

## Dachau, the Town and the People

Because of the Nazi detention camp of the same name, the lovely, quaint, 1200 year-old town of Dachau has been vilified by the world. The residents had no say when the Nazis built the camp in 1933. From the arrival of the first prisoners until the camp was liberated on April 29, 1945, many of the townspeople, facing arrest or possible execution, tried to help the concentration camp prisoners who worked on roads and buildings outside the camp by feeding them and providing warm blankets. The day before the camp was liberated, the residents of Dachau revolted against the SS. Several citizens were killed before the SS suppressed the insurrection.

## Goebbels, Joseph: Minister for Public Enlightenment and Propaganda

As the Russians advanced toward Berlin, Goebbels and his family moved into the Vorbunker, an area connected to the lower Fuhrerbunker under the Reich Chancellery gardens in central Berlin. On April 29, 1945, along with four others, Goebbels witnessed Hitler's Last Will and Testament. After the Fuhrer's suicide on April 30th, Goebbels arranged for SS dentist, Helmet Kunz, to kill his six children by injecting them with morphine and then, when they were unconscious, crushing an ampule of cyanide in each of their mouths. According to Kunz's testimony, he gave the children the morphine injections but it was their mother, Magda Goebbels, and Hitler's personal doctor who actually administered the cyanide. Shortly thereafter, Goebbels and his wife killed themselves in the Chancellery garden. There are three different accounts of the suicides:

1. Goebbels shot himself and Magda took poison.
2. Both Goebbels and Magda took cyanide and then were shot by an SS trooper
3. Goebbels shot Magda and then himself.

The bodies of Joseph and Magda Goebbels his wife were burned in a shell crater, but due to the lack of fuel, the burning was only partly effective, and their bodies were easily identifiable.

## Goering, Herman: Reichsmarshall and Commander in Chief of the Luftwaffe:

Goring was captured by troops of the United States Seventh Army on May 9, 1945. In 1946, he was brought before the International Military Tribunal at Nuremberg, where he defended himself with skill and aggressiveness, demanding that he not be questioned about the party's program because, "he knew nothing about it." The judges disagreed, saying 'his guilt is unique in its enormity. The record discloses no excuses for this man." Goering was found guilty on all four counts brought against him: Count 1, conspiracy to commit crimes alleged in other counts; Count 2, crimes against peace; Count 3, war crimes; Count 4, crimes against humanity. He was sentenced to death by hanging, but on October 15, 1946, two hours before he was to meet his fate, he committed suicide by taking a potassium cyanide capsule that, according to different reports, was hidden in his skincare cream or concealed in a copper cartridge shell. At the time Goering had been scheduled to die, guards brought his body into the gymnasium on a stretcher where the hangings were taking place. Because the army didn't want rumors of Goering's escape to spread, the colonel in charge of the proceedings ordered the blanket removed so witnesses and Allied correspondents could see that Goering was dead. At the order of the court, Goring was cremated and his ashes were thrown into the last remaining incinerator at Dachau.

### Himmler, Heinrich: Reichsfuhrer of the SS, Chief of German Police, Minister of the Interior

After Hitler's death, Himmler unsuccessfully tried to influence the victors by granting last-minute reprieves for Jews and important prisoners. He was arrested on May 22, 1945, and was scheduled to stand trial with other German leaders at Nuremberg. However, on May 23rd, he committed suicide in Luneburg prison, taking a potassium chloride capsule before the interrogation could begin. There are varying accounts of Goebbels' death. One reports that his last words were *Ich bin Heinrich Himmler!* ("I am Heinrich Himmler!"). Another version has Himmler biting into a hidden cyanide pill embedded in one of his teeth, when searched by a British doctor, who then yelled, "He has done it!" Several attempts to revive Himmler were unsuccessful. His body was buried in an unmarked grave on the Luneburg Green. The precise location of his gravesite remains unknown.

### Hippke, Erich: Chief Luftwaffe Surgeon

American investigators determined that Hippke was the source of the ideas for the experiments Rascher conducted at Dachau. It was through Hippke that Rascher was able to obtain the decompression chamber from the Luftwaffe's Aviation Institute. One-hundred individuals died in the High Flight Tests and 300 more died during the freezing experiments. Hippke was never charged with a crime. Ironically, his successor, Oskar Schroeder, who took over on May 15, 1944, long after the Dachau experiments were over, was charged and sentenced to life in prison.

## Hitler, Adolf: Fuehrer and Chancellor of the Third Reich

When the war was hopelessly lost, Hitler moved his headquarters to the Fuhrerbunker below the chancellery garden. There, in the midst of his flunkies, and in a state of extreme nervous exhaustion, he spent hours perusing giant war maps and shifting colored pins around to locate units that no longer existed. With the exception of his secretaries, Goebbels, Martin Bormann, and several others, his lieutenants had begun to desert him. At the end he denounced Goering for trying to usurp his leadership and Himmler for seeking to negotiate with the Allies. At last, acknowledging defeat, feeling the German people had been unworthy of his genius, and unwilling to meet the same humiliating fate of his ally, Benito Mussolini, whose corpse was hanged upside down and abused by angry Italian mobs, the Fuehrer decided to commit suicide. In the early hours of April 29, 1945, Hitler married Eva Braun, his longtime mistress, in a civil service in his private sitting room. In keeping with Nazi requirements, the official asked both Hitler and Eva whether they were of pure Aryan blood and whether they were free from hereditary illness. After a small wedding breakfast, Hitler dictated his last will and political testament, in which he justified his life and work. The next day, with the Soviets less than 500 meters from the bunker, and learning from Fieldmarshall Keitel that ammunition was running out, Hitler retreated into his suite and shot himself, while Eva took poison to end her life. In accordance with his instructions, the bodies were wrapped in blankets carried to the Reich Chancellery garden, dumped into a trough, doused with gasoline and burned.

## Mandel, Maria—SS Oberaufseherin at Ravensbruck

On May 15, 1939 Mandel was assigned as an aufseherin at the newly opened Ravensbruck Concentration Camp near Berlin. She quickly impressed her superiors and, on April 1, 1941, was elevated to the rank of a SS-Oberaufseherin. In that capacity she oversaw daily roll calls, assignments for the Aufseherinnen, and punishments. In October 1942, she was transferred to the Auschwitz-Birkenau camp where she was directly responsible for the death of over 500,000 female prisoners and, because of her cruelty, came to be known as "The Beast." On August 10, 1945, she was arrested by the United States army and handed over to the Republic of Poland. She was tried in a Krakow courtroom in the Auschwitz trial and sentenced to death. Mandel was hanged on January 24, 1948, at the age of 36.

## Mischlinge: Individuals of Mixed Race

The fate of the Mischlinge was an important topic at the Wannsee Conference of January 20, 1942, at which the Final Solution to the Jewish problem was discussed. The Mischlinge matter was never resolved. In the end, the Mischlinge were not deported, sterilized, nor exterminated. They remained non-Aryans under earlier decrees. Most of the Mischlinge survived the war.

## Munich

In 1943 British planes carried out one of the worst air raids on Munich. Four-hundred-thirty-five were injured, 205 died and 9000 were left homeless. From spring 1944, American bombers bombed Munich by day and the British bombed the city by night. In April 1945, the US Army occupied Munich.

## Rascher, Sigmund: German SS Doctor

Rascher and his wife, Nini, attempted to please Himmler by demonstrating that population growth could be accelerated by extending the childbearing age. Rascher publicized the fact that his wife had given birth to three children after age forty-eight. Himmler then used a photograph of Rascher's family as propaganda material. However, during her fourth "pregnancy" Nini Rascher was arrested for trying to kidnap a baby. An investigation revealed that her other three children had been either bought or kidnapped. Himmler felt personally betrayed by this conduct, and Rascher was arrested in April 1944. As well as complicity in the kidnappings of the three infants, he was accused of financial irregularities, the murder of one of his assistants, and scientific fraud. Rascher was shot in Dachau shortly before its liberation by American forces.

## Rosenberg, Alfred: Party Philosopher and Minister for the Eastern Occupied Area

The defendants at Nuremberg were separately charged on two, three or four counts. Twelve men, including Rosenberg, were charged on all four (see Goering). Rosenberg was found guilty on all four counts and was hanged on the morning of October 16th, 1946.

## Ravensbruck: Frauenlager (concentration Camp specializing in women inmates)

About 50,000 prisoners perished at Ravensbruck. On April 25, 1945, the frauenlager was captured by the allies, and its remaining prisoners were liberated.

## Sievers, Wolfram, Doctor: Chief of the Institute for Military Scientific Research, Colonel SS

Sievers was tried at the Nuremberg in the Doctor's Trial. He was convicted, but not for anything having to do with the experiments that took place at Dachau. He was hanged on June 2, 1948.

## Weiss, Martin Gottfried,–SS Obersturmbannfuhrer at Dachau

Weiss was twice assigned as commandant of the Dachau main camp (1942-1943 and April 1945). He also commanded the satellite-camp of Muhldorf (1944-1945). Weiss was tried during the Dachau Trials of November 1945. These trials, which were held for all war criminals caught in the United States zones in occupied Germany and Austria, were held within the walls of the former concentration camp to underline the moral corruptness of the Nazi Regime. On December 13, 1945, Weiss was sentenced to death for atrocities committed during his first command at Dachau, which included the initial construction of the camp's gas chamber and human experimentation conducted using camp inmates. He was found guilty and executed in Luneburg prison on May 29, 1946.

67549950R00274

Made in the USA
Lexington, KY
16 September 2017